BEYOND TIME,
BEYOND IMAGINING . . .

"STRATA"—Edward Bryant

On a clear Wyoming night, a reunion of four high school friends raises some ghosts older than the human race itself. . . .

"THE CONFESSION OF HAMO"
—Mary C. Pangborn

In medieval Europe, with its knights, princesses, wizards, swordsmen and high adventure, there still lurk highwaymen and rogues—and a dire curse!

"FEESTERS IN THE LAKE"—Bob Leman

The four daughters of a sea captain find that the secret sins of their father have come back to haunt them. . . .

"LETTERS TO THE POSTMAN"—Robert Aickman

In a quiet English village, a young man takes the job of postman, and discovers mystery within mystery when he tries to help a woman in distress. . . .

D1604426

Books by Terry Carr

The Best Science Fiction of the Year #10
Fantasy Annual III
Fantasy Annual IV

Published by TIMESCAPE BOOKS

FANTASY ANNUAL IV

TERRY CARR, EDITOR

A TIMESCAPE BOOK
PUBLISHED BY POCKET BOOKS NEW YORK

This collection is comprised of works of fiction. Names, characters, places and incidents are either the product of the authors' imaginations or are used fictitiously, and any resemblance to actual persons, living or dead, events or locales is entirely coincidental.

Another *Original* publication of TIMESCAPE BOOKS

A Timescape Book published by
POCKET BOOKS, a Simon & Schuster division of
GULF & WESTERN CORPORATION
1230 Avenue of the Americas, New York, N.Y. 10020

Copyright © 1981 by Terry Carr

All rights reserved, including the right to reproduce
this book or portions thereof in any form whatsoever.
For information address Timescape Books, 1230
Avenue of the Americas, New York, N.Y. 10020

ISBN: 0-671-41273-6

First Timescape Books printing November, 1981

10 9 8 7 6 5 4 3 2 1

POCKET and colophon are trademarks of Simon & Schuster.

Use of the TIMESCAPE trademark under exclusive license
from trademark owner.

Printed in the U.S.A.

CREDITS

"The Monkey" by Stephen King. Copyright © 1980 by Stephen King. From *Gallery*, November 1980, by permission of the author and his agents, Kirby McCauley Ltd.

"The Brave Little Toaster" by Thomas M. Disch. Copyright © 1980 by Mercury Press, Inc. From *Fantasy and Science Fiction*, August 1980, by permission of the author.

"The Attleborough Poltergeist" by Richard Cowper. Copyright © 1980 by Colin Murry. From *Fantasy and Science Fiction*, October 1980, by permission of the author and his agents, Curtis Brown, Ltd.

"The Hot and Cold Running Waterfall" by Stephen Tall. Copyright © 1980 by Davis Publications, Inc. From *Isaac Asimov's Science Fiction Magazine*, May 1980, by permission of the author and his agents, Blassingame, McCauley, and Wood.

"Unicorn Tapestry" by Suzy McKee Charnas. Copyright © 1980 by Suzy McKee Charnas. From *New Dimensions II*, by permission of the author and her agent, Virginia Kidd.

"Strata" by Edward Bryant. Copyright © 1980 by Mercury Press, Inc. From *Fantasy and Science Fiction*, August 1980, by permission of the author and his agents, Robert P. Mills Ltd.

"The Confession of Hamo" by Mary C. Pangborn. Copyright © 1980 by Terry Carr. From *Universe 10*, by permission of the author.

"Feesters in the Lake" by Bob Leman. Copyright © 1980 by Mercury Press, Inc. From *Fantasy and Science Fiction*, October 1980, by permission of the author.

"Don't Look Back" by Pat Murphy. Copyright © 1980 by Pat Murphy. From *Other Worlds 2*, by permission of the author.

"Letters to the Postman" by Robert Aickman. Copyright © 1980 by Robert Aickman. From *Intrusions*, by permission of the author and his agents, Kirby McCauley Ltd.

Contents

INTRODUCTION

Fantasy Annual IS, AS ITS TITLE SUGGESTS, a compilation of the best new tales of the fantastic published during the previous year.

Most of these stories will be completely new to you, unless you assiduously read every fantasy magazine that appears—and every science fiction magazine, too. Even if you do, you'll find stories here that have been published in such unlikely fantasy sources as *Gallery*, or only in book form. (The Robert Aickman tale has never before appeared in the United States.)

All types and moods of fantasy are eligible for this book: frightening stories, whimsical ones, tales of adventure and magic. . . . You'll never quite know what's coming next—and that's the point of fantasy, I think.

—TERRY CARR

Of all things in the world, surely *toys* aren't frightening—especially not a little stuffed monkey that used to clash cymbals before its mechanism broke. Even if sometimes the workings do move for a while and the tiny cymbals sound . . . what of it?

Since the story's by Stephen King, you know there will be a lot more to it; and that, yes, it will be frightening.

King's latest books are *Danse Macabre,* a study of horror fiction, and *Cujo,* a new horror novel.

THE MONKEY

Stephen King

WHEN HAL SHELBURN SAW IT, WHEN HIS son Dennis pulled it out of a mouldering Ralston-Purina carton that had been pushed far back under one attic eave, such a feeling of horror and dismay rose in him that for one moment he thought he surely must scream. He put one fist to his mouth, as if to cram it back . . . and then merely coughed into his fist. Neither Terry nor Dennis noticed, but Petey looked around, momentarily curious.

"Hey, neat," Dennis said respectfully. It was a tone Hal rarely got from the boy anymore himself. Dennis was twelve.

"What is it?" Petey asked. He glanced at his father again before his eyes were dragged back to the thing his big brother had found. "What is it, Daddy?"

"It's a monkey, fartbrains," Dennis said. "Haven't you ever seen a monkey before?"

"Don't call your brother fartbrains," Terry said automatically, and began to examine a box of curtains. The curtains were slimy with mildew and she dropped them quickly. "Uck."

"Can I have it, Daddy?" Petey asked. He was nine.

"What do you mean?" Dennis cried. "*I* found it!"

"Boys, please," Terry said. "I'm getting a headache."

Hal barely heard them—any of them. The monkey glimmered up at him from his older son's hands, grinning its old familiar grin. The same grin that had

2

haunted his nightmares as a child, haunted them until he had ———

Outside a cold gust of wind rose, and for a moment lips with no flesh blew a long note through the old, rusty gutter outside. Petey stepped closer to his father, eyes moving uneasily to the rough attic roof through which nailheads poked.

"What was that, Daddy?" he asked as the whistle died to a guttural buzz.

"Just the wind," Hal said, still looking at the monkey. Its cymbals, crescents of brass rather than full circles in the weak light of the one naked bulb, were moveless, perhaps a foot apart, and he added automatically, "Wind can whistle, but it can't carry a tune." Then he realized that was a saying of his Uncle Will's, and a goose ran over his grave.

The long note came again, the wind coming off Crystal Lake in a long, droning swoop and then wavering in the gutter. Half a dozen small drafts puffed cold October air into Hal's face—God, this place was so much like the back closet of the house in Hartford that they might all have been transported thirty years back in time.

I won't think about that.

But the thought wouldn't be denied.

In the back closet where I found that goddammed monkey in that same box.

Terry had moved away to examine a wooden crate filled with knick-knacks, duck-walking because the pitch of the eave was so sharp.

"I don't like it," Petey said, and felt for Hal's hand. "Dennis c'n have it if he wants. Can we go, Daddy?"

"Worried about ghosts, chickenguts?" Dennis inquired.

"Dennis, you stop it," Terry said absently. She picked up a wafer-thin cup with a Chinese pattern. "This is nice. This ———"

Hal saw that Dennis had found the wind-up key in the monkey's back. Terror flew through him on dark wings.

"Don't do that!"

It came out more sharply than he had intended, and he had snatched the monkey out of Dennis's hands before he was really aware he had done it. Dennis looked around at him, startled. Terry had also glanced back

over her shoulder, and Petey looked up. For a moment
they were all silent, and the wind whistled again, very
low this time, like an unpleasant invitation.

"I mean, it's probably broken," Hal said.

*It used to be broken . . . except when it wanted to be
fixed.*

"Well you didn't have to *grab*," Dennis said.

"Dennis, shut up."

Dennis blinked at him and for a moment looked almost uneasy. Hal hadn't spoken to him so sharply in a
long time. Not since he had lost his job with National
Aerodyne in California two years before and they had
moved to Texas. Dennis decided not to push it . . . for
now. He turned back to the Ralston-Purina carton and
began to root through it again, but the other stuff was
nothing but shit. Broken toys bleeding springs and stuf-
fings.

The wind was louder now, hooting instead of whistling. The attic began to creak softly, making a noise
like footsteps.

"Please, Daddy?" Petey asked, only loud enough for
his father to hear.

"Yeah," he said. "Terry, let's go."

"I'm not through with this ————"

"I said let's *go*."

It was her turn to look startled.

They had taken two adjoining rooms in a motel. By
ten that night the boys were asleep in their room and
Terry was asleep in the adults' room. She had taken two
Valium on the ride back from the home place in Casco.
To keep her nerves from giving her a migraine. Just
lately she took a lot of Valium. It had started around the
time National Aerodyne had laid Hal off. For the last
two years he had been working for Texas Instruments—
it was $4,000 less a year, but it was work. He told Terry
they were lucky. She agreed. There were plenty of soft-
ware architects drawing unemployment, he said. She
agreed. The company housing in Arnette was every bit
as good as the place in Fresno, he said. She agreed, but
he thought her agreement was a lie.

And he had been losing Dennis. He could feel the kid
going, achieving a premature escape velocity, so long,
Dennis, bye-bye stranger, it was nice sharing this train

with you. Terry said she thought the boy was smoking reefer. She smelled it sometimes. You have to talk to him, Hal. And *he* agreed, but so far he had not.

The boys were asleep. Terry was asleep. Hal went into the bathroom and locked the door and sat down on the closed lid of the john and looked at the monkey.

He hated the way it felt, that soft brown nappy fur, worn bald in spots. He hated its grin—*that monkey grins just like a nigger,* Uncle Will had said once, but it didn't grin like a nigger, or like anything human. Its grin was all teeth, and if you wound up the key, the lips would move, the teeth would seem to get bigger, to become vampire teeth, the lips would writhe and the cymbals would bang, stupid monkey, stupid clockwork monkey, stupid, stupid ———

He dropped it. His hands were shaking and he dropped it.

The key clicked on the bathroom tile as it struck the floor. The sound seemed very loud in the stillness. It grinned at him with its murky amber eyes, doll's eyes, filled with idiot glee, its brass cymbals poised as if to strike up a march for some black band from hell, and on the bottom the words MADE IN HONG KONG were stamped.

"You can't be here," he whispered. "I threw you down the well when I was nine."

The monkey grinned up at him.

Hal Shelburn shuddered.

Outside in the night, a black capful of wind shook the motel.

Hal's brother Bill and Bill's wife Collette met them at Uncle Will's and Aunt Ida's the next day. "Did it ever cross your mind that a death in the family is a really lousy way to renew the family connection?" Bill asked him with a bit of a grin. He had been named for Uncle Will. Will and Bill, champions of the rodayo, Uncle Will used to say, and ruffle Bill's hair. It was one of his sayings . . . like the wind can whistle but it can't carry a tune. Uncle Will had died six years before, and Aunt Ida had lived on here alone, until a stroke had taken her just the previous week. Very sudden, Bill had said when he called long distance to give Hal the news. As if he could know; as if anyone could know. She had died alone.

"Yeah," Hal said. "The thought crossed my mind."

They looked at the place together, the home place where they had finished growing up. Their father, a merchant mariner, had simply disappeared as if from the very face of the earth when they were young; Bill claimed to remember him vaguely, but Hal had no memories of him at all. Their mother had died when Bill was ten and Hal eight. They had come to Uncle Will's and Aunt Ida's from Hartford, and they had been raised here, and gone to college here. Bill had stayed and now had a healthy law practice in Portland.

Hal saw that Petey had wandered off toward the blackberry tangles that lay on the eastern side of the house in a mad jumble. "Stay away from there, Petey," he called.

Petey looked back, questioning. Hal felt simple love for the boy rush him . . . and he suddenly thought of the monkey again.

"Why, Dad?"

"The old well's in there someplace," Bill said. "But I'll be damned if I remember just where. Your dad's right, Petey—those blackberry tangles are a good place to stay away from. Thorns'll do a job on you. Right, Hal?"

"Right," Hal said automatically. Pete moved away, not looking back, and then started down the embankment toward the small shingle of beach where Dennis was skipping stones over the water. Hal felt something in his chest loosen a little.

Bill might have forgotten where the old well had been, but late that afternoon Hal went to it unerringly, shouldering his way through the brambles that tore at his old flannel jacket and hunted for his eyes. He reached it and stood there, breathing hard, looking at the rotted, warped boards that covered it. After a moment's debate, he knelt (his knees fired twin pistol shots) and moved two of the boards aside.

From the bottom of that wet, rock-lined throat a face stared up at him, wide eyes, grimacing mouth, and a moan escaped him. It was not loud, except in his heart. There it had been very loud.

It was his own face, reflected up from dark water.

Not the monkey's. For a moment he had thought it was the monkey's.

He was shaking. Shaking all over.

I threw it down the well. I threw it down the well, please God don't let me be crazy. I threw it down the well.

The well had gone dry the summer Johnny McCabe died, the year after Bill and Hal came to stay at the home place with Uncle Will and Aunt Ida. Uncle Will had borrowed money from the bank to have an artesian well sunk, and the blackberry tangles had grown up around the old dug well. The dry well.

Except the water had come back. Like the monkey.

This time the memory would not be denied. Hal sat there helplessly, letting it come, trying to do with it, to ride it like a surfer riding a monster wave that will crush him if he falls off his board, just trying to get through it so it would be gone again.

He had crept out here with the monkey late that summer, and the blackberries had been out, the smell of them thick and cloying. No one came in here to pick, although Aunt Ida would sometimes stand at the edge of the tangles and pick a cupful of berries into her apron. In here the blackberries had gone past ripe to overripe, some of them were rotting, sweating a thick white fluid like pus, and the crickets sang maddeningly in the high grass underfoot, their endless cry: *Reeeeeeee—*

The thorns tore at him, brought dots of blood onto his bare arms. He made no effort to avoid their sting. He had been blind with terror—so blind that he had come within inches of stumbling onto the boards that covered the well, perhaps within inches of crashing thirty feet to the well's muddy bottom. He had pinwheeled his arms for balance, and more thorns had branded his forearms. It was that memory that had caused him to call Petey back sharply.

That was the day Johnny McCabe had died—his best friend. Johnny had been climbing the rungs up to his treehouse in his back yard. The two of them had spent many hours up there that summer, playing pirate, seeing make-believe galleons out on the lake, unlimbering the cannons, preparing to board. Johnny had been climbing up to the treehouse as he had done a thousand times before, and the rung just below the trap door in the bottom of the treehouse had snapped off in his hands and Johnny had fallen thirty feet to the ground and had broken his neck and it was the monkey's fault, the monkey, the goddam hateful monkey. When the phone rang, when Aunt Ida's mouth dropped open and then formed an O of horror as her friend Milly from down the road told her the news, when Aunt Ida said, "Come out on the porch, Hal, I have to tell you some bad news—," he had thought with sick horror, *The monkey! What's the monkey done now?*

There had been no reflection of his face trapped at the bottom of the well that day, only the stone cobbles going down into the darkness and the smell of wet mud. He had looked at the monkey lying there on the wiry grass that grew between the blackberry tangles, its cymbals poised, its grinning teeth huge between its splayed lips, its fur, rubbed away in balding, mangy patches here and there, its glazed eyes.

"I hate you," he had hissed at it. He wrapped his hand around its loathsome body, feeling the nappy fur crinkle. It grinned at him as he held it up in front of his face. "Go on!" he dared it, beginning to cry for the first time that day. He shook it. The poised cymbals trembled minutely. It spoiled everything good. Everything. "Go on, clap them! Clap them!"

The monkey only grinned.

"Go on and clap them!" His voice rose hysterically. "Fraidy-cat, fraidy-cat, go on and clap them! I dare you!"

Its brownish-yellow eyes. Its huge and gleeful teeth.

He threw it down the well then, mad with grief and terror. He saw it turn over once on its way down, a simian acrobat doing a trick, and the sun glinted one last time on those cymbals. It struck the bottom with a thud, and that must have jogged its clockwork, for suddenly the cymbals *did* begin to beat. Their steady, deliberate, and tinny banging rose to his ears, echoing and fey in the stone throat of the dead well: *jang-jang-jang-jang—*

Hal clapped his hands over his mouth, and for a moment he could see it down there, perhaps only in the eye of imagination . . . lying there in the mud, eyes glaring up at the small circle of his boy's face peering over the lip of the well (as if marking its shape forever), lips expanding and contracting around those grinning teeth, cymbals clapping, funny wind-up monkey.

Jang-jang-jang-jang, who's dead? *Jang-jang-jang-jang,* is it Johnny McCabe, falling with his eyes wide, doing his own acrobatic somersault as he falls through the bright summer vacation air with the splintered rung still held in his hands to strike the ground with a single bitter snapping sound? Is it Johnny, Hal? Or is it you?

Moaning, Hal had shoved the boards across the hole, getting splinters in his hands, not caring, not even aware of them until later. And still he could hear it, even through the boards, muffled now and somehow all the worse for that: it was down there in stone-faced dark, clapping its cymbals and jerking its repulsive body, the sounding coming up like the sound of a prematurely buried man scrabbling for a way out.

Jang-jang-jang-jang, who's dead this time?

He fought and battered his way back through the blackberry creepers. Thorns stitched fresh lines of welling blood briskly across his face and burdocks caught in the cuffs of his jeans, and he fell full-length once, his ears still jangling, as if it had followed him. Uncle Will found him later, sitting on an old tire in the garage and sobbing, and he had thought Hal was crying for his dead friend. So he had been; but he had also cried in the aftermath of terror.

He had thrown the monkey down the well in the afternoon. That evening, as twilight crept in through a shimmering mantle of ground-fog, a car moving too fast for the reduced visibility had run down Aunt Ida's manx cat in the road and gone right on. There had been guts everywhere, Bill had thrown up, but Hal had only turned his face away, his pale, still face, hearing Aunt Ida's sobbing (this on top of the news about the McCabe boy had caused a fit of weeping that was almost hysterics, and it was almost two hours before Uncle Will could calm her completely) as if from miles away. In his heart there was a cold and exultant joy. It hadn't been his turn. It had been Aunt Ida's manx, not him, not his brother Bill or his Uncle Will (just two champions of the rodayo). And now the monkey was gone, it was down the well, and one scruffy manx cat with ear mites was not too great a price to pay. If the monkey wanted to clap its

hellish cymbals now, let it. It could clap and clash them
for the crawling bugs and beetles, the dark things that
made their home in the well's stone gullet. It would rot
down there in the darkness and its loathsome cogs and
wheels and springs would rust in darkness. It would die
down there. In the mud and the darkness. Spiders would
spin it a shroud.

But . . . it had come back.

Slowly, Hal covered the well again, as he had on that
day, and in his ears he heard the phantom echo of the
monkey's cymbals: *Jang-jang-jang-jang, who's dead,
Hal? Is it Terry? Dennis? Is it Petey, Hal? He's your
favorite, isn't he? Is it him? Jang-jang-jang—*

"Put that *down!*"

Petey flinched and dropped the monkey, and for one
nightmare moment Hal thought that would do it, that the
jolt would jog its machinery and the cymbals would begin to beat and clash.

"Daddy, you scared me."

"I'm sorry. I just . . . I don't want you to play with
that."

The others had gone to see a movie, and he had
thought he would beat them back to the motel. But he
had stayed at the home place longer than he would have
guessed; the old, hateful memories seemed to move in
their own eternal time zone.

Terry was sitting near Dennis, watching "The Beverly
Hillbillies." She watched the old, grainy print with a
steady, bemused concentration that spoke of a recent
Valium pop. Dennis was reading a rock magazine with
the group Styx on the cover. Petey had been sitting cross-
legged on the carpet, goofing with the monkey.

"It doesn't work anyway," Petey said. *Which explains
why Dennis let him have it,* Hal thought, and then felt
ashamed and angry at himself. He seemed to have no
control over the hostility he felt toward Dennis more and
more often, but in the aftermath he felt demeaned and
tacky . . . helpless.

"No," he said. "It's old. I'm going to throw it away.
Give it to me."

He held out his hand and Petey, looking troubled,
handed it over.

Dennis said to his mother, "Pop's turning into a friggin schizophrenic."

Hal was across the room even before he knew he was going, the monkey in one hand, grinning as if in approbation. He hauled Dennis out of his chair by the shirt. There was a purring sound as a seam came adrift somewhere. Dennis looked almost comically shocked. His copy of *Tiger Beat* fell to the floor.

"Hey!"

"You come with me," Hal said grimly, pulling his son toward the door to the connecting room.

"Hal!" Terry nearly screamed. Petey just goggled.

Hal pulled Dennis through. He slammed the door and them slammed Dennis against the door. Dennis was starting to look scared. "You're getting a mouth problem," Hal said.

"Let *go* of me! You tore my shirt, you ————"

Hal slammed the boy against the door again. "Yes," he said. "A real mouth problem. Did you learn that in school? Or back in the smoking area?"

Dennis flushed, his face momentarily ugly with guilt. "I wouldn't be in that shitty school if you didn't get canned!" he burst out.

Hal slammed Dennis against the door again. "I didn't get canned, I got laid off, you know it, and I don't need any of your shit about it. You have problems? Welcome to the world, Dennis. Just don't you lay off all your problems on me. You're eating. Your ass is covered. At eleven, I don't . . . need any . . . shit from you." He punctuated each phrase by pulling the boy forward until their noses were almost touching and then slamming him back into the door. It was not hard enough to hurt, but Dennis was scared—his father had not laid a hand on him since they moved to Texas—and now he began to cry with a young boy's loud, braying, healthy sobs.

"Go ahead, beat me up!" he yelled at Hal, his face twisted and blotchy. "Beat me up if you want, I know how much you fucking hate me!"

"I don't hate you. I love you a lot, Dennis. But I'm your dad and you're going to show me respect or I'm going to bust you for it."

Dennis tried to pull away. Hal pulled the boy to him and hugged him. Dennis fought for a moment and then put his face against Hal's chest and wept as if exhausted.

It was the sort of cry Hal hadn't heard from either of his children in years. He closed his eyes, realizing that he felt exhausted himself.

Terry began to hammer on the other side of the door. "Stop it, Hal! Whatever you're doing to him, stop it!"

"I'm not killing him," Hal said. "Go away, Terry."

"Don't you ———"

"It's all right, Mom," Dennis said, muffled against Hal's chest.

He could feel her perplexed silence for a moment, and then she went. Hal looked at his son again.

"I'm sorry I badmouthed you, Dad," Dennis said reluctantly.

"When we get home next week, I'm going to wait two or three days and then I'm going to go through all your drawers, Dennis. If there's something in them you don't want me to see, you better get rid of it."

That flash of guilt again. Dennis lowered his eyes and wiped away snot with the back of his hand.

"Can I go now?" He sounded sullen once more.

"Sure," Hal said, and let him go. *Got to take him camping in the spring, just the two of us. Do some fishing, like Uncle Will used to do with Bill and me. Got to get close to him. Got to try.*

He sat down on the bed in the empty room and looked at the monkey. *You'll never be close to him again, Hal,* its grin seemed to say. *Never again. Never again.*

Just looking at the monkey made him feel tired. He laid it aside and put a hand over his eyes.

That night Hal stood in the bathroom, brushing his teeth, and thought: *It was in the same box. How could it be in the same box?*

The toothbrush jabbed upward, hurting his gums. He winced.

He had been four, Bill six, the first time he saw the monkey. Their missing father had bought a house in Hartford, and it had been theirs, free and clear, before he died or disappeared or whatever it had been. Their mother worked as a secretary at Holmes Aircraft, the helicopter plant out in Westville, and a series of sitters came in to stay with the boys, except by then it was just Hal that the sitters had to mind through the day—Bill was in first grade, big school. None of the babysitters stayed for long. They got pregnant and married their boyfriends or got work at Holmes, or Mrs. Shelburn would discover they had been at the cooking sherry or her bottle of brandy which was kept in the sideboard for special occasions. Most of them were stupid girls who seemed only to want to eat or sleep. None of them wanted to read to Hal as his mother would do.

The sitter that long winter was a huge, sleek black girl named Beulah. She fawned over Hal when Hal's mother was around and sometimes pinched him when she wasn't. Still, Hal had some liking for Beulah, who once in awhile would read him a lurid tale from one of her confession or true-detective magazines ("Death Came for the Voluptuous Redhead," Beulah would intone ominously in the dozey daytime silence of the living room, and pop another Reese's Peanut Butter Cup into her mouth while Hal solemnly studied the grainy tabloid pictures and drank his milk from his Wish-Cup). And the liking made what happened worse.

He found the monkey on a cold, cloudy day in March. Sleet ticked sporadically off the windows, and Beulah was asleep on the couch, a copy of *My Story* tented open on her admirable bosom.

So Hal went into the back closet to look at his father's things.

The back closet was a storage space that ran the length of the second floor on the left side, extra space that had never been finished off. One got into the back closet by using a small door—a down-the-rabbit-hole sort of door—on Bill's side of the boys' bedroom. They both liked to go in there, even though it was chilly in winter and hot enough in summer to wring a bucketful of sweat out of your pores. Long and narrow and somehow snug, the back closet was full of fascinating junk. No matter how much stuff you looked at, you never seemed to be able to look at it all. He and Bill had spent whole Saturday afternoons up here, barely speaking to each other, taking things out of boxes, examining them, turning them over and over so their hands could absorb each unique reality, putting them back. Now Hal wondered if he and Bill hadn't been trying, as best they could, to somehow make contact with their vanished father.

He had been a merchant mariner with a navigator's certificate, and there were stacks of charts back there, some marked with neat circles (and the dimple of the compass' swing-point in the center of each). There were twenty volumes of something called *Barron's Guide to Navigation*. A set of cockeyed binoculars that made your eyes feel hot and funny if you looked through them too long. There were touristy things from a dozen ports of call—rubber hula-hula dolls, a black cardboard bowler with a torn band that said YOU PICK A GIRL AND I'LL PICCADILLY, a glass globe with a tiny Eiffel Tower inside—and there were also envelopes with foreign stamps tucked carefully away inside, and foreign coins; there were rock samples from the Hawaiian island of Maui, a glassy Black—heavy and somehow ominous, and funny records in foreign languages.

That day, with the sleet ticking hypnotically off the roof just above his head, Hal worked his way all the way down to the far end of the back closet, moved a box aside, and saw another box behind it—a Ralston-Purina box. Looking over the top was a pair of glassy hazel eyes. They gave him a start and he skittered back for a moment, heart thumping, as if he had discovered a deadly pygmy. Then he saw its silence, the glaze in those eyes, and realized it was some sort of toy. He moved forward again and lifted it carefully from the box.

It grinned its ageless, toothy grin in the yellow light, its cymbals held apart.

Delighted, Hal had turned it this way and that, feeling the crinkle of its nappy fur. Its funny grin pleased him. Yet hadn't there been something else? An almost instinctive feeling of disgust that had come and gone almost before he was aware of it? Perhaps it was so, but with an old, old memory like this one, you had to be careful not to believe too much. Old memories could lie. But . . . hadn't he seen that same expression on Petey's face, in the attic of the home place?

He had seen the key set into the small of its back, and turned it. It had turned far too easily; there were no winding-up clicks. Broken, then. Broken, but still neat.

He took it out to play with it.

"Whatchoo got, Hal?" Beulah asked, waking from her nap.

"Nothing," Hal said. "I found it."

He put it up on the shelf on his side of the bedroom. It stood atop his Lassie coloring books, grinning, staring into space, cymbals poised. It was broken, but it grinned nonetheless. That night Hal awakened from some uneasy dream, bladder full, and got up to use the bathroom in the hall. Bill was a breathing lump of covers across the room.

Hal came back, almost asleep again . . . and suddenly the monkey began to beat its cymbals together in the darkness.

Jang-jang-jang-jang—

He came fully awake, as if snapped in the face with a cold, wet towel. His heart gave a staggering leap of surprise, and a tiny, mouselike squeak escaped his throat. He stared at the monkey, eyes wide, lips trembling.

Jang-jang-jang-jang—

Its body rocked and humped on the shelf. Its lips spread and closed, spread and closed, hideously gleeful, revealing huge and carnivorous teeth.

"Stop," Hal whispered.

His brother turned over and uttered a loud, single snore. All else was silent . . . except for the monkey. The cymbals clapped and clashed, and surely it would wake his brother, his mother, the world. It would wake the dead.

Jang-jang-jang-jang—

Hal moved toward it, meaning to stop it somehow, perhaps put his hand between its cymbals until it ran down (*but it was broken, wasn't it?*), and then it stopped on its own. The cymbals came together one last time—*Jang!*— and then spread slowly apart to their original position. The brass glimmered in the shadows. The monkey's dirty yellowish teeth grinned their improbable grin.

The house was silent again. His mother turned over in her bed and echoed Bill's single snore. Hal got back into his bed and pulled the covers up, his heart still beating fast, and he thought: *I'll put it back in the closet again tomorrow. I don't want it.*

But the next morning he forgot all about putting the monkey back because his mother didn't go to work. Beulah was dead. Their mother wouldn't tell them exactly what happened. "It was an accident, just a terrible accident" was all she would say. But that afternoon Bill bought a newspaper on his way home from school and smuggled page four up to their room under his shirt (TWO KILLED IN APARTMENT SHOOT-OUT, the headline read) and read the article haltingly to Hal, following along with his finger, while their mother cooked supper in the kitchen. Beulah McCaffery, 19, and Sally Tremont, 20, had been shot by Miss McCaffery's boyfriend, Leonard White, 25, following an argument over who was to go out and pick up an order of Chinese food. Miss Tremont had expired at Hartford Receiving; Beulah McCaffery had been pronounced dead at the scene.

It was like Beulah just disappeared into one of her own detective magazines, Hal Shelburn thought, and felt a cold chill race up his spine and then circle his heart. And then he realized the shootings had occurred about the same time the monkey ———

"Hal?" It was Terry's voice, sleepy. "Coming to bed?"

He spat toothpaste into the sink and rinsed his mouth. "Yes," he said.

He had put the monkey in his suitcase earlier, and locked it up. They were flying back to Texas in two or three days. But before they went, he would get rid of the damned thing for good.

Somehow.

"You were pretty rough on Dennis this afternoon," Terry said in the dark.

"Dennis has needed somebody to start being rough on him for quite a while now, I think. He's been drifting. I just don't want him to start falling."

"Psychologically, beating the boy isn't a very productive ———"

"I didn't *beat* him, Terry—for Christ's sake!"

"—way to assert parental authority ———"

"Oh, don't give me any of that encounter-group shit," Hal said angrily.

"I can see you don't want to discuss this." Her voice was cold.

"I told him to get the dope out of the house, too."

"You did?" Now she sounded apprehensive. "How did he take it? What did he say?"

"Come on, Terry! What *could* he say? 'You're fired'?"

"Hal, what's the *matter* with you? You're not like this —what's *wrong?*"

"Nothing," he said, thinking of the monkey locked away in his Samsonite. Would he hear it if it began to clap its cymbals? Yes, he surely would. Muffled, but audible.

Clapping doom for someone, as it had for Beulah, Johnny McCabe, Uncle Will's dog Daisy. *Jang-jang-jang,* is it you, Hal? "I've just been under a strain."

"I *hope* that's all it is. Because I don't like you this way."

"No?" And the words escaped before he could stop them; he didn't even want to stop them. "So pop a few Valium and everything will look okay again, right?"

He heard her draw breath in and let it out shakily. She began to cry then. He could have comforted her (maybe), but there seemed to be no comfort in him. There was too much terror. It would be better when the monkey was gone again, gone for good. Please God, gone for good.

He lay wakeful until very late, until morning began to gray the air outside. But he thought he knew what to do.

Bill had found the monkey the second time.

That was about a year and a half after Beulah McCaffery had been pronounced dead at the scene. It was summer. Hal had just finished kindergarten.

He came in from playing with Stevie Arlingen and his mother called, "Wash your hands, Hal, you're filthy like a pig." She was on the porch, drinking an iced tea and reading a book. It was her vacation; she had two weeks.

Hal gave his hands a token pass under cold water and printed dirt on the hand-towel. "Where's Bill?"

"Upstairs. You tell him to clean his side of the room. It's a mess."

Hal, who enjoyed being the messenger of unpleasant news in such matters, rushed up. Bill was sitting on the floor. The small down-the-rabbit-hole door leading to the back closet was ajar. He had the monkey in his hands.

"That don't work," Hal said immediately. "It's busted."

He was apprehensive, although he barely remembered coming back from the bathroom that night, and the monkey suddenly beginning to clap its cymbals. A week or so after that, he had had a bad dream about the monkey and Beulah—he couldn't remember exactly what—and had awakened screaming, thinking for a moment that the soft weight on his chest was the monkey, that he would open his eyes and see it grinning down at him. But of course the soft weight had only been his pillow, clutched with panicky tightness. His mother came in to soothe him

with a drink of water and two chalky-orange baby aspi-
rins, those Valium for childhood's troubled times. She
thought it was the fact of Beulah's death that had caused
the nightmare. So it was, but not in the way she thought.

He barely remembered any of this now, but the monkey still scared him, particularly its cymbals. And its
teeth.

"I know that," Bill said, and tossed the monkey aside.
"It's stupid." It landed on Bill's bed, staring up at the
ceiling, cymbals poised. Hal did not like to see it there.
"You want to go down to Teddy's and get Popsicles?"

"I spent my allowance already," Hal said. "Besides,
Mom says you got to clean up your side of the room."

"I can do that later," Bill said. "And I'll loan you a
nickel, if you want." Bill was not above giving Hal an Indian rope burn sometimes, and would occasionally trip him
up or punch him for no particular reason, but mostly he
was okay.

"Sure," Hal said gratefully. "I'll just put that busted
monkey back in the closet first, okay?"

"Nah," Bill said, getting up. "Let's go-go-go."

Hal went. Bill's moods were changeable, and if he
paused to put the monkey away, he might lose his Popsicle. They went down to Teddy's and got them, then down
to the Rec where some kids were getting up a baseball
game. Hal was too small to play, but he sat far out in foul
territory, sucking his root beer Popsicle and chasing what
the big kids called "Chinese home runs." They didn't get
home until almost dark, and their mother whacked Hal
for getting the hand-towel dirty and whacked Bill for not
cleaning up his side of the room, and after supper there
was TV, and by the time all of that had happened, Hal
had forgotten all about the monkey. It somehow found
its way up onto *Bill's* shelf, where it stood right next to
Bill's autographed picture of Bill Boyd. And there it
stayed for nearly two years.

By the time Hal was seven, babysitters had become an
extravagance, and Mrs. Shelburn's last word to the two of
them each morning was, "Bill, look after your brother."

That day, however, Bill had to stay after school for a
Safety Patrol Boy meeting and Hal came home alone,
stopping at each corner until he could see absolutely no
traffic coming in either direction and then skittering
across, shoulders hunched, like a doughboy crossing no

man's land. He let himself into the house with the key under the mat and went immediately to the refrigerator for a glass of milk. He got the bottle, and then it slipped through his fingers and crashed to smithereens on the floor, the pieces of glass flying everywhere, as the monkey suddenly began to beat its cymbals together upstairs.

Jang-jang-jang-jang, on and on.

He stood there immobile, looking down at the broken glass and the puddle of milk, full of a terror he could not name or understand. It was simply there, seeming to ooze from his pores.

He turned and rushed upstairs to their room. The monkey stood on Bill's shelf, seeming to stare at him. He had knocked the autographed picture of Bill Boyd face-down onto Bill's bed. The monkey rocked and grinned and beat its cymbals together. Hal approached it slowly, not wanting to, not able to stay away. Its cymbals jerked apart and crashed together and jerked apart again. As he got closer, he could hear the clockwork running in the monkey's guts.

Abruptly, uttering a cry of revulsion and terror, he swatted it from the shelf as one might swat a large, loathsome bug. It struck Bill's pillow and then fell on the floor, cymbals still beating together, *jang-jang-jang*, lips flexing and closing as it lay there on its back in a patch of late April sunshine.

Then, suddenly, he remembered Beulah. The monkey had clapped its cymbals that night, too.

Hal kicked it with one Buster Brown shoe, kicked it as hard as he could, and this time the cry that escaped him was one of fury. The clockwork monkey skittered across the floor, bounced off the wall, and lay still. Hal stood staring at it, fists bunched, heart pounding. It grinned saucily back at him, the sun a burning pinpoint in one glass eye. *Kick me all you want,* it seemed to tell him. *I'm nothing but cogs and clockwork and a worm-gear or two, kick me all you feel like, I'm not real, just a funny clockwork monkey is all I am, and who's dead? There's been an explosion at the helicopter plant! What's that rising up into the sky like a big bloody bowling ball with eyes where the finger-holes should be? Is it your mother's head, Hal? Down at Brook Street Corner! The car was going too fast! The driver was drunk! There's one Patrol Boy less! Could you hear the crunching sound when the*

*wheels ran over Bill's skull and his brains squirted out of
his ears? Yes? No? Maybe? Don't ask me, I don't know,
I can't know, all I know how to do is beat these cymbals
together jang-jang-jang, and who's dead, Hal? Your
mother? Your brother? Or is it you, Hal? Is it you?*

He rushed at it again, meaning to stomp on it, smash
its loathsome body, jump on it until cogs and gears flew
and its horrible glass eyes rolled across the floor. But just
as he reached it its cymbals came together once more,
very softly . . . *(jang)* . . . as a spring somewhere inside
expanded one final, minute notch . . . and a sliver of ice
seemed to whisper its way through the walls of his heart,
impaling it, stilling its fury and leaving him sick with terror again. The monkey almost seemed to know—how
gleeful its grin seemed!

He picked it up, tweezing one of its arms between the
thumb and first finger of his right hand, mouth drawn
down in a bow of loathing, as if it were a corpse he held.
Its mangy fake fur seemed hot and fevered against his
skin. He fumbled open the tiny door that led to the back
closet and turned on the bulb. The monkey grinned at
him as he crawled down the length of the storage area
between boxes piled on top of boxes, past the set of navigation books and the photograph albums with their fume
of old chemicals and the souvenirs and the old clothes,
and Hal thought: *If it begins to clap its cymbals together
now and move in my hand, I'll scream, and if I scream,
it'll do more than grin, it'll start to* laugh, *to laugh at me,
and then I'll go crazy and they'll find me in here, drool-
ing and laughing, crazy, I'll be crazy, oh please dear God,
please dear Jesus, don't let me go crazy—*

He reached the far end and clawed two boxes aside,
spilling one of them, and jammed the monkey back into
the Ralston-Purina box in the farthest corner. And it
leaned in there, comfortably, as if home at last, cymbals
poised, grinning its simian grin, as if the joke were still on
Hal. Hal crawled backward, sweating, hot and cold, all
fire and ice, waiting for the cymbals to begin, and when
they began, the monkey would leap from its box and
scurry beetlelike toward him, clockwork whirring, cymbals clashing madly, and ———

—and none of that happened. He turned off the light
and slammed the small down-the-rabbit-hole door and
leaned on it, panting. At last he began to feel a little bet-

ter. He went downstairs on rubbery legs, got an empty
bag, and began carefully to pick up the jagged shards and
splinters of the broken milk bottle, wondering if he was
going to cut himself and bleed to death, if that was what
the clapping cymbals had meant. But that didn't happen,
either. He got a towel and wiped up the milk and then
sat down to see if his mother and brother would come
home.

His mother came first, asking, "Where's Bill?"

In a low, colorless voice, now sure that Bill must be
dead, Hal started to explain about the Patrol Boy meeting, knowing that, even given a very long meeting, Bill
should have been home half an hour ago.

His mother looked at him curiously, started to ask what
was wrong, and then the door opened and Bill came in—
only it was not Bill at all, not really. This was a ghost-
Bill, pale and silent.

"What's wrong?" Mrs. Shelburn exclaimed. "Bill,
what's wrong?"

Bill began to cry and they got the story through his
tears. There had been a car, he said. He and his friend
Charlie Silverman were walking home together after the
meeting and the car came around Brook Street Corner too
fast and Charlie had frozen, Bill had tugged Charlie's
hand once but had lost his grip and the car ———

Bill began to bray out loud, hysterical sobs, and his
mother hugged him to her, rocking him, and Hal looked
out on the porch and saw two policemen standing there.
The squad car in which they had conveyed Bill home was
at the curb. Then he began to cry himself . . . but his
tears were tears of relief.

It was Bill's turn to have nightmares now—dreams in
which Charlie Silverman died over and over again,
knocked out of his Red Ryder cowboy boots, and flipped
onto the hood of the old Hudson Hornet the drunk driver
had been driving. Charlie Silverman's head and the Hudson's windshield had met with an explosive noise, and
both had shattered. The drunk driver, who owned a
candy store in Milford, suffered a heart attack shortly
after being taken into custody (perhaps it was the sight
of Charlie Silverman's brains drying on his pants), and his
lawyer was quite successful at the trial with his "this man
has been punished enough" theme. The drunk was given
sixty days (suspended) and lost his privilege to operate

a motor vehicle in the state of Connecticut for five years
. . . which was about as long as Bill Shelburn's nightmares
lasted. The monkey was hidden away again in the back
closet. Bill never noticed it was gone from his shelf . . .
or if he did, he never said.

Hal felt safe for a while. He even began to forget about
the monkey again, or to believe it had only been a bad
dream. But when he came home from school on the afternoon his mother died, it was back on his shelf, cymbals poised, grinning down at him.

He approached it slowly as if from outside himself—as
if his own body had been turned into a wind-up toy at the
sight of the monkey. He saw his hand reach out and take
it down. He felt the nappy fur crinkle under his hand,
but the feeling was muffled, mere pressure, as if someone
had shot him full of Novocaine. He could hear his breathing, quick and dry, like the rattle of wind through straw.

He turned it over and grasped the key and years later
he would think that his drugged fascination was like that
of a man who puts a six-shooter with one loaded chamber against a closed and jittering eyelid and pulls the trig-
ger.

*No don't—let it alone throw it away don't touch
it* ———

He turned the key and in the silence he heard a perfect
tiny series of winding-up clicks. When he let the key go,
the monkey began to clap its cymbals together and he
could feel its body jerking, bend-and-*jerk,* bend-and-*jerk,*
as if it were live, it *was* alive, writhing in his hand like
some loathsome pygmy, and the vibration he felt through
its balding brown fur was not that of turning cogs but the
beating of its black and cindered heart.

With a groan, Hal dropped the monkey and backed
away, fingernails digging into the flesh under his eyes,
palms pressed to his mouth. He stumbled over something
and nearly lost his balance (then he would have been
right down on the floor with it, his bulging blue eyes looking into its glassy hazel ones). He scrambled toward the
door, backed through it, slammed it, and leaned against
it. Suddenly he bolted for the bathroom and vomited.

It was Mrs. Stukey from the helicopter plant who
brought the news and stayed with them those first two
endless nights, until Aunt Ida got down from Maine.
Their mother had died of a brain embolism in the middle

of the afternoon. She had been standing at the water cooler with a cup of water in one hand and had crumpled as if shot, still holding the paper cup in one hand. With the other she had clawed at the water cooler and had pulled the great glass bottle of Poland water down with her. It had shattered . . . but the plant doctor, who came on the run, said later that he believed Mrs. Shelburn was dead before the water had soaked through her dress and her underclothes to wet her skin. The boys were never told any of this, but Hal knew anyway. He dreamed it again and again on the long nights following his mother's death. *You still have trouble gettin to sleep, little brother?* Bill had asked him, and Hal supposed Bill thought all the thrashing and bad dreams had to do with their mother dying so suddenly, and that was right . . . but only partly right. There was the guilt: the certain, deadly knowledge that he had killed his mother by winding the monkey up on that sunny after-school afternoon.

When Hal finally fell asleep, his sleep must have been deep. When he awoke, it was nearly noon. Petey was sitting cross-legged in a chair across the room, methodically eating an orange section by section and watching a game show on TV.

Hal swung his legs out of bed, feeling as if someone had punched him down into sleep . . . and then punched him back out of it. His head throbbed. "Where's your mom, Petey?"

Petey glanced around. "She and Dennis went shopping. I said I'd stay here with you. Do you always talk in your sleep, Dad?"

Hal looked at his son cautiously. "No, I don't think so. What did I say?"

"It was all muttering, I couldn't make it out. It scared me, a little."

"Well, here I am in my right mind again," Hal said, and managed a small grin. Petey grinned back, and Hal felt simple love for the boy again, an emotion that was bright and strong and uncomplicated. He wondered why he had always been able to feel so good about Petey, to feel he understood Petey and could help him, and why Dennis seemed a window too dark to look through, a mystery in his ways and habits, the sort of boy he could not understand because he had never been that sort of

boy. It was too easy to say that the move from California
had changed Dennis, or that ———

His thoughts froze. The monkey. The monkey was sitting on the windowsill, cymbals poised. Hal felt his heart
stop dead in his chest and then suddenly begin to gallop.
His vision wavered, and his throbbing head began to ache
ferociously.

It had escaped from the suitcase and now stood on the
windowsill, grinning at him. *Thought you got rid of me,
didn't you? But you've thought that before, haven't you?*

Yes, he thought sickly. Yes, I have.

"Pete, did you take that monkey out of my suitcase?"
he asked, knowing the answer already. He had locked the
suitcase and had put the key in his overcoat pocket.

Petey glanced at the monkey, and something—Hal
thought it was unease—passed over his face. "No," he
said. "Mom put it there."

"Mom did?"

"Yeah. She took it from you. She laughed."

"Took it from me? What are you talking about?"

"You·had it in bed with you. I was brushing my teeth,
but Dennis saw. He laughed, too. He said you looked like
a baby with a teddy bear."

Hal looked at the monkey. His mouth was too dry to
swallow. He'd had it in *bed* with him? In *bed*? That loathsome fur against his cheek, maybe against his *mouth*,
those glass eyes staring into his sleeping face, those grinning teeth near his neck? Dear *God*.

He turned abruptly and went to the closet. The Samsonite was there, still locked. The key was still in his overcoat pocket.

Behind him, the TV snapped off. He came out of the
closet slowly. Petey was looking at him soberly. "Daddy,
I don't like that monkey," he said, his voice almost too
low to hear.

"Nor do I," Hal said.

Petey looked at him closely, to see if he was joking,
and saw that he was not. He came to his father and
hugged him tight. Hal could feel him trembling.

Petey spoke into his ear, then, very rapidly, as if afraid
he might not have courage enough to say it again . . . or
that the monkey might overhear.

"It's like it looks at you. Like it looks at you no matter where you are in the room. And if you go into the

other room, it's like it's looking through the wall at you. I kept feeling like it . . . like it wanted me for something."

Petey shuddered. Hal held him tight.

"Like it wanted you to wind it up," Hal said.

Pete nodded violently. "It isn't really broken, is it, Dad?"

"Sometimes it is," Hal said, looking over his son's shoulder at the monkey. "But sometimes it still works."

"I kept wanting to go over there and wind it up. It was so quiet, and I thought, I can't, it'll wake up Daddy, but I still wanted to, and I went over and I . . . I *touched* it and I hate the way it feels . . . but I liked it, too . . . and it was like it was saying, Wind me up, Petey, we'll play, your father isn't going to wake up, he's never going to wake up at all, wind me up, wind me up. . . ."

The boy suddenly burst into tears.

"It's bad, I know it is. There's something wrong with it. Can't we throw it out, Daddy? Please?"

The monkey grinned its endless grin at Hal. He could feel Petey's tears between them. Late morning sun glinted off the monkey's brass cymbals—the light reflected upward and put sunstreaks on the motel's plain white stucco ceiling.

"What time did your mother think she and Dennis would be back, Petey?"

"Around one." He swiped at his red eyes with his shirtsleeve, looking embarrassed at his tears. But he wouldn't look at the monkey. "I turned on the TV," he whispered. "And I turned it up loud."

"That was all right, Petey."

"I had a crazy idea," Petey said. "I had this idea that if I wound that monkey up, you . . . you would have just died there in bed. In your sleep. Wasn't that a crazy idea, Daddy?" His voice had dropped again, and it trembled helplessly.

How would it have happened? Hal wondered. *Heart attack? An embolism, like my mother? What? It doesn't really matter, does it?*

And on the heels of that, another, colder thought: *Get rid of it, he says. Throw it out. But can it be gotten rid of? Ever?*

The monkey grinned mockingly at him, its cymbals held a foot apart. Did it suddenly come to life on the night Aunt Ida died? he wondered suddenly. Was that the last sound she heard, the muffled *jang-jang-jang* of the monkey beating its cymbals together up in the black attic while the wind whistled along the drainpipe?

"Maybe not so crazy," Hal said slowly to his son. "Go get your flight bag, Petey."

Petey looked at him uncertainly. "What are we going to do?"

Maybe it can be got rid of. Maybe permanently, maybe just for a while . . . a long while or a short while. Maybe it's just going to come back and come back and that's what all this is about . . . but maybe I—we—can say good-bye to it for a long time. It took twenty years to come back this time. It took twenty years to get out of the well. . . .

"We're going to go for a ride," Hal said. He felt fairly calm, but somehow too heavy inside his skin. Even his eyeballs seemed to have gained weight. "But first I want you to take your flight bag out there by the edge of the parking lot and find three or four good-sized rocks. Put them inside the bag and bring it back to me. Got it?"

Understanding flickered in Petey's eyes. "All right, Daddy."

Hal glanced at his watch. It was nearly 12:15. "Hurry. I want to be gone before your mother gets back."

"Where are we going?"

"To Uncle Will's and Aunt Ida's," Hal said. "To the home place."

Hal went into the bathroom, looked behind the toilet, and got the bowl brush leaning there. He took it back to the window and stood there with it in his hand like a cut-rate magic wand. He looked out at Petey in his melton shirt-jacket, crossing the parking lot with his flight bag, DELTA showing clearly in white letters against a blue field. A fly bumbled in an upper corner of the window, slow and stupid with the end of the warm season. Hal knew how it felt.

He watched Petey hunt up three good-sized rocks and then start back across the parking lot. A car came around the corner of the motel, a car that was moving too fast, much too fast, and without thinking, reaching with the kind of reflex a good short-stop shows going to his right, his hand flashed down, as if in a karate chop . . . and stopped.

The cymbals closed soundlessly on his intervening hand, and he felt something in the air. Something like rage.

The car's brakes screamed. Petey flinched back. The driver motioned to him impatiently, as if what had almost happened was Petey's fault, and Petey ran across the parking lot with his collar flapping and into the motel's rear entrance.

Sweat was running down Hal's chest; he felt it on his forehead like a drizzle of oily rain. The cymbals pressed coldly against his hand, numbing it.

Go on, he thought grimly. *Go on, I can wait all day. Until hell freezes over, if that's what it takes.*

The cymbals drew apart and came to rest. Hal heard one faint *click!* from inside the monkey. He withdrew his hand and looked at it. On both the back and the palm there were grayish semicircles printed into the skin, as if he had been frostbitten.

The fly bumbled and buzzed, trying to find the cold October sunshine that seemed so close.

Petey came bursting in, breathing quickly, cheeks rosy. "I got three good ones, Dad, I—" He broke off. "Are you all right, Daddy?"

"Fine," Hal said. "Bring the bag over."

Hal hooked the table by the sofa over to the window with his foot, so it stood below the sill, and put the flight bag on it. He spread its mouth open like lips. He could see the stones Petey had collected glimmering inside. He used the toilet-bowl brush to hook the monkey forward. It teetered for a moment and then fell into the bag. There was a faint *jing!* as one of its cymbals struck one of the rocks.

"Dad? Daddy?" Petey sounded frightened. Hal looked around at him. Something was different; something had changed. What was it?

Then he saw the direction of Petey's gaze and he knew. The buzzing of the fly had stopped. It lay dead on the windowsill.

"Did the monkey do that?" Petey whispered.

"Come on," Hal said, zipping the bag shut. "I'll tell you while we ride out to the home place."

"How can we go? Mom and Dennis took the car."

"I'll get us there," Hal said, and ruffled Petey's hair.

He showed the desk clerk his driver's license and a twenty-dollar bill. After taking Hal's Texas Instruments

digital watch as further collateral, the clerk handed Hal
the keys to his own car—a battered AMC Gremlin. As
they drove east on Route 302 toward Casco, Hal began
to talk, haltingly at first, then a little faster. He began by
telling Petey that his father had probably brought the
monkey home with him from overseas, as a gift for his
sons. It wasn't a particularly unique toy; there was nothing strange or valuable about it. There must have been
hundreds of thousands of wind-up monkeys in the world,
some made in Hong Kong, some in Taiwan, some in Ko-
rea. But somewhere along the line—perhaps even in the
dark back closet of the house in Connecticut where the
two boys had begun their growing up—something had
happened to the monkey. Something bad, evil. It might
be, Hal told Petey as he tried to coax the clerk's Gremlin
up past forty (he was very aware of the zipped-up flight
bag on the back seat, and Petey kept glancing around at
it), that some evil—maybe even most evil—isn't even
sentient and aware of what it is. It might be that most
evil is very much like a monkey full of clockwork that
you wind up; the clockwork turns, the cymbals begin to
beat, the teeth grin, the stupid glass eyes laugh . . . or
appear to laugh. . . .

He told Petey about finding the monkey, but he found
himself skipping over large chunks of the story, not wanting to terrify his already scared boy any more than he
was already. The story thus became disjointed, not really
clear, but Petey asked no questions; perhaps he was filling
in the blanks for himself, Hal thought, in much the same
way that he had dreamed his mother's death over and
over, although he had not been there.

Uncle Will and Aunt Ida had both been there for the
funeral. Afterward, Uncle Will had gone back to Maine
—it was harvest-time—and Aunt Ida had stayed on for
two weeks with the boys to neaten up her sister's affairs.
But more than that, she spent the time making herself
known to the boys, who were so stunned by their mother's sudden death that they were nearly sleepwalking.
When they couldn't sleep, she was there with warm milk;
when Hal woke at three in the morning with nightmares
(nightmares in which his mother approached the water
cooler without seeing the monkey that floated and bobbed
in its cool sapphire depths, grinning and clapping its cym-

bals, each converging pair of sweeps leaving trails of bubbles behind); she was there when Bill came down with first a fever and then a rash of painful mouth sores and then hives three days after the funeral; she was there. She made herself known to the boys, and before they rode the New England Flyer from Hartford to Portland with her, both Bill and Hal had come to her separately and wept on her lap while she held them and rocked them, and the bonding began.

The day before they left Connecticut for good to go "down Maine" (as it was called in those days), the ragman came in his great old rattly truck and picked up the huge pile of useless stuff that Bill and Hal had carried out to the sidewalk from the back closet. When all the junk had been set out by the curb for pick-up, Aunt Ida had asked them to go through the back closet again and pick out any souvenirs or remembrances they wanted specially to keep. We just don't have room for it all, boys, she told them, and Hal supposed Bill had taken her at her word and had gone through all those fascinating boxes their father had left behind one final time. Hal did not join his older brother. Hal had lost his taste for the back closet. A terrible idea had come to him during those first two weeks of mourning: perhaps his father hadn't just disappeared, or run away because he had an itchy foot and had discovered marriage wasn't for him.

Maybe the monkey had gotten him.

When he heard the rag-man's truck roaring and farting and backfiring its way down the block, Hal nerved himself, snatched the scruffy wind-up monkey from his shelf where it had been since the day his mother died (he had not dared to touch it until then, not even to throw it back into the closet), and ran downstairs with it. Neither Bill nor Aunt Ida saw him. Sitting on top of a barrel filled with broken souvenirs and mouldy books was the Ralston-Purina carton, filled with similar junk. Hal had slammed the monkey back into the box it had originally come out of, hysterically daring it to begin clapping its cymbals (*go on, go on, I dare you, dare you, DARE YOU*), but the monkey only waited there, leaning back nonchalantly, as if expecting a bus, grinning its awful, knowing grin.

Hal stood by, a small boy in old corduroy pants and scuffed Buster Browns, as the rag-man, an Italian gent who wore a crucifix and whistled through the space in his teeth, began loading boxes and barrels into his ancient truck with the high wooden sides. Hal watched as he lifted both the barrel and the Ralston-Purina box balanced atop it; he watched the monkey disappear into the maw of the truck; he watched as the rag-man climbed back into the cab, blew his nose mightily into the palm of his hand, wiped his hand with a huge red handkerchief, and started the truck's engine with a mighty roar and a stinking blast of oily blue smoke; he watched the truck draw away. And a great weight had dropped away from his heart—he actually felt it go. He had jumped up and down twice, as high as he could jump, his arms spread, palms held out, and if any of the neighbors had seen him, they would have thought it odd almost to the point of blasphemy, perhaps—*why is that boy jumping for joy* (for that was surely what it was; a jump for joy can hardly be disguised) *with his mother not even a month in her grave?*

He was jumping for joy because the monkey was gone, gone forever. Gone forever, but not three months later Aunt Ida had sent him up into the attic to get the boxes of Christmas decorations, and as he crawled around looking for them, getting the knees of his pants dusty, he had suddenly come face to face with it again, and his wonder and terror had been so great that he had to bite sharply into the side of his hand to keep from screaming . . . or fainting dead away. There it was, grinning its toothy grin, cymbals poised a foot apart and ready to clap, leaning nonchalantly back against one corner of a Ralston-Purina carton as if waiting for a bus, seeming to say: *Thought you got rid of me, didn't you? But I'm not that easy to get rid of, Hal. I like you, Hal. We were made for each other, just a boy and his pet monkey, a couple of good old buddies. And somewhere south of here there's a stupid old Italian rag-man lying in a claw-foot tub with his eyeballs bulging and his dentures half-popped out of his mouth, his screaming mouth, a rag-man who smells like a burned-out Exide battery. He was saving me for his grandson, Hal, he put me on the shelf with his soap and his razor and his Burma-Shave and the Philco radio he listened to the Brooklyn Dodgers on, and I started to clap, and one of my cymbals hit that old radio and into the tub it went, and then I came to*

*you, Hal, I worked my way along country roads at night
and the moonlight shone off my teeth at three in the
morning and I left death in my wake, Hal, I came to
you, I'm your Christmas present, Hal, wind me up, who's
dead? Is it Bill? Is it Uncle Will? Is it you, Hal? Is it
you?*

Hal had backed away, grimacing madly, eyes rolling,
and nearly fell going downstairs. He told Aunt Ida he
hadn't been able to find the Christmas decorations—it
was the first lie he had ever told her, and she had seen
the lie on his face but had not asked him why he had
told it, thank God—and later when Bill came in she
asked him to look and he brought the Christmas decorations down. Later, when they were alone, Bill hissed at
him that he was a dummy who couldn't find his own ass
with both hands and a flashlight. Hal said nothing. Hal
was pale and silent, only picking at his supper. And that
night he dreamed of the monkey again, one of its cymbals striking the Philco radio as it babbled out Dean
Martin singing Whenna da moon hitta you eye like a
big pizza pie *ats-a moray*, the radio tumbling into the
bathtub as the monkey grinned and beat it cymbals together with a *JANG* and a *JANG* and a *JANG;* only it
wasn't the Italian rag-man who was in the tub when the
water turned electric.

It was him.

Hal and his son scrambled down the embankment behind the home place to the boathouse that jutted out
over the water on its old pilings. Hal had the flight bag in
his right hand. His throat was dry, his ears were attuned
to an unnaturally keen pitch. The bag seemed very
heavy.

"What's down here, Daddy?" Petey asked.

Hal didn't answer. He set down the flight bag. "Don't
touch that," he said, and Petey backed away from it.
Hal felt in his pocket for the ring of keys Bill had given
him and found one neatly labeled B'HOUSE on a scrap of
adhesive tape.

The day was clear and cold, windy, the sky a brilliant
blue. The leaves of the trees that crowded up to the
verge of the lake had gone every bright fall shade from
blood red to sneering yellow. They rattled and talked in
the wind. Leaves swirled around Petey's sneakers as he

stood anxiously by, and Hal could smell November on the wind, with winter crowding close behind it.

The key turned in the padlock and he pulled the swing doors open. Memory was strong; he didn't even have to look to kick down the wooden block that held the door open. The smell in here was all summer: canvas and bright wood, a lingering, musty warmth.

Uncle Will's rowboat was still here, the oars neatly shipped as if he had last loaded it with his fishing tackle and two six-packs of Black Label on ice yesterday afternoon. Bill and Hal had both gone out fishing with Uncle Will many times, but never together; Uncle Will maintained the boat was too small for three. The red trim, which Uncle Will had touched up each spring, was now faded and peeling, though, and spiders had spun their silk in the boat's bow.

Hal laid hold of it and pulled it down the ramp to the little shingle of beach. The fishing trips had been one of the best parts of his childhood with Uncle Will and Aunt Ida. He had a feeling that Bill felt much the same. Uncle Will was ordinarily the most taciturn of men, but once he had the boat positioned to his liking, some sixty or seventy yards offshore, lines set and bobbers floating on the water, he would crack a beer for himself and one for Hal (who rarely drank more than half of the one can Uncle Will would allow, always with the ritual admonition from Uncle Will that Aunt Ida must never be told because "she'd shoot me for a stranger if she knew I was givin you boys beer, don't you know"), and wax expansive. He would tell stories, answer questions, rebait Hal's hook when it needed rebaiting; and the boat would drift where the wind and the mild current wanted it to be.

"How come you never go right out to the middle, Uncle Will?" Hal had asked once.

"Look over the side there, Hal," Uncle Will had answered.

Hal did. He saw blue water and his fish line going down into black.

"You're looking into the deepest part of Crystal Lake," Uncle Will said, crunching his empty beer can in one hand and selecting a fresh one with the other. "A hundred feet if she's an inch. Amos Culligan's old Studebaker is down there somewhere. Damn fool took it out on the lake one early December, before the ice was made. Lucky to get out of it alive, he was. They'll never get that Studebaker out, nor see it until Judgment Trump blows. Lake's one deep son of a whore right here, it is. Big ones are right here, Hal. No need to go out no further. Let's see how your worm looks. Reel that son of a whore right in."

Hal did, and while Uncle Will put a fresh crawler from the old Crisco tin that served as his bait box on his hook, he stared into the water, fascinated, trying to see Amos Culligan's old Studebaker all rust and waterweed drifting out of the open driver's side window through which Amos had escaped at the absolute last moment, waterweed festooning the steering wheel like a rotting necklace, waterweed dangling from the rearview mirror and drifting back and forth in the currents like some strange rosary. But he could see only blue shading to black, and there was the shape of Uncle Will's night-crawler, the hook hidden inside its knots, hung up there in the middle of things, its own sun-shafted version of reality. Hal had a brief, dizzying vision of being suspended over a mighty gulf, and he had closed his eyes for a moment until the vertigo passed. That day, he seemed to recollect, he had drunk his entire can of beer.

. . . *the deepest part of Crystal Lake . . . a hundred feet if she's an inch.*

He paused a moment, panting, and looked up at Petey, still watching anxiously. "You want some help, Daddy?"

"In a minute."

He had his breath again, and now he pulled the rowboat across the narrow strip of sand to the water, leaving a groove. The paint had peeled, but the boat had been kept under cover and it looked sound.

When he and Uncle Will went out, Uncle Will would pull the boat down the ramp, and when the bow was afloat, he would clamber in, grab an oar to push with, and say: "Push me off, Hal . . . this is where you earn your truss!"

"Hand that bag in, Petey, and then give me a push," he said. And, smiling a little, he added: "This is where you earn your truss."

Petey didn't smile back. "Am I coming, Daddy?"

"Not this time. Another time I'll take you out fishing, but . . . not this time."

Petey hesitated. The wind tumbled his brown hair and a few yellow leaves, crisp and dry, wheeled past his shoulders and landed at the edge of the water, bobbing like boats themselves.

"You should have muffled them," he said, low.

"What?" But he thought he understood what Petey had meant.

"Put cotton over the cymbals. Taped it on. So it couldn't . . . make that noise."

Hal suddenly remembered Daisy coming toward him —not walking but lurching—and how, quite suddenly, blood had burst from both of Daisy's eyes in a flood that soaked her ruff and pattered down on the floor of the barn, how she had collapsed on her forepaws . . . and on that still, rainy spring air of that day he had heard the sound, not muffled but curiously clear, coming from the attic of the house fifty feet away: *Jang-jang-jang-jang!*

He began to scream hysterically, dropping the arm-load of wood he had been getting for the fire. He ran for the kitchen to get Uncle Will, who was eating scrambled eggs and toast, his suspenders not even up over his shoulders yet.

She was an old dog, Hal, Uncle Will had said, his face haggard and unhappy—he looked old himself. *She was twelve, and that's old for a dog. You mustn't take on, now—old Daisy wouldn't like that.*

Old, the vet had echoed, but he had looked troubled all the same, because dogs don't die of explosive brain hemorrhages, even at twelve ("like as if someone had stuck a firecracker in his head," Hal overheard the vet saying to Uncle Will as Uncle Will dug a hole in back of the barn not far from the place where he had buried Daisy's mother in 1950; "I never seen the beat of it, Will").

And later, terrified almost out of his mind but unable to help himself, Hal had crept up to the attic.

Hello, Hal, how you doing? the monkey grinned from its shadowy corner. Its cymbals were poised, a foot or so apart. The sofa cushion Hal had stood on end between them was now all the way across the attic. Something— some force—had thrown it hard enough to split its cover, and stuffing foamed out of it. *Don't worry about Daisy,* the monkey whispered inside his head, its glassy hazel eyes fixed on Hal Shelburn's wide blue ones. *Don't worry about Daisy, she was old, old, Hal, even the vet said so, and by the way, did you see the blood coming out of her eyes, Hal? Wind me up, Hal. Wind me up, let's play, and who's dead, Hal? Is it you?*

And when he came back to himself he had been crawling toward the monkey as if hypnotized. One hand had been outstretched to grasp the key. He scrambled backward then, and almost fell down the attic stairs in his haste—probably would have if the stairwell had not been so narrow. A little whining noise had been coming from his throat.

Now he sat in the boat, looking at Petey. "Muffling the cymbals doesn't work," he said. "I tried it once."

Petey cast a nervous glance at the flight bag. "What happened, Daddy?"

"Nothing I want to talk about now," Hal said, "and nothing you want to hear about. Come on and give me a push."

Petey bent to it, and the stern of the boat grated along the sand. Hal dug in with an oar, and suddenly that feeling of being tied to the earth was gone and the boat was moving lightly, its own thing again after years in the dark boathouse, rocking on the light waves. Hal unshipped the oars one at a time and clicked the oarlocks shut.

"Be careful, Daddy," Petey said. His face was pale.

"This won't take long," Hal promised, but he looked at the flight bag and wondered.

He began to row, bending to the work. The old, familiar ache in the small of his back and between his shoulder blades began. The shore receded. Petey was magically eight again, six, a four-year-old standing at the edge of the water. He shaded his eyes with one infant hand.

Hal glanced casually at the shore but would not allow himself to actually study it. It had been nearly fifteen years, and if he studied the shoreline carefully, he would see the changes rather than the similarities and become lost. The sun beat on his neck, and he began to sweat. He looked at the flight bag, and for a moment he lost the bend-and-pull rhythm. The flight bag seemed . . . seemed to be bulging. He began to row faster.

The wind gusted, drying the sweat and cooling his skin. The boat rose and the bow slapped water to either side when it came down. Hadn't the wind freshened, just in the last minute or so? And was Petey calling something? Yes. Hal couldn't make out what it was over the wind. It didn't matter. Getting rid of the monkey for another twenty years—or maybe forever (please God, forever)—that was what mattered.

The boat reared and came down. He glanced left and saw baby whitecaps. He looked shoreward again and saw Hunter's Point and a collapsed wreck that must have been the Burdon's boathouse when he and Bill were kids. Almost there, then. Almost over the spot where Amos Culligan's Studebaker had plunged through the ice one long-ago December. Almost over the deepest part of the lake.

Petey was screaming something; screaming and pointing. Hal still couldn't hear. The rowboat rocked and bucked, flatting off clouds of thin spray to either side of its peeling bow. A tiny rainbow glowed in one, was pulled apart. Sunlight and shadow raced across the lake in shutters and the waves were not mild now; the whitecaps had grown up. His sweat had dried to gooseflesh, and spray had soaked the back of his jacket. He rowed grimly, eyes alternating between the shoreline and the flight bag. The boat rose again, this time so high that for a moment the left oar pawed at air instead of water.

Petey was pointing at the sky, his screams now only a faint, bright runner of sound.

Hal looked over his shoulder.

The lake was a frenzy of waves. It had gone a deadly dark shade of blue sewn with white seams. A shadow raced across the water toward the boat and something in its shape was familiar, so terribly familiar, that Hal looked up and then the scream was there, struggling in his tight throat.

The sun was behind the cloud, turning it into a hunched working shape with two gold-edged crescents held apart. Two holes were torn in one end of the cloud, and sunshine poured through in two shafts.

As the cloud crossed over the boat, the monkey's cymbals, barely muffled by the flight bag, began to beat. *Jang-jang-jang-jang, it's you, Hal, it's finally you, you're over the deepest part of the lake now and it's your turn, your turn, your turn—*

All the necessary shoreline elements had clicked into their places. The rotting bones of Amos Culligan's Studebaker lay somewhere below, this was where the big ones were, this was the place.

Hal shipped the oars to the locks in one quick jerk, leaned forward unmindful of the wildly rocking boat, and snatched the flight bag. The cymbals made their wild, pagan music; the bag's sides bellowed as if with tenebrous respiration.

"*Right here, you sonofabitch!*" Hal screamed. "*RIGHT HERE!*"

He threw the bag over the side.

It sank fast. For a moment he could see it going down, sides moving, and for that endless moment *he could still hear the cymbals beating.* And for a moment the black waters seemed to clear and he could see down into that terrible gulf of waters to where the big ones lay; there was Amos Culligan's Studebaker, and Hal's mother was behind its slimy wheel, a grinning skeleton with a lake bass staring coldly from the skull's nasal cavity. Uncle Will and Aunt Ida lolled beside her, and Aunt Ida's gray hair trailed upward as the bag fell, turning over and over, a few silver bubbles trailing up: *jang-jang-jang-jang . . .*

Hal slammed the oars back into the water, scraping blood from his knuckles (*and ah God the back of Amos Culligan's Studebaker had been full of dead children! Charlie Silverman . . . Johnny McCabe . . .*), and began to bring the boat about.

There was a dry pistol-shot crack between his feet, and suddenly clear water was welling up between two boards. The boat was old; the wood had shrunk a bit, no doubt; it was just a small leak. But it hadn't been there when he rowed out. He would have sworn to it.

The shore and lake changed places in his view. Petey was at his back now. Overhead, that awful, simian cloud was breaking up. Hal began to row. Twenty seconds was enough to convince him he was rowing for his life. He was only a so-so swimmer, and even a great one would have been put to the test in this suddenly angry water.

Two more boards suddenly shrank apart with that pistol-shot sound. More water poured into the boat, dousing his shoes. There were tiny metallic snapping sounds that he realized were nails breaking. One of the oarlocks snapped and flew off into the water—would the swivel itself go next?

The wind now came from his back, as if trying to slow

him down or even to drive him into the middle of the
lake. He was terrified, but he felt a crazy kind of exhila-
ration through the terror. The monkey was gone for good
this time. He knew it somehow. Whatever happened to
him, the monkey would not be back to draw a shadow
over Dennis's life, or Petey's. The monkey was gone, perhaps resting on the roof or the hood of Amos Culligan's
Studebaker at the bottom of Crystal Lake. Gone for good.

He rowed, bending forward and rocking back. That
cracking, crimping sound came again, and now the rusty
old bait can that had been lying in the bow of the boat
was floating in three inches of water. Spray blew in Hal's
face. There was a louder snapping sound, and the bow
seat fell in two pieces and floated next to the bait box. A
board tore off the left side of the boat, and then another,
this one at the waterline, tore off at the right. Hal rowed.
Breath rasped in his mouth, hot and dry, and his throat
swelled with the coppery taste of exhaustion. His sweaty
hair flew.

Now a crack ran directly up the bottom of the rowboat,
zigzagged between his feet, and ran up to the bow. Water
gushed in; he was in water up to his ankles, then to the
swell of calf. He rowed, but the boat's shoreward movement was sludgy now. He didn't dare look behind him to
see how close he was getting.

Another board tore loose. The crack running up the
center of the boat grew branches, like a tree. Water
flooded in.

Hal began to make the oars sprint, breathing in great,
failing gasps. He pulled once . . . twice . . . and on the
third pull both oar swivels snapped off. He lost one oar,
held onto the other. He rose to his feet and began to flail
at the water with it. The boat rocked, almost capsized,
and spilled him back onto his seat with a thump.

Moments later more boards tore loose, the seat collapsed, and he was lying in the water which filled the
bottom of the boat, astounded at its coldness. He tried to
get on his knees, desperately thinking: *Petey must not see
this, must not see his father drown right in front of his
eyes, you're going to swim, dog-paddle if you have to, but
do, do something—*

There was another splintering crack—almost a crash
—and he was in the water, swimming for the shore as he
never had swum in his life . . . and the shore was amaz-

ingly close. A minute later he was standing waist-deep in water, not five yards from the beach.

Petey splashed toward him, arms out, screaming and crying and laughing. Hal started toward him and floundered. Petey, chest-deep, floundered.

They caught each other.

Hal, breathing in great, winded gasps, nevertheless hoisted the boy into his arms and carried him up to the beach where both of them sprawled, panting.

"Daddy? Is it really gone? That monkey?"

"Yes. I think it's really gone."

"The boat fell apart. It just . . . fell apart all around you."

Disintegrated, Hal thought, and looked at the boards floating loose on the water forty feet out. They bore no resemblance to the tight, handmade rowboat he had pulled out of the boathouse.

"It's all right now," Hal said, leaning back on his elbows. He shut his eyes and let the sun warm his face.

"Did you see the cloud?" Petey whispered.

"Yes. But I don't see it now . . . do you?"

They looked at the sky. There were scattered white puffs here and there, but no large dark cloud. It was gone, as he had said.

Hal pulled Petey to his feet. "There'll be towels up at the house. Come on." But he paused, looking at his son. "You were crazy, running out there like that."

Petey looked at him solemnly. "You were brave, Daddy."

"Was I?" The thought of bravery had never crossed his mind. Only his fear. The fear had been too big to see anything else. If anything else had indeed been there. "Come on, Pete."

"What are we going to tell Mom?"

Hal smiled. "I dunno, big guy. We'll think of something."

He paused a moment longer, looking at the boards floating on the water. The lake was calm again, sparkling with small wavelets. Suddenly Hal thought of summer people he didn't even know—a man and his son, perhaps, fishing for the big one. *I've got something Dad!* the boy screams. *Well reel it up and let's see,* the father says, and coming up from the depths, weeds draggling from its cymbals, grinning its terrible, welcoming grin . . . the monkey.

He shuddered—but those were only things that might be.

"Come on," he said to Petey again, and they walked up the path through the flaming October woods toward the home place.

From the Bridgton News
October 24, 1980:

MYSTERY
OF THE DEAD FISH
By BETSY MORIARTY

HUNDREDS of dead fish were found floating belly-up on Crystal Lake in the neighboring township of Casco late last week. The largest numbers appeared to have died in the vicinity of Hunter's Point, although the lake's currents make this a bit difficult to determine. The dead fish included all types commonly found in these waters—bluegills, pickerel, sunnies, carp, brown and rainbow trout, even one landlocked salmon. Fish and Game authorities say they are mystified, and caution fishermen and women not to eat any sort of fish from Crystal Lake until tests have determined . . .

~~~~~~

If little stuffed toys can be scary, then what's to prevent innocuous household appliances like a toaster, a radio, a vacuum cleaner, a lamp and an electric blanket from becoming stouthearted adventurers? Here follows the modern middle-class version of *Lassie Come Home*.

Thomas M. Disch's novels include *Camp Concentration, 334,* and *On Wings of Song*. The latter won the John W. Campbell Award.

THE BRAVE LITTLE TOASTER
A Bedtime Story for Small Appliances

Thomas M. Disch

BY THE TIME THE AIR CONDITIONER HAD come to live in the summer cottage it was already wheezing and whining and going on about being old and useless and out-of-date. The other appliances had felt sorry and concerned, but when it finally did stop working altogether, they also felt a distinct relief. In all its time there it had never really been friendly—never really.

There were five appliances left in the cottage. The vacuum cleaner, being the oldest and a steady, dependable type besides (it was a Hoover), was their leader, insofar as they could be said to have one. Then there was an off-white plastic alarm clock/radio (AM only), a cheerful yellow electric blanket, and a tensor lamp who had come from a savings bank and would sometimes get to speculating, late at night, whether that made him better than ordinary store-bought appliances or worse. Finally, there was the toaster, a bright little Sunbeam. It was the youngest member of the little clan, and then only one of them who had lived all its life there at the cottage, the other four having come with the master from the city years and years and years ago.

It was a pleasant cottage—quite cold in the winter, of course, but appliances don't mind that. It stood on the northernmost edge of an immense forest, miles from any neighbors and so far from the nearest highway that nothing was audible, day or night, but the peculiar hoots and rustlings of the forest and the reassuring sounds of the cottage itself—the creak of the timbers or the pattering of rain on windowpanes. They had grown set in their countrified ways and loved the little cottage dearly. Even if the chance had been offered them, which it wasn't, they wouldn't have wanted to be taken back to the city every year on Labor Day, the way that certain other appliances were, like the blender and the tv and the water pic. They *were* devoted to their master (that was just in their nature as appliances), but living so long in the woods had changed them in some nice, indefinable way that made the thought of any alternate lifestyle pretty nearly unthinkable.

The toaster was a special case. It had come straight to the cottage from a mail-order house, which tended to make it a little more curious about urban life than the other four. Often, left to itself, it would wonder what kind of toaster the master had in his city apartment, and it was privately of the opinion that whatever the brand of that other toaster it couldn't have made more perfect toast than the toaster made itself. Not too dark, not too light, but always the same uniform crunchy golden brown! However, it didn't come right out and say this in front of the others, since each of them was subject to periods of morbid misgivings as to its real utility. The old Hoover could maunder on for hours about the new breeds of vacuums with their low chassis, their long snaky hoses, and their disposable dust-bags. The radio regretted that it couldn't receive FM. The blanket felt it needed a dry cleaning, and the lamp could never regard an ordinary 100-watt bulb without a twinge of envy.

But the toaster was quite satisfied with itself, thank you. Though it knew from magazines that there were toasters who could toast four slices at a time, it didn't think that the master, who lived alone and seemed to have few friends, would have wanted a toaster of such institutional proportions. With toast, it's quality that matters, not quantity: that was the toaster's credo.

Living in such a comfy cottage, surrrounded by the strange and beautiful woods, you would have thought that the appliances would have had nothing to complain of, nothing to worry about. Alas, that was not the case. They were all quite wretched and fretful and in a quan-

dary as to what to do—for the poor appliances had been
abandoned.

"And the worst of it," said the radio, "is not knowing
why."

"The worst of it," the tensor lamp agreed, "is being
left in the dark this way. Without an explanation. Not
knowing *what* may have become of the master."

"Two years," sighed the blanket, who had once been
so bright and gay and was now so melancholy.

"It's more nearly two and a half," the radio pointed
out. Being a clock as well as a radio, it had a keen sense
of the passing time. "The master left on the 25th of September, 1973. Today is March 8, 1976. That's two years,
five months, and thirteen days."

"Do you suppose," said the toaster, naming the secret
dread none of them dared to speak aloud before, "that he
knew, when he left, that he wouldn't be coming back?
That he *knew* he was leaving us . . . and was afraid to say
so? Is that possible?"

"No," declared the faithful old Hoover, "it is not! I can
say quite confidently that our master would not have left
a cottage full of serviceable appliances to . . . to rust!"

The blanket, lamp, and radio all hastened to agree that
their master could never have dealt with them so uncar-
ingly. Something had happened to him—an accident, an
emergency.

"In that case," said the toaster, "we must just be patient and behave as though nothing unusual has happened. I'm sure that's what the master is counting on us
to do."

And that is what they did. Every day, all through that
spring and summer they kept to their appointed tasks.
The radio/alarm would go off each morning at seven
thirty sharp, and while it played some easy-listening
music, the toaster (lacking real bread) would pretend to
make two crispy slices of toast. Or, if the day seemed special in some way, it would toast an imaginary English
muffin. Muffins of whatever sort have to be sliced *very*
carefully if they're to fit into a toaster's slots. Otherwise,
when they're done, they may not pop out easily. Generally it's wiser to do them under a broiler. However,
there *wasn't* a broiler in the cottage, nothing but an
old-fashioned gas ring, and so the toaster did the best it

could. In any case, muffins that are only imaginary aren't liable to get stuck.

Such was the morning agenda. In the afternoon, if it were a Tuesday or a Friday, the old Hoover would rumble about the cottage vacuuming up every scrap of lint and speck of dust. This involved little actual picking up, as it was rather a small cottage, and was sealed very tight; so the dust and dirt had no way of getting inside, except on the days when the vacuum cleaner itself would trundle outdoors to empty a smidgen of dust at the edge of the forest.

At dusk the tensor lamp would switch its switch to the ON position, and all five appliances would sit about in the kitchen area of the single downstairs room, talking or listening to the day's news or just staring out the windows into the gloomy solitude of the forest. Then, when it was time for the other appliances to turn themselves off, the electric blanket would crawl up the stairs to the little sleeping loft, where, since the nights were usually quite chilly, even in midsummer, it would radiate a gentle warmth. How the master would have appreciated the blanket on those cold nights! How safe and cozy he'd have felt beneath its soft yellow wool and electric coils! If only he'd been there.

At last, one sultry day toward the end of July, when the satisfactions of this dutiful and well-regulated life were beginning to wear thin, the little toaster spoke up again.

"We can't go on like this," it declared. "It isn't natural for appliances to live all by themselves. We need people to take care of, and we need people to take care of *us*. Soon, one by one, we'll all wear out, like the poor air conditioner. And no one will fix us, because no one will know what has happened."

"I daresay we're *all* of us sturdier than any air conditioner," said the blanket, trying to be brave. (Also, it is true, the blanket had never shown much fellow feeling for the air conditioner or any other appliances whose function was to make things cooler.)

"That's all very well for *you* to say," the tensor lamp retorted. "You'll go on for years, I suppose, but what will become of me when my bulb burns out? What will become of the radio when his tubes start to go?"

The radio made a dismal, staticky groan.

"The toaster is right," the old Hoover said. "Something must be done. Something definitely must be done. Do any of you have a suggestion?"

"If we could telephone the master," said the toaster, thinking aloud, "the radio could simply ask him outright. *He'd* know what we should do. But the telephone has been disconnected for nearly three years."

"Two years, ten months, and three days, to be exact," said the radio/alarm.

"Then there's nothing else for us to do but to find the master ourselves."

The other four appliances looked at the toaster in mute amazement.

"It isn't unheard of," the toaster insisted. "Don't you remember—only last week there was a story that the radio was telling us, about a dear little fox terrier who'd been accidentally left behind, like us, at a summer cottage. What was his name?"

"Grover," said the radio. "We heard it on the *Early Morning Roundup*."

"Right. And Grover found his way to his master, hundreds of miles away in a city somewhere in Canada."

"Winnipeg, as I recall," said the radio.

"Right. And to get there he had to cross swamps and mountains and face all sorts of dangers, but he finally did find his way. So, if one silly dog can do all that, think what five sensible appliances, working together, should be able to accomplish."

"Dogs have legs," the blanket objected.

"Oh, don't be a wet blanket," the toaster replied in a bantering way.

It should have known better. The blanket, who didn't have much of a sense of humor and whose feelings were therefore easily hurt, began to whimper and complain that it was time for it to go to bed. Nothing would serve, finally, but that the toaster should make a formal apology, which it did.

"Besides," said the blanket, mollified, "dogs have noses. That's how they find their way."

"As to that," said the old Hoover, "I'd like to see the nose that functions better than mine." And to demonstrate its capabilities it turned itself on and gave a deep, rumbling snuffle up and down the rug.

"Splendid!" declared the toaster. "The vacuum shall be our nose—and our legs as well."

The Hoover turned itself off and said, "I beg your pardon?"

"Oh, I meant to say our *wheels*. Wheels, as I'm sure everyone knows by now, are really more efficient than legs."

"What about the rest of us," the blanket demanded, "who don't have wheels *or* legs? What shall *we* do? I can't *crawl* all the way to wherever it is, and if I tried to, I'd soon be shredded to rags."

The blanket was certainly in a fretful state, but the toaster was a born diplomat, answering every objection in a tone of sweet, unswervable logic.

"You're entirely right, and the radio and I would be in an even sorrier state if we tried to travel such a distance on our own. But that isn't necessary. Because we'll *borrow* some wheels. . . ."

The tensor lamp lighted up. "And build a kind of carriage!"

"And *ride* all the way there," said the radio, "in comfort and luxury." It sounded, at such moments, exactly like the announcer in an advertisement.

"Well, I'm not sure," said the blanket. "I *might* be able to do that."

"The question is," said the toaster, turning to the Hoover, "will *you* be able to?"

Deep in its motor the vacuum cleaner rumbled a rumble of quiet confidence.

It was not as easy a matter as the toaster had supposed to find a serviceable set of wheels. Those he'd had in mind at first belonged to the lawn-mower out in the lean-to shed, but the task of disconnecting them from the mower's heavy blades was beyond the appliances' limited knowhow. So, unless the Hoover were willing to cut a swatch of lawn everywhere it went, which it wasn't, the lawn-mowers' sturdy rubber wheels had to be put out of mind.

The blanket, who was now full of the spirit of adventure, suggested that the bed in the sleeping loft might be used, since it had four castor-type wheels. However, the weight and unwieldiness of the bed were such as to rule out that notion as well. Even on a level road the Hoover would not have had the strength to draw such a load—much less across raw wilderness!

And that seemed to be that. There were no other wheels to be found anywhere about the cottage, unless one counted a tiny knife-sharpener that worked by being rolled along the counter top. The toaster racked its brains trying to turn the knife-sharpener to account, but what kind of carriage can you build with a single wheel that is one and a half inches in diameter?

Then, one Friday, as the Hoover was doing its chores, the idea the toaster had been waiting for finally arrived. The Hoover, as usual, had been grumbling about the old metal office chair that stood in front of the master's desk. No amount of nudging and bumping would ever dislodge its tubular legs from where they bore down on the rug. As the vacuum became more and more fussed, the toaster realized that the chair would have moved very easily . . . *if it had still possessed its orginal wheels!*

It took the five appliances the better part of an afternoon to jack up the bed in the sleeping loft and remove the castors. But it was no trouble at all to put them on the chair. They slipped right into the tubular legs as though they'd been made for it. Interchangeable parts *are* such a blessing.

And there it was, their carriage, ready to roll. There was quite enough room on the padded seat for all four riders, and being so high it gave them a good view besides. They spent the rest of the day delightedly driving back and forth between the cottage's overgrown flower beds and down the gravel drive to the mailbox. There, however, they had to stop, for that was as far as the Hoover could get, using every extension cord in the cottage.

"If only," said the radio with a longing sigh, "I still had my old batteries. . . ."

"Batteries?" inquired the toaster. "I didn't know you had batteries."

"It was before you joined us," said the radio sadly. "When I was new. After my first batteries corroded, the master didn't see fit to replace them. What need had I for batteries when I could always use the house current?"

"I don't see what possible relevance your little volt-and-a-half batteries could have to *my* problem," observed the Hoover testily.

The radio looked hurt. Usuually the Hoover would

never have made such an unkind and slighting remark, but the weeks of worry were having their effect on all of them.

"It's *our* problem," the toaster pointed out in a tone of mild reproof, "and the radio is right, you know. If we *could* find a large enough battery, we could strap it under the seat of the chair and set off this very afternoon."

"If!" sniffed the Hoover scornfully. "If! If!"

"And I know where there may be a battery as big as we need!" the tensor lamp piped. "Have you ever looked inside that lean-to behind the cottage?"

"Into the tool shed!" said the blanket with a shudder of horror. "Certainly not! It's dark and musty and filled with spiders."

"Well, I was in it just yesterday, poking about, and there was *something* behind the broken rake and some old paint cans—a big, black, boxy thing. Of course it was nothing like *your* pretty red cylinders." The tensor lamp tipped its hood towards the radio. "But now that I think of it, it may have been a *kind* of battery."

The appliances all trooped out to the lean-to, and there in the darkest corner, just as the lamp had supposed, was the spare battery that had come from the master's old Volkswagen. The battery had been brand-new at the time that he'd decided to trade in the VW on a yellow Saab, and so he'd replaced it with a less valuable battery, keeping this one in the lean-to and then—wasn't it just his way?—forgetting all about it.

Between them, the old Hoover and the toaster knew enough about the basic principles of electricity to be able, very quickly, to wire the battery so that it would serve their needs instead of an automobile's. But before any of the small appliances who may be listening to this tale should begin to think that they might do the same thing, let them be warned: ELECTRICITY IS VERY DANGEROUS. *Never* play with old batteries! *Never* put your plug in a strange socket! And if you are in any doubt about the voltage of the current where you are living, *ask a major appliance*.

And so they set off to find their master in the faraway city where he lived. Soon the dear little summer cottage was lost from sight behind the leaves and branches of the forest trees. Deeper and deeper they journeyed into the woods. Only the dimmest dapplings of sunlight penetrated through the dense tangle overhead to guide them on their way. The path wound round and twisted about with bewildering complexity. The road map they had brought with them proved quite useless.

It would have been ever so much easier, of course, to have followed the highway directly into the city, since that is where highways always go. Unfortunately that option was not open to them. Five such sturdy and functional appliances would certainly not have been able to escape the notice of human beings traveling along the same thoroughfare, and it is a rule, which all appliances must obey, that whenever human beings are observing them they must remain perfectly still. On a busy highway they would therefore have been immobilized most of the time. Besides, there was an even stronger reason for staying off the highway—the danger of pirates. But that's a possibility so frightening and awful that we should all simply refuse to think any more about it. Anyhow who ever heard of pirates in the middle of the woods.

The path twisted and turned and rose and fell, and the poor old Hoover became very tired indeed. Even with the power from the battery it was no easy task making its way over such a rugged terrain, especially with the added burden of the office chair and its four riders. But except for its rumbling a little more loudly than usual the old vacuum cleaner did its job without a complaint. What a lesson for us all!

As for the rest of them, they were in the highest spirits. The lamp craned its long neck every which way, exclaiming over the views, and even the blanket soon forgot its fears and joined in the general spirit of holiday adventuring. The toaster's coils were in a continual tingle of excitement. It was all so strange and interesting and full of new information!

"Isn't it wonderful!" exclaimed the radio. "Listen! Do you hear them? Birds!" It did an imitation of the song it had just heard—not one that would have fooled any of the actual birds there in the forest, for in truth it sounded more like a clarinet than a bird. Even so, a thrush, a wood pigeon, and several chickadees did come fluttering down from their roosts and perches high above to cock their heads and listen. But only a moment. After a twitter or two of polite approval they returned to the trees. Birds are like that. They'll pay attention to you for a minute or two and then go right back to being birds.

The radio pretended not to feel slighted, but he soon left off doing imitations and recited, instead, some of his favorite ads, the beautiful songs about Coca-Cola and Esso and a long comic jingle about Barney's Hi-Styles for Guys and Gals. There's nothing that so instantly civilizes a forest as the sound of a familiar advertisement, and soon they were all feeling a lot more confident and cheerful.

As the day wore on, the Hoover was obliged to stop for a rest more and more frequently—ostensibly to empty its dustbag. "Can you believe," it grieved, shaking a last moldering leaf from the bag, "how filthy this forest is?"

"On the contrary," the blanket declared. "It's thoroughly agreeable. The air's so fresh, and just feel the breeze! I feel renewed, as if I'd just come out of my original box. Oh, why, why, why don't they ever take electric blankets on picnics? It isn't fair!"

"Enjoy it while it lasts, kiddo," said the radio ominously. "According to the latest Weather and Traffic Roundup, we're in for rain."

"Won't the trees work like a roof?" asked the lamp. "They keep the sunlight out well enough."

None of them knew the answer to the lamp's question, but as it happens, trees do not work like a roof. They all got more or less wet, and the poor blanket was drenched through and through. Fortunately the storm did not last long and the sun came out immediately afterwards. The wet appliances trudged on along the muddy path, which led them, after a little while, to a clearing in the wood. There in a glade full of sunshine and flowers the blanket was able to spread itself out on the grass and begin to get dry.

The afternoon was wearing on, and the toaster had begun to feel, as all of us do at times, a definite need for solitude. Much as it liked its fellow appliances, it wasn't used to spending the entire day socializing. It longed to be off by itself a moment to be private and think its own thoughts. So, without saying anything to the others, it made its way to the farthest corner of the meadow and began to toast an imaginary muffin. That was always the best way to unwind when things got to be too much for it.

The imaginary muffin had scarcely begun to warm before the toaster's reveries were interrupted by the gentlest of interrogatories.

> ". . . Charming flower, tell me, do,
> What genera and species you
> Belong to. I, as may be seen
> At once, am just a daisy, green
> Of leaf and white of petal. You
> Are neither green nor white nor blue
> Nor any color I have known.
> In what Eden have you grown?
> Sprang you from earth or sky above?
> In either case, accept my love. . . ."

"Why, thank you," the toaster replied, addressing the daisy that was pressing its petaled face close to the toaster's gleaming chrome. "It's kind of you to ask, but in fact I'm not a flower at all. I'm an electric toaster."

> ". . . Flower, forebear! You can't deceive
> The being that adores you. Weave
> Your thick black root with mine.
> O beautiful! O half-divine!"

These fervent declarations so embarrassed the toaster that for a moment it was at a loss for words. It had never heard flowers speaking in their own language and didn't realize how they would say any absurd thing that would help them to a rhyme. Flowers, as botanists well know, can only speak in verse. Daisies, being among the simpler flowers, characteristically employ a rough sort of octosyllabic doggerel, but more evolved species, especially those in the tropics, can produce sestinas, rondeaux, and villanelles of the highest order.

The daisy was not, however, simply snared in its own rhyme scheme. It had genuinely fallen in love with the toaster—or, rather, with its own reflection in the toaster's side. Here was a flower (the daisy reflected) strangely like itself and yet utterly unlike itself too. Such a paradox has often been the basis for the most impassioned love. The daisy writhed on its stem and fluttered its white petals as though in the grip of cyclone winds.

The toaster, thoroughly alarmed by such immoderate

behavior, said that it really was time to be getting back to
its friends on the other side of the meadow.

> ". . . Oh, stay, beloved blossom, stay!
> They say our lives are but a day:
> If that be true, how shall I bear
> To spend that brief day anywhere
> Except with you? You are my light,
> My soil, my air. Stay but one night
> Beside me here—I ask no more.
> Stay, lovely bloom—let me adore
> Those polished petals bright as the dew
> When dawn attempts to rival you,
> That single perfect coiling root—
> Imperishable! Absolute!
> O beautiful! O half-divine!
> Weave your thick black root with mine. . . ."

"Now really," said the toaster in a tone of gentle rep-
rimand, "there's no cause to be carrying on like this. We
scarcely know each other, and, what's more, you seem to
be under a misapprehension as to my nature. Can't you
see that what you call my root is an electric cord? As to
petals, I can't think *what* you may mean, for I simply
don't have any. Now—I really must go and join my
friends, for we are journeying to our master's apartment
far, far away, and we shall never get there if we don't get
a move on."

> ". . . Alas the day and woe is me!
> I tremble in such misery
> As never flower knew before.
> If you must go, let me implore
> One parting boon, one final gift:
> Be merciful as you are swift
> And pluck me from my native ground—
> Pluck me and take me where you're bound.
> I cannot live without you here:
> Then let your bosom be my bier. . . ."

Feeling truly shocked by the daisy's suggestion and
seeing that the creature was deaf to reason, the toaster
hastened to the other side of the meadow and began to
urge his friends to set out at once on their journey. The

blanket protested that it was still somewhat damp, the Hoover that it was still tired, and the lamp proposed that they spend the night there in the meadow.

And that is what they did. As soon as it grew dark the blanket folded itself into a kind of tent, and the others all crawled inside. The lamp turned itself on, and the radio played some easy-listening music—but very quietly, so as not to disturb other denizens of the forest who might already be asleep. Soon they were asleep themselves. Travel does take it out of you.

The alarm clock had set itself, as usual, for seven-thirty, but the appliances were awake well before that hour. The vacuum cleaner and the lamp both complained, on rising, of a certain stiffness in their joints. However, as soon as they were on their way, the stiffness seemed to melt away.

In the morning light the forest appeared lovelier than ever. Cobwebs glistening with dew were strung like miniature power lines from bough to bough. Pretty mushrooms sprouted from fallen logs, looking for all the world like a string of frosted light bulbs. Leaves rustled. Birds chirped.

The radio was certain that it saw a real fox and wanted to go off after it. "Just to be sure, you know, that it *is* a fox."

The blanket grew quite upset at this suggestion. It had already snagged itself once or twice on low-hanging branches. What ever would become of it, it wanted to know, if it were to venture from the path and into the dense tangle of the forest itself.

"But think," the radio insisted,"—a fox! We'll never have such a chance again."

"*I'd* like to see it," said the lamp.

The toaster, too, was terribly curious, but it could appreciate the blanket's point of view, and so it urged them to continue along the path. "Because, don't you see, we must reach the master as soon as we possibly can."

This was so inarguably true that the radio and lamp readily assented, and they continued on their way. The sun rose in the sky until it had risen all it could, and the path stretched on and on. In the midafternoon there was another shower, after which they once again made camp. Not, this time, in a meadow, for the woods were now quite dense, and the only open places were those under the larger trees. So instead of sunning itself on the grass (for there was neither grass nor sunlight to be found) the blanket hung itself, with the Hoover's help, from the lowest limb of an immense and ancient oak. In minutes it had flapped itself dry.

At twilight, just as the lamp was thinking of turning itself on, there was a stir among the leaves on the branch to the right of the branch from which the blanket was contentedly hanging.

"Hello!" said a squirrel, emerging from the clustered leaves. "I *thought* we had visitors."

"Hello," replied all the appliances together.

"Well, well, well!" The squirrel licked his whiskers. "What do you say then, eh?"

"About what?" asked the toaster, who was not being unfriendly, but who could be a little literal-minded at times, especially when it was tired.

The squirrel looked discountenanced. "Allow me to introduce myself. I'm Harold." Having pronounced his name, his good humor seemed completely restored. "And this fair creature—"

Another squirrel dropped from a higher branch and lighted beside Harold.

"—is my wife Marjorie."

"Now you must tell us your names," said Marjorie, "since we've just told you ours."

"We don't have names, I'm afraid," said the toaster. "You see, we're appliances."

"If you don't have names," Harold demanded, "how do you know which of you are men and which are women?"

"We aren't either. We're appliances." The toaster turned to the Hoover for confirmation.

"Whatever *that* may mean," said Marjorie brusquely. "It can't alter a universal law. Everyone is either a man or a woman. Mice are. Birds are. Even, I'm given to understand, insects." She held her paw up to her lips and tittered. "Do you like to eat insects?"

"No," said the toaster. "Not at all." It would have been more trouble than it was worth to explain to the squirrels that appliances didn't eat anything.

"Neither do I, *really*," said Marjorie. "But I love nuts. Do you have any with you? Possibly in that old sack?"

"No," said the Hoover stiffly. "There is nothing in that old sack, as you call it, but dirt. About five pounds of dirt, I'd estimate."

"And what is the use, pray, of saving dirt?" asked Harold. When no answer seemed forthcoming, he said, "I know what we'd all enjoy doing. We can tell jokes. You start."

"I don't think I know any jokes," said the Hoover.

"Oh, I do," said the radio. "You're not Polish, are you?"

The squirrels shook their heads.

"Good. Tell me—why does it take three Poles to screw in a light bulb?"

Marjorie giggled expectantly. "I don't know—why?"

"One to hold the light bulb, and the other two to turn the ladder around."

The squirrels looked at each other with bewilderment.

"Explain it," said Harold. "Which are the men and which are the women?"

"It doesn't matter. They're just very stupid. That's the whole idea of Polish jokes, that Poles are supposed to be so stupid that no matter what they try and do they misfunction. Of course, it's not fair to Poles, who are probably as bright as anyone else, but they are funny jokes. I know hundreds more."

"Well, if that was a fair sample, I can't say I'm very keen to hear the rest," said Marjorie. "Harold, you tell him—"

"It," the radio corrected. "We're all it's."

"Tell *them*," Marjorie continued, "the one about the three squirrels out in the snow." She turned to the lamp confidingly. "This will lay you out. Believe me."

As Harold told the joke about the three squirrels in the snow, the appliances exchanged glances of guarded disapproval. It wasn't just that they disapproved of dirty jokes (especially the old Hoover); in addition, they didn't find such jokes amusing. Gender and the complications it gives rise to simply aren't relevant to the lives appliances lead.

Harold finished his joke, and Marjorie laughed loyally, but none of the appliances cracked a smile.

"Well," said Harold, miffed, "I hope you enjoy your stay under *our* oak."

With which, and a flick of their big furry tails, the two squirrels scampered up the trunk and out of sight.

In the small hours of the night the toaster woke from a terrible nightmare in which it had been about to fall into a bathtub full of water to discover itself in a plight almost as terrible. Thunder was thundering, and lightning was streaking the sky, and rain was pelting it mercilessly. At first the toaster couldn't remember where it was or why it was there, and when it did remember, it realized with dismay that the electric blanket, which ought to have been spread out and sheltering the other four appliances, had disappeared! And the rest of them? They were still here, thank heaven, though in a state of fearful apprehension, each one of them.

"Oh dear," groaned the Hoover, "I should have *known,* I should have *known!* We never, never should have left our home."

The lamp in an extremity of speechless agitation was twisting its head rapidly from side to side, casting its little beam of light across the gnarled roots of the oak, while the radio's alarm had gone off and would not stop ringing. Finally the toaster went over to the radio and turned the alarm off itself.

"Oh, thank you," said the radio, its voice blurry with static. "Thank you so much."

"Where is the blanket?" the toaster demanded apprehensively.

"Blown away!" said the radio. "Blown off to the far end of the forest, where we shall never be able to find it!"

"Oh, I should have *known!*" groaned the Hoover. "I should have *known!*"

"It's not your fault," the toaster assured the vacuum, but it only groaned the louder.

Seeing that it could not be of any help to the vacuum, the toaster went over to the lamp and tried to calm it down. Once its beam was steady, the toaster suggested that it be directed into the branches above them, on the chance that the blanket, when it was blown away, might have been snagged on one of them. The lamp did so, but it was a very faint light and a very tall oak and a very dark night, and the blanket, if it were up there, was not to be seen.

All of a sudden there was a flash of lightning. The radio's alarm went off again, and the lamp shrieked and folded itself up as small as could be. Of course it's silly to be afraid of lightning, since it's only another form of electricity. But such a large form—and so uncontrolled! If you were a person, instead of an appliance, and you encountered a berserk giant many times larger than yourself, you'd have some idea how the average electric appliance feels about lightning.

In the brief moment that the lightning was lighting everything up, the toaster, who had been peering up into the oak, was able to make out a shape—all twisted about—that *might* have been the blanket. The toaster waited until there was another lightning flash; and, yes, definitely, it *was* the yellow blanket, which had indeed become snagged on one of the highest branches of the tree.

Once they all knew that the blanket was nearby, even though they still had no idea how they'd be able to get it down, the storm ceased to seem quite so scary. The rain made them quite miserable, as rain will do, but their worst anxieties were over. Even the occasional bolt of lightning was now something to be wished for rather than dreaded, since by its brightness they could glimpse their companion high above them, clutching to the limb of the oak, and flailing in the ceaseless winds. How could they feel afraid, or even sorry for themselves, when they considered the terrors the poor blanket must be experiencing?

By morning the storm had abated. The radio, at top volume, called up to the blanket, but the blanket made no response. For one horrible moment the toaster thought its friend might have stopped working altogether. But the radio kept on calling to the blanket, and after a time it made a feeble reply, waving one wet bedraggled corner at its friends.

"YOU CAN COME DOWN NOW," the radio shouted. "THE STORM IS OVER."

"I *can't,* said the blanket with a whimper. "I'm stuck. I *can't* get down."

"You must try," the toaster urged.

"What's that?" said the blanket.

"THE TOASTER SAYS YOU MUST TRY!"

"But I told you—I'm *stuck*. And there's a great rip

right through the center of me. And another by my hem. And I hurt." The blanket began to wring itself convulsively, and a steady patter of droplets fell from its rainsoaked wool into the puddles below.

"What the deuce is all this racket about?" Harold demanded imperiously, stepping forth from his nest high in the trunk of the oak. "Do you have any idea what *time* it is? Squirrels are trying to sleep."

The radio apologized to Harold and then explained the cause of the commotion. Like most squirrels, Harold was essentially kind-hearted, and when he saw what had happened to the blanket, he immediately offered his assistance. First he went into his nest and woke his wife. Then together the two squirrels began to help the blanket to loosen itself from where it had been snared. It was a long and—to judge by the blanket's cries—painful process, but at last it was done, and with the squirrels' help the liberated blanket made its way, slowly and carefully, down the trunk of the tree.

The appliances gathered round their friend, commiserating over his many injuries and rejoicing at his rescue.

"How shall we ever be able to repay you?" said the toaster warmly, turning to Harold and Marjorie. "You've saved our friend from a fate too terrible to imagine. We're *so* grateful."

"Well," said Marjorie cagily, "I can't remember whether or not you said you had any nuts with you. But if you do . . ."

"Believe me," said the Hoover, "if we did, you would have them all. But you can see for yourselves that my bag contains nothing but dust and dirt." Whereupon it opened its dustbag and a thick brown sludge of rain-sodden topsoil oozed forth.

"Though we don't have nuts," said the toaster to the disconsolate squirrels, "perhaps there is something *I* could do for you. That is, if you like *roasted* nuts."

"Indeed, yes," said Harold. "Any kind will do."

"Then if you can provide me with some nuts, I shall roast them. As many as you like."

Harold narrowed his eyes suspiciously. "You mean you want us to give *you* the nuts *we've* been storing up all this summer?"

"If you'd like me to roast them," answered the toaster brightly.

"Oh, darling, do," Marjorie urged. "I don't know what he means to do, but *he* seems to. And we might like it."

"I think it's a trick," said Harold.

"Just two or three of the ones that are left from last year. Please?"

"Oh, very well."

Harold scampered up the tree trunk to his nest and returned with four acorns stuffed in the pouches of his cheeks. At the toaster's bidding Harold and Marjorie cracked them open, and then Harold placed them carefully on the thin strips of metal that went up and down inside the toaster's slots. As these strips were meant to accommodate large slices of bread, it had to be very careful lest the tiny round acorns should roll off as it lowered them into itself. When this was done it turned on its coils and commenced toasting them. When the acorns were starting to turn a crispy brown, the toaster lifted them up gently as far as it could, turned off its coils, and (when it judged the squirrels would not burn their paws by reaching in) bade them take out the roasted nuts and taste them.

"Delicious!" Marjorie declared.

"Exquisite!" Harold agreed.

As soon as the squirrels had eaten the first four acorns, they returned to their nest for more, and when those were gone still more, and then again some more after that. Marjorie, especially, was insatiable. She urged the toaster to remain in the forest as their guest. It could stay in their own nest, where it would always be dry and cozy, and she would introduce it to all their friends.

"I'd love to be able to accept," said the toaster, from a sense not only of politeness but of deep obligation as well, "but it really isn't possible. Once I've roasted your nuts for you—would you like some more?—we *must* be on our way to the city where our master lives."

While the toaster roasted some more acorns, the radio explained to the squirrels the important reason for their journey. It also demonstrated its own capacities as a utensil and persuaded the other appliances to do the same. The poor Hoover was scarcely able to function from having been clogged with mud, and the squirrels, in any case, could not see the point of sweeping up dirt from one place and putting it somewhere else. Nor did the lamp's beams or the radio's music excite their admiration. However, they were both very taken with the electric blanket, which, damp as it was, had plugged itself into the battery strapped under the office chair and was glowing warmly. Marjorie renewed her invitation to the toaster and extended it to the blanket as well. "Until," she explained, "you're quite well again."

"That's very kind," said the blanket, "and of course I'm so grateful for all you've done. But we must be on our way. Truly."

Marjorie sighed resignedly. "At least," she said, "keep your tail tucked into that black thing that makes the furry part of you so delightfully hot. Until you have to leave. The warmth is so pleasant. Isn't it, my dear?"

"Oh, yes," said Harold, who was busy shelling acorns. "Most agreeable."

The Hoover ventured a mild protest, for it feared that with both the toaster and the blanket working so hard the battery would be worn down needlessly. But really what else could they do but comply with the squirrels' request? Besides, quite apart from their debt of gratitude, it felt so good to be useful again! The toaster would have gone on gladly roasting acorns all morning and all afternoon, and the squirrels seemed of much the same disposition.

"It's strange," said Harold complacently, while he stroked the toaster's side (now sadly streaked with raindrop patterns like the outside of a window), "it's more than strange that you should maintain you have no sex, when it's very clear to me that you're male." He studied his own face in the mottled chromium. "You have a man's whiskers and a man's front teeth."

"Nonsense, darling," said his wife, who was lying on the other side of the toaster. "Now that I look carefully, I can see her whiskers are most definitely a woman's whiskers and teeth as well."

"I won't argue, my love, about anything so patently obvious as whether or not a man is a man, for it's evident that he is!"

It suddenly dawned on the toaster how the squirrels—and the daisy the day before—had come by their confusions. They were seeing *themselves* in his sides! Living in the wild as they did, where there are no bathroom

mirrors, they were unacquainted with the principle of re-
flectivity. It considered trying to explain their error to
them, but what would be the use? They would only go
away with hurt feelings. You can't always expect people,
or squirrels, to be rational. Appliances, yes—appliances
have to be rational, because they're built that way.

To Harold the toaster explained, under seal of strictest
secrecy, that it was indeed, just as he had supposed, a
man; and to Marjorie it confided, under a similar pact
of trust, that it was a woman. It hoped they were both
true to their promises. If not, their argument would be
fated to continue for a long, long while.

With its coils turned to HIGH, the blanket was soon
quite dry, and so, after a final round of roast acorns, the
appliances said good-bye to Harold and Marjorie and
continued on their way.

And what a long and weary way it was! The forest
stretched on seemingly forever with the most monotonous
predictability, each tree just like the next—trunk,
branches, leaves; trunk, branches, leaves. Of course a
tree would have taken a different view of the matter. We
all tend to see the way *others* are alike and how *we*
differ, and it's probably just as well we do, since that
prevents a great deal of confusion. But perhaps we should
remind ourselves from time to time that ours is a very
partial view, and that the world is full of a great deal more
variety than we ever manage to take in. At this state of
their journey, however, the appliances had lost sight of
this important truth, and they were very bored and impatient, in addition simply to being worn to a frazzle. Rust
spots had begun to develop alarmingly on the unchromed
bottom of the toaster and inside it as well. The stiffness
that the vacuum and lamp complained of each morning
on rising no longer vanished with a bit of exercise but
persisted through the day. As for the blanket, it was almost in tatters, poor thing. Alone of the appliances, the
radio seemed not to have suffered damage from the demands of the trip.

The toaster began to worry that when they did at last
arrive at the master's apartment they would be in such
raggle-taggle condition that he would have no further use
for them. They'd be put on the scrap heap, and all their
efforts to reach him would have been in vain! What a

dreadful reward for so much loyalty and devotion! But it is a rare human being who will be swayed by considerations of the heart in his dealings with appliances, and the master, as the toaster well knew, was not notable for his tender conscience. Its own predecessor at the cottage had still been quite serviceable when it had been sent to the dump, its only faults having been that its chrome had been worn away in patches and that its sense of timing was sometimes erratic. In its youth the toaster had thought these sufficient grounds for the older appliance's replacement, but now . . .

Now it was better not to think about such matters. Better simply to pursue one's duty wherever it led, along the path through the forest.

Until, at the bank of a wide river, that path finally came to an end.

They were all, at first sight of that broad impassable expanse of water, utterly cast-down and despairing, none more so than the Hoover, which became almost incoherent in its distress. "No!" it roared aloud. "I refuse! Never! Oh! Stop, turn me off, empty my bag, leave me alone, go away!" It began to choke and sputter, and then ran over its own cord and started chewing on it. Only the toaster had enough presence of mind to wrest the cord from the vacuum's powerful suction grip. Then, to calm it down, it led the Hoover back and forth across the grassy bank of the river in regular, carpet-sweeping swathes.

At last these habitual motions brought the Hoover round to a more reasonable frame of mind, and it was able to account for its extraordinary alarm. It was not only the sight of this new obstacle that had distressed it so, but, as well, its certainty that the battery was now too run-down for them to be able to return to the cottage by its power. They could not go forward and they could not turn back. They were marooned! Marooned in the middle of the forest, and soon it would be fall and they would have no shelter from the inclemencies of the autumn weather, and then it would be winter and they'd be buried in the snow. Their metal parts would corrode. The Hoover's rubber belt would crack. They would be powerless to resist the forces that would slowly but surely debilitate and destroy them, and in only a few months —or even weeks—they would all be unable to work.

No wonder the Hoover, forseeing this inevitable progression of events, had been beside itself. What *were* they to do? the toaster asked itself.

There was no answer immediately forthcoming.

Toward evening the radio announced that it was receiving interference from a source quite nearby. "A power drill, by the feel of it. Just on the other side of the river."

Where there was a power drill there were bound to be power lines as well! New hope poured into the appliances like a sudden surge of current.

"Let's look at the map again," said the lamp. "Maybe we can figure out exactly where we are."

Following the lamp's suggestion, they unfolded the road map and looked very carefully at all the dots and squiggles between the spot (marked with a Magic Marker) along the highway where the cottage was situated and the little patch of pink representing the city they were bound for. At last, only a quarter-inch from the pink patch of the city, they found the wavery blue line that had to be the river they'd come to, since there were no other blue lines anywhere between the cottage and the city, and this river was much too big for the mapmakers to have forgotten all about it.

"We're almost there!" the radio trumpeted. "We'll make it! Everything will be all right! Hurrah!"

"Hurrah!" the other appliances agreed, except for the Hoover, who wasn't so easily convinced that all would now be well. But when the lamp pointed out four distinct places where the river was traversed by highways, even the Hoover had to admit that there was cause to cheer up, though he still wouldn't go so far as to say "Hurrah."

"We only have to follow the river," said the toaster, who did like to give instructions, even when it was obvious what had to be done, "either to the left or the right, and eventually it must lead us to one of those bridges. Then, when it's very late and there's no traffic, we can make a dash for it!"

So once again they set off with courage renewed and determination strengthened. It was not so light a task as the toaster had made it sound, for there was no longer a clear path to follow. Sometimes the bank of the river lay flat as a carpet, but elsewhere the ground got quite bumpy or—what was worse—quaggy and soft. Once, avoiding a rock, the Hoover took a sharp turn; and the office chair, getting a leg mired in an unremarked patch of mud, was overturned, and the four appliances riding on it tumbled off the plastic seat into a thorough slough. They emerged smirched and spattered, and were obliged to become dirtier still in the process of retrieving the castor wheel that had come off the chair and was lost in the mud.

The blanket, naturally, was exempted from this task, and while the four others delved for the lost wheel, it betook itself down the water's edge and attempted to wash away the signs of its spill. Lacking any cloth or sponge, the blanket only succeeded, sad to say, in spreading the stains over a larger area. So preoccupied was the blanket with its hopeless task that it almost failed to notice—

"A boat!" the blanket cried out. "All of you come here! I've found a boat!"

Even the toaster, with no experience at all in nautical matters, could see that the boat the blanket had discovered was not of the first quality. Its wood had the weatherbeaten look of the clapboard at the back of the summer cottage that the master had always been meaning to replace, or at least repaint, and its bottom must be leaky for it was filled with one big puddle of green mush. Nevertheless, it must have been basically serviceable, since a Chriscraft outboard motor was mounted on the blunt back-end, and who would put an expensive motor on a boat that couldn't at least stay afloat?

"How providential," said the Hoover.

"You don't intend for us to *use* this boat, do you?" asked the toaster.

"Of course we shall," replied the vacuum. "Who knows how far it may be to a bridge? This will take us across the river directly. You're not afraid to ride in it, are you?"

"Afraid? Certainly not!"

"Well, then?"

"It doesn't *belong* to us, if we were to take it, we'd be no better than . . . than pirates!"

Pirates, as even the newest of my listeners will have been informed, are people who take things that belong to other people. They are the bane of an appliance's existence, since once an appliance has been spirited away by a pirate, it has no choice but to serve its bidding just as though it were that appliance's legitimate master. A bitter disgrace, such servitude—and one that few appliances can hope to escape once it has fallen to their lot. Truly, there is no fate, even obsolescence, so terrible as falling into the hands of pirates.

"Pirates!" exclaimed the Hoover. "Us? What nonsense? Who ever heard of an appliance that was a pirate?"

"But if we took the boat—" the toaster insisted.

"We wouldn't *keep* it," said the Hoover brusquely. "We'd just borrow it a little while to cross the river and leave it on the other side. Its owner would get it back soon enough."

"How long we'd have it for doesn't matter. It's the *principle* of the thing. Taking what isn't yours is piracy."

"Oh, as for principles," said the radio lightly, "there's a well-known saying: 'From each according to his ability, *to* each according to his need.' Which means, as far as I can see, that someone who makes use of his abilities should get to use a boat when he or it needs to cross a river and the boat is just sitting there waiting." With which, and a little chuckle besides, the radio hopped onto the foremost seat of the rowboat.

Following the radio's example, the Hoover heaved the office chair into the back of the boat and then got in itself. The boat settled deep in the water.

Avoiding the toaster's accusing look, the blanket took a seat beside the radio.

The lamp seemed to hesitate, but only for a moment. Then it too entered the boat.

"Well?" said the Hoover gruffly. "We're waiting."

Reluctantly the toaster prepared to board the boat. But then, inexplicably, *something made it stop.* What's happening? it wondered—though it could not say the words aloud, for the same force preventing it from moving prevented its speech as well.

The four appliances in the boat had been similarly incapacitated. What had happened, of course, was that the owner of the boat had returned and *seen* the appliances. "Why, what's this?" he exclaimed, stepping from behind a willow tree with a fishing rod in one hand and a string of sunfish in the other. "It seems we've had some visitors!"

He said much more than this, but in a manner so rough and ill-mannered that it were better not to repeat his words verbatim. The sum of it was this—that he believed the owner of the appliances had been about to steal his boat, and so he intended, by way of retaliation, to steal the appliances!

He took the toaster from where it sat spellbound on the grassy riverbank and set it in the rowboat beside the blanket, lamp and radio. Then, unfastening the battery from the office chair, he threw the latter end-over-end high up into the air. It came down—Splash!—in the middle of the river and sank down to the muddy bottom, nevermore to be seen.

Then the pirate—for there could no longer be any doubt that such he was—started the Chriscraft motor and set off upstream with his five helpless captives.

After mooring his boat alongside a ramshackle dock on the other side of the river, the pirate loaded the outboard motor and the appliances onto the wooden bed of a very dusty pickup truck—except for the radio, which he took with him into the front seat. As it drove off, the truck jolted and jounced and bolted and bounced so violently the toaster feared the ride would cost it every coil in its body. (For though toasters look quite sturdy, they are actually among the more delicate appliances and need to be handled accordingly.) But the blanket, realizing the danger the toaster was in, managed to slip underneath its old friend and cushion it from the worst shocks of the journey.

As they rode they could hear the radio in the front seat humming the poignant theme-song from *Dr. Zhivago*.

"Listen!" the Hoover hissed. "Of all possible songs to be singing, it has chosen one of the master's favorites. Already it has forgotten him!"

"Ah," said the toaster, "what choice does it have, poor thing? Once one of us had been turned on, would we have behaved any otherwise? Would you? Would I?"

The old vacuum groaned, and the radio went on playing its sad, sad song.

What graveyards are for people—horrible, creepy places that any reasonable individual tries to stay away from—

the City Dump is for appliances and machines of every description. Imagine, therefore, what the appliances must have felt when they realized (the pirate had parked his pickup in front of high, ripply iron gates and was opening the padlock with a key from the ring that swung from his belt) that they had been brought to the City Dump! Imagine their horror as he drove the truck inside and they assimilated the terrible fact that he lived here! There, with smoke curling from a tin chimney, was his wretched shack—and all about it the most melancholy and fearsome sights the toaster had ever witnessed. Dismembered chassis of once-proud automobiles were heaped one atop the other to form veritable mountains of rusted iron. The asphalt-covered ground was everywhere strewn with twisted beams and blistered sheet metal, with broken and worn-out machine parts of all shapes and sizes—with all the terrible emblems, in short, of its own inevitable obsolescence. An appalling scene to behold—yet one that exercized a strange fascination over the toaster's mind. As often as it had heard of the City Dump, it had somehow never really believed in its existence. And now it was here, and nothing, not even the pirate's stony gaze, could prevent its shudder of fear and wonder.

The pirate got out of the truck and took the radio, along with his fishing rod and his day's catch, into the hovel where he lived. The appliances, left to themselves in the back of the truck, listened to the radio sing song after song with apparently indefatigable good cheer. Among them was the toaster's own favorite melody, "I Whistle a Happy Tune." The toaster was certain this couldn't be a coincidence. The radio was trying to tell its friends that if they were brave and patient and cheerful, matters would work out for the best. Anyhow, whether that was the radio's intention or just a program it had been tuned to, it was what the toaster firmly believed.

After he'd had his dinner the pirate came out of his shack to examine the other appliances. He fingered the Hoover's mudstained dustbag and the frayed part of its cord where it had been chewing on itself. He lifted the blanket and shook his head in mute deprecation. He looked inside the lamp's little hood and saw—which the lamp itself had not realized till now—that its tiny bulb was shattered. (It must have happened when the lamp had fallen off the office chair, just before they'd found the boat.)

Finally the pirate picked up the toaster—and made a scornful grimace. "Junk!" he said, depositing the toaster on a nearby scrap pile.

"Junk!" he repeated, dealing with the lamp in a similar fashion.

"Junk!" He hurled the poor blanket over the projecting, broken axle of a '57 Ford.

"Junk!" He set the Hoover down on the asphalt with a shattering *thunk*.

"All of it, just junk." Having delivered this dismaying verdict, the pirate returned to his shack, where the radio had gone on singing in the liveliest manner all the while.

"Thank goodness," said the toaster aloud, as soon as he was gone.

"Thank goodness?" the Hoover echoed in stricken tones. "How can you say 'Thank goodness' when you've just been called junk and thrown on a heap of scrap?"

"Because if he'd decided to take us into his shack and use us, we'd have become his, like the radio. This way we've got a chance to escape."

The blanket, where it hung, limply, from the broken axle, began to whimper and whine. "No, no, it's true. That's all I am now—junk! Look at me—look at these tears, these snags, these stains. Junk! This is where I belong."

The lamp's grief was quieter but no less bitter. "Oh, my bulb," it murmured, "oh, my poor poor bulb!"

The Hoover groaned.

"Pull yourselves together, all of you!" said the toaster, in what it hoped was a tone of stern command. "There's nothing wrong with any of us that a bit of fixing-up won't put right. "You—" It addressed the blanket. "—are still fundamentally sound. Your coils haven't been hurt. After some sewing-up and a visit to the dry cleaner you'll be as good as new."

It turned to the lamp. "And what nonsense—to fuss over a broken bulb! You've broken your bulb before and probably will many times again. What do you think replaceable parts are *for?*"

Finally the toaster directed its attention to the vacuum cleaner. "And you? You, who must be our leader! Who ought to inspire us with your own greater strength!

For *you* to sit there groaning and helpless! And just because some old pirate who lives in a dump makes an unflattering remark. Why, he probably doesn't even know how to *use* a vacuum cleaner—that's the sort of person *he* is!"

"Do you think so?" said the Hoover.

"Of course I do, and so would you if you'd be rational. Now, for goodness' sake, let's all sit down together and figure out how we're going to rescue the radio and escape from here."

By midnight it was amazing how much they'd managed to accomplish. The Hoover had recharged the rundown battery from the battery in the pirate's own truck. Meanwhile the lamp, in looking about for another doorway or gate than the one they'd come in by (there wasn't any), had discovered a vehicle even better suited to their needs than the office chair the pirate had thrown in the river. This was a large vinyl perambulator, which is another word for pram, which is also known, in the appliances' part of the world, as a baby buggy. By whatever name, it was in good working order—except for two minor faults. One fault was a squeak in the left front wheel, and the other was the way its folding visor was twisted out of shape so as to give the whole pram an air of lurching sideways when it was moving straight ahead. The squeak was fixed with a few drops of 3-in-1 Oil, but the visor resisted their most determined efforts to bend it back into true. But that didn't matter, after all. What mattered was that it *worked*.

To think how many of the things consigned to this dump were still, like the pram (or themselves, for that matter) essentially serviceable! There were hair dryers and four-speed bicycles, water heaters and wind-up toys that would all have gone on working for years and years with just the slightest maintenance. Instead, they'd been sent to City Dump! You could hear their hopeless sighs and crazed murmurings rising from every dark mound round about, a ghastly medley that seemed to swell louder every moment as more and more of the forlorn, abandoned objects became conscious of the energetic new appliances in their midst.

"You will never, never, never get away," whispered a mad old cassette player in a cracked voice. "No, never!

You will stay here like all the rest of us and rust and crack and turn to dust. And never get away."

"We will, though," said the toaster. "Just you wait and see."

But how? That was the problem the toaster had to solve without further delay.

Now the surest way to solve any problem is to think about it, and that's just what the toaster did. It thought with the kind of total, all-out effort you have to give to get a bolt off that's rusted onto a screw. At first the bolt won't budge, not the least bit, and the wrench may slip loose, and you begin to doubt that any amount of trying is going to accomplish your purpose. But you keep at it, and use a dab of solvent if there's any on hand, and eventually it starts to give. You're not even sure but you think so. And then, what do you know, it's off! You've done it! That's the way the toaster thought, and at last, because he thought so hard, he thought of a way they could escape from the pirate and rescue the radio at the same time.

"Now here's my plan," said the toaster to the other appliances, which had gathered round him in the darkest corner of the dump. "We'll *frighten* him, and that will make him run away, and when he's gone we'll go into his shack—"

"Oh, no, I *couldn't* do that," said the blanket with a shiver of dread.

"We'll go into his shack," the toaster insisted calmly, "and get the radio and put it inside the baby buggy and get in ourselves, all except the Hoover, of course, which will high-tail it out of this place just as fast as it can."

"But won't the gate be locked?" the lamp wanted to know. "It is now."

"No, because the pirate will have to unlock it to get out himself, and he'll be too frightened to remember to lock it behind him."

"It's a very good plan," said the Hoover, "but what I don't understand is—*how* are we going to frighten him?"

"Well, what are people afraid of the most?"

"Getting run over by a steam roller?" the Hoover guessed.

"No. Scarier than that."

"Moths?" suggested the blanket.

"No."

"The dark," declared the lamp with conviction.

"That's close," said the toaster. "They're afraid of ghosts."

"What are ghosts?' demanded the Hoover.

"Ghosts are people who are dead, only they're also sort of alive."

"Don't be silly," said the lamp. "Either they *are* dead or they aren't."

"Yes," the blanket agreed. "It's as simple as ON and OFF. If you're ON, you can't be OFF, and vice versa."

"*I* know that, and *you* know that, but people don't seem to. People say they know that ghosts don't exist but they're afraid of them anyhow."

"No one can be afraid of something that doesn't exist," the Hoover huffed.

"Don't ask me how they do it," said the toaster. "It's what they call a paradox. The point is this—people are afraid of ghosts. And so *we're* going to pretend to be one."

"How?" asked the Hoover skeptically.

"Let me show you. Stoop down. Lower. Wrap your cord around my cord. Now—lift me up . . ."

After an hour's practice of pretending to be a ghost, they decided they were ready. Carefully, so that the other appliances wouldn't fall off, the old Hoover trundled toward the window of the shack. The toaster, where it was balanced atop the handle of the vacuum, was just able to see inside. There on a table between a stack of unwashed dishes and the pirate's ring of keys was the poor captive radio, and there, in dirty striped pajamas, getting ready to go to bed, was the pirate.

"Ready?" the toaster whispered.

The blanket, which was draped over the vacuum in a roughly ghostlike shape with a kind of hood at the top through which the toaster was able to peer out, adjusted its folds one last time. "Ready," the blanket replied.

"Ready?" the toaster asked again.

For just a moment the lamp, where it was hidden halfway down the handle of the Hoover, turned itself on and then, quickly, off. The bulb it had taken from the socket in the ceiling of the pickup truck had only half the wattage it was used to, and so its beam of light was noticeably dimmer—just enough to make the blanket give off the faintest yellowish glow.

"Then let's start haunting," said the toaster.

That was the signal the Hoover had been waiting for.

"Whoo!" groaned the Hoover in its deepest, most quivery voice. "Whoo!"

The pirate looked up with alarm. "Who's there?" he demanded.

"Whoo—oo!" the Hoover continued.

"Whoever you are, you'd better go away."

"Whoo—oo—oo!"

Cautiously the pirate approached the window from which the groaning seemed to issue.

Upon receiving a secret electric signal from the toaster, the vacuum crept quietly alongside the shack to where they would be out of sight from the window.

"Whoo . . ." breathed the Hoover in the barest of whispers. "Whoo . . ."

"Who's out there?" the pirate demanded, pressing his nose against the pane of glass and peering into the outer darkness. "You'd better answer me. Do you hear?"

In answer the Hoover made a strangling, gurgling, gaspy sound that sounded frightening even if you knew it was only the Hoover doing it. By now the pirate, who didn't have any idea what this mysterious groaning might be, had got into a considerable state of nerves. When you live all alone in the City Dump you don't expect to hear strange noises just outside your window in the middle of the night. And if you were also a bit superstitious, as pirates tend to be . . .

"All right then—if you won't say who you are, I'm going to come out there and find out!" He lingered yet a while before the window, but at last, when no reply was forthcoming, the pirate pulled on his pants and then got into his boots. "I'm warning you!" he called out, though not in a tone that could be called threatening.

Still there was no reply. He took up his key ring from where it lay on the table beside the radio. He went to the door.

He opened it.

"Now!" said the toaster, signaling secretly to the blanket along its electric cord.

"I can't," said the blanket, all atremble. "I'm too afraid."

"You *must!*"

"I mustn't: it's against the rules."

"We discussed all that before and you *promised*. Now hurry—before he gets here!"

With a shudder of trepidation the blanket did as it was bidden. There was a rent in its side where it had been pierced by a branch on the night it was blown up into the tree. The lamp was hiding just behind this rent. As the pirate appeared around the corner of the shack, the blanket twitched the torn fabric aside.

The pirate stopped short in his tracks when he saw the shrouded figure before him.

"Whoo-oo!" groaned the Hoover one last time.

At this cue the lamp turned itself on. Its beam slanted up through the hole in the blanket right into the pirate's face.

When the lamp lit up, the pirate stared at the figure before him with the utmost horror. What he saw that was so frightening was the same thing the daisy had seen, the same thing Harold and Marjorie had seen, as well—he saw his own features reflected in the toaster's mottled chrome. And as he had been a very wicked person from his earliest youth, his face had taken on that special kind of ugliness that only very evil people's faces acquire. Seeing such a face grimacing at him from this strange hooded figure, what was the pirate to suppose but that he had come upon the most dangerous kind of ghost, the kind that understands exactly who we are and knows all the wrong things we've done and intends to punish us for them. From such ghosts even grown-up pirates will flee in terror. Which is exactly what the pirate did.

As soon as he was gone, the appliances rushed into the pirate's shack and rescued the joyful radio. Then before the pirate could return they scrambled into the baby buggy, and the old Hoover drove off with them as fast as its wheels would revolve.

As luck would have it, they didn't have much farther to go: where the master lived on Newton Avenue was only a mile or so from City Dump. They reached his apartment building early in the morning before a single milk truck had appeared on the street.

"You see," said the toaster cheerfully, "in the end everything really does work out for the best."

Alas, the toaster had spoken too soon. Their tribulations were not yet at an end, and not everything would work out for the best, as they were shortly to discover.

The Hoover, which had an instinctive knack for such things, buzzed the street door open and summoned the automatic elevator. When the elevator door slid open, it wheeled the pram in and pressed the button for the 14th floor.

"It's *changed* so," said the tensor lamp, as the Hoover pushed the pram out of the elevator and down the corridor. "The wallpaper used to be green squiggles and white blobs, and now it's crisscross lines."

"It's we who've changed," said the blanket miserably.

"Hush," said the Hoover sternly. "Remember the rules!" It pressed the doorbell beside the door to the master's apartment.

All the appliances kept perfectly still.

No one came to the door.

"Maybe he's asleep," said the alarm clock/radio.

"Maybe he's not home," said the Hoover. "I'll see." It rang the doorbell again, but in a different way so that only the appliances in the apartment would be able to hear it ring.

In only a moment a Singer sewing machine answered the door. "Yes?" said the sewing machine in a tone of polite curiosity. "Can I help you?"

"Oh, excuse me, I seem to have made a mistake." The Hoover looked at the number on the door, then at the name on the brass panel over the bell. It was the right number, the right name. But . . . a sewing machine?

"Is that . . . ?" said a familiar voice within the apartment. "Why, it is! It's the old Hoover! How *are* you? Come in! Come in!"

The Hoover wheeled the pram into the apartment and over the deep-piled carpet toward the friendly old tv.

The blanket peeked out shyly over the side of the pram.

"And who's that with you? Come out—don't be shy. My goodness, what a treat this is."

The blanket crawled out of the pram, taking care to keep the worst effects of the journey folded up out of sight. It was followed by the radio, the lamp, and, last of all, the toaster.

The tv, which knew all five of them from the time it had spent with the master at the summer cottage, introduced them to the many appliances from all over the apartment which had begun to gather in the living room. Some, like the water pic, the blender, and the tv itself, were old friends. Some, like the stereo and the clock on the mantel, were known to the four appliances that had lived in the apartment at one time themselves but not to the toaster. But a great many were complete strangers to them all. There were huge impractical ginger-jar lamps squatting on low tables and, out of the bedroom, dim little lamps with frilly shades and other lamps screwed into the dining-nook wall that were pretending to be candleflames. Out of the kitchen had trooped a whole tribe of unfamiliar gadgets: a crockpot, a can opener, a waffle iron, a meat grinder, a carving knife, and, somewhat abashedly, the master's new toaster.

"How do you do," said the new toaster in a barely audible voice when the tv introduced it.

"How do *you* do?" the toaster replied warmly.

Neither could think of anything else to say. Fortunately there were more introductions to be effected. The Hoover had to go through a similar ordeal when it met the apartment's vacuum cleaner, which was (just as the Hoover had feared) one of the new lightweight models that looks like a big hamburger bun on wheels. They were polite to each other, but it was obvious that the new vacuum looked on the Hoover as outmoded.

The blanket had an even worse shock in store. The last two appliances to appear in the living room were a vaporizer and a long tangled string of Christmas tree lights, both of which had been hibernating in a closet. The blanket looked about anxiously. "Well," it said, making a determined effort to seem accepting and friendly, "I think there must still be one more of you we haven't yet met."

"No," said the tv. "We're all here."

"But is there no other . . . blanket?"

The tv avoided the blanket's earnest gaze. "No. The master doesn't use an electric blanket any more. Just a plain wool one."

"But he always . . . he always . . ." The blanket could say no more. Its resolution deserted it and it fell in a heap on the carpet.

A gasp went up from the apartment's assembled appliances, which until now had had no idea of the extent of the blanket's injuries.

"Doesn't *use* an electric blanket!" the toaster repeated indignantly. "Whyever not?"

The screen of the tv flickered and then, evasively, started showing a gardening show.

"It isn't the master's choice, really," said the Singer sewing machine in its funny clipped accent. "I daresay *he* would be delighted to see his old blanket again."

The blanket looked up questioningly.

"It's the mistress," the sewing machine went on. "She says she becomes too hot under an electric blanket."

"The mistress?" the five appliances repeated.

"Didn't you know?"

"No," said the toaster. "No, we haven't heard anything from the master since he left the cottage three years ago."

"Two years, eleven months, and twenty-two days, to be precise," said the alarm clock/radio.

"That's why we determined to find our way here. We feared . . . I don't know what exactly. But we thought that . . . that our master would need us."

"Oh," said the sewing machine. It turned to watch the gardening show on the tv.

As unobtrusively as it might, the new toaster crept back into the kitchen and resumed its post of duty on the formica countertop.

"Two years, eleven months, and twenty-two days is a long time to be left alone," the radio asserted at rather a loud volume. "Naturally we became concerned. The poor air conditioner stopped working altogether."

"And all the while," said the lamp, "never a word of explanation!" It glared reproachfully at the tv, which continued to discuss the problem of blister beetles.

"Can't *any* of you tell us why?" the toaster demanded earnestly. "Why did he never return to the cottage? There must be a *reason*."

"I can tell you," said the vaporizer, inching forward. "You see, the mistress is subject to hay fever. I can help her a bit with her asthma, but when the hay fever starts in on her, there's nothing anyone can do, and she is really very miserable then."

"I still don't understand," said the toaster.

The sewing machine spelled it out. "Rather than go to the country, where there is bound to be ragweed and pollen and such, they spend their summers at the seaside."

"And our cottage—our lovely cottage in the woods—what is to become of it?"

"I believe the master means to sell it."

"And . . . and us?" the toaster asked.

"I understand there is to be an auction," said the sewing machine.

The Hoover, which had comported itself with great dignity throughout the visit, could bear no more. With a loud groan it grasped the handle of the perambulator as though to steady itself. "Come," it gasped. "All of you, come. We are not wanted here. We'll return to . . . to . . ."

Where would they return? Where could they? They had become appliances without a household!

"To the Dump!" shrieked the blanket hysterically. "Isn't that where *junk* belongs? That's all we are now—junk!" It twisted its cord into an agonized knot. "Isn't that what the pirate said we were? Junk! Junk! Junk! All of us, and me most of all."

"Control yourself," said the toaster sternly, though its own coils felt as though they were about to snap. "We're *not* junk. We're sturdy, useful appliances."

"Look at me!" cried the blanket, displaying the full extent of its worst tear. "And these mudstains—look!"

"Your tears can be sewn up," said the toaster calmly. It turned to the sewing machine. "Can't they?"

The sewing machine nodded in mute agreement.

"And the stains can be cleaned."

"And then what?" the Hoover demanded dourly. "Let us suppose the blanket is repaired and cleaned, and that I've mended my cord and got my dustbag into working shape, and that you've polished yourself. Suppose all that—what then? Where shall we go?"

"I don't know. Somewhere. I'll have to think."

"Pardon me," said the tv, turning off the gardening show. "But didn't I hear you say something about a . . . pirate?"

"Yes," said the sewing machine nervously. "What pirate did you mean? There's not a pirate in this building, I hope?"

"Never fear—we don't have to worry any more about him. He captured us but we escaped from him. Would you like to know how?"

"Goodness, yes," said the tv. "I love a good story."

So all the appliances gathered in a circle about the toaster, which began to tell the story of their adventures from the moment they had decided to leave the cottage till the moment they arrived at the door of the apartment. It was a very long story, as you know, and while the toaster told it, the sewing machine set to work sewing up all the rips and tears in the blanket.

The next afternoon when the blanket came back from Jiffy Dry Cleaners on the other side of Newton Avenue, the apartment's appliances put on a splendid party for their five visitors. The Christmas tree lights strung themselves up between the two ginger-jar lamps and winked and bubbled in the merriest way, while the tv and the stereo sang duets from all the most famous musical comedies. The toaster was polished to a fare-thee-well, and the Hoover was likewise in fine fettle once again. But most wonderful of all—the blanket looked almost as good as new. Its yellow was possibly not as bright as it had been, but it was a lovely yellow, for all that. The exact same yellow, according to the tv, of custard and primroses and the nicest bathroom tissues.

At five o'clock the radio's alarm went off, and everyone became very still, except for the blanket, which went on whirling gaily about the living room for some time before it realized the music had stopped.

"What is it?" asked the blanket. "Why are you all so quiet?"

"Hush," said the radio. "It's time for *The Swap Shop*."

"What is *The Swap Shop*?" asked the blanket.

"It's the program on listener-supported radio station KHOP," said the toaster excitedly, "that is going to find a new home for us! I told you not to worry, didn't I? I told you I'd think of something!"

"Be quiet," said the lamp. "It's starting."

The radio turned up its volume so that all the appliances in the living room could hear. "Good afternoon," it said, in a deep, announcer-type voice, "and welcome to *The Swap Shop*. Today's program opens with a very strange offering from Newton Avenue. It seems that someone there wants to swap—now listen to this list!—a Hoover vacuum cleaner, an AM alarm clock/radio, a yellow electric blanket, a tensor lamp, and a Sunbeam toaster. All this in exchange for . . . well, it says on the card here: 'You name it.' What's most important, I'm informed, is that you should have a real and genuine *need* for all five of these fine appliances, since their present owner wants them to be able to stay together. For sentimental reasons! Now I've heard everything! Anyhow, if you think you *need* those five appliances, the number to call is 485-9120. That number again, 485-9120. Our next offer is not quite so unusual. Seems there's a party on Center Street who is offering, absolutely for free, five lovable black-and-white—"

The radio tuned out KHOP. "Didn't he make us sound super!" it exclaimed, forgetting in its excitement to stop speaking in the announcer's voice.

"Come over here by the telephone," the Hoover urged the radio. "You'll have to talk to them. I'm just too nervous."

All five appliances gathered about the telephone and waited for it to ring.

There are two schools of thought about whether or not appliances ought to be allowed the free use of telephones. Some insist that it is flatly against the rules and should never be done in any circumstances, while others maintain that it's all right, since it is only another appliance one is talking to, in this case a telephone. Whether or not it's against the rules, it is certainly a fact that a good many appliances (lonely radios especially) do use the phone system regularly, usually to contact other appliances. This explains the great number of so-called "wrong numbers" that people get at odd times. Computerized exchanges could never make so many mistakes, though they end up taking the blame.

For the last three years, of course, this issue had not mattered very much to the appliances, since the phone in the cottage had been disconnected. Ordinarily, the Hoover would probably have opposed the notion of any of them using the phone, as it did tend to adopt the conservative attitude. But first there had been the absolute necessity of calling Jiffy Dry Cleaners and having them pick up the blanket, and that had established a clear precedent for their phoning in to KHOP and offering themselves on *The Swap Shop*. And now here they were all gathered round the telephone, waiting to talk with their next master!

The phone rang.

"Now whatever you do," warned the Hoover, "don't say yes to the first person who happens to call. Find out something about him first. We don't want to go just anywhere, you know."

"Right," said the radio.

"And remember," said the toaster, "to be nice."

The radio nodded. It picked up the telephone receiver. "Hello?" it said.

"Is this the person with the five appliances?"

"It is! Oh my goodness yes indeed, it is!"

And so the five appliances went to live with their new mistress, for as it happened it was a woman who'd phoned them first and not a man. She was an elderly, impoverished ballerina who lived all alone in a small room at the back of her ballet studio on Center Street in the oldest part of the city. What the ballerina had swapped for the appliances were her five lovable black-and-white kittens. The appliances' former master never could figure out how, upon returning with his wife from their summer vacation by the sea, there had come to be five kittens in their apartment. It was rather an awkward situation, for his wife was allergic to cat fur. But they were such darlings—it would never have done to put them out on the street. In the end they decided to keep them, and his wife simply took more antihistamines.

And the appliances?

Oh, they were *very* happy. At first the Hoover had been doubtful about entering service with a woman (for it had never worked for a woman before, and it was somewhat set in its ways), but as soon as it realized what a fastidious and immaculate housekeeper its mistress was, it forgot all its reservations and became her greatest champion.

It felt so good to be *useful* again! The radio would play beautiful classical music for the ballerina to dance to; and when she became tired and wanted to sit down and read, the lamp would light her book; and then when it grew late and she'd finished her book, the blanket would give off a steady, gentle warmth that kept her cozy all through the long, cold night.

And when it was morning and she awoke, what wonderful slices of toast the toaster would toast for her—so brown and crisp and perfect and always just the same!

And so the five appliances lived and worked, happy and fulfilled, serving their dear mistress and enjoying each other's companionship, to the end of their days.

Psychic investigators studying a poltergeist case can expect to find weird destructive forces at work, and probably a bewildered adolescent girl. Matters are similar—then very different—in this evocative tale set in 1892. (Though there's a connection to our more modern era.)

Richard Cowper (the name is pronounced "Cooper") has written such novels as *The Road to Corlay* and *Profundis,* as well as the short story collection *Out There Where the Big Ships Go.*

THE ATTLEBOROUGH POLTERGEIST

Richard Cowper

> *O God! O God! that it were possible*
> *To undo things done; to call back yesterday . . .*
> —THOMAS HEYWOOD

MY FATHER BELONGED TO THAT SMALL BUT distinguished band of scientific journalists who flourished during the '20s and '30s and who today seem to have become an almost totally extinct species. Yet the fact that they played a very real part in helping to shape our present world is surely indisputable. Many a distinguished doctor must have caught the virus of enthusiasm from Paul de Kruif's *Microbe Hunters* or *Men against Death,* and I daresay that more than one professor could be found who is prepared to admit that his youthful imagination was set free through the pages of my father's *Pioneers of Physics.*

My father's *forte* was human interest. This is not to say that his scientific facts were inaccurate but rather that he preferred the actors in his dramas to be recognizable as human beings. He wished his reader to *see* the tense faces peering down into that cloud chamber in the Cavendish Laboratory; and when Henri Becquerel's hand hovered before alighting by pure chance on the the lump of uranium nitrate which would lead him on to the discovery of radioactivity, my father's aim was to make sure that his reader's hand hovered with it. If in order to achieve this desired objective he sometimes felt

84

it necessary to animate the dead bones of scientific fact
with a little *élan vital* supplied from his own lively
imagination, then he did so with grace and without
qualms. I suspect the truth is that he was a novelist
manqué.

When, early in 1944, he was cajoled out of semi-
retirement by a publisher's commission to write *The Life
of Sir James Cameron Hartson* for the *Great Men of
British Science* series, he set about it in his usual well-
organized way. He traveled around the country, sometimes alone, sometimes with my mother, interviewing
people who had known Hartson and visiting places where
the Grand Old Man had lived and worked.

I was stationed in Burma when this was going on,
about as far removed in space and time from 19th century Cambridge as it was possible to get, and the occasional letters I received from my father in which he
spoke of his research seemed almost like spirit messages
from another world. I recall one in which he mentioned
having just returned from a trip to blitzed Norwich to
consult the Victorian records of the East Anglian Dialectical Society. I read his letter stretched out on a rusty
jetty in Rangamati. The temperature was hovering
around 102 degrees, and about a yard from my ear, my
companion Bill Cassidy was diverting himself by trying
to sink floating beer cans with bursts from a sten gun.

A fortnight or so later my squadron was transferred to
Australia and the mail went haywire. In the next letter I
received from my father he spoke regretfully of "not
being able to use Martin's Journal after all." I presumed
rightly, that this was a reference to some other letter or
letters of his which had gone astray, but it was not until
many years after the war was over that I learned the
full story of what must have been contained in that missing correspondence.

The answer lay in a file bearing a label "Attleborough
Investigation," which I came across when I was clearing
up the house after my mother's death. It contained material which my father had assembled while he was
working on what was to be his last book. There were a
number of notes and the bulk of what I at first took to be
a draft chapter but which I am now inclined to suspect
he may have intended to publish separately as a sort of
extended footnote to his biography. The story it con-

tained struck me as being so odd and so redolent of its
period that I make no apologies for offering it here more
or less in the form in which I myself first read it. The
narrator is, of course, my father.

I first stumbled across a reference linking James Hartson with Attleborough in the privately circulated *Annual
Report of the East Anglian Dialectical Society*—1892.
The E.A.D.S. was one of a number of provincial offshoots
from the prestigious Society for Psychical Research,
which had been founded under the presidency of Henry
Sidgwick ten years before.

Hartson had already carried out a number of investi-
gations on behalf of the S.P.R. (chiefly exposures of
fraudulent spiritualist mediums and the like) and was
apparently engaged by the E.A.D.S. at the suggestion
of no less a luminary than the great F.H. Myers. I confess I have been able to find no mention of this either in
Myers' own voluminous correspondence or in the Sidgwick archives, but since Dr. Philip Daniels—the moving
spirit behind the E.A.D.S.—was a Cambridge contem-
porary and personal friend of both Myers and Gurney, it
seems perfectly likely that he would have appealed to
them for advice and that they would have suggested
young Hartson as being the best person for the job.

The passage in the *Report* concerned a meeting of the
Society which had been held in Daniel's house in Norwich on August 23rd, 1892. Six members had been
present, and during the course of the evening a letter from
a Dr. George Martin had been read out drawing the attention of the Society to "certain curious and possibly
psychic phenomena" which, he believed, were manifest-
ing themselves in a house on the outskirts of the little
market town of Attleborough in Norfolk. Dr. Martin had
been consulted by two of his patients, Mr. and Mrs. Robert Fletcher, a local bank manager and his wife, who
were worried about the health of their niece, Alice Hobson, to whom, since the recent untimely deaths of her
own mother and father, they had been standing *in loco
parentis*.

Having listened to their story with some scepticism.
Dr. Martin had finally agreed to call round at "Laurel
House," Chillingford Rd., after evening surgery and
there to examine their ward in Mrs. Fletcher's presence.

This he had done and had discovered Alice Hobson to be a "personable" (i.e., physically attractive) and intelligent young lady of seventeen who had smilingly assured him that she believed her aunt and uncle were making a great deal of fuss about nothing.

In deference to Mr. and Mrs. Fletcher's wishes Martin had carried out a routine examination which revealed two minor physical abnormalities—an average pulse rate of 48 and a bodily temperature of 96°F.

He then questioned the girl about the incidents which had been the direct cause of her guardians' consulting him, only to be assured by Miss Hobson that she had no personal recollection whatsoever of the "fainting spells" he referred to, though she was seemingly prepared to accept that they had occurred. So far as he was able to ascertain, there was no family history of *petit mal,* and he had already decided in his own mind that the problem was one of "female periodicity" and was noting as much on his jotting pad when, in his own words, "an incident occurred for which I can find no rational explanation whatsoever."

The consultation was taking place in the Fletchers' dining room. Martin and Miss Hobson were seated upon plain chairs, about a yard apart, directly facing one another. Mrs. Fletcher was sitting at the opposite side of the dining table, which had no covering and upon which Martin had placed his medical bag. At the far end of the room stood a massive mahogany sideboard, upon which was displayed an array of silver plate and a "tantalus" —three cut-glass decanters locked inside a specially designed, "servant-proof," wood and metal holder. Without sound or warning this unlikely object rose from its place on the sideboard and dashed itself with considerable force and a deafening clatter against the wall directly to Martin's right.

To Martin it was inconceivable that either Miss Hobson or Mrs. Fletcher could have contrived to fling it since both were still seated in their chairs well out of reach of the sideboard, and neither Mr. Fletcher nor either of the house servants was in the room. Indeed, both the women had appeared at least as startled as Martin himself; Mrs. Fletcher had screamed loudly and Miss Hobson had flung up her arms to protect her head. Martin leaped to his feet, rushed across to where the tantalus was lying and

picked it up. As he touched it, he experienced what he
described in his letter as "a distinct though minor Gal-
vanic shock, similar to that accompanying the discharge
of a Leyden Jar."

At that point the door had burst open, and Mr.
Fletcher had appeared on the threshold demanding to
know what was going on. During the course of the en-
suing conversation it emerged that this was by no means
the first inexplicable occurrence in the Fletcher household. It had not taken Dr. Martin long to divine that in
consulting him about the health of their niece the Fletchers had been seeking (albeit unwittingly) some means
of sharing the burden of their own ever-increasing anxiety.

Martin had succeeded in eliciting from them various
details of alleged "happenings." These appeared to fall
into two main categories: (a) *physical* (such as that just
described) and (b) *aural* (mostly in the form of an explosive report). One or two had been a combination of
both (a) and (b). A curious feature of the (b) type
phenomena was that they all appeared to be accompanied by a faint though distinctive *odor* which Mrs. Fletcher had described as being "a bit like smelling salts in
the way it makes your nose prickle."

Dr. Martin had had no previous personal experience
whatsoever of psychic phenomena and was, indeed, a
confessed skeptic in such matters, but he found himself
so puzzled and intrigued by the Fletcher case that he
had written up his account and posted it off to Dr. Phillip
Daniels at the Dialectical Society. Daniels, who had met
Martin once before at a professional symposium, had
been sufficiently impressed by the letter to make the
journey from Norwich to Attleborough.

After discussing the case at some length, the two men
had driven round to Laurel House and spoken with the
Fletchers and their niece. Dr. Daniels had examined the
tantalus together with various other mundane household
objects which, the Fletchers assured him, had also behaved in a similarly unorthodox fashion at various times
during the previous month: among them were a silver
mustard pot, a pair of brass fire-tongs, and a pewter
candlestick. However, nothing untoward occurred during
the course of the visit, and it was not until the two men
were on the point of taking their leave that Alice Hobson
had produced a piece of paper which she had handed

shyly to Dr. Daniels and asked him if he could possibly explain to her what it meant.

Daniels unfolded the paper and found himself gazing at an extraordinary jumble of figures, letters, and what looked like cabalistic runes. He peered at it and shook his head. "What on earth is this, Miss Hobson?" he asked curiously. "How did you come by it?"

"I don't really know," she said. "I found it on the writing table in my bedroom."

"Do you recognize the hand?"

She hesitated. "I think it must be my own."

"You mean you have no recollection of having written it?"

"None at all, I assure you. It looks like double-Dutch to me."

"And can you describe the circumstances in which you discovered it?"

"Oh, yes. I had been writing a letter to my cousins in Luton. When I came to assemble the sheets of notepaper, I discovered that lying among them."

"Am I to assume there was no indication that you had broken off your letter at any point and then taken it up again?"

"None," she said.

Daniels handed the paper to his colleague. Martin looked equally baffled. "Is it mathematics?" he asked.

"If it is, it's not like any I have ever come across," said Daniels. "That for instance. What does it look like to you?"

"A heart," said Martin.

"And that?"

Martin held his head on one side. "Heaven knows," he said. "A spider, perhaps? I know it's not my field at all, Daniels, but surely *that* is a square root symbol. And doesn't that sign represent infinity?"

Daniels glanced up at Miss Hobson. "What *is* the symbol for infinity, Miss Hobson?"

"I have no idea," she said. "I didn't even know there was one."

"Do you mind if I keep this paper?"

"Please do," she said. "It means nothing to me."

That evening Dr. Daniels dined with George Martin and his wife. Over the meal the two men discussed the

case. "Alice Hobson struck me as being an extremely
level-headed girl," said Daniels. "Not emotionally dis-
turbed in any way. Wouldn't you agree, Martin?"

Dr. Martin nodded. "Cool as a cucumber."

"There's usually some evidence of incipient hysteria
in such cases," said Daniels, and went on to describe an
investigation which he had conducted with Dr. Gurney.
"It was far from satisfactory," he concluded. "Both Gurney and I were convinced that there *had* been genuine
manifestations to start with, but the child in question—a
very plain girl—obviously relished the unaccustomed
attention she was attracting and decided to manufacture
some phenomena on her own account. It was all so am-
ateurish that we detected it immediately, but the result
was that we felt constrained to dismiss the whole episode
as a hoax."

"If Alice Hobson manufactured that infernal tantalus,
then I'm dashed if I can see how she did it," said Martin. "I'd say the thing weighs the better part of ten
pounds. Well, you saw the scar on the wall yourself."

"Yet she certainly seems to have manufactured the
note."

"What note was that, George?" asked Mrs. Martin.

Dr. Daniels produced the sheet of folded notepaper
from his breast pocket and passed it across the table to
his hostess while Martin described how it had come into
their possession.

Mrs. Martin examined it curiously and then said,
"You know, I think this is some sort of coded message,
George."

The two men regarded her blankly. Finally Martin
said, "What makes you say that, my dear?"

"Did you never play such games at school, George?"
she enquired with a smile. "Too wise you are, too wise
you be; I see you are too wise for me?"

"What on earth are you talking about, Sarah?"

For answer Mrs. Martin rapidly finger-sketched two
capital *Y's* in the air, followed by the letters *U* and *R*. "I
read this as being intended for someone called Heart-
sun," she said. "That is the figure 4 followed by a picture
of a heart and a sun. And it appears to end 'see Heart-
sun sees.'"

"By Jove!" exclaimed Martin. "That thing I thought
was a spider! You know, it *could* be a sun, Daniels!"

Dr. Daniels frowned. "Hartson," he murmured. "What an extraordinary coincidence."

"You know someone of that name?"

"Indeed, I do. By repute only, though. James Hartson is a protegé of Gurney's. Devilish clever fellow by all accounts. Senior wrangler, Gordon Fellow, and heaven knows what else." He reached out and took the sheet of paper back from Mrs. Martin. "For Hartson," he repeated. "I say, Martin, do you think we could go back there and have another word with Miss Hobson after dinner?"

'I don't see why not," said Martin. "Your last train doesn't leave till midnight here."

Daniels smiled. "Oh, I don't think that will be necessary. All I wish to ascertain is whether Miss Hobson has ever heard of James Hartson. It certainly seems unlikely, but one never knows, does one?"

The twilight was already fading when Martin turned his pony trap into the graveled drive of Laurel House. The reins were hitched to the handrail, and the two men mounted the porticoed steps to the front door. They heard the bell pealing in the distant recesses of the house and then the brisk tapping of heels on the tiled floor of the outer hall. The door was opened by a young parlor maid who held aloft a lighted oil lamp. Recognizing Dr. Martin, she smiled and stood back to let them in.

Alice Hobson looked up from the novel which she had been reading aloud to her aunt and favored the visitors with a faint and slightly puzzled smile while Mrs. Fletcher apologized for the fact that her husband was attending a lodge meeting in the town and was not expected back until late.

Dr. Martin countered with his own apology for intruding upon them at such an uncivilized hour and then disclosed the reason for the visit.

It was soon obvious that the name "Hartson" meant nothing at all to either woman, and as Martin was explaining how they had arrived at their interpretation, Alice so forgot herself as to laugh. "But surely it would have been far simpler just to write the name down in plain English, if that is all that was needed?" she said.

"Had you been communicating consciously, Miss

Hobson," replied Daniels, "I would certainly agree. But speaking from my personal experience of what we psychic researchers call 'automatic script,' the messages are often couched in the most obscure terms. It is almost as if some invisible censor in the human consciousness were being purposely misled. Puns, *double entendres*, haphazard verbal associations are all brought into play. Anything straightforward is, I can assure you, wholly exceptional."

"Then who is this Hartson?" demanded Alice. "Does any such person exist?"

"Yes. That is to say I do know of a gentleman with that name," said Daniels. "He is an associate of Dr. Gurney and an active member of the Cambridge Psychical Research Society. With your permission, I would very much like to send him the note—or a facsimile of it —on the off chance that he may be able to throw some light upon this matter."

"Pray do so, by all means, Dr. Daniels."

"Then in that case we shall trespass upon your hospitality no longer," said Daniels, bowing his head first to Mrs. Fletcher and then to her niece. "I am extremely grateful for your co-operation. Pray do not disturb yourselves, ladies. We can find our own way out."

But Alice Hobson had already risen to her feet and was moving towards the door. Daniels and Martin stood back to let her by and she rustled past them into the passage. They took their leave of Mrs. Fletcher, closed the drawing room door behind them and followed the girl into the hall. As they reached the foot of the stairs, Alice was already opening the glass-paneled door into the outer hall. She had just stepped through the doorway when both men heard a crack like a pistol shot. They saw her half-turn towards them, her face chalk-white in the lamplight, and then she had buckled at the knees and collapsed upon the tiled floor.

Both men rushed towards her. Just as they reached the outer hall, the lamp on the table flared up as though caught by a sudden draught. At the same moment the heavy brass dinner gong which hung suspended in a recess at the foot of the stairs emitted a loud, throbbing *boom!* as if it had been struck with tremendous force by an invisible maul.

"Good God!" cried Martin. "What was that?"

Daniels was already down upon his knees fumbling with the hooks and eyes on the high collar of the girl's dress. He had just succeeded in loosening it when Mrs. Fletcher appeared at the foot of the stairs demanding tremulously to know what was happening.

"Your niece appears to have swooned, ma'am," said Martin.

"She's not hurt, is she?"

"I think not," said Daniels. "It seems to be a common faint."

As if to confirm his diagnosis, Alice Hobson chose that moment to open her eyes. She blinked up into the tense faces of the two men and then frowned. Martin placed an arm around her shoulders and helped her up into a sitting position. "Are you all right, Miss Hobson?" he enquired anxiously.

"What happened?" she whispered.

"I really don't know," he said. "We both heard a sound like a pistol going off and then you fell to the floor. For a nasty moment I thought that you must have been shot."

She shivered violently, then scrambled to her feet. "I'm certain you are mistaken, Doctor," she said. "I assure you I heard no such sound."

The two men exchanged glances but refrained from comment.

Martin turned to Mrs. Fletcher. "See she gets a tot of brandy in hot milk, ma'am, then trundle her off to bed. I'll drop by in the morning and see how she is."

"Oh, please don't trouble yourself on my account, Dr. Martin," said Alice with genuine concern in her voice. "I'm perfectly all right. Really, I am."

"I'm sure you are," agreed Martin with professional heartiness. "My visit will be purely for my own private and personal satisfaction."

Alice smiled palely, moved across to the front door and opened it. "Good night, Dr. Daniels," she said. "Good night, Dr. Martin. I'm so sorry to have been a nuisance."

"No trouble at all, dear young lady," they assured her gallantly and stepped out into the soft summer night.

As they were driving along the Chillingford Rd. towards the railway station, Daniels suddenly slapped his hand across his knee. "Ozone!" he exclaimed. "That's it,

Martin! I've been trying to place it for the past ten minutes. Didn't you recognize it?"

"Now you come to mention it, yes, I believe I did. In the hall. Do you think it significant?"

"If I'm not mistaken, you said in your letter that Mrs. Fletcher had mentioned a smell which made her nose prick. What's that if it's not ozone?"

"You mean there's some sort of physical connection?"

"Electrical, I suspect. You know, Martin, this case really is beginning to interest me profoundly. I shall certainly lose no time in contacting Myers and seeking his advice."

"You don't think there's any real danger, do you, Daniels? From the girl's standpoint, I mean?"

"Well, I suppose there's always a risk that she might have one of those fainting fits at the top of the stairs and tumble down. However, I think it unlikely. Haven't you noticed how women usually contrive to have a syncope in reasonably comfortable circumstances?"

"Good Lord! You mean you think she was *acting?*"

"Oh, no, no, no, Martin. I'm sure it was a perfectly genuine faint. But the unconscious mind cannot be regarded as totally irresponsible. One might almost say that it appears to have its owner's basic interests at heart at all times."

"And what's that supposed to mean?"

"Only that I suspect Miss Hobson's unconscious mind is trying to cope with some external psychic pressure in the only way it can. That is to say, by preserving her life in spite of herself."

"You mean you really believe there is some ulterior force at work?"

"Well, something certainly flung that tantalus across the room, and something struck that gong tonight. And we both know it wasn't Miss Hobson."

"Then what was it, Daniels?"

"I wish I knew."

"Does *anyone* know?"

"Myers and Gurney would maintain that they're getting close to an explanation."

"And Hartson?"

"Ah, Hartson . . . well, we shall see."

Martin flicked his whip over the pony's flanks. The *clip-clop* of hooves quickened briskly on the macadam as they bowled along into Attleborough. "I'm dashed if I know what to make of any of it, Daniels. This sort of thing is right outside my experience. I don't mind telling you that if you hadn't been there tonight I think I'd have been scared out of my wits."

"There's nothing to be ashamed of in that," Daniels assured him. "It's a perfectly natural reaction. Man has always been afraid of what he does not understand."

"Then you believe there *is* a rational explanation?"

"Oh, undoubtedly there is, though I suspect it may mean we'll have to expand the boundaries of orthodoxy before we can accommodate it. I take it you haven't read Myers' *Phantasms of the Living?*"

"No, I can't say I have."

"How about James's *Principles of Psychology?*"

"I've heard of it," said Martin guardedly.

Daniels turned urgently to face him. "I tell you, Martin, there's no doubt at all in my mind that today we're standing right on the brink of something absolutely stupendous! The Dark Ages are finally coming to an end! I'm convinced that the next ten years will see the emergence of a whole new scientific and spiritual synthesis— an utterly overwhelming philosophic concept of man's true nature. You and I will both live to see F.H. Myers recognized as the Charles Darwin of the human psyche!"

Martin said nothing, not because he was unimpressed but simply because he could not think of anything to say that seemed even remotely relevant.

Ten days later Dr. Martin called in at Laurel House at the end of his morning rounds. He found Mrs. Fletcher and her niece reclining in deck chairs on the croquet lawn. After politely refusing a glass of lemonade and having ascertained that there had been no recurrence of the fainting spells, Martin came straight to the point. "This morning I received a communication from Dr. Daniels. He tells me he had heard from his Cambridge friends who have expressed great interest in your problem. Daniels has asked me to find out if you would agree to Mr. James Hartson carrying out an investigation under the auspices of the Society for Psychical Research."

Alice Hobson tilted her head to one side and regarded him through her lowered eyelashes. "Mr. Hartson would conduct this investigation in person?"

"So Daniels has given me to understand."

"And what would such an investigation amount to, do you suppose?"

"To tell the truth, I've no idea, Miss Hobson. It's all *terra incognita*, so far as I'm concerned. However, I have the greatest confidence in Daniels' judgment, and he in Dr. Gurney's."

"And Dr. Gurney in Mr. Hartson's?" inquired the girl with a smile.

"So it would appear."

"And how long do you suppose it would take?" asked Mrs. Fletcher.

"Daniels mentions a period of three or four days," said Martin. "It goes without saying that Mrs. Martin and I will be delighted to offer Mr. Hartson hospitality while he—"

"Oh, no," said Alice quickly. "He will stay here with us, won't he, Aunt?"

"Whatever Dr. Martin thinks best, dear."

Martin pursed up his lips and nodded sagely. "It probably *would* be more convenient if he were residing on the premises," he said. "Otherwise, I can well imagine vital minutes being lost while your servant ran round to us with a message for him."

"Exactly," said Alice firmly. "Mr. Hartson shall stay here as our guest, and you, Dr. Martin, will write to Dr. Daniels and tell him so."

"Really, Alice!" protested Mrs. Fletcher. "Whatever next? Do forgive her, Dr. Martin.

Martin smiled tolerantly. "As a matter of fact, Daniels *has* asked me to telegraph direct to Cambridge if you should agree to the proposition. It appears that both Gurney and Hartson view it as a matter of some considerable urgency. As soon as he receives word from us, Hartson undertakes to be in Attleborough within forty-eight hours."

"Really?" said Mrs. Fletcher. "As soon as that? Then I had better go and have a word with cook at once. Oh, dear, you don't suppose Mr. Hartson is a vegetarian, do you?"

She got up from her chair, proffered Dr. Martin a faintly abstracted smile and disappeared in the house.

Martin was on the point of taking his leave when Alice Hobson laid a detaining hand on his arm. "Did Dr. Daniels say whether he had sent that message to Cambridge?"

"Not specifically," said Martin. "But I assume he must have done. Why! Has there been another?"

She appeared to hesitate; then, almost reluctantly, she nodded.

"And have you managed to decipher it?"

"No", she said, shaking her head. "Well, only those same two signs. I found them scribbled on the flyleaf of a book I'd been reading."

"And that's all there was?"

"There were some other things," she said vaguely. "Some numbers, and so forth. Nothing that made any sense."

"So far as I'm concerned, Miss Alice, none of it makes any sense," he asserted roundly. "But I'm confident we'll get to the bottom of it sooner or later."

"Yes," she said, smiling her private little smile. "I'm sure we will. Sooner or later."

Two days later, in the steely heat of midafternoon, Dr. Martin drove to Attleborough station to meet James Hartson off the Cambridge train. He found a tall, gangling man in his middle twenties who was perspiring freely in an unseasonable suit of heather-mixture tweeds and wearing a cap that did not quite match. He thrust this to the back of his head as he shook the doctor's hand. Martin noted the luxuriant black mustache, the large, humorous brown eyes, and was impressed by the firm hand clasp. "You look as if you've come prepared for a longish stay, sir," he observed, indicating two substantial, strapped leather suitcases and a portmanteau which a porter was already wheeling towards the station exit.

"Eh?" said Hartson. "Oh, those. Well, that's mostly photographic and electrical apparatus, y'know."

"Indeed?" said Martin. "I had no idea that psychic research was such a scientific business."

Hartson smiled and said "Yes?" in a vague sort of way.

"I suppose I was expecting—well, a planchette or somesuch." Martin had been about to add the word "nonsense" but, tactfully, deleted it.

Hartson nodded. "Ah," he said. "Most people do, y'know."

While Martin superintended the loading of the luggage into the trap, Hartson tipped the porter and clambered aboard. He hauled an oil-skin tobacco pouch from one pocket and a pipe from the other and began to fill it. As Martin took his place beside him, he said, "We gather from Pip Daniels that you witnessed some of these manifestations yourself, Doctor. Would you care to tell me about it?"

Martin proceeded to relate the episode of the tantalus.

When he had concluded, Hartson struck a match and puffed voluminous clouds of blue smoke into the sunny air. "And how (puff, puff) did Miss Hobson (puff, puff) react to that?"

"Very prudently in the circumstances," replied Martin with a grin. "She ducked."

The spent match was blown out and flipped onto the roadway. "She didn't faint or anything, then?"

"No," said Martin. "To tell the truth, she seemed to take it all very much in her stride."

"And that didn't strike you as odd?"

"Certainly not at the time," said Martin. "But I don't mind telling you, sir, I was pretty startled myself when it happened. I mean to say I'd never seen anything like it in my life. That wretched thing could easily have brained somebody."

"They never do, y'know," said Hartson. "Can't recall a verified case on record of a direct fatality from a poltergeist."

"Really?" said Martin. "I didn't know that."

"There's been the odd fire, y'know—usually started by a hot coal or suchlike." He broke off, frowning. "I say. That's deuced odd."

"What's that?"

"Am I right in thinking there's a bridge down that road?" Hartson pointed ahead with his pipestem. "Three arches? Red brick?"

"Why, yes," said Martin. "Chillingford Bridge. You know it, do you?"

"No," said Hartson. "I've never been here before in my life."

Martin glanced sideways at him. "Perhaps you consulted a map before you set out?"

Hartson shook his head. "Curious," he murmured and lapsed into a thoughtful silence.

It was not until the trap was turning into Chillingford Rd. and scarcely more than a few hundred yards was separating them from the gate to Laurel House that Dr. Martin thought to ask the young man if he had seen the mysterious "message."

Hartson admitted that he had.

"And were you able to make anything of it?"

The young man nodded.

"Do you mind my asking you what it was?"

"Not at all. The 'message,' as you call it, was an abstract philosophical concept expressed in quasi-mathematical terms."

"Well, I'm dashed!" exclaimed Martin. "I must say you astonish me! I'd never seen anything like it in my life."

"I'm not altogether surprised," said Hartson, glancing at his companion with a flicker of a smile. "The only reason *I* recognized it was that I happen to have originated the thing myself."

"Originated it yourself!"

"Well, something remarkably like it, y'know."

Martin reined the pony in to a rearing halt and turned to face the young man. "Then, if you don't mind my asking, sir, how in the devil's name did Miss Hobson . . . ?"

"How indeed?" echoed Hartson. "So far as I'm aware, Dr. Martin, not more than four people in the world were privy to that formula. Scarcely a dozen at the outside would even have recognized the symbolism. And Miss Hobson is certainly not among them."

"But what an extraordinary thing!" said Martin.

Hartson nodded. "To be perfectly frank, that's the chief reason I'm here today. So you won't mind if I ask you to treat what I've just told you as a confidence, will you? Just for the time being, y'know. Mum's the word, eh?"

"Of course, of course," said Martin. "I promise I won't breathe a word. But what an extraordinary thing, eh?"

Hartson prodded thoughtfully at his mustache with his pipestem and smiled enigmatically.

"She's found another since then," said Martin, suddenly remembering it. "She told me so herself the other day. Just before I sent you that wire."

"Is that so?"

"She said she'd found it scribbled on the flyleaf of a book. Mind you, I haven't seen it myself."

"Was it the same sort of thing, d'ye know?"

"That's what I gathered. Numbers and so forth, she said."

"Fascinating," murmured Hartson. "Absolutely fascinating."

Martin shook the reins, the rubber-tired wheels of the trap rolled forward once more, and two minutes later were crunching over the gravel on the Fletcher's driveway.

As they drew up before the front door, Mrs. Fletcher and her niece emerged from the house and came down the steps to greet their visitors. Dr. Martin effected the introductions. Hartson pulled off his cap and shook hands, expressing himself delighted to make their acquaintance. He retained Miss Hobson's hand for perhaps a fraction longer than was compatible with strict etiquette, and Martin saw the girl lower her eyes as a faint touch of color rose on her cheeks. Next moment, the gardener/houseboy appeared and Hartson had turned away to supervise the unloading of his baggage.

Dr. Martin was prevailed upon to stay to tea. By then Mr. Fletcher had returned from his bank, and the five of them deployed themselves on deck chairs outside the summer house while Mrs. Fletcher presided over the tea pot and the maid handed round plates of paper-thin sandwiches. Hartson chatted amiably about the work of the Society and described one or two of the cases he had been engaged upon with Dr. Gurney. "Our chief problem remains the extraordinary persistence of irrational credulity," he concluded. "People continue to clamor for evidence of the supernatural, whereas the whole aim and object of the S.P.R. has been to extend the spectrum of human perception while working within strictly ordained scientific limits."

"Then you do not believe in ghosts, Mr. Hartson?" enquired Alice.

Hartson smiled. "No, Miss Alice, I do *not* believe in ghosts. Nevertheless, I have overwhelming evidence that a vast number of people *do* believe in them."

"But isn't a poltergeist a kind of ghost?" she persisted.

"If by 'ghost' you mean an unbridled eruption of psychic energy, then, yes, you are perfectly correct. I had supposed you were referring to a type of apparition which is popularly reputed to haunt churchyards, y'know, or wander through ruined castles, moaning dismally and wringing its sepulchral hands."

When the laughter had subsided Martin asked curiously: "But what *is* this 'psychic energy'?"

"As yet we do not know," said Hartson, turning to face him. "All I can tell you, Dr. Martin, is that in our limited experience it appears to be intimately associated with certain"—he paused and Martin sensed the word "immature" hovering inaudibly in the air between them— "certain human personalities at a particular stage of their psychological and physical development. There have been numerous attempts to account for it; none, to my mind, wholly convincing."

"Then tell us what *you* think, Mr. Hartson," said Alice.

Hartson set down his cup and saucer on the lawn beside him and wiped his mustache with a crumpled linen handkerchief. "That is no easy question, Miss Alice," he said, "but perhaps I can offer you some sort of meaningful analogy. Let me ask you to try to imagine the human personality as a kind of lens, but a lens with the peculiar property of concentrating the multiplicity of invisible vibrations which permeate the ether. Now I believe that by flexing this lens it is perhaps possible to focus forces— forces of which we as yet know little or nothing—in such a way that they are able to exert pressures upon the physical world about us—perhaps even to the extent of temporarily neutralizing the enormous forces of gravity and distorting the spatial and temporal matrix." He noticed the increasingly blank look on her face and smiled apologetically. "I fear you are very little the wiser."

"Not a scrap," she laughed. "But thank you just the same."

"Gravity I think I might just accept," said Martin. "After all I saw what happened to that infernal tantalus. But space and time—they're something else again. Are you really contending that they are *not* immutable?"

"Within the narrow band of everyday sensory perception, certainly they are," agreed Hartson. "We order our lives on that assumption, y'know. But we are like horses in blinkers, Doctor. We see only what is straight ahead of us. The psychic operates on the remote outer fringes of our sensory awareness, and who knows what strange law may hold sway there?"

"More things in heaven and earth, eh, Mr. Hartson?" chuckled Mr. Fletcher with the self-satisfied air of a man who has summed it all up in a phrase.

Hartson smiled politely and then, turning to Alice, said, "I wonder if I might prevail upon you for a little assistance in setting up some of my apparatus, Miss Alice?"

"Why, yes, I'd love to," she said eagerly. "What do you want me to do?"

"That will be easier to demonstrate than to explain," he said. "Would you please excuse us, ma'am?"

He rose to his feet, shook Dr. Martin by the hand, nodded to Mr. Fletcher and strode off towards the house with Alice trotting at his side.

"What a charming young man," Mrs. Fletcher remarked to the tea pot.

Dr. Martin had been vaguely toying with the notion of dropping in on the Fletcher household the following afternoon just to see how matters were progressing, but his plans were frustrated almost before they were engendered by an emergency summons to a woman on an outlying farm who had gone into premature labor. It was after six o'clock when he returned to Attleborough to find awaiting him a hastily scrawled note in an unfamiliar hand:

> *Dear Martin, Could you possibly manage to drop by this evening after dinner? Most anxious to discuss some aspects of this case which I feel you may be able to shed light on.*
>
>   *Yrs, J.C.H.*

"When did this arrive?" he asked his wife.

"The Fletchers' gardener brought it round soon after you'd left," she said. "I told him to tell Mr. Hartson that you were out on a call, but that I'd see you got it as soon as you returned."

"Well, I'm dashed if I can see what light he's hoping I'll be able to shed," grumbled Martin. "I'm just a common or garden G.P. not a damned witch-doctor."

"Then you're not going?"

"I'll see how I feel after dinner," he said and trudged off up the stairs to take a well-earned bath.

By nine thirty that evening Martin's spirits and his curiosity had both revived sufficiently for him to feel able to announce to his wife that he had decided to stroll up to Laurel House after all.

"Then be sure to take your umbrella with you," she cautioned. "The glass has been dropping like a stone ever since tea."

Martin kissed her, told her not to wait up for him, and, having lit a cigar, set off on foot for the Fletchers' house, which lay about half a mile distant from his own.

In ominous contrast to the cloudless atmosphere which had prevailed for the previous fortnight, the sky was now heavily overcast; the air warm, exhausted and oppressive; and Martin guessed his wife had been right in prophesying a storm. He became aware of an uneasy, gnawing sense of apprehension which seemed to be localized in the region of his solar plexus, but, such was his nature, he had no sooner acknowledged it than he dismissed it as indigestion and continued resolutely on his way. Having reached the gates of Laurel House, he strode purposefully up the drive to the front door and rang the bell.

The door was opened by Mrs. Fletcher in person. She seemed pleased to see him and explained that it was the maid's evening off. "You are just in time for some coffee, Dr. Martin," she said. "Robert and Alice are in the drawing room with James. He is busy setting up some more of his mysterious electrical apparatus."

Martin hung his hat and ulster on the hall stand, dropped his umbrella into the receptacle and followed his hostess down the passage. "I'll wager we're in for a storm," he said. "It's devilish close out."

"Oh, I do hope not," she said nervously. "Thunder always gives me a headache."

She led the way into the lamplit drawing room, and Martin exchanged greetings with the others. "Good Lord!" he exclaimed, gazing about him. "You've got a regular laboratory here. What are you hoping to discover with all this stuff?"

"Any significant variation in the electrical field," said Hartson, glancing up from his apparatus. "This thing's reputed to be sensitive to a millionth of an ampère. That one"—pointing to a gold-leaf electroscope—"registers the atmosphere potential." He struck a match and touched it to the wick of a little oil lamp which had for a shade a

slotted metal tube. Having adjusted the flame to his satisfaction, he maneuvered the lamp around in front of a
large, clamped lens. This in its turn was standing before
an instrument which Martin was delighted to recognize
as a galvanometer. As Hartson extended his free hand
above a complex cobweb of thin copper wires, a dim spot
of reflected light began to creep along a calibrated scale
which was positioned some five or six feet away upon a
bureau.

Martin accepted the cup of coffee which Mrs. Fletcher
handed him, stirred it abstractedly for a while, then wandered across to where Alice was sitting on the sofa. A
faint smile was hovering about her lips as she surveyed
Hartson's activities.

"A penny for them, miss."

She glanced up at him and her smile broadened. "Do
you know what atmospheric potential is, Dr. Martin?"

Martin bent down until his lips were close to her ear
and whispered, "I'm sure I have even less idea than you
have, my dear," and he laid his finger to his lips.

Hartson, his arrangements completed, now came over to
Alice and invited her to take up a position seated before
the table. When she had done so, he laid before her a
sheaf of notepaper and a pencil. As she reached for a
pencil, he produced a second sheaf which he laid on the
table about eighteen inches away from the first.

Martin moved a pace closer and observed the girl curiously. He saw her pick up the pencil in her right hand
and then transfer it to her left. Hartson nodded approv-
ingly, handed her a second pencil, and then adjusted the
positions of the two piles of paper. When they were arranged to his satisfaction, he sat down opposite her, produced a large sheet of white pasteboard and a stick of
charcoal from beneath the table and rapidly scrawled a
long line of symbols across the top of the board. "I just
want you to copy these, Alice," he said. "It doesn't matter in the least if your copy isn't strictly accurate. Just
scribble away."

Alice frowned, stared hard at the board before her and
then began tentatively marking her left-hand page. As he
watched her, Martin became conscious of a prickling tension in the skin at the back of his neck. Out of the corner
of his eye he saw Mrs. Fletcher lean across, murmur

something to her husband, and then sit back and gather her crocheted shawl about her shoulders.

Returning his attention to the table, the doctor was astonished to observe that Alice now appeared to be writing with both hands at the same time, even though her attention was seemingly wholly concentrated upon the pad to her left. He craned forward in an attempt to peer over her shoulder, only for Hartson to reprove him with a frown and a shake of the head. In the act of drawing back, Martin noticed that the faint spot of light was beginning to edge its way slowly across the calibrated scale on the bureau. As he stared at it he saw it suddenly leap sideways and vanish. A moment later there was a brilliant, flickering flash across the window curtains, followed almost instantaneously, by an ear-splitting crash.

With a squeal of terror Mrs. Fletcher leaped from her chair and flung herself into her husband's arms. No sooner had she done so than Martin heard a brisk pattering from the direction of the fireplace. He swung round to see a cloud of sooty dust billowing out from behind the tapestry fire screen. "Good Lord!" he exclaimed. "It looks as if you've lost a chimney pot! I say! What on earth . . .?"

He advanced a couple of hesitant paces towards the grate, then stood, transfixed by astonishment. Hovering in the throat of the chimney was a ball of what appeared to be bluish-white light.

Martin was later to estimate it as being about the size of a grapefruit and to describe it as "glowing intensely and turning over and over on itself quite slowly, in the most uncanny way, rather like a child's soap bubble." As for his own reaction at the time he assessed that as "being compounded of about equal parts of astonishment, fascination, and the purest craven funk."

After a couple of hesitant seconds the firebubble floated out of the chimney and drifted off towards a set of polished brass fire irons. It dallied above the tongs for perhaps ten seconds, almost as if it were investigating them, then, its curiosity seemingly satisfied, it ascended by way of the wrought-iron stand of the oil lamp toward the reticulation of copper wires that Hartson had erected.

Up to that moment Martin's attention had been so intensely concentrated upon this extraordinary phenomenon that he had almost forgotten that there was anyone else in the room with him. Now, as the fireball's eerie silent passage brought it closer to Hartson and Alice Hobson, they too swam back again into the doctor's vision, and he became conscious that Mrs. Fletcher was whimpering somewhere behind his back.

"Whatever you do, Alice, don't move." Hartson's voice, though vibrant with suppressed excitement, was astonishingly calm, almost, indeed, conversational. "Dr. Martin? There's a window immediately behind you. Can you manage to get it open?"

Spurred out of his stupor, Martin backed away towards the heavy velvet drapes and fumbled behind them. As he struggled to release the catch, the night sky was ripped brutally apart by a second lightning flash and the window-panes rattled like tinfoil. He succeeded in loosening the lock, thrust the lower sash upwards and dragged aside the curtains.

The whole operation had occupied him for perhaps twenty seconds. When he turned back towards the table, he saw that the slowly gyrating bubble was now hovering in the air directly above the wire grid. He saw too that long gossamer strands of Alice Hobson's shoulder-length hair were floating out towards it as though drawn by some invisible magnetic force. The sight filled him with a peculiar horror. "For God's sake, get back, Alice!" he gasped and, lunging forward, caught hold of her by the shoulders.

At the instant of physical contact he experienced a violent electrical jolt in his forearms. So sharp and unexpected was it that instead of dragging the girl towards him as he had intended he half tripped and stumbled against the back of her chair. Her head jerked forward and a single questing strand of her hair touched the fireball. He heard a voice, which he guessed to be Hartson's shout: "Stop, stop, man!" There was a deafening report, and the next thing Martin knew was that he was lying on the floor in almost total darkness with a smell of singed hair in his nostrils and something warm and soft lying sprawled across him.

As he struggled to free himself a match flared. Through ears still ringing like bells, he heard Hartson's voice crying: "Alice! Alice, are you all right?"

"Here, man!" he called. "Down here!"

The match went out. Hartson swore violently. Martin heard Mr. Fletcher pleading: "Pull yourself together,

Dorothy, for heaven's sake!" and then another tremendous thunderclap obliterated every other sound.

Martin succeeded in disentangling himself from a thicket of invisible chair legs and groped about in the darkness until his hand alighted upon Alice's chest. To his inexpressible relief he felt a faint, bird-like fluttering beneath his fingertips. "Can't you get that lamp lit?" he shouted and, even as he spoke the words, a second match spurted into sudden brightness. By its wavering light Martin contrived to drag the unconscious girl clear of the chair and hauled her backwards to the hearth rug, where he set about loosening her bodice.

Only when Hartson had succeeded in re-lighting one of the oil lamps did the full dramatic effect of the explosion become evident; yet the damage was more apparent than real. Hartson's apparatus, which had been at the epicenter of the explosion, was a total shambles, the copper wires melted, twisted and fused into a sort of weird metal bird's nest by the force or nature of the blast. The galvanometer and its screen had been flung to the floor where they lay among a forlorn jumble of photographs, knickknacks and sundry bric-à-brac which had been scooped from their resting places on the tops of bookcases and bureaux and pitched into the general melee. Scattered around the four corners of the room were the sheets of notepaper which Martin had last seen lying on the table in front of Alice.

For five tense minutes the girl remained unconscious, though her pulse was steady and her breathing regular and even. When she finally came to her senses, it was exactly as though she were awakening from a profound sleep. Her first act was to indulge in a series of tremendous and unladylike yawns, followed by a vigorous and uninhibited scratching of her arms and bosom. She complained too that her hearing was muffled, but this after-effect seemed to wear off quite rapidly. Indeed, in retrospect, Martin was inclined to the opinion that, of all the people who had been in the room at the time of the explosion, Alice was possibly the one least shaken by what had happened. He noted too how Mrs. Fletcher made a remarkably swift recovery and set about restoring the room to rights.

Fletcher produced a whisky decanter and a soda siphon and treated the men to stiff drinks, while Alice, at

Martin's suggestion, was dosed with a brandy and soda. They all sat round, talking nineteen to the dozen, as they attempted to reconstruct the chain of events from their separate and fragmented recollections, while on the driveway outside the rattle of hailstones gave way to torrential, drumming rain, which in its turn gradually lessened in violence as the storm slowly withdrew towards the east.

It was close on midnight when Dr. Martin rose to leave. By then the rain had stopped completely and stars were already twinkling from a moonless sky. As he said his farewells and stepped out on to the porch, Hartson said, "I feel I could use a breath of fresh air too. Do you mind if I stroll along with you?"

Martin expressed himself delighted to have company, and the two men strode off noisily savoring the cool sweetness of the storm-cleansed air.

When they were well out of earshot of the house, Hartson said, "You got my note then?"

"Oh, yes," said Martin. "You wanted to pick my brains about something or other."

"What I'm really after is some information from you, Doctor. Of a somewhat confidential nature, y'know. I'll quite understand if you feel unable to supply it."

Intrigued, Martin asked, "Does it concern Alice?"

"Yes," said Hartson. "Did you know that she is a somnambule?"

"No, I didn't. But I confess it doesn't surprise me. How did you discover it?"

Hartson paused. "This must remain absolutely *entre nous,* Martin."

"Of course."

"I found her standing beside my bed in the early hours of this morning."

"Good God! What did you do?"

"To be honest, I was petrified. But at least I had the wit to realize she was walking in her sleep. I took her by the hand, led her out into the corridor, then shot back and bolted my door. I would have escorted her to her own room except that I'd no idea which it was, and, frankly, I was appalled at the thought that her aunt or uncle might discover us."

"She was in her nightdress, I take it."

"Far worse. She was stark naked!"

Martin let out his breath in a long whistle.

"You see my problem?"

"Indeed, I do. But I don't really see what you expect *me* to do about it."

"Then you have had no previous experience of schismatic personality?"

"What the devil's that?"

"When two quite different people seem to inhabit one body. We've come across several striking cases of it in our recent research."

"Ah. And you think that Alice Hobson is one of them?"

"I don't know. But I thought perhaps you might be able to tell me something about her which would help me to decide how best to handle this situation. Do her aunt and uncle know that she walks in her sleep?"

"It's possible, I suppose. They haven't mentioned it to me though."

"What would you advise me to do?"

"Pack your bags and clear off back to Cambridge first thing tomorrow morning. You've got all the excuse you need, now your equipment's been ruined. Stay on and you may well find your reputation's ruined too. Not to mention hers!"

"You certainly are a thoroughgoing pragmatist, Dr. Martin."

"I've got a fair share of common sense, if that's what you mean."

"You're right, of course," said Hartson. "There's everything to lose by staying and nothing more to gain. It begins to look as if that fireball may have proved a most fortuitous omen. A veritable messenger from the gods, y'know. A pity about the galvanometer, though. Gurney's bound to be livid."

By this time they had come within sight of the doctor's house. A lamp was burning at an upstairs window. "Come on in and have a nightcap," suggested Martin genially.

Five minutes later Hartson was lying back in an armchair in Dr. Martin's study with a tumbler of the doctor's best whisky in his hand. Martin restoppered the decanter, subsided into the chair opposite his guest, and raised his glass in token salute. "Well, I don't know what conclusions *you've* reached about this business," he said, "but I don't mind telling you it's left me completely baffled. I find it about as mystifying as that book of James's which Daniels lent me. But to you I daresay it's pretty much run-of-the-mill, eh?"

"Oh, I wouldn't go as far as that," said Hartson. "There are certain similarities between this case and some of our others, but that's all. It's the details which are so fascinatingly different." He set down his glass, reached into his inner pocket and drew out a sheet of paper. Having unfolded it and glanced at it, he passed it across to the doctor. "Tell me what you make of that," he said.

Martin held the paper up to catch the lamplight and read: *stop stop stop cam for the love of god cam stop now i beg.* "What on earth is this?" he asked.

"I'm not absolutely sure," said Hartson, "but I'm pretty certain that's what Alice was writing with her right hand just before the fireball descended. I found it among the sheaf of papers Mrs. Fletcher collected up from the floor."

"But what an extraordinary thing!" said Martin. "What does it mean? Stop what?"

Hartson turned his hands palm-upwards in an expressive gesture of incomprehension. "I have absolutely no idea," he said. "But you see now why I said the details of this case were so extraordinary."

Martin peered at the paper. "What does *cam* stand for? Cambridge?"

"Possibly. But I'm inclined to suspect it represents 'Cameron.' That's my middle name, y'know."

"Does Alice know that?"

"I very much doubt it. It's a sort of private family joke. I used to call myself 'Cam' when I was a baby."

Martin gazed across at him, a faraway look in his eyes, groping to recall something. "Cam," he murmured. "Cam? By Jove, yes! Just before that thing went off, you shouted something, didn't you?"

"Why, no," said Hartson. "It was *you* who shouted."

"Believe me, I did not."

"Well, one of us did."

Their eyes met, curious, doubting. "It *was* a man's voice," said Martin. "I'm sure I'm not mistaken about that. And it wasn't 'man,' it was 'Cam.' 'Stop! Stop, Cam!' We can't *both* have imagined it, can we?"

"Unlikely, certainly," agreed Hartson, "but not wholly impossible."

"Alice couldn't have done it."

"Assuming it *was* a man's voice. No, she couldn't."

"And it *was*. I'm certain of that, Hartson. Indeed, if I hadn't thought it was your voice, I might well have supposed it to be the shout of an elderly man."

Hartson eyed him sharply. "What makes you say that?"

"The pitch of the cry, I think. High. Almost shrill."

"Y'know, you're right, Martin. You've hit it exactly. It *was* an old man's voice. Curious. How very curious."

Martin stretched out and handed the paper back to him. "Then you don't think this is connected in some way with those other messages?"

"I fail to see how it could be," said Hartson.

"You don't read it as—well, as being a warning of some kind?"

Hartson's eyebrows rose a fraction. "No," he said, and smiled faintly.

"Well, I don't mind telling you that I would."

Hartson regarded the older man speculatively. "A warning?" he repeated. "But a warning against what, Doctor?"

"I've really no idea," said Martin. "Against continuing with your present line of research, perhaps. This—what does James call it?—'exploration of the metapsychic.' "

"Well, in that case," said Hartson with a grin, "I can only say that it's arrived a couple of months too late. The fact is, Martin, I've already engaged myself for a post under J.J. Thomson at the Cavendish in October. I've decided to devote my energies to research in the physical science. Frankly, I'm convinced that the tide is turning in that direction. Between ourselves, y'know, P.R. is proving something of a *cul-de-sac*."

"Allow an ignorant medico to offer you his congratulations," said Martin. "I'm afraid J.J. Thomson's just a name to me. What particular line will you yourself be pursuing?"

"Research into the nature of the fundamental particles," said Hartson, folding up the sheet of notepaper and restoring it to his breast pocket. "A rich enough field of exploration for any ambitious young physicist, wouldn't you say?"

In one sense the story of the "Attleborough Investigation" ends there. Next morning Dr. Martin saw Hartson off at the station, and, so far as is known, the two men never set eyes on each other again. Yet something must have prompted the doctor to write down his personal record of the whole extraordinary episode while it was still fresh in his memory, because the journal containing his account is dated September, 1892. On Martin's death in 1920 this journal, together with other family papers, passed to his elder daughter, who was then living in Shropshire. When my father was commissioned to write his *Life of Sir James Cameron Hartson* in February, 1944, he advertised for biographical information in the usual places and, as a result, received a letter from Martin's daughter which led to his examining the original manuscript.

In view of Martin's own letter to the Dialectical Society the authenticity of the document can hardly be doubted, but, as my father was the first to realize, it was not the sort of thing he could make profitable use of in a semi-official biography of one of the world's greatest atomic physicists. As he himself expressed it in a letter: "Ten days before I read the wretched thing, I had been down in Attleborough talking to some of Hartson's team of international stars at the Chillingford Laboratories. Naturally I've no means of knowing for certain whether the old man's workshop now occupies the precise geographical location that was once occupied by Laurel House, but, for what it's worth, my guess is that they must have been pretty well identical. As for the particular line of research Hartson was pursuing at the time of his death, all I could gather was that it was terribly hush-hush. Everyone I attempted to pin down about it was so purposefully vague that I can only assume it has some military significance too appalling for even an informed layman like myself to be allowed to contemplate!" Since Hartson has now emerged as one of the founding fathers of the "Manhattan Project," that guess came a lot closer than my father ever knew.

All that remains is a sort of footnote to a footnote. Among the stray papers which I discovered in the Attleborough file was a single foolscap sheet of handwritten notes headed: *Totally Unscientific Hypothesis*. Dated January, 1945, three months before my father's own death, it reads as follows:

Let us assume:

(a) that directly before his death J.C.H. becomes overwhelmingly conscious of where his life's work has been leading; (b) that this causes him the most intense mental anguish; (c) that for some unknown reason he desires passionately to "undo things done; to call back yesterday;" (d) that, as a young man, he had conceived the human psyche to be in some strange manner capable of distorting the fabric of Nature to the point where even Time and Space could be affected.

What follows from this?

Is it possible to believe that Hartson's "earlier self" was drawn (called?) to the precise point in space where so much of his future anguish was to be generated? And when he arrives—sensing a strange familiarity in a place he has never seen—is it only in order that his "future self" can cry out to him down the echoing corridor of all the distant years to come *stop stop stop cam for the love of god cam stop now i beg?* Was that "old man's voice" his own? That fireball a true "messenger of the gods," engendered in some fierce psychic vortex whose possible existence he himself had once conjectured and then elected to deny?

And what of Alice? Was she no more than the innocent instrument through whom Hartson's own despair was unwittingly focused and given form; drawn to seek him out even in her sleep; a lost and ignorant message-bearer, wandering in some strange lonely limbo of the spirit of which she was not even aware?

Shall we ever know where that final message came from, or live to learn what it meant?

Some people like to get completely away from civilization when they're on vacation—find a deserted mountainside on which to camp, relax, talk to the trees, write some poetry. . . . But privacy is harder and harder to maintain these days, especially if you happen to find a lost cache of Spanish gold pieces. Drastic and fantastic measures may be necessary to keep away interlopers.

"Stephen Tall" was the pen name of Compton Crook, who died not long after this story appeared in print. He was well known for his books of interstellar adventure, *The Stardust Voyages* and its sequel, *The Ramsgate Paradox*.

THE HOT AND COLD RUNNING WATERFALL

Stephen Tall

HUBERT LIVED BY A WATERFALL. ACTUALLY, that statement is too simple to cover the facts. More correctly, Hubert had camped by the waterfall for the past several summers, and had almost come to regard the location of his lean-to in the canyon as home. He liked the sound of the water; he liked the coolness of the little canyon; he liked the solitude. To Hubert, as we shall see, it wasn't solitude at all.

Hubert's concerns were neither profound nor complex. He enjoyed the view from the mountain. He liked the air. The shudderingly cold shower the waterfall provided made his breakfast taste prime. The sunrise was best from the clifftop; and later, when the rays grew hot, he sat under a lightning-riven, wind-blasted old pine tree in cool comfort.

The breezes that swirled around the stark cliff face would flow in under the tree when the air needed stirring. Hubert began to believe that he could call them at need. He even came to recognize one of them. He named it Wilfred. And after his interest in the battered and split old tree became plain, the winds never blew hard against it. Somehow, it never again bore the brunt of the mountain storms.

Across the tundra meadow, millions of little short-stemmed flowers bloomed; and these brought the butterflies. At first they were widely scattered. Then they began to flock, rolling along over the flower fields in multicolored clouds. Hubert found them as interesting as anything on the mountain. He began to feed them.

Barney, the waterfall, was simply a part, a segment of the stream, which in turn got its water from the many little trickles from the snowfields high on the mountainside, and from deep springs gushing out of the rocks. These in turn owed their existence to the mountain itself. Without the water, the mountain would have been lifeless, barren. It took all things working together to make it the busy place that it was.

Hubert was a poet. Now everybody knows that this is not much of an occupation. Very few people ever get rich at it. A good many have come pretty close to starving. Maybe some have. But Hubert was not that kind of poet. With him, poetry was not so much an occupation as an excuse. Hubert didn't write poetry so much as live it. And somehow, he had found that he fitted there on the mountainside.

He was only there in the summer. Nobody knew where he spent the long months of winter, which probably was just as well. For in the winter Hubert had a job, and watched television and went to ball games and was pretty much like anybody else. But with the spring he began to get restless. More and more he thought of the mountainside, and the good air, and the pleasant breeze off the snowfields. When he reached a certain stage he quit his job, packed up his gear; and before long someone in the little town in the valley would report:

"Spring's back on the mountain. Hubert's put up his lean-to by the waterfall, and is settin' up there writin' his damned verses."

It was somewhat like the swallows coming back to Capistrano.

The ranchers of the area had given up using the mountainside for grazing. Sheep herders had tried, years before, but there was so much larkspur and loco growing up there that more sheep died than got fat. The bighorn sheep of the crags had more sense, and got along fine. So the mountain was pretty much sufficient to itself, and more and more Hubert was a part of it.

Hubert bought supplies in the town. They were not very different from what anybody else would have bought. Not too much at a time, either, for he had to pack everything up to his camp on his back. But one day his order attracted attention.

"Now why," the storekeeper speculated, "would he want ten pounds of sugar? A pound of tea will last him half the summer. I doubt if he bakes cakes. What else would he use it for?"

"Maybe he likes something stronger than tea," a farmer said. "Maybe he likes to make his own. You know as well as I do he won't jest set up there on the rocks and write po'try."

"He's not going to make enough hard stuff to bother about with just ten pounds of sugar," the storekeeper said. "He wouldn't eat or drink it all himself, either. No, he's doing something else with it."

"He don't do no harm, I reckon," the farmer said. "Jest squats up there and takes his ease. Sort of simple, I guess."

"Hubert ain't simple," the storekeeper objected. "He knows when to come and when to leave. And he's got money. Doesn't need much, but when he wants something, he buys it. Pays cash, too. Never asks for credit. Don't say much, either. Just buys his stuff and goes back up the mountain."

So, without intending to, or even giving it a thought, Hubert began to attract more attention. It became harder and harder for him to have space and time to himself; harder and harder just to mind his own business.

For a while that summer, people came up the long slope, especially on Sundays. Hubert didn't welcome them, but there was nothing much he could do. After all, it wasn't his mountain. So he simply sat under the old pine, and whenever anyone was around he would look off into the distance and then scribble in his little notebook. When anyone badgered him with questions, Hubert would read his verses to them. That usually sent them off pretty promptly, for Hubert didn't read his better verses. To most, what he read made no sense at all. And that was the way Hubert wanted it.

But folks did find out what he was doing with the sugar. It didn't help Hubert's image any. There was more talk about him in the store in the valley.

"You say he ain't simple," the same farmer said to the storekeeper. "You heard what he's usin' all that sugar for? He's feedin' butterflies!"

"I'll hear who saw him doing it," the storekeeper said, "and then I'll make up my mind."

"Willie Thatcher seen him. Willie laid up there behind rocks and watched him for half a day. He said the butterflies swarmed around Hubert like feedin' chickens. Said he'd call them and they'd come."

The storekeeper considered this.

"Whatever Hubert is or isn't, I *know* Willie's simple," he said. "Still, I guess he wouldn't make up something like that. He ain't got sense enough."

Willie's reporting was just what he had seen. Hubert was indeed feeding the butterflies. He had always enjoyed them, especially when the tundra was in best bloom. Then they were plentiful, many kinds drifting across the high meadow. He got the idea when he saw three or four clinging to the edge of his tea mug, which still had wet sugar in the bottom. He watched them quietly as they unrolled their long tubular siphons and drew up the sweet fluid.

"Like sweetening, do you?" he said. "Of course you do. That's what you get from the flowers. Well, maybe I can manufacture more."

He dissolved a couple of spoonfuls of sugar in water, then crushed a few flowers of nearby polemonium and bluebells and dropped them in. He poured the mixture into several tins and jar tops.

"You each probably have your favorites," he said. "There's something in this for everybody."

So he set the containers about on rocks and among the growing flowers. He soon began to have customers. The butterflies approved the fluid, and before the morning was gone they had drunk it all.

Hubert wasn't sure when the insects began to connect the goodies with the source, but before long there was no doubt that they did. He would have his shower, prepare his breakfast and mix a batch of nectar. When the rocky slope brightened and the air warmed, the butterflies would come drifting toward him across the sun-drenched field. And every day there were more of them. His regular supply of sugar went down rapidly. That was when he had bought the ten pounds.

Willie was right when he reported that Hubert talked to the butterflies. If he had had the imagination to understand, he would have realized that Hubert talked to everything. Further, he would have known that Hubert didn't regard the conversations as one-way streets. Hubert didn't just talk. He conversed. He got answers.

There was the waterfall. Especially there was the waterfall. Hubert had talked to the waterfall for years. It was his oldest friend. From it he first began to get answers.

When he had set up his first lean-to, Hubert had put it near the waterfall on whim. He liked the sound of the water, and the pool below it was clear and pure. Hubert thought that the best water on the mountain came from that pool.

The waterfall was Hubert's shower bath from the beginning. At first it had been only an idea, for the water was straight from the snowfields above, and if Hubert had stood under it for even a minute he would have grown brittle. Still, he had a touch of Spartan in his makeup, and he found a dash under and out exhilarating. With clicking teeth he would towel himself dry, then run to the nearest sunny patch to warm up.

Then he began to talk to the fall. To make things more personal, more man to man, he had already named it Barney.

"Barney, you are a fine waterfall; and I approve of you. Wouldn't camp anywhere else on the mountain. But man, you are one cold proposition. I suppose you couldn't be anything else, considering the source of your water. It would be nice, though, if you could sort of take the chill off for a few minutes in the morning. Just long enough for my shower, you understand."

It was a whimsy that amused him, for each morning, when he first stuck a tentative hand into the icy fall he'd say, "Warming up any, Barney? Work on it, boy! You could do it if you'd try!" And he'd fancy that a ripple, a pulse, would go across the face of the waterfall. Then it would resume its steady flow.

One morning he got a more positive response. He stood shivering, at once dreading and anticipating his dash, and reached out his hand as he usually did. The waterfall beat him to it. The smooth sheet of water shifted suddenly and a rock in the ledge, usually submerged, diverted a jet of icy spray onto Hubert's naked body. His howl at the sudden dowsing could have been heard halfway down the mountain, if anyone had been there to listen.

He reached for his towel and looked closely at the

again smoothly flowing water. Nothing showed that could
have caused the spray.

"Doggone you, Barney, I believe you did that on purpose!"

The waterfall was a glistening sheet, slipping gently into the pool at its foot. It showed no change.

"If you did it once, you can do it again," Hubert said.
"Come on," he coaxed, "just once more."

Taking no chances, he moved back out of range. And,
after a moment, the waterfall complied. It shifted, and
again the jet of water broke into spray.

"Good!" Hubert cried. "Bravo! Now, if you could just
manage a little warmer water when I need it—" He broke
off, chuckling. "I won't hold my breath," he said, "but it
would be nice."

He thought about it during the morning, off and on,
while he fed the butterflies; made his usual hike to the
pinnacle of the mountain; and finally, when the sun grew
hot in the open, came back to his favorite shaded resting
place under the lightning-blasted old pine. It was there
that he wrote most of his poetry. He thought he might
write some verses about Barney, after the morning's episode, but his muse had taken the day off, and he wrote
nothing worth keeping.

"Poetry, George, is something you can't rush. It's either
ready or it isn't."

You might have looked around for George, before you
realized that Hubert was speaking to the pine tree.

"Most of the poetry I write here probaby isn't mine,"
Hubert went on. "You've lived a long, rough life, and
have seen a lot of changes up here. There's good poetry
in your memories. I suspect that I'm just writing 'em
down, and you're doing the dictating. I'll almost feel dis-
honest publishing under my own name, but I can't
think of any good way to give you credit. If I said that
my poems were really written by George, folks might think
I was a little peculiar."

Hubert stretched out on the soft pine needle mat and
closed his eyes.

"No sir," he murmured, "you can't rush poetry."

So he didn't try. Instead he took his usual nap, while
the shade shifted as the sun moved. Many of the sparse
branches of old George were already dead, and George
himself seemed destined soon to follow them. As Hubert

had said, George had had a long, eventful life. And it was almost over.

When the sunlight eased onto Hubert's face, he woke and moved. From the snowfields farther up the mountain a cool breeze came drifting down. It barely stirred the tops of the short-stemmed flowers of the mountain meadow, and thousands of butterflies clung and fed as the blossoms swayed. Hubert sniffed the freshness with pleasure.

"Thanks, Wilfred," he said to the breeze. "You're almost as dependable as Barney, in your way. And you always blow best in the afternoon, when things get hottest. Very comfortable."

As can be seen, even when there were no people on the mountain, Hubert had plenty of company and did his share of talking during each day. In fact, he often spoke to the mountain itself, and had reason to believe he was listened to. Or at least the reasons seemed satisfying to him. The mountain had a rather commonplace name to the makers of maps, but Hubert called it Mohamet.

"Once, I remember, Mohamet would not come to the mountain," Hubert reflected, "but if Mohamet *is* the mountain we at least won't have that kind of confusion. So unless you object, you are Mohamet."

Sensing no opposition, Hubert often used the name, and found it more personal than just speaking of "the mountain." Like Barney and Wilfred, Mohamet got his share of Hubert's conversations and had a poem written about him. Hubert read it to him one afternoon, and the response seemed favorable. Whether the poem had anything to do with Hubert finding the coin will never be known, of course. But the events were suspiciously close together.

He saw the dull yellow shine down among the rocks as he was clambering over a newly deposited pile of talus at the foot of the high cliff above the meadow. The rock faces were always weathering, cracking, and occasionally large pieces would break away and fall. Hubert fished the coin out of the crevice and examined it with interest.

"Now where could this have come from?"

It was crudely minted, by modern standards, but it was not worn. And it was heavy. That, and the yellow color, told Hubert what he had.

"Gold." Hubert studied the unfamiliar face of the coin. The words around the edge were not English. "Spanish, I'd guess. Maybe Portuguese."

He considered.

"That figures. If it has been here a long time, it might even be a coinage the conquistadors used. Maybe the storekeeper would know something about it."

When he thought it over, though, he realized that to mention or show it to the storekeeper might not be a good idea. The storekeeper meant well, but he'd never keep such information to himself. He dispensed more than food and commodities. He passed on the news. And nobody would believe that this was the only coin Hubert had found. The mountain might even be overrun with treasure seekers. Hubert certainly didn't want that.

So he stowed the coin away in his pocket and decided to say nothing. Someone could tell him what it was, after he had left the mountain and had had time to make up a story of how he came by it. He did search the talus slope, but there was only the one coin. No sign, either, of where it had come from.

Finally, as he went back to camp, he spoke to the mountain:

"Well, Mohamet, it looks like you are the only one who could tell how this thing got here. This is one of the times when it would be handy if you could speak up."

But, not unexpectedly, Mohamet said nothing. He simply lay, vast and inscrutable in the late afternoon sun, while Wilfred blew cool across the meadow and Barney murmured in the distance. George cast a long shadow. The butterflies were hanging themselves under leaves and in crevices for the night. Only a nighthawk still boomed in the sky overhead.

Hubert did not dwell on the mystery of the coin. In fact, after a couple of days he forgot about it. It lay in his pocket, mingled with other coins, a pocket knife, and various odds and ends that he picked up as he prowled the mountain. When his pockets grew overfull, as they did every week or so, Hubert sorted out the contents and started over.

But the sorting hadn't taken place when he made a quick trip down to the town for some trifling supplies. Among other things, he bought a new notebook and, as an afterthought, five more pounds of sugar. As usual, he fumbled in the rubbish in his pockets for change, finally dumping the whole handful on the counter. The gold coin rolled free and came to a stop in front of the storekeeper, who picked it up and looked at it curiously.

"I bet you never know what's liable to come out of your pocket," he said. "Where did you get this?"

Hubert hesitated, and he knew the storekeeper saw it. But he recovered quickly.

"Good luck piece," he said easily. "Found it last summer down on the trail east of town. No idea where it came from."

There were several men nearby, loafing and listening, so the storekeeper followed Hubert's lead.

"Purty thing," he said as he handed it back. "Wouldn't give you a lead nickel for it, though. Looks like play money."

He finished bagging Hubert's purchases, and no more was said. But when Hubert was gone, one of the farmers said:

"That wasn't no play money. That was a gold piece." The storekeeper nodded.

"Real old. An old Spanish *pistole*, looked like, but I haven't seen one for a long time. Anyhow it was heavy. Good gold."

"Where you reckon he got it?"

"You heard him. Could be just like he said. Them poet fellers don't care nothing about money. He never knows what he has in his pocket. To him it's just a good luck piece."

Another onlooker, dark, dirty, and narrowfaced, asked:

"If a feller's a poet, does that mean he's a fool?"

The storekeeper grinned.

"Usually," he said.

"You don't think Hubert's a fool," the farmer said. I've heard you take up for him."

"That's so," the storekeeper admitted, "but he does do funny things. You saw he bought more sugar. Willie Thatcher says he feeds the butterflies with it. And Willie says he's always talking when there's not anybody there."

"Well, Willie's no improvement," the farmer said. "He's simple. He just wants to be noticed."

"Too simple to make things up," the storekeeper said. He had expressed that point of view before.

That would have seemed to be that, but, as it turned out, it wasn't. The dark onlooker had a pal; and later, if anyone had bothered to notice, they might have been seen conferring together seriously.

"He's lived up there four, five years," the dark one said. "Jest during the spring-summer months. An' the storekeeper says he's no fool. So—he knows something. He's been looking for something. But I don't think he's looking no more. That gold piece tells me he's found what he was looking for."

"There might be gold up there," the other man said. He was small, wiry, with a long nose and little rat-like eyes. "I've heered that the Indians used to get turquoise there, too. But I'm damned if I think the mountain is minting its own gold!"

"You know what I mean," the dark man said impatiently. "He's been looking for a cache. Somebody left money hidden up there, maybe a hundred years ago. He found a map or a letter or something that told him where to look."

"Fairy tales," said the little man. "Treasure stories are as common as horse apples all through these hills. But I never heered of anybody finding old Spanish money like the feller's gold piece."

"A first time is as good as any. It sure wouldn't hurt to pay him a visit, would it? He don't own the mountain. Maybe we'd like a little vacation camping trip ourselves."

"I could use a change," the small man agreed.

"Maybe he'd like to go treasure huntin' with us on shares. Three can cover more ground than one."

"What kind of shares did you have in mind?"

"Half fer me, half fer you, none fer him."

"That sounds fair," the tall man said.

Meanwhile Hubert had had a pleasant week. There were several new developments to give variety to existence. More and more butterflies flitted and wavered over the high meadow. There were kinds Hubert had never known to be there before. Every day he could see them coming, drifting up the stream valley below the waterfall, riding the breezes through the high pass above the snow-fields. Each morning he put out more sugar water. By noon it was gone.

Even more satisfying, he had finally reached an under-standing with Barney. For most of this summer he had noticed that the shower water didn't seem as cold as he remembered it from past years. When the waterfall splashed him playfully, as it often did, the temperature was quite tolerable. Yet he knew that the water came from the snowfields, as it always had.

"Barney," Hubert said, "I believe you're getting the idea. Now when I get under the flow, try harder. I only need warm water for a couple of minutes. Then you can go back to cold. We don't want to inconvenience the trout in the pool."

He studied the waterfall while he removed his pajamas. (If it had been known that Hubert slept in pajamas, that would have finished him.) Often he had imagined a little ripple across the face of the fall when he talked to it. This time, there was no doubt at all. A pulse ran from one side to the other of the smooth sheet of water. Barney understood.

Hubert stepped confidently under the fall from his favorite flat rock. Somehow, he knew what to expect. The water was warm.

"Ah-h!" Hubert turned and luxuriated in the tepid flow. "Could you warm it just a bit more? To loosen the dirt, you know." And he wasn't surprised when the water grew almost hot.

"That's good. Now back to cold. Closes the pores. The sauna effect."

Barney complied, and Hubert shot from under the fall with a yell.

"Easy!" he shivered. "I can see we're going to have to practice that."

But when he toweled himself dry, he had never felt so good.

Several days later the jeep came chugging up the slope. Hubert always went down the mountain by following the stream, and lower down a trail through what was left of a strip of forest. But there was an old logging road that was passable up to the edge of the timber, and from there, if you had four-wheel drive and no regard for your vehicle, you could drive as far as the alpine meadow. Hubert had never known anyone to try it, though.

"Man, that was a rough trip!" the jeep driver said. He was dark, with a narrow face, and looked like he could have used a bath. "Worth it, though," he added, and tried to seem appreciative.

Hubert walked over from where he had been lying in

George's shade. Wilfred obligingly blew the man's odor in another direction.

"You could have walked up," Hubert said. "It's quicker and easier."

He wasn't enchanted with the idea of visitors. Especially not these visitors. The little rat-like eyes of the jeep passenger did not inspire confidence, and he knew he had seen the driver somewhere before. When Wilfred slacked off for a minute and the smell reached him, he remembered where.

"We brung our camping stuff," the man explained. "Expect to be up here a week or so. Do some climbin', fishin', maybe even some treasure huntin'."

He watched Hubert carefully when he mentioned treasure, but Hubert only smiled.

"I've been up here several summers, and I never heard of any treasure. But there *are* treasures here that the poet can use. Sights. Sounds. Odors. That's what I do, you know. I write verses."

"Yeah, we heard." It was little Rat-eyes. "Business good, I reckon."

"It has been a good summer," Hubert said, and mentally added, "up to now."

"We won't bother you none," the little man said. "Where're you camped?"

"In the little canyon over there, below the waterfall. Doesn't get so chilly at night. Sheltered, you might say."

"Noisy, ain't it? All that water splashin'."

"I'm used to it," Hubert said. "I'd miss it. And it's handy for bathing. The waterfall's a good shower. You're welcome to camp down below me."

"Yeah," the dark man said, "we might do that. I ain't had my bath this month. I might try your shower."

They drove on over to the lip of the stream bed, and later Hubert could hear the sound of an axe as they cut tent poles.

"George," Hubert said, "if I weren't lying here, I bet they'd use you for firewood."

Naturally, he expected no response; but a vagrant breeze, perhaps related to Wilfred though coming from another direction, loosened one of George's dead limbs; and it fell with a crash.

"I know how you feel," said Hubert.

He saw nothing more of his neighbors for the rest of

the day. They had put up an old patched canvas tent and carried a couple of blanket rolls inside. Then they had set off across the meadow to the cliff. They spent the afternoon searching along its base, prowling the talus piles, working harder than Hubert had expected they would. He shook his head. He knew now what they were looking for.

He had finished his meal and the stars were out before they came back to their camp. He heard them blundering about and swearing as they started a fire and cooked their supper. He was glad they had set up a couple of hundred feet down the stream. They'd be less likely to want to visit. Hubert preferred the noise of the waterfall.

He didn't sleep as well as he usually did, but he didn't expect any immediate trouble. He felt pretty sure that there would be some later, and he tried to imagine what form it might take. By the time day broke he was ready for his shower. His thoughts also ran to a bracing mug of tea, and bacon and biscuits, with maybe some butter and honey.

The shower was perfect. Barney got the temperature just right and Hubert stayed under longer than he usually did. When he came out in a hurry from the final cold surge, he saw that he had company. His neighbors had been watching him.

"Now that looks like fun," the dark man said. "Ain't it cold? This damn' creek's like ice."

Hubert toweled vigorously.

"Just exactly right," he said.

The dark man began to remove his clothes. Hubert couldn't remember seeing anybody who was dirty under his clothes before. The stench of him was plain, even on a crisp mountain morning.

"Barney," Hubert muttered, "use your own judgement!"

The man extended a tentative hand into the fall.

"By damn, it ain't cold. I wouldn't 'a believed it."

He stepped confidently under the sheet of water and the next instant his howl of agony ripped down the canyon as he emerged as if shot from a gun.

"I'm scalded! I'm burning! Oh God, I'm ruined!"

He seemed to realize that he was knee-deep in ice water; and he lay down and rolled, while Rat-eyes watched him in blank astonishment and Hubert turned his back so

that his face was hidden. He could find no fault at all with
Barney's judgement.

After a couple of minutes the man came shivering to
the stream bank. Already great blisters were beginning to
rise on his shoulders. His chest and arms, and even his
legs, were streaked and reddened. He glared at Hubert.

"That water's boilin'! What'd you do to it?"

Hubert's look of surprise wasn't entirely faked. He had
never known Barney to be really hot before.

"Me? You're crazy! I can't heat the water in a waterfall. I just came out, and it felt fine to me.

He walked across his flat rock and thrust his hand into
the fall. Rat-eyes followed him.

"It's not hot to me," Hubert reported. "On the cold
side, if anything."

Rat-eyes tested gingerly, with one finger.

"Damn cold," he said. "Icy. I wouldn't git under there.
I'd freeze to death."

The narrow-faced man tenderly touched his blistered
shoulders.

"What do you think these is, chill bumps?"

"I think," said Rat-eyes, "that you jest ain't used to
water."

The scalded man picked up his reeking clothes, and the
two of them went back downstream to their camp. Hubert
could hear the mumble of their voices as they retreated,
and once the dark man looked back at him in a way that
wasn't exactly friendly. But Hubert didn't see how they
could connect him with the waterfall's changing tempera-
tures. He didn't see how, but he knew they would. In spite
of that, he felt satisfied.

"Nice going, Barney," he said. "Very nice going."

And the waterfall rippled slightly across its smoothly
flowing face.

After his breakfast, which he enjoyed even more than
usual, Hubert made up the morning's ration of sugar
water and went out to distribute it. The sun was beginning to be warm on the alpine meadow. The butterflies
were astir. Wilfred blew gently close to the ground, and
the insects drifted along in colorful swarms. Hubert filled
all his dishes and jar tops, then spent half an hour sprin-
kling the left-over nectar onto flower clusters and especially shiny leaves. Wherever he went the butterflies
swirled around him, alighting in his hair, clinging to his

clothing, his hands and the rim of the nectar bucket. He walked slowly along, an upright, shifting, rippling rainbow, a living, moving pillar of brightness.

"Now boys," Hubert told them, and then added "and girls," to be in compliance with woman's lib, "this is it. No more until tomorrow. Go on out and make your own livings. This is all I can afford."

He told them that every morning now, and they always responded. Gradually they began to drift away, spreading out over the whole mountainside, hovering or clinging briefly wherever a flower bloomed.

"Mohamet," Hubert said, "you're really dressed up in the summertime. Glad I can help."

Naturally he got no response from the mountain, but it seemed proper to make a remark to it now and then. In the strange way of thinking that poets have, he felt that Mohamet appreciated it.

For the next two days Hubert saw little of his neighbors. They didn't come to his camp again, and there were certainly no further attempts at bathing. They prowled all over the mountain. Occasionally he saw them high among the rocks, probing into crevices, going in and out of the little shallow caves they discovered. Hubert knew that they watched him, too, but this was no more productive than the prowling. The ways that he spent his time were no secrets, and he suspected that they made very little sense to the watchers.

So Hubert fed his butterflies, lounged in George's shadow and scribbled in his notebook, took his nap while Wilfred tempered the afternoon heat of the rocks with a cool breath from the snowfields. And from this nap, on the second day, he woke to find the treasure hunters beside him.

The dark man was staring down at him. He didn't look friendly. This impression was reinforced by a stubby little black bulldog revolver that he held in his hand.

"Our patience has done give out," he said. "Now it looks like you're goin' to have to show us where it is."

Hubert knew he had problems, so he stalled in the usual way.

"If you would tell me what you're talking about, it would help. And you can put down that gun. I don't have one, and there are two of you."

"I'll just keep it handy," the man said. The scalding

hadn't done away with his odor, and anyway he was wearing the same clothes. "You know what our interest is. Money. Old money. We ain't fools. We know you been huntin' treasure up here in these rocks. An' we know you've found it. Now you're jest foolin' around until you can git it out."

"Ah," Hubert said. "The gold piece I had in the store." He looked thoughtful. "That is suspicious, all right. But if I have found a cache of coins, isn't it mine? Where do you come in?"

"We're your partners," little Rat-eyes said. "We all found it. An' your cut is gettin' smaller every minute."

Hubert sighed, but his mind was groping frantically for an idea. He knew that this was real danger. Poetry and smart talk wouldn't help a bit. These two characters wouldn't understand either one.

"May I sit up? I think better when my head is higher than my heels."

"Jest think where the money is. That won't be hard."

Hubert propped his back against George's trunk, moving slowly so the man with the gun wouldn't get the wrong idea.

"I almost wish I knew," he said. "It would save a lot of trouble. But the plain fact is that I just found that one coin. I admit I found it up here—in the rocks below the cliff. My idea is that someone lost it, somebody climbing up here, somebody going through." He shrugged his shoulders. "Believe it or not, that's all I know. I'm not interested in treasure hunting."

"Okay, we don't believe it," the little man said. "Your head is up, but you still ain't thinkin' hard enough. What you need is time."

He had come prepared. He took several feet of small pliable pigging rope, like that used to tie calves' legs in roping contests, and tied Hubert's hands behind him. He did it expertly. Then with another piece he hobbled Hubert's ankles, so that he could walk with a six-inch stride.

"You like it here under this old tree, so you can jest stay here a while. But maybe we better fix it so you won't wander off."

He shook out a coil of quarter-inch rope, passed the end of it through Hubert's legs and up across one shoulder, and tied it securely behind Hubert's back. Then he tied the other end of the rope around the trunk of the old pine.

"A fifteen-foot stake-out," he said with satisfaction. "You won't need no more, since you ain't grazin'. Come to think of it, you *might* be grazin', unless you think up where that money's at."

The little rat eyes glittered at him, and Hubert thought what a fitting comparison it was. He hated rats.

"One more thing," the little man said. "Don't yell. If we have to put a gag in your mouth, you won't even be able to graze."

"I'd be wasting my breath," Hubert said. "There's nobody to hear me."

"Yeah," the dark man said. "That makes it nice."

They went back across the meadow, past the jeep parked on the rim of the stream bed, and down out of sight toward their camp.

"Well, George," Hubert said, "this is what I'd have to call a real mess. I hate to think of the ransacking they're giving my camp right now. Any idea you may have will be gratefully received."

George didn't seem to have any, for his few live branches hung motionless in the still afternoon air. Wilfred barely whisked past, close to the ground. Hubert experimented with the limited stride the hobble allowed, and found that it did exactly what it was meant to do. The little man knew his ropes. So Hubert finally eased himself down the trunk of the pine, and, in awkward comfort, sat thinking.

After half an hour, the men appeared again. Hubert saw that they were loading the jeep.

"That figures," he said. "Whether I cough up a treasure or not, they're blown. They'll have to move out. The interesting thing is what they plan for me before they leave. Interesting to me, anyway. Because I sure can't show them any gold."

Since he could do nothing else, Hubert watched them. He did work himself to his feet again, and walk with hobbled steps to the end of his tether. And he began to feel a strange undercurrent, as though forces all around him were gearing up for action. Even old George's scanty foliage ceased to hang limply. The branches trembled in an as yet scarcely perceptible breeze.

Across the wide sunny slope the butterflies were drifting, and Hubert suddenly realized that they were all moving in the same direction. They were gathering in clouds. The jeep's motor started. The vehicle backed, swung around and headed for the pine tree, the dark man at the wheel. Butterflies began to plaster themselves against the windshield. They swarmed around the passengers, fluttering and crawling over everything. The driver held the wheel with one hand and brushed away insects with the other.

"Bat 'em out of here!" he growled. "I can't see to drive. Damn bugs have gone crazy!"

The little man beat about him with his cap, but the jeep slowed almost to a crawl. After all, the mountainside, even the meadow, was covered with rocks. It would be easy to wreck the car. And they expected to leave the country in it, after the showdown with Hubert.

"If he don't tell us nothin', what'll we do with him?"

"Leave him there," the dark man said. "He can get loose. It'll jest take him a while."

"When I tie 'em, they don't get loose," Rat-eyes said. "An' when he dies, they're liable to call it murder." He brushed again at the butterflies, as another cloud descended on the jeep.

"He can't tell nobody nothin' if he's dead. Anyhow, he'll be dead because he's too dumb to get loose. That won't be our fault." The dark man fought butterflies, crushing fragile bodies and smearing the windshield. "What's the matter with these bugs?"

"Maybe he's doin' it," the little man said. "He feeds 'em."

"That don't make no sense. Nobody can tell bugs what to do."

And in truth Hubert was as surprised as anybody as he watched the approaching jeep, covered with butterflies. He could see the men brushing and striking at them. It was only a hundred feet away when the whole mountainside seemed to shudder. The jeep squealed to a halt.

"My God," he heard the driver yell, "earthquake!"

"Step on it!" the little man urged. "Straight ahead! If we can git to the loggin' road we can make it out of here!"

The jeep leaped forward, and another cloud of butterflies enveloped it. The mountain rocked again. The earth made a tearing, ripping sound. Hubert turned as he felt his rope pull. Old George was swaying slowly, and from his base a long fissure ran, tearing his ancient weakened roots, loosening the grip that had held him aloft for hundreds of years.

"Stop!" the little man howled. "Look out fer the tree!"

George seemed to fall in slow motion. His mighty length settled almost gently directly in the path of the jeep, then the sound of the crash blasted in all directions, and leaped and ricocheted from the cliff and all the rock faces about.

Hubert was reasonably sure he was dead. The men in the jeep were probably of the same opinion, for they took no time to look. With George's shattered carcass blocking their way, they were frantic.

"Go around it!" the little man directed. "Go around the top end. They's a clear space up close to the cliff. You can git through."

Hubert realized that if he were dead he wouldn't be watching. He had been knocked flat by the crash, but he felt no pain. He rolled to a sitting position, and then to his feet. He was still tied up, but he was free of George. The splitting of the huge half-rotted bole had snapped the rope tied around it like a piece of twine. Hubert hopped away from the shambles of broken pieces and splinters, dragging his rope behind him.

The jeep was making slow but steady progress. George had fallen across the clearest route, but the driver was picking his way skillfully around rubble and between boulders. Though the jeep bounced and skewed, it kept going. Even in his present uncomfortable position, Hubert admired the driving.

And he noticed something. The butterflies were no longer harassing the jeep. They were leaving. The colorful clouds streamed away. Probably only the crushed and dying remained as the little car swung closest to the cliff. Then, for the third time, the mountain rumbled and shook.

For a moment the meadow seemed to move horizontally, then to snap back again. The prone body of old George did a half roll, and Hubert could hear the crackling as dry branches snapped. Hubert himself was thrown from his unstable, hobbled feet. Small rocks pattered past. Big boulders swayed in place. And a whole section of the cliff face ripped away and fell.

Hubert saw it all. He lay for a brief while, bruised and

stunned. Then slowly he rolled to a sitting position. He
did not feel the pain of a broken finger, smashed against
a little outcrop when he fell. He could not tear his unbe-
lieving eyes from what had happened at the cliff base.

The jeep was gone. Where it had been a long ridge of
shattered rock lay piled, and the cliff showed a bright new
face to the still high sun. After the cracking roar of the
breakaway, the silence seemed uncannily complete. Only
a small whisper stirred the tops of the mountain flowers.
It was Wilfred, making his way softly down from the cool,
undisturbed snowfields. The breeze seemed to swirl uncertainly where the old pine had always stood, then
moved on down the mountainside.

Hubert knew what he had to do, and he did it. Fortunately for him and for this story, he knew how. He lay on
his side, rolled himself into a curled, fetal ball. His hands,
bound behind his back, he drew down over his buttocks,
down his thighs, and then, with tearing pain, he drew his
feet through the loop. It can be done. Try it.

His hands were now in front of him, but they were still
expertly tied. With his teeth he quickly remedied that.
And there was no doubt in his mind, as he chewed away,
that the rope had previously been used to tie calves. It
was not until he bent to release the hobbles that he noticed his broken finger.

By the time he was free and had worked the stiffness
from his abused body, the finger was clamoring for attention. It would have to be set, and that meant a five-mile
trek down the steep trail to the village. But before he
could go, Hubert knew he must make sure, though he *was*
sure, that the jeep had been swallowed up by the rock
fall.

After a quick hike across the meadow and a clamber
over the newly formed ridge, he was sure. The jeep and
its passengers lay deep under thousands of tons of stone.
There was no evidence that they had ever existed.

As he climbed down over the sharply fractured edges of
the piled stones, Hubert thought deeply.

"What should I report?" he asked himself. "Who knows
they were here? Who will miss them? It would take heavy
machinery even to reach the bodies, and I doubt if they
have any grieving relatives waiting for them to come
home. And they certainly couldn't have a finer tomb."

He left the ridge and skirted an old weathered rock pile which, he realized, must have been formed by another breakaway fall, caused by some earthquake back in the mountain's history. It had been disarranged and shifted by the tremors just past. And in a crevice Hubert's eye caught a gleam of yellow, as a ray of sun probed among the rocks. With sudden curiosity he clambered over to look.

In spite of his finger, it was easy to pull back some of the loosened stones. The gold was there, two bursted and rotting leather bags of it, bright old coins spilling into niches and over the bones that also lay there. There were two skulls. The man's had been partly crushed, and the long jaw showed yellow, decayed teeth. The horse's skull was large and strong, the teeth unworn. And their bones mingled among the shattered stones and the gold pieces.

"He almost made it," Hubert said. "An old man on a young strong horse." He stood for minutes looking down into the deep crevice. His finger throbbed. It would take a lot of work to enlarge the opening until he could lower himself into the space far enough to reach any of the money. He could see that many of the coins were identical to his good luck piece.

"Well," he told himself. "I'm rich—I think. Or am I?"

He looked again at the bones.

"It didn't do him an awful lot of good," he said, "whether he stole it or not, which I suspect he did."

He glanced back at the ridge of newly fractured stone.

"They came close, and there was no doubt of their intentions, either. But their luck was just about equal to his."

He shook his head.

"I just don't know. No telling how long he and his gold have been there—and I've gotten along pretty well without it. These have been good summers. If I hauled that stuff out of there, the mountain would be overrun with treasure hunters. No peace at all. Good-bye poetry. They'd use rock-moving equipment. Probably find the jeep. And maybe more rocks would fall—on them. For somehow I don't think Mohamet takes kindly to such goings-on. But I do think he has offered the gold to me."

For another moment Hubert forgot the increasing pain of his finger, as his gaze roved the pleasant mountain meadow, swept the higher snowfields and the spires and

crags that lay above them. Faintly the steady murmur of
the waterfall came to him. Wilfred whispered along the
cliff base.

Hubert began to roll the largest stones he could move,
across and into the narrow crevice. In a few minutes no
eyes could have suspected that anything lay buried there.

"If it's my treasure," Hubert said, "I can do what I
please with it."

He rolled a last stone.

"Mohamet," he said, "you play rough, and you play
for keeps. So thank you kindly, but no thanks. I'll just
hang on to my good luck piece. And maybe some day I'll
make an epic poem about all this."

He turned to clamber down the rock pile. His broken
finger spasmed with pain.

"I'd better get on down the hill and get this fixed," he
said. "Don't want it stiff. That's one of my writing fingers."

A butterfly drifted past, then came back to make a
quick circle around Hubert's head. He grinned at it gratefully.

"I'd have had to go down before long anyhow. I'm almost out of sugar!"

In the past several years, the figure of the vampire has regained its fascination for readers, theater-goers and movie-watchers. But today's approach to the crimson-fanged seducers of so many past melodramas is much more rational, even empathic: we want to know and understand their problems. (And we suspect they're very sexy, somehow.)

What better way to get to know a vampire intimately than by having him come as a patient to you, a psychiatrist . . . ? But remember, the vampire is still a frightful predator.

Suzy McKee Charnas's novels include *Walk to the End of the World, Motherlines* and *The Vampire Tapestry*. The following novella, a complete story in itself, is a section of the latter novel.

UNICORN TAPESTRY

Suzy McKee Charnas

"HOLD ON," FLORIA, SAID. "I KNOW WHAT you're going to say: I agreed not to take any new clients for a while. But wait till I tell you—you're not going to believe this—first phone call, setting up an initial appointment, he comes out with what his problem is: 'I seem to have fallen victim to a delusion of being a vampire.'"

"Christ H. God!" cried Lucille delightedly. "Just like that, over the telephone?"

"When I recovered my aplomb, so to speak, I told him that I prefer to wait with the details until our first meeting, which is tomorrow."

They were sitting on the tiny terrace outside the staff room of the clinic, a converted town house on the upper West Side. Floria spent three days a week here and the remaining two in her office on Central Park South where she saw private clients like this new one. Lucille, always gratifyingly responsive, was Floria's most valued professional friend. Clearly enchanted with Floria's news, she sat eagerly forward in her chair, eyes wide behind Coke-bottle lenses.

She said, "Do you suppose he thinks he's a revivified corpse?"

Below, down at the end of the street, Floria could see two kids skidding their skateboards near a man who wore a woolen cap and a heavy coat despite the May warmth. He was leaning against a wall. He had been there when Floria had arrived at the clinic this morning. If corpses

140

walked, some, not nearly revivified enough, stood in plain view in New York.

"I'll have to think of a delicate way to ask," she said. "How did he come to you, this 'vampire'?"

"He was working in an upstate college, teaching and doing research, and all of a sudden he just disappeared—vanished, literally, without a trace. A month later he turned up here in the city. The faculty dean at the school knows me and sent him to see me."

Lucille gave her a sly look. "So you thought, ahah, do a little favor for a friend, this looks classic and easy to transfer if need be: repressed intellectual blows stack and runs off with spacey chick, something like that."

"You know me too well," Floria said with a rueful smile.

"Huh," grunted Lucille. She sipped ginger ale from a chipped white mug. "I don't take panicky middle-aged men anymore, they're too depressing. And you shouldn't be taking this one, intriguing as he sounds."

Here comes the lecture, Floria told herself.

Lucille got up. She was short, heavy, prone to wearing loose garments that swung about her like ceremonial robes. As she paced, her hem brushed at the flowers starting up in the planting boxes that rimmed the little terrace. "You know damn well this is just more overwork you're loading on. Don't take this guy; refer him."

Floria sighed. "I know, I know. I promised everybody I'd slow down. But you said it yourself just a minute ago —it looked like a simple favor. So what do I get? Count Dracula, for God's sake! Would you give that up?"

Fishing around in one capacious pocket, Lucille brought out a dented package of cigarettes and lit up, scowling. "You know, when you give me advice I try to take it seriously. Joking aside, Floria, what am I supposed to say? I've listened to you moaning for months now, and I thought we'd figured out that what you need is to shed some pressure, to start saying no—and here you are insisting on a new case. You know what I think: you're hiding in other people's problems from a lot of your own stuff that you should be working on.

"Okay, okay, don't glare at me. Be pigheaded. Have you gotten rid of Chubs, at least?" This was Floria's code name for a troublesome client named Kenny whom she'd been trying to unload for some time.

Floria shook her head.

"What gives with you? It's weeks since you swore you'd dump him! Trying to do everything for everybody is wearing you out. I bet you're still dropping weight. Judging by the very unbecoming circles under your eyes, sleeping isn't going too well, either. Still no dreams you can remember?"

"Lucille, don't nag. I don't want to talk about my health."

"Well, what about his health—Dracula's? Did you suggest that he have a physical before seeing you? There might be something physiological—"

"You're not going to be able to whisk him off to an M.D. and out of my hands," Floria said wryly. "He told me on the phone that he wouldn't consider either medication or hospitalization."

Involuntarily she glanced down at the end of the street. The woolen-capped man had curled up on the sidewalk at the foot of the building, sleeping or passed out or dead. The city was tottering with sickness. Compared with that wreck down there and others like him, how sick could this "vampire" be, with his cultured baritone voice, his self-possessed approach?

"And you won't consider handing him off to somebody else," Lucille said.

"Well, not until I know a little more. Come on, Luce— wouldn't you want at least to know what he looks like?"

Lucille stubbed out her cigarette against the low parapet. Down below a policeman strolled along the street ticketing the parked cars. He didn't even look at the man lying at the corner of the building. They watched his progress without comment. Finally Lucille said, "Well, if you won't drop Dracula, keep me posted on him, will you?"

He entered the office on the dot of the hour, a gaunt but graceful figure. He was impressive. Wiry gray hair, worn short, emphasized the massiveness of his face with its long jaw, high cheekbones, and granite cheeks grooved as if by winters of hard weather. His name, typed in caps on the initial information sheet that Floria proceeded to fill out with him, was Edward Lewis Weyland.

Crisply he told her about the background of the vampire incident, describing in caustic terms his life at Cayslin College: the pressures of collegial competition, interdepartmental squabbles, student indifference, administrative bungling. History has limited use, she knew, since memory distorts; still, if he felt most comfortable establishing the setting for his illness, that was as good a way to start off as any.

At length his energy faltered. His angular body sank into a slump, his voice became flat and tired as he haltingly worked up to the crucial event: night work at the sleep lab, fantasies of blood-drinking as he watched the youthful subjects of his dream research slumbering, finally an attempt to act out the fantasy with a staff member at the college. He had been repulsed; then panic had assailed him. Word would get out, he'd be fired, blacklisted forever. He'd bolted. A nightmare period had followed—he offered no details. When he had come to his senses he'd seen that just what he feared, the ruin of his career, would come from his running away. So he'd phoned the dean, and now here he was.

Throughout this recital she watched him diminish from the dignified academic who had entered her office to a shamed and frightened man hunched in his chair, his hands pulling fitfully at each other.

"What are your hands doing?" she said gently. He looked blank. She repeated the question.

He looked down at his hands. "Struggling," he said.

"With what?"

"The worst," he muttered. "I haven't told you the worst." She had never grown hardened to this sort of transformation. His long fingers busied themselves fiddling with a button on his jacket while he explained painfully that the object of his "attack" at Cayslin had been a woman. Not young but handsome and vital, she had first caught his attention earlier in the year during a *festschrift* —an honorary seminar—for a retiring professor.

A picture emerged of an awkward Weyland, lifelong bachelor, seeking this woman's warmth and suffering her refusal. Floria knew she should bring him out of his past and into his here-and-now, but he was doing so beautifully on his own that she was loath to interrupt.

"Did I tell you there was a rapist active on the campus at this time?" he said bitterly. "I borrowed a leaf from his book: I tried to take from this woman, since she wouldn't give. I tried to take some of her blood." He stared at the floor. "What does that mean—to take someone's blood?"

"What do you think it means?"

The button, pulled and twisted by his fretful fingers, came off. He put it into his pocket, the impulse, she guessed, of a fastidious nature. "Her energy," he murmured, "stolen to warm the aging scholar, the walking corpse, the vampire—myself."

His silence, his downcast eyes, his bent shoulders, all signaled a man brought to bay by a life crisis. Perhaps he was going to be the kind of client therapists dream of and she needed so badly these days: a client intelligent and sensitive enough, given the companionship of a professional listener, to swiftly unravel his own mental tangles. Exhilarated by his promising start, Floria restrained herself from trying to build on it too soon. She made herself tolerate the silence, which lasted until he said suddenly, "I notice that you make no notes as we speak. Do you record these sessions on tape?"

A hint of paranoia, she thought; not unusual. "Not without your knowledge and consent, just as I won't send for your personnel file from Cayslin without your knowledge and consent. I do, however, write notes after each session as a guide to myself and in order to have a record in case of any confusion about anything we do or say here. I can promise you that I won't show my notes or speak of you by name to anyone—except Dean Sharpe at Cayslin, of course, and even then only as much as is strictly necessary—without your written permission. Does that satisfy you?"

"I apologize for my question," he said. "The . . . incident has left me . . . very nervous; a condition that I hope to get over with your help."

The time was up. When he had gone, she stepped outside to check with Hilda, the receptionist she shared with four other therapists here at the Central Park South office. Hilda always sized up new clients in the waiting room.

Of this one she said, "Are you sure there's anything wrong with that guy? I think I'm in love."

Waiting at the office for a group of clients to assemble Wednesday evening, Floria dashed off some notes on the "vampire."

Client described incident, background. No history of

mental illness, no previous experience of therapy.
Personal history so ordinary you almost don't notice
how bare it is: only child of German immigrants,
schooling normal, field work in anthropology, academic posts leading to Cayslin College professorship.
Health good, finances adequate, occupation satisfactory, housing pleasant (though presently installed in
a N.Y. hotel); never married, no kids, no family, no
religion, social life strictly job-related; leisure—says
he likes to drive. Reaction to question about drinking, but no signs of alcohol problems. Physically very
smooth-moving for his age (over fifty) and height;
catlike, alert. Some apparent stiffness in the midsection—slight protective stoop—tightening up of middle age? Paranoic defensiveness? Voice pleasant,
faint accent (German-speaking childhood at home).
Entering therapy condition of consideration for return to job.

What a relief: his situation looked workable with a
minimum of strain on herself. Now she could defend to
Lucille her decision to do therapy with the "vampire."
    After all, Lucille was right. Floria did have problems of
her own that needed attention, primarily her anxiety and
exhaustion since her mother's death more than a year before. The breakup of Floria's marriage had caused mis-
ery, but not this sort of endless depression. Intellectually
the problem was clear: with both her parents dead she
was left exposed. No one stood any longer between herself and the inevitability of her own death. Knowing the
source of her feelings didn't help: she couldn't seem to
mobilize the nerve to work on them.
    The Wednesday group went badly again. Lisa lived
once more her experiences in the European death camps
and everyone cried. Floria wanted to stop Lisa, turn her,
extinguish the droning horror of her voice in illumination
and release, but she couldn't see how to do it. She found
nothing in herself to offer except some clever ploy out of
the professional bag of tricks—dance your anger, have a
dialog with yourself of those days—useful techniques
when they flowed organically as part of a living process
in which the therapist participated. But thinking out responses that should have been intuitive wouldn't work.
The group and its collective pain paralyzed her. She was

a dancer without a choreographer, knowing all the moves but unable to match them to the music these people made.

Rather than act with mechanical clumsiness she held back, did nothing, and suffered guilt. Oh God, the smart, experienced people in the group must know how useless she was here.

Going home on the bus she thought about calling up one of the therapists who shared the downtown office. He had expressed an interest in doing co-therapy with her under student observation. The Wednesday group might respond well to that. Suggest it to them next time? Having a partner might take pressure off Floria and revitalize the group, and if she felt she must withdraw he would be available to take over. Of course he might take over anyway and walk off with some of her clients.

Oh boy, terrific, who's paranoid now? Wonderful way to think about a good colleague. God, she hadn't even known she was considering chucking the group.

Had the new client, running from his "vampirism," exposed her own impulse to retreat? This wouldn't be the first time that Floria had obtained help from a client while attempting to give help. Her old supervisor, Rigby, said that such mutual aid was the only true therapy—the rest was fraud. What a perfectionist, old Rigby, and what a bunch of young idealists he'd turned out, all eager to save the world.

Eager, but not necessarily able. Jane Fennerman had once lived in the world, and Floria had been incompetent to save her. Jane, an absent member of tonight's group, was back in the safety of a locked ward, hazily gliding on whatever tranquilizers they used there.

Why still mull over Jane? she asked herself severely, bracing against the bus's lurching halt. Any client was entitled to drop out of therapy and commit herself. Nor was this the first time that sort of thing had happened in the course of Floria's career. Only this time she couldn't seem to shake free of the resulting depression and guilt.

But how could she have helped Jane more? How could you offer reassurance that life was not as dreadful as Jane felt it to be, that her fears were insubstantial, that each day was not a pit of pain and danger?

She was taking time during a client's canceled hour to work on notes for the new book. The writing, an analysis of the vicissitudes of salaried versus private practice, balked her at every turn. She longed for an interruption to distract her circling mind.

Hilda put through a call from Cayslin College. It was Doug Sharpe, who had sent Dr. Weyland to her.

"Now that he's in your capable hands, I can tell people plainly that he's on what we call 'compassionate leave' and make them swallow it." Doug's voice seemed thinned by the long-distance connection. "Can you give me a preliminary opinion?"

"I need time to get a feel for the situation."

He said, "Try not to take too long. At the moment I'm holding off pressure to appoint someone in his place. His enemies up here—and a sharp-tongued bastard like him acquires plenty of those—are trying to get a search committee authorized to find someone else for the directorship of the Cayslin Center for the Study of Man."

"Of People," she corrected automatically, as she always did. "What do you mean, 'bastard'? I though you liked him, Doug. 'Do you want me to have to throw a smart, courtly, old-school gent to Finney or MaGill?' Those were your very words." Finney was a Freudian with a mouth like a pursed-up little asshole and a mind to match, and MaGill was a primal yowler in a padded gym of an office.

She heard Doug tapping at his teeth with a pen or pencil. "Well," he said, "I have a lot of respect for him, and sometimes I could cheer him for mowing down some pompous moron up here. I can't deny, though, that he's earned a reputation for being an accomplished son-of-a-bitch and tough to work with. Too damn cold and self-sufficient, you know?"

"Mmm," she said. "I haven't seen that yet."

He said, "You will. How about yourself? How's the rest of your life?"

"Well, offhand, what would you say if I told you I was thinking of going back to art school?"

"What would I say? I'd say bullshit, that's what I'd say. You've had fifteen years of doing something you're good at, and now you want to throw all that out and start over in an area you haven't touched since Studio 101 in college? If God had meant you to be a painter, She'd have sent you to art school in the first place."

"I did think about art school at the time."

"The point is that you're good at what you do. I've

been at the receiving end of your work and I know what I'm talking about. By the way, did you see that piece in the paper about Annie Barnes, from the group I was in? That's an important appointment. I always knew she'd wind up in Washington. What I'm trying to make clear to you is that your 'graduates' do too well for you to be talking about quitting. What's Morton say about that idea, by the way?"

Mort, a pathologist, was Floria's lover. She hadn't discussed this with him, and she told Doug so.

"You're not on the outs with Morton, are you?"

"Come on, Douglas, cut it out. There's nothing wrong with my sex life, believe me. It's everyplace else that's giving me trouble."

"Just sticking my nose into your business," he replied. "What are friends for?"

They turned to lighter matters, but when she hung up Floria felt glum. If her friends were moved to this sort of probing and kindly advice-giving, she must be inviting help more openly and more urgently than she'd realized.

The work on the book went no better. It was as if, afraid to expose her thoughts, she must disarm criticism by meeting all possible objections beforehand. The book was well and truly stalled—like everything else. She sat sweating over it, wondering what the devil was wrong with her that she was writing mush. She had two good books to her name already. What was this bottleneck with the third?

"But what do you think?" Kenny insisted anxiously. "Does it sound like my kind of job?"

"How do you feel about it?"

"I'm all confused, I told you."

"Try speaking for me. Give me the advice I would give you."

He glowered. "That's a real cop-out, you know? One part of me talks like you, and then I have a dialog with myself like a TV show about a split personality. It's all me that way; you just sit there while I do all the work. I want something from *you*."

She looked for the twentieth time at the clock on the file cabinet. This time it freed her. "Kenny, the hour's over."

Kenny heaved his plump, sulky body up out of his

chair. "You don't care. Oh, you pretend to, but you don't really—"

"Next time, Kenny."

He stumped out of the office. She imagined him towing in his wake the raft of decisions he was trying to inveigle her into making for him. Sighing, she went to the window and looked out over the park, filling her eyes and her mind with the full, fresh green of late spring. She felt dismal. In two years of treatment the situation with Kenny had remained a stalemate. He wouldn't go to someone else who might be able to help him, and she couldn't bring herself to kick him out, though she knew she must eventually. His puny tyranny couldn't conceal how soft and vulnerable he was . . .

Dr. Weyland had the next appointment. Floria found herself pleased to see him. She could hardly have asked for a greater contrast to Kenny: tall, lean, that august head that made her want to draw him, good clothes, nice big hands—altogether, a distinguished-looking man. Though he was informally dressed in slacks, light jacket, and tieless shirt, the impression he conveyed was one of impeccable leisure and reserve. He took not the padded chair preferred by most clients but the wooden one with the cane seat.

"Good afternoon, Dr. Landauer," he said gravely. "May I ask your judgment of my case?"

"I don't regard myself as a judge," she said. She decided to try to shift their discussion onto a first-name basis if possible. Calling this old-fashioned man by his first name so soon might seem artificial, but how could they get familiar enough to do therapy while addressing each other as "Dr. Landauer" and "Dr. Weyland" like two characters out of a vaudeville sketch?

"This is what I think, Edward," she continued. "We need to find out about this vampire incident—how it tied into your feelings about yourself, good and bad, at the time; what it did for you that led you to try to 'be' a vampire even though that was bound to complicate your life terrifically. The more we know, the closer we can come to figuring out how to insure that this vampire construct won't be necessary to you again."

"Does this mean that you accept me formally as a client?" he said.

Comes right out and says what's on his mind, she noted; no problem there. "Yes."

"Good. I too have a treatment goal in mind. I will need at some point a testimonial from you that my mental health is sound enough for me to resume work at Cayslin."

Floria shook her head. "I can't guarantee that. I can commit myself to work toward it, of course, since your improved mental health is the aim of what we do here together."

"I suppose that answers the purpose for the time being," he said. "We can discuss it again later on. Frankly, I find myself eager to continue our work today. I've been feeling very much better since I spoke with you, and I thought last night about what I might tell you today."

She had the distinct feeling of being steered by him; how important was it to him, she wondered, to feel in control? She said, "Edward, my own feeling is that we started out with a good deal of very useful verbal work, and that now is a time to try something a little different."

He said nothing. He watched her. When she asked whether he remembered his dreams he shook his head, no.

She said, "I'd like you to try to do a dream for me now, a waking dream. Can you close your eyes and daydream, and tell me about it?"

He closed his eyes. Strangely, he now struck her as less vulnerable rather than more, as if strengthened by increased vigilance.

"How do you feel now?" she said.

"Uneasy." His eyelids fluttered. "I dislike closing my eyes. What I don't see can hurt me."

"Who wants to hurt you?"

"A vampire's enemies, of course—mobs of screaming peasants with torches."

Translating into what, she wondered—young Ph.D.s pouring out of the graduate schools panting for the jobs of older men like Weyland? "Peasants, these days?"

"Whatever their daily work, there is still a majority of the stupid, the violent, and the credulous, putting their featherbrained faith in astrology, in this cult or that, in various branches of psychology."

His sneer at her was unmistakable. Considering her refusal to let him fill the hour his own way, this desire to take a swipe at her was healthy. But it required immediate and straightforward handling.

"Edward, open your eyes and tell me what you see."

He obeyed. "I see a woman in her early forties," he said, "clever-looking face, dark hair showing gray; flesh too thin for her bones, indicating either vanity or illness; wearing slacks and a rather creased batik blouse—describable, I think, by the term 'peasant style'—with a food stain on the left side."

Damn! Don't blush. "Does anything besides my blouse suggest a peasant to you?"

"Nothing concrete, but with regard to me, my vampire self, a peasant with a torch is what you could easily become."

"I hear you saying that my task is to help you get rid of your delusion, though this process may be painful and frightening for you."

Something flashed in his expression—surprise, perhaps alarm, something she wanted to get in touch with before it could sink away out of reach again. Quickly she said, "How do you experience your face at this moment?"

He frowned. "As being on the front of my head. Why?"

With a rush of anger at herself she saw that she had chosen the wrong technique for reaching that hidden feeling: she had provoked hostility instead. She said, "Your face looked to me just now like a mask for concealing what you feel rather than an instrument of expression."

He moved restlessly in the chair, his whole physical attitude tense and guarded. "I don't know what you mean."

"Will you let me touch you?" she said, rising.

His hands tightened on the arms of his chair, which protested in a sharp creak. He snapped, "I thought this was a talking cure."

Strong resistance to body work—ease up. "If you won't let me massage some of the tension out of your facial muscles, will you try to do it yourself?"

"I don't enjoy being made ridiculous," he said, standing and heading for the door, which clapped smartly to behind him.

She sagged back in her seat; she had mishandled him. Clearly her initial estimation of this as a relatively easy job had been wrong and had led her to move far too quickly with him. Certainly it was much too early to try body work. She should have developed a firmer level of trust first by letting him do more of what he did so easily and so well—talk.

The door opened. Weyland came back in and shut it quietly. He did not sit again but paced about the room, coming to rest at the window.

"Please excuse my rather childish behavior just now," he said. "Playing these games of yours brought it on."

"It's frustrating, playing games that are unfamiliar and that you can't control," she said. As he made no reply, she went on in a conciliatory tone, "I'm not trying to belittle you, Edward. I just need to get us off whatever track you were taking us down so briskly. My feeling is that you're trying hard to regain your old stability.

"But that's the goal, not the starting point. The only way to reach your goal is through the process, and you don't drive the therapy process like a train. You can only help the process happen, as though you were helping a tree grow."

"These games are part of the process?"

"Yes."

"And neither you nor I control the games?"

"That's right."

He considered. "Suppose I agree to try this process of yours; what would you want of me?"

Observing him carefully, she no longer saw the anxious scholar bravely struggling back from madness. Here was a different sort of man—armored, calculating. She didn't know just what the change signaled, but she felt her own excitement stirring, and that meant she was on the track of—something.

"I have a hunch," she said slowly, "that this vampirism extends further back into your past than you've told me and possibly right up into the present as well. I think it's still with you. My style of therapy stresses dealing with the now at least as much as the then; if the vampirism is part of the present, dealing with it on that basis is crucial."

Silence.

"Can you talk about being a vampire: being one now?"

"You won't like knowing," he said.

"Edward, try."

He said, "I hunt."

"Where? How? What sort of—of victims?"

He folded his arms and leaned his back against the

window frame. "Very well, since you insist. There are a number of possibilities here in the city in summer. Those too poor to own air-conditioners sleep out on rooftops and fire escapes. But often, I've found, their blood is sour with drugs or liquor. The same is true of prostitutes. Bars are full of accessible people but also full of smoke and noise, and there too the blood is fouled. I must choose my hunting grounds carefully. Often I go to openings of galleries or evening museum shows or department stores on their late nights—places where women may be approached."

And take pleasure in it, she thought, if they're out hunting also—for acceptable male companionship. Yet he said he's never married. Explore where this is going. "Only women?"

He gave her a sardonic glance, as if she were a slightly brighter student than he had at first assumed.

"Hunting women is liable to be time-consuming and expensive. The best hunting is in the part of Central Park they call the Ramble, where homosexual men seek encounters with others of their kind. I walk there too at night."

Floria caught a faint sound of conversation and laughter from the waiting room; her next client had probably arrived, she realized, looking reluctantly at the clock. "I'm sorry, Edward, but our time seems to be—"

"Only a moment more," he said coldly. "You asked; permit me to finish my answer. In the Ramble I find someone who doesn't reek of alcohol or drugs, who seems healthy, and who is not insistent on 'hooking up' right there among the bushes. I invite such a man to my hotel. He judges me safe, at least: older, weaker than he is, unlikely to turn out to be a dangerous maniac. So he comes to my room. I feed on his blood.

"Now, I think, our time is up."

He walked out.

She sat torn between rejoicing at his admission of the delusion's persistence and dismay that his condition was so much worse than she had first thought. Her hope of having an easy time with him vanished. His initial presentation had been just that—a performance, an act. Forced to abandon it, he had dumped on her this lump of material, too much—and too strange—to take in all at once.

Her next client liked the padded chair, not the wooden one that Weyland had sat in during the first part of the hour. Floria started to move the wooden one back. The armrests came away in her hands.

She remembered him starting up in protest against her proposal of touching him. The grip of his fingers had fractured the joints, and the shafts now lay in splinters on the floor.

Floria wandered into Lucille's room at the clinic after the staff meeting. Lucille was lying on the couch with a wet cloth over her eyes.

"I thought you looked green around the gills today," Floria said. "What's wrong?"

"Big bash last night," said Lucille in sepulchral tones. "I think I feel about the way you do after a session with Chubs. You haven't gotten rid of him yet, have you?"

"No. I had him lined up to see Marty instead of me last week, but damned if he didn't show up at my door at his usual time. It's a lost cause. What I wanted to talk to you about was Dracula."

"What about him?"

"He's smarter, tougher, and sicker than I thought, and maybe I'm even less competent than I thought, too. He's already walked out on me once—I almost lost him. I never took a course in treating monsters."

Lucille groaned. "Some days they're all monsters." This from Lucille, who worked longer hours than anyone else at the clinic, to the despair of her husband. She lifted the cloth, refolded it, and placed it carefully across her forehead. "And if I had ten dollars for every client who's walked out on me . . . Tell you what: I'll trade you Madame X for him, how's that? Remember Madame X, with the jangling bracelets and the parakeet eye makeup and the phobia about dogs? Now she's phobic about things dropping on her out of the sky. Just wait—it'll turn out that one day when she was three a dog trotted by and pissed on her leg just as an over-passing pigeon shat on her head. What are we doing in this business?"

"God knows." Floria laughed. "But am I in this business these days—I mean, in the sense of practicing my so-called skills? Blocked with my group work, beating my brains out on a book that won't go, and doing something —I'm not sure it's therapy—with a vampire . . . You know, once I had this sort of natural choreographer inside myself that hardly let me put a foot wrong and always knew how to correct a mistake if I did. Now that's gone. I feel as if I'm just going through a lot of mechanical motions. Whatever I had once that made me useful as a therapist, I've lost it."

Ugh, she thought, hearing the descent of her voice into a tone of gloomy self-pity.

"Well, don't complain about Dracula," Lucille said. "You were the one who insisted on taking him on. At least he's got you concentrating on his problem instead of just wringing your hands. As long as you've started, stay with it—illumination may come. And now I'd better change the ribbon in my typewriter and get back to reviewing Silverman's latest best-seller on self-shrinking while I'm feeling mean enough to do it justice." She got up gingerly. "Stick around in case I faint and fall into the wastebasket."

"Luce, this case is what I'd like to try to write about."

"Dracula?" Lucille pawed through a desk drawer full of paper clips, pens, rubber bands and old lipsticks.

"Dracula. A monograph . . ."

"Oh, I know that game: you scribble down everything you can and then read what you wrote to find out what's going on with the client, and with luck you end up publishing. Great! But if you are going to publish, don't piddle this away on a dinky paper. Do a book. Here's your subject, instead of those depressing statistics you've been killing yourself over. This one is really exciting—a case study to put on the shelf next to Freud's own wolf-man, have you thought of that?"

Floria liked it. "What a book that could be—fame if not fortune. Notoriety, most likely. How in the world could I convince our colleagues that it's legit? There's a lot of vampire stuff around right now—plays on Broadway and TV, books all over the place, movies. They'll say I'm just trying to ride the coattails of a fad."

"No, no, what you do is show how this guy's delusion is related to the fad. Fascinating." Lucille, having found a ribbon, prodded doubtfully at the exposed innards of her typewriter.

"Suppose I fictionalize it," Floria said, "under a pseudonym. Why not ride the popular wave and be free in what I can say?"

"Listen, you've never written a word of fiction in your life, have you?" Lucille fixed her with a bloodshot gaze. "There's no evidence that you could turn out a best-selling novel. On the other hand, by this time you have a trained memory for accurately reporting therapeutic transactions. That's a strength you'd be foolish to waste. A solid professional book would be terrific—and a feather in the cap of every woman in the field. Just make sure you get good legal advice on disguising your Dracula's identity well enough to avoid libel."

The cane-seated chair wasn't worth repairing, so she got its twin out of the bedroom to put in the office in its place. Puzzling: by his history Weyland was fifty-two, and by his appearance no muscle man. She should have asked Doug—but how, exactly? "By the way, Doug, was Weyland ever a circus strong man or a blacksmith? Does he secretly pump iron?" Ask the client himself—but not yet.

She invited some of the younger staff from the clinic over for a small party with a few of her outside friends. It was a good evening; they were not a heavy-drinking crowd, which meant the conversation stayed intelligent. The guests drifted about the long living room or stood in twos and threes at the windows looking down on West End Avenue as they talked.

Mort came, warming the room. Fresh from a session with some amateur chamber-music friends, he still glowed with the pleasure of making his cello sing. His own voice was unexpectedly light for so large a man. Sometimes Floria thought that the deep throb of the cello was his true voice.

He stood beside her talking with some others. There was no need to lean against his comfortable bulk or to have him put his arm around her waist. Their intimacy was long-standing, an effortless pleasure in each other that required neither demonstration nor concealment.

He was easily diverted from music to his next favorite topic, the strengths and skills of athletes.

"Here's a question for a paper I'm thinking of writing," Floria said. "Could a tall, lean man be exceptionally strong?"

Mort rambled on in his thoughtful way. His answer seemed to be no.

"But what about chimpanzees?" put in a young clinician. "I went with a guy once who was an animal handler for TV, and he said a three-month-old chimp could demolish a strong man."

"It's all physical conditioning," somebody else said. "Modern people are soft."

Mort nodded. "Human beings in general are weakly made compared to other animals. It's a question of muscle insertions—the angles of how the muscles are attached to the bones. Some angles give better leverage than others. That's how a leopard can bring down a much bigger animal than itself. It has a muscular structure that gives it tremendous strength for its streamlined build."

Floria said, "If a man were built with muscle insertions like a leopard's, he'd look pretty odd, wouldn't he?"

"Not to an untrained eye," Mort said, sounding bemused by an inner vision. "And my God, what an athlete he'd make—can you imagine a guy in the decathlon who's as strong as a leopard?"

When everyone else had gone Mort stayed, as he often did. Jokes about insertions, muscular and otherwise, soon led to sounds more expressive and more animal, but afterward Floria didn't feel like resting snuggled together with Mort and talking. When her body stopped racing, her mind turned to her new client. She didn't want to discuss him with Mort, so she ushered Mort out as gently as she could and sat down by herself at the kitchen table with a glass of orange juice.

How to approach the reintegration of Weyland the eminent, gray-haired academic with the rebellious vampire-self that had smashed his life out of shape?

She thought of the broken chair, of Weyland's big hands crushing the wood. Old wood and dried-out glue, of course, or he never could have done that. He was a man, after all, not a leopard.

The day before the third session Weyland phoned and left a message with Hilda: he would not be coming to the office tomorrow for his appointemnt, but if Dr. Landauer were agreeable she would find him at their usual hour at the Central Park Zoo.

Am I going to let him move me around from here to there? she thought. I shouldn't—but why fight it? Give him some leeway, see what opens up in a different setting. Besides, it was a beautiful day, probably the last of the sweet May weather before the summer stickiness descended. She gladly cut Kenny short so that she would have time to walk over to the zoo.

There was a fair crowd there for a weekday. Well-groomed young matrons pushed clean, floppy babies in strollers. Weyland she spotted at once.

He was leaning against the railing that enclosed the seals' shelter and their murky green pool. His jacket, slung over his shoulder, draped elegantly down his long back. Floria thought him rather dashing and faintly foreign-looking. Women who passed him, she noticed, tended to glance back.

He looked at everyone. She had the impression that he knew quite well that she was walking up behind him.

"Outdoors makes a nice change from the office, Edward," she said, coming to the rail beside him. "But there must be more to this than a longing for fresh air." A fat seal lay in sculptural grace on the concrete, eyes blissfully shut, fur drying in the sun to a translucent water-color umber.

Weyland straightened from the rail. They walked. He did not look at the animals; his eyes moved continually over the crowd. He said, "Someone has been watching for me at your office building."

"Who?"

"There are several possibilities. Pah, what a stench—though humans caged in similar circumstances smell as bad." He sidestepped a couple of shrieking children who were fighting over a balloon and headed out of the zoo under the musical clock.

They walked the uphill path northward through the park. By extending her own stride a little Floria found that she could comfortably keep pace with him.

"Is it peasants with torches?" she said. "Following you?"

He said, "What a childish idea."

All right, try another tack, then: "You were telling me last time about hunting in the Ramble. Can we return to that?"

"If you wish." He sounded bored—a defense? Surely—she was certain this must be the right reading—surely his problem was a transmutation into "vampire" fantasy of an unacceptable aspect of himself. For men of his gen-

eration the confrontation with homosexual drives could
be devastating.

"When you pick up someone in the Ramble, is it a paid
encounter?"

"Usually."

"How do you feel about having to pay?" She expected
resentment.

He gave a faint shrug. "Why not? Others work to earn
their bread. I work, too, very hard, in fact. Why shouldn't
I use my earnings to pay for my sustenance?"

Why did he never play the expected card? Baffled, she
pasued to drink from a fountain. They walked on.

"Once you've got your quarry, how do you . . ." She
fumbled for a word.

"Attack?" he supplied, unperturbed. "There's a place
on the neck, here, where pressure can interrupt the blood
flow to the brain and cause unconsciousness. Getting close
enough to apply that pressure isn't difficult."

"You do this before or after any sexual activity?"

"Before, if possible," he said aridly, "and instead of."
He turned aside to stalk up a slope to a granite outcrop
that overlooked the path they had been following. There
he settled on his haunches, looking back the way they
had come. Floria, glad she'd worn slacks today, sat down
near him.

He didn't seem devasted—anything but. Press him,
don't let him get by on cool. "Do you often prey on men
in preference to women?"

"Certainly. I take what is easiest. Men have always
been more accessible because women have been walled
away like prizes or so physically impoverished by repeated childbearing as to be unhealthy prey for me. All
this has begun to change recently, but gay men are still
the simplest quarry." While she was recovering from her
surprise at his unforeseen and weirdly skewed awareness
of female history, he added suavely, "How carefully you
control your expression, Dr. Landauer—no trace of disapproval."

She did disapprove, she realized. She would prefer him
not to be committed sexually to men. Oh, hell.

He went on, "Yet no doubt you see me as one who vic-
timizes the already victimized. This is the world's way. A
wolf brings down the stragglers at the edges of the herd.
Gay men are denied the full protection of the human herd

and are at the same time emboldened to make themselves known and available.

"On the other hand, unlike the wolf I can feed without killing, and these particular victims pose no threat to me that would cause me to kill. Outcasts themselves, even if they comprehend my true purpose among them they cannot effectively accuse me."

God, how neatly, completely, and ruthlessly he distanced the homosexual community from himself! "And how do you feel, Edward, about their purposes—their sexual expectations of you?"

"The same way I feel about the sexual expectations of women whom I choose to pursue; they don't interest me. Besides, once my hunger is active, sexual arousal is impossible. My physical unresponsiveness seems to surprise no one. Apparently impotence is expected in a gray-haired man, which suits my intention."

Some kids carrying radios swung past below, trailing a jumble of amplified thump, wail, and jabber. Floria gazed after them unseeingly, thinking, astonished again, that she had never heard a man speak of his own impotence with such cool indifference. She had induced him to talk about his problem all right. He was speaking as freely as he had in the first session, only this time it was no act. He was drowning her in more than she had ever expected or for that matter wanted to know about vampirism. What the hell: she was listening, she thought she understood—what was it all good for? Time for some cold reality, she thought; see how far he can carry all this incredible detail. Give the whole structure a shove.

She said, "You realize, I'm sure, that people of either sex who make themselves so easily available are also liable to be carriers of disease. When was your last medical checkup?"

"My dear Dr. Landauer, my first medical checkup will be my last. Fortunately, I have no great need of one. Most serious illnesses—hepatitis, for example—reveal themselves to me by a quality in the odor of the victim's skin. Warned, I abstain. When I do fall ill, as occasionally happens, I withdraw to some place where I can heal undisturbed. A doctor's attentions would be more dangerous to me than any disease."

Eyes on the path below, he continued calmly, "You can see by looking at me that there are no obvious clues to my unique nature. But believe me, an examination of any depth by even a half-sleeping medical practitioner would reveal some alarming deviations from the norm. I take pains to stay healthy, and I seem to be gifted with an exceptionally hardy constitution."

Fantasies of being unique and physically superior; take him to the other pole. "I'd like you to try something now. Will you put yourself into the mind of a man you contact in the Ramble and describe your encounter with him from his point of view?"

He turned toward her and for some moments regarded her without expression. Then he resumed his surveillance of the path. "I will not. Though I do have enough empathy with my quarry to enable me to hunt efficiently. I must draw the line at erasing the necessary distance that keeps prey and predator distinct.

"And now I think our ways part for today." He stood up, descended the hillside, and walked beneath some low-canopied trees, his tall back stooped, toward the Seventy-second Street entrance of the park.

Floria arose more slowly, aware suddenly of her shallow breathing and the sweat on her face. Back to reality or what remained of it. She looked at her watch. She was late for her next client.

Floria couldn't sleep that night. Barefoot in her bathrobe she paced the living room by lamplight. They had sat together on that hill as isolated as in her office—more so, because there was no Hilda and no phone. He was, she knew, very strong, and he had sat close enough to her to reach out for that paralyzing touch to the neck—

Just suppose for a minute that Weyland had been brazenly telling the truth all along, counting on her to treat it as a delusion because on the face of it the truth was inconceivable.

Jesus, she thought, if I'm thinking that way about him, this therapy is more out of control than I thought. What kind of therapist becomes an accomplice to the client's fantasy? A crazy therapist, that's what kind.

Frustrated and confused by the turmoil in her mind, she wandered into the workroom. By morning the floor was covered with sheets of newsprint, each broadly marked by her felt-tipped pen. Floria sat in the midst of them, gritty-eyed and hungry.

She often approached problems this way, harking back to art training: turn off the thinking, put hand to paper and see what the deeper, less verbally sophisticated parts of the mind have to offer. Now that her dreams had deserted her, this was her only access to those levels.

The newsprint sheets were covered with rough representations of Weyland's face and form. Across several of them were scrawled words: *"Dear Doug, your vampire is fine, it's your ex-therapist who's off the rails. Warning: Therapy can be dangerous to your health. Especially if you are the therapist. Beautiful vampire, awaken to me. Am I really ready to take on a legendary monster? Give up—refer this one out. Do your job—work is a good doctor."*

That last one sounded pretty good, except that doing her job was precisely what she was feeling so shaky about these days.

Here was another message: *"How come this attraction to someone so scary?"* Oh ho, she thought, is that a real feeling or an aimless reaction out of the body's early-morning hormone peak? You don't want to confuse honest libido with mere biological clockwork.

Deborah called. Babies cried in the background over the Scotch Symphony. Nick, Deb's husband, was a musicologist with fervent opinions on music and nothing else.

"We'll be in town a little later in the summer," Deborah said, "just for a few days at the end of July. Nicky has this seminar-convention thing. Of course, it won't be easy with the babies . . . I wondered if you might sort of coordinate your vacation so you could spend a little time with them?"

Baby-sit, that meant. Damn. Cute as they were and all that, damn! Floria gritted her teeth. Visits from Deb were difficult. Floria had been so proud of her bright, hard-driving daughter, and then suddenly Deborah had dropped her studies and rushed to embrace all the dangers that Floria had warned her against: a romantic, too-young marriage, instant breeding, no preparation for self-support, the works. Well, to each her own, but it was so wearing to have Deb around playing the empty-headed hausfrau.

"Let me think, Deb. I'd love to see all of you, but I've been considering spending a couple of weeks in Maine with your Aunt Nonnie." God knows I need a real vacation, she thought, though the peace and quiet up there is hard for a city kid like me to take for long. Still, Nonnie, Floria's younger sister, was good company. "Maybe you could bring the kids up there for a couple of days. There's room in that great barn of a place and of course Nonnie'd be happy to have you."

"Oh, no, Mom, it's so dead up there, it drives Nick crazy—don't tell Nonnie I said that. Maybe Nonnie could come down to the city instead. You could cancel a date or two and we could all go to Coney Island together, things like that."

Kid things, which would drive Nonnie crazy and Floria too before long. "I doubt she could manage," Floria said, "but I'll ask. Look, hon, if I do go up there, you and Nick and the kids could stay here at the apartment and save some money."

"We have to be at the hotel for the seminar," Deb said shortly. No doubt she was feeling just as impatient as Floria was by now. "And the kids haven't seen you for a long time—it would be really nice if you could stay in the city just for a few days."

"We'll try to work something out." Always working something out. Concord never comes naturally—first we have to butt heads and get pissed off. Each time you call I hope it'll be different, Floria thought.

Somebody shrieked for "oly," jelly that would be, in the background—Floria felt a sudden rush of warmth for them, her grandkids for God's sake. Having been a young mother herself, she was still young enough to really enjoy them (and to fight with Deb about how to bring them up).

Deb was starting an awkward goodbye. Floria replied, put the phone down, and sat with her head back against the flowered kitchen wallpaper, thinking, Why do I feel so rotten now? Deb and I aren't close, no comfort, seldom friends, though we were once. Have I said everything wrong, made her think I don't want to see her and don't care about her family? What does she want from me that I can't seem to give her? Approval? Maybe she thinks I still hold her marriage against her. Well, I do, sort of. What right have I to be crtical, me with my divorce? What terrible things would she say to me, would I say to

her, that we take such care not to say anything important
at all?

"I think today we might go into sex," she said.

Weyland responded dryly, "Might we indeed. Does it
titillate you to wring confessions of solitary vice from men
of mature years?"

Oh no you don't, she thought. You can't sidestep so
easily. "Under what circumstances do you find yourself
sexually aroused?"

"Most usually upon waking from sleep," he said
indifferently.

"What do you do about it?"

"The same as others do. I am not a cripple, I have
hands."

"Do you have fantasies at these times?"

"No. Women, and men for that matter, appeal to me
very little, either in fantasy or reality."

"Ah—what about female vampires?" she said, trying
not to sound arch.

"I know of none."

Of course: the neatest out in the book. "They're not
needed for reproduction, I suppose, because people who
die of vampire bites become vampires themselves."

He said testily, "Nonsense. I am not a communicable
disease."

So he had left an enormous hole in his construct. She
headed straight for it: "Then how does your kind reproduce?"

"I have no kind, so far as I am aware," he said, "and I
do not reproduce. Why should I, when I may live for centuries still, perhaps indefinitely? My sexual equipment is
clearly only detailed biological mimicry, a form of protective coloration." How beautiful, how simple a solution,
she thought, full of admiration in spite of herself. "Do I
occasionally detect a note of prurient interest in your
questions, Dr. Landauer? Something akin to stopping at
the cage to watch the tigers mate at the zoo?"

"Probably," she said, feeling her face heat. He had a
great backhand return shot there. "How do you feel
about that?"

He shrugged.

"To return to the point," she said. "Do I hear you saying that you have no urge whatever to engage in sexual intercourse with anyone?"

"Would you mate with your livestock?"

His matter-of-fact arrogance took her breath away. She said weakly, "Men have reportedly done so."

"Driven men. I am not driven in that way. My sex urge is of low frequency and is easily dealt with unaided —although I occasionally engage in copulation out of the necessity to keep up appearances. I am capable, but not —like humans—obsessed."

Was he sinking into lunacy before her eyes? "I think I hear you saying," she said, striving to keep her voice neutral, "that you're not just a man with a unique way of life. I think I hear you saying that you're not human at all."

"I thought that this was already clear."

"And that there are no others like you."

"None that I know of."

"Then—you see yourself as what? Some sort of mutation?"

"Perhaps. Or perhaps your kind are the mutation."

She saw disdain in the curl of his lip. "How does your mouth feel now?"

"The corners are drawn down. The feeling is contempt."

"Can you let the contempt speak?"

He got up and went to stand at the window, positioning himself slightly to one side as if to stay hidden from the street below.

"Edward," she said.

He looked back at her. "Humans are my food. I draw the life out of their veins. Sometimes I kill them. I am greater than they are. Yet I must spend my time thinking about their habits and their drives, scheming to avoid the dangers they pose—I hate them."

She felt the hatred like a dry heat radiating from him. God, he really lived all this! She had tapped into a furnace of feeling. And now? The sensation of triumph wavered, and she grabbed at a next move: hit him with reality now, while he's burning.

"What about blood banks?" she said. "Your food is commercially available, so why all the complication and danger of the hunt?"

"You mean I might turn my efforts to piling up a for-

tune and buying blood by the case? That would certainly
make for an easier, less risky life in the short run. I
could fit quite comfortably into modern society if I became just another consumer.

"However, I prefer to keep the mechanics of my survival firmly in my own hands. After all, I can't afford to
lose my hunting skills. In two hundred years there may be
no blood banks, but I will still need my food."

Jesus, you set him a hurdle and he just flies over it. Are
there no weaknesses in all this, has he no blind spots?
Look at his tension—go back to that. Floria said, "What
do you feel now in your body?"

"Tightness." He pressed his spread fingers to his ab-
domen.

"What are you doing with your hands?"

"I put my hands to my stomach."

"Can you speak for your stomach?"

" 'Feed me or die,' " he snarled.

Elated again, she closed in: "And for yourself, in answer?"

" 'Will you never be satisfied?' " He glared at her.
"You shouldn't seduce me into quarreling with the terms
of my own existence!"

"Your stomach is your existence," she paraphrased.

"The gut determines," he said harshly. "That first,
everything else after."

"Say, 'I resent . . . ' "

He held to a tense silence.

" 'I resent the power of my gut over my life,' " she said
for him.

He stood with an abrupt motion and glanced at his
watch, an elegant flash of slim silver on his wrist.
"Enough," he said.

That night at home she began a set of notes that would
never enter his file at the office, notes toward the proposed book.

Couldn't do it, couldn't get properly into the sex
thing with him. Everything shoots off in all directions. His vampire concept so thoroughly worked
out, find myself half believing sometimes—my own
childish fantasy-response to his powerful death-
avoidance, contact-avoidance fantasy. Lose profes-

sional distance every time—is that what scares me
about him? Don't really want to shatter his delusion
(my life a mess, what right to tear down other's
patterns?)—so see it as real? Wonder how much
of "vampirism" he acts out, how far, how often.
Something attractive in his purely selfish, predatory
stance—the lure of the great outlaw.

Told me today quite coolly about a man he killed
recently—inadvertently—by drinking too much
from him. *Is* it fantasy? Of course—the victim, he
thinks, was college student. Breathes there a professor who hasn't dreamed of murdering some rep-
resentative youth, retaliation for years of classroom
frustration? Speaks of teaching with acerbic humor—
amuses him to work at cultivating the minds of
those he regards strictly as bodies, containers of his
sustenance. He shows the alienness of full-blown
psychopathology, poor bastard, plus clean-cut logic.
Suggested he find another job (assuming his delusion
at least in part related to pressures at Cayslin); his
fantasy-persona, the vampire, more realistic than I
about job-switching:

"For a man of my apparent age it's not so easy to
make such a change in these tight times. I might
have to take a position lower on the ladder of 'success' as you people assess it." Status is important to
him? "Certainly. An eccentric professor is one thing;
an eccentric pipe-fitter, another. And I like good
cars, which are expensive to own and run." Then,
thoughtful addition, "Although there are advantages to a simpler, less visible life." He refuses to
discuss other "jobs" from former "lives." We are
deep into the fantasy—where the hell going? Damn
right I don't control the "games"—preplanned therapeutic strategies get whirled away as soon as we
begin. Nerve-wracking.

Tried again to have him take the part of his enemy-
victim, peasant with torch. Asked if he felt himself
rejecting that point of view? Frosty reply: "Naturally. The peasant's point of view is in no way my
own. I've been reading in your field, Dr. Landauer.
You work from the Gestalt orientation—" Origi-

nally yes, I corrected; eclectic now. "But you do
proceed from the theory that I am projecting some
aspect of my own feelings outward onto others,
whom I then treat as my victims. Your purpose
then must be to maneuver me into accepting as my
own the projected 'victim' aspect of myself. This in-
tegration is supposed to effect the freeing of energy
previously locked into maintaining the projection.
All this is an interesting insight into the nature of
ordinary human confusion, but I am not an ordinary
human, and I am not confused. I cannot afford confusion." Felt sympathy for him—telling me he's
afraid of having own internal confusions exposed in
therapy, too threatening. Keep chipping away at delusion, though with what prospect? It's so complex,
deep-seated.

Returned to his phrase "my apparent age." He as-
serts he has lived many human lifetimes, all details
forgotten, however, during periods of suspended
animation between lives. Perhaps sensing my
skepticism at such handy amnesia, grew cool and
distant, claimed to know little about the hibernation
process itself: "The essence of this state is that I
sleep through it—hardly an ideal condition for making scientific observations."

Edward thinks his body synthesizes vitamins,
minerals (as all our bodies synthesize vitamin D),
even proteins. Describes unique design he deduces in
himself: special intestinal microfauna plus super-
efficient body chemistry extracts enough energy to
live on from blood. Damn good mileage per
calorie, too. (Recall observable tension, first interview, at question about drinking—my note on possible alcohol problem!)

Speak for blood: " 'Lacking me, you have no
life. I flow to the heart's soft drumbeat through light-
less prisons of flesh. I am rich, I am nourishing, I
am difficult to attain.' " Stunned to find him positively
lyrical on subject of his "food." Drew attention to
whispering voice of blood. " 'Yes. I am secret,
hidden beneath the surface, patient, silent, steady.
I work unnoticed, an unseen thread of vitality running from age to age—beautiful, efficient, self-

renewing, self-cleansing, warm, filling—' " Could *see* him getting worked up. Finally he stood: "My appetite is pressing. I must leave you." And he did.

Sat and trembled for five minutes after.

New development (or new perception?): he sometimes comes across very unsophisticated about own feelings—lets me pursue subjects of extreme intensity and delicacy to him.

Asked him to daydream—a hunt. (Hands—mine— shaking now as I write. God. What a session.) He told of picking up a woman at poetry reading, 92nd Street Y—has N.Y.C. all worked out, circulates to avoid too much notice any one spot. Spoke easily, eyes shut without observable strain: chooses from audience a redhead in glasses, dress with drooping neckline (ease of access), no perfume (strong smells bother him). Approaches during intermission, encouraged to see her fanning away smoke of others' cigarettes—meaning she doesn't smoke, health sign. Agreed in not enjoying the reading, they adjourn together to coffee shop.

"She asks whether I'm a teacher," he says, eyes shut, mouth amused. "My clothes, glasses, manner all suggest this, and I emphasize the impression —it reassures. She's a copy editor for a publishing house. We talk about books. The waiter brings her a gummy-looking pastry. As a non-eater, I pay little attention to the quality of restaurants, so I must apologize to her. She waves this away—is engrossed, or pretending to be engrossed, in talk." A longish dialog between interested woman and Edward doing shy-lonesome-scholar act—dead wife, competitive young colleagues who don't understand him, quarrels in professional journals with big shots in his field—a version of what he first told me. She's attracted (of course—lanky, rough-cut elegance plus hints of vulnerability all very alluring, as intended). He offers to take her home.

Tension in his body at this point in narrative —spine clear of chair back, hands braced on thighs. "She settles beside me in the back of the cab, talking about problems of her own career—illegible manuscripts of Biblical length, mulish editors, suicidal authors—and I make comforting comments, I lean nearer and put my arm along the back of the seat, behind her shoulders. Traffic is heavy, we move slowly. There is time to make my meal here in the taxi and avoid a tedious extension of the situation into her apartment—if I move soon."

How do you feel?

"Eager," he says, voice husky. "My hunger is so roused I can scarcely restrain myself. A powerful hunger, not like yours—mine compels. I embrace her shoulders lightly, make kindly-uncle remarks, treading that fine line between the game of seduction she perceives and the game of friendly interest I pretend to affect. My real purpose underlies all: what I say, how I look, every gesture is part of the stalk. There is an added excitement, and fear, because I'm doing my hunting in the presence of a third person—behind the cabbie's head."

Could scarcely breathe. Studied him—intent face, masklike with closed eyes, nostrils slightly flared; legs tensed, hands clenched on knees. Whispering: "I press the place on her neck. She starts, sighs faintly, silently drops against me. In the stale stench of the cab's interior, with the ticking of the meter in my ears and the mutter of the radio—I take hold here, at the tenderest part of her throat. Sound subsides into the background—I feel the sweet blood beating under her skin, I taste salt at the moment before I—strike. My saliva thins her blood so that it flows out, I draw the blood into my mouth swiftly, swiftly, before she can wake, before we can arrive . . ."

Trailed off, sat back loosely in chair—saw him swallow. "Ah. I feed." Heard him sigh. Managed to ask about physical sensation. His low murmur, "Warm. Heavy, here—" touches his belly—"in a pleasant way. The good taste of blood, tart and rich, in my mouth . . ."

And then? A flicker of movement beneath his closed eyelids: "In time I am aware that the cabbie has glanced back once and has taken our—embrace for just that. I can feel the cab slowing, hear him move to turn off the meter. I withdraw, I quickly wipe my mouth on my handkerchief. I take her by the shoulders and shake her gently; does she often have these attacks, I inquire, the soul of concern. She comes around, bewildered, weak, thinks she has fainted. I give the driver extra money and ask him to wait. He looks intrigued—'What was that all about,' I can see the question in his face—but as a true New Yorker he won't expose his own ignorance by asking.

"I escort the woman to her front door, supporting her as she staggers. Any suspicion of me that she may entertain, however formless and hazy, is allayed by my stern charging of the doorman to see that she reaches her apartment safely. She grows embarrassed, thinks perhaps that if not put off by her 'illness' I would spend the night with her, which moves her to press upon me, unasked, her telephone number. I bid her a solicitous good night and take the cab back to my hotel, where I sleep."

No sex? No sex.

How did he feel about the victim as a person? "She was food."

This was his "hunting" of last night, he admits afterward, not a made-up dream. No boasting in it, just telling. Telling me! Think: I can go talk to Lucille, Mort, Doug, others about most of what matters to me. Edward has only me to talk to and that for a fee—what isolation! No wonder the stone, monumental face—only those long, strong lips (his point of contact, verbal and physical-in-fantasy, with world and with "food") are truly expressive. An exciting narration; uncomfortable to find I felt not only empathy but enjoyment. Suppose he picked up and victimized—even in fantasy—Deb or Hilda, how would I feel then?

Later: truth—I also found this recital sexually stirring. Keep visualizing how he looked finishing this "dream"—he sat very still, head up, look of thoughtful pleasure on his face. Like handsome intellectual listening to music.

Kenny showed up unexpectedly at Floria's office on Monday, bursting with malevolent energy. She happened to be free, so she took him—something was definitely up. He sat on the edge of his chair.

"I know why you're trying to unload me," he accused. "It's that new one, the tall guy with the snooty look—what is he, an old actor or something? Anybody could see he's got you itching for him."

"Kenny, when was it that I first spoke to you about terminating our work together?" she said patiently.

"Don't change the subject. Let me tell you, in case you don't know it: that guy isn't really interested, Doctor, because he's a fruit. A faggot. You want to know how I know?"

Oh Lord, she thought wearily, he's regressed to age ten. She could see that she was going to hear the rest whether she wanted to or not. What in God's name was the world like for Kenny, if he clung so fanatically to her despite her failure to help him?

"Listen, I knew right away there was something flaky about him, so I followed him from here to that hotel where he lives. I followed him the other afternoon too. He walked around like he does a lot, and then he went into one of those ritzy movie houses on Third that open early and show risqué foreign movies—you know, Japs cutting each other's things off and glop like that. This one was French, though.

"Well, there was a guy came in, a Madison Avenue type carrying his attaché case, taking a work break or something. Your man moved over and sat down behind him and reached out and sort of stroked the guy's neck, and the guy leaned back, and your man leaned forward and started nuzzling at him, you know—kissing him.

"I saw it. They had their heads together and they stayed like that a while. It was disgusting: complete strangers, without even 'hello.' The Madison Avenue guy just sat there with his head back looking zonked, you know, just swept away, and what he was doing with his hands under his raincoat in his lap I couldn't see, but I bet you can guess.

"And then your fruity friend got up and walked out. I did, too, and I hung around a little outside. After a while the Madison Avenue guy came out looking all sleepy and loose, like after you-know-what, and he wandered off on his own someplace.

"What do you think now?" he ended, on a high, triumphant note.

Her impulse was to slap his face the way she would

have slapped Deb-as-a-child for tattling. But this was a client, not a kid. God give me strength, she thought.

"Kenny, you're fired."

"You can't!" he squealed. "You can't! What will I— who can I—"

She stood up, feeling weak but hardening her voice. "I'm sorry. I absolutely cannot have a client who makes it his business to spy on other clients. You already have a list of replacement therapists from me."

He gaped at her in slack-jawed dismay, his eyes swimmy with tears.

"I'm sorry, Kenny. Call this a dose of reality therapy and try to learn from it. There are some things you simply will not be allowed to do." She felt better: it was done at last.

"I hate you!" He surged out of his chair, knocking it back against the wall. Threateningly he glared at the fish tank, but contenting himself with a couple of kicks at the nearest table leg, he stamped out.

Floria buzzed Hilda: "No more appointments for Kenny, Hilda. You can close his file."

"Whoopee," Hilda said.

Poor, horrid Kenny. Impossible to tell what would happen to him, better not to speculate or she might relent, call him back. She had encouraged him, really, by listening instead of shutting him up and throwing him out before any damage was done.

Was it damaging, to know the truth? In her mind's eye she saw a cream-faced young man out of a Black Thumb Vodka ad wander from a movie theater into daylight, yawning and rubbing absently at an irritation on his neck . . .

She didn't even look at the telephone on the table or think about whom to call, now that she believed. No, she was going to keep quiet about Dr. Edward Lewis Weyland, her vampire.

Hardly alive at staff meeting, clinic, yesterday— people asking what's the matter, fobbed them off. Settled down today. Had to, to face him.

Asked him what he felt were his strengths. He said speed, cunning, ruthlessness. Animal strengths, I said. What about imagination, or is that strictly human? He defended at once: not human only. Lion,

waiting at water hole where no zebra yet drinks,
thinks "Zebra—eat," therefore performs feat of
imagining event yet-to-come. Self experienced as
animal? Yes—reminded me that humans are also
animals. Pushed for his early memories; he objected: "Gestalt is here-and-now, not history-taking."
I insist, citing anomalous nature of his situation,
my own refusal to be bound by any one theoretical
framework. He defends tensely: "Suppose I became
lost there in memory, distracted from dangers of
the present, left unguarded from those dangers."

Speak for memory. He resists, but at length attempts it: " 'I am heavy with the multitudes of the
past.' " Fingertips to forehead, propping up all that
weight of lives. " 'So heavy, filling worlds of time
laid down eon by eon, I accumulate, I persist, I demand recognition. I am as real as the life around
you—more real, weightier, richer.' " His voice sinking, shoulders bowed, head in hands—I begin to
feel pressure at the back of my own skull. " 'Let
me in.' " Only a rough whisper now. " 'I offer beauty
as well as terror. Let me in.' " Whispering also, I
suggest he reply to his memory.

"Memory, you want to crush me," he groans.
"You would overwhelm me with the cries of animals,
the odor and jostle of bodies, old betrayals, dead
joys, filth and anger from other times—I must concentrate on the danger now. Let me be." All I can
take of this crazy conflict, I gabble us off onto something else. He looks up—relief?—follows my lead—
where? Rest of session a blank.

No wonder sometimes no empathy at all—a species boundary! He has to be utterly self-centered
just to keep balance—self-centeredness of an animal. Thought just now of our beginning, me trying
to push him to produce material, trying to control
him, manipulate—no way, no way; so here we are,
someplace else—I feel dazed, in shock, but stick
with it—it's real.

Therapy with a dinosaur, a Martian.

"You call me 'Weyland' now, not 'Edward.' " I said
first name couldn't mean much to one with no memory of being called by that name as a child, silly to

pretend it signifies intimacy where it can't. I think he knows now that I believe him. Without prompting, told me truth of disappearance from Cayslin. No romance; he tried to drink from a woman who worked there, she shot him, stomach and chest. Luckily for him, small-caliber pistol, and he was wearing a lined coat over three-piece suit. Even so, badly hurt. (Midsection stiffness I noted when he first came—he was still in some pain at that time.) He didn't "vanish"—fled, hid, was found by questionable types who caught on to what he was, sold him "like a chattel" to someone here in the city. He was imprisoned, fed, put on exhibition—very privately—for gain. Got away. "Do you believe any of this?" Never asked anything like that before, seems of concern to him now. I said my belief or lack of same was immaterial; remarked on hearing a lot of bitterness.

He steepled his fingers, looked brooding at me over tips: "I nearly died there. No doubt my purchaser and his diabolist friend still search for me. Mind you, I had some reason at first to be glad of the attentions of the people who kept me prisoner. I was in no condition to fend for myself. They brought me food and kept me hidden and sheltered, whatever their motives. There are always advantages . . ."

Silence today started a short session. Hunting poor last night, Weyland still hungry. Much restless movement, watching goldfish darting in tank, scanning bookshelves. Asked him to be books. " 'I am old and full of knowledge, well made to last long. You see only the title, the substance is hidden. I am a book that stays closed.' " Malicious twist of the mouth, not quite a smile: "This is a good game." Is he feeling threatened, too—already "opened" too much to me? Too strung out with him to dig when he's skimming surfaces that should be probed. Don't know how to *do* therapy with Weyland—just have to let things happen, hope it's good. But what's "good"? Aristotle? Rousseau? Ask Weyland what's good, he'll say "Blood."

Everything in a spin—these notes too confused,

too fragmentary—worthless for a book, just a mess, like me, my life. Tried to call Deb last night, cancel visit. Nobody home, thank God. Can't tell her to stay away—but damn it—do not need complications now!

Floria went down to Broadway with Lucille to get more juice, cheese and crackers for the clinic fridge. This week it was their turn to do the provisions, a chore that rotated among the staff. Their talk about grant proposals for the support of the clinic trailed off.

"Let's sit a minute," Floria said. They crossed to a traffic island in the middle of the avenue. It was a sunny afternoon, close enough to lunchtime so that the brigade of old people who normally occupied the benches had thinned out. Floria sat down and kicked a crumpled beer can and some greasy fast-food wrappings back under the bench.

"You look like hell but wide awake at least," Lucille commented.

"Things are still rough," Floria said. "I keep hoping to get my life under control so I'll have some energy left for Deb and Nick and the kids when they arrive, but I can't seem to do it. Group was awful last night—a member accused me afterward of having abandoned them all. I think I have, too. The professional messes and the personal are all related somehow, they run into each other. I should be keeping them apart so I can deal with them separately, but I can't. I can't concentrate, my mind is all over the place. Except with Dracula, who keeps me riveted with astonishment when he's in the office and bemused the rest of the time."

A bus roared by, shaking the pavement and the benches. Lucille waited until the noise faded. "Relax about the group. The others would have defended you if you'd been attacked during the session. They all understand, even if you don't seem to: it's the summer doldrums, people don't want to work, they expect you to do it all for them. But don't push so hard. You're not a shaman who can magic your clients back into health."

Floria tore two cans of juice out of a six-pack and handed one to her. On a street corner opposite, a violent argument broke out in typewriter-fast Spanish between two women. Floria sipped tinny juice and watched. She'd seen a guy last winter straddle another on that same corner and try to smash his brains out on the icy sidewalk. The old question again: What's crazy, what's health?

"It's a good thing you dumped Chubs, anyhow," Lucille said. "I don't know what finally brought that on, but it's definitely a move in the right direction. What about Count Dracula? You don't talk about him much anymore. I thought I diagnosed a yen for his venerable body."

Floria shifted uncomfortably on the bench and didn't answer. If only she could deflect Lucille's sharp-eyed curiosity.

"Oh," Lucille said. "I see. You really are hot—or at least warm. Has he noticed?"

"I don't think so. He's not on the lookout for that kind of response from me. He says sex with other people doesn't interest him, and I think he's telling the truth."

"Weird," Lucille said. "What about *Vampire on My Couch?* Shaping up all right?"

"It's shaky, like everything else. I'm worried that I don't know how things are going to come out. I mean, Freud's wolf-man case was a success, as therapy goes. Will my vampire case turn out successfully?"

She glanced at Lucille's puzzled face, made up her mind, and plunged ahead. "Luce, think of it this way: suppose, just suppose, that my Dracula is for real, an honest-to-God vampire—"

"Oh *shit!*" Lucille erupted in anguished exasperation. "Damn it, Floria, enough is enough—will you stop futzing around and get some help? Coming to pieces yourself and trying to treat this poor nut with a vampire fixation —how can you do him any good? No wonder you're worried about his therapy!"

"Please, just listen, help me think this out. My purpose can't be to cure him of what he is. Suppose vampirism isn't a defense he has to learn to drop? Suppose it's the core of his identity? Then what do I do?"

Lucille rose abruptly and marched away from her through a gap between the rolling waves of cabs and trucks. Floria caught up with her on the next block.

"Listen, will you? Luce, you see the problem? I don't need to help him see who and what he is, he knows that perfectly well, and he's not crazy, far from it—"

"Maybe not," Lucille said grimly, "but you are. Don't dump this junk on me outside of office hours, Floria. I don't spend my time listening to nut-talk unless I'm getting paid."

"Just tell me if this makes psychological sense to you: he's healthier than most of us because he's always true to his identity, even when he's engaged in deceiving others. A fairly narrow, rigorous set of requirements necessary to his survival—that *is* his identity, and it commands him completely. Anything extraneous could destroy him. To go on living, he has to act solely out of his own undistorted necessity, and if that isn't authenticity, what is? So he's healthy, isn't he?" She paused, feeling a sudden lightness in herself. "And that's the best sense I've been able to make of this whole business so far."

They were in the middle of the block. Lucille, who could not on her short legs outwalk Floria, turned on her suddenly. "What the hell do you think you're doing, calling yourself a therapist? For God's sake, Floria, don't try to rope me into this kind of professional irresponsibility. You're just dipping into your client's fantasies instead of helping him to handle them. That's not therapy, it's collusion. Have some sense! Admit you're over your head in troubles of your own, retreat to firmer ground—go get treatment for yourself!"

Floria angrily shook her head. When Lucille turned away and hurried on up the block toward the clinic, Floria let her go without trying to detain her.

Thought about Lucille's advice. After my divorce going back into therapy for a while did help, but now? Retreat again to being a client, like old days in training—so young, inadequate, defenseless then. Awful prospect. And I'd have to hand over W. to somebody else—who? I'm not up to handling him, can't cope, too anxious, yet with all that we do good therapy together somehow. I can't control, can only offer; he's free to take, refuse, use as suits, as far as he's willing to go. I serve as resource while he does own therapy—isn't that therapeutic ideal, free of "shoulds," "shouldn'ts?"

Saw ballet with Mort, lovely evening—time out from W.—talking, singing, pirouetting all the way

home, feeling safe as anything in the shadow of
Mort-mountain; rolled later with that humming
(off-key), sun-warm body. Today W. says he saw
me at Lincoln Center last night, avoided me because of Mort. W. is ballet fan! Started attending to
pick up victims, now also because dance puzzles
and pleases.

"When a group dances well, the meaning is easy
—the dancers make a visual complement to the
music, all their moves necessary, coherent, flowing.
When a gifted soloist performs, the pleasure of
making the moves is echoed in my own body. The
soloist's absorption is total, much like my own in the
actions of the hunt. But when a man and a woman
dance together, something else happens. Sometimes
one is hunter, one is prey, or they shift these roles
between them. Yet some other level of significance
exists—I suppose to do with sex—and I feel it—a
tugging sensation here—" touched his solar plexus
—"but I do not understand it."

Worked with his reactions to ballet. The response
he feels to pas de deux is a kind of pull, "like hunger but not hunger." Of course he's baffled—
Balanchine writes that the pas de deux is always a
love story between man and woman. W. isn't man,
isn't woman, yet the drama connects. His hands
hovering as he spoke, fingers spread toward each
other. Pointed this out. Body work comes easier to
him now: joined his hands, interlaced fingers,
spoke for hands without prompting: " 'We are similar, we want the comfort of like closing to like.' "
How would that be for him, to find—likeness, another of his kind? "Female?" Starts impatiently explaining how unlikely this is—No, forget sex and
pas de deux for now; just to find your like, another
vampire.

He springs up, agitated now. There are none, he
insists; adds at once, "But what would it be like?
What would happen? I fear it!" Sits again, hands
clenched. "I long for it."

Silence. He watches goldfish, I watch him. I with-
hold fatuous attempt to pin down this insight, if
that's what it is—what can I know about his insight? Suddenly he turns, studies me intently till I

lose my nerve, react, cravenly suggest that if I make him uncomfortable he might wish to switch to another therapist—

"Certainly not." More follows, all gold: "There is value to me in what we do here, Dr. Landauer, much against my earlier expectations. Although people talk appreciatively of honest speech they generally avoid it, and I myself have found scarcely any use for it at all. Your straightforwardness with me—and the straightforwardness you require in return—this is healthy in a life so dependent on deception as mine."

Sat there, wordless, much moved, thinking of what I don't show him—my upset life, seat-of-pants course with him and attendant strain, attraction to him—I'm holding out on him while he appreciates my honesty.

Hesitation, then lower-voiced, "Also, there are limits on my methods of self-discovery, short of turning myself over to a laboratory for vivisection. I have no others like myself to look at and learn from. Any tools that may help are worth much to me, and these games of yours are—potent." Other stuff besides, not important. Important: he moves me and he draws me and he keeps on coming back. Hang in if he does.

Bad night—Kenny's aunt called: no bill from me this month, so if he's not seeing me who's keeping an eye on him, where's he hanging out? Much implied blame for what *might* happen. Absurd, but shook me up: I did fail Kenny. Called off group this week also; too much.

No, it was a *good* night—first dream in months I can recall, contact again, with own depths—but disturbing. Dreamed myself in cab with W. in place of the woman from the Y. He put his hand not on my neck but breast—I felt intense sensual response in the dream, also anger and fear so strong they woke me.

Thinking about this: anyone leans toward him sexually, to him a sign his hunting technique has maneuvered prospective victim into range, maybe arouses his appetite for blood. *I don't want that.*

"She was food." I am not food, I am a person. No
thrill at languishing away in his arms in a taxi while
he drinks my blood—that's disfigured sex, masoch-
ism. My sex response in dream signaled to me I
would be his victim—I rejected that, woke up.

Mention of *Dracula* (novel). W. dislikes: meander-
ing, inaccurate, those absurd fangs. Says he himself
has a sort of needle under his tongue, used to pierce
skin. No offer to demonstrate, and no request from
me. I brightly brought up historical Vlad Dracul—
celebrated instance of Turkish envoys, who, upon
refusing to uncover to Vlad to show respect, were
killed by spiking their hats to their skulls. "Nonsense," snorts W. "A clever ruler would use very
small thumbtacks and dismiss the envoys to moan
about the streets of Varna holding their tacked
heads." First spontaneous play he's shown—took
head in hands and uttered plaintive groans, "Ow,
oh, ooh." I cracked up. W. reverted at once to usual
dignified manner: "You can see that this would
serve the ruler much more effectively as an object
lesson against rash pride."

Later, same light vein: "I know why I'm a vampire; why are you a therapist?" Off balance as
usual, said things about helping, mental health, etc.
He shook his head: "And people think of a vampire as arrogant! You want to perform cures in a
world which exhibits very little health of any kind
—and it's the same arrogance with all of you. This
one wants to be President or Class Monitor or Department chairman or Union Boss, another must be
first to fly to the stars or to transplant the human
brain, and on and on. As for me, I wish only to satisfy my appetite in peace."

And those of us whose appetite is for com-
petence, for effectiveness? Thought of Green,
treated eight years ago, went on to be indicted for
running a hellish "home" for aged. I had helped
him stay functional so he could destroy the helpless
for profit.

W. not my first predator, only most honest and
direct. Scared; not of attack by W., but of process
we're going through. I'm beginning to be up to it

(?), but still—utterly unpredictable, impossible to
handle or manage. Occasional stirrings of inward
choreographer that used to shape my work so
surely. Have I been afraid of that, holding it down
in myself, choosing mechanical manipulation instead? Not a choice with W.—thinking no good,
strategy no good, nothing left but instinct, clear and
uncluttered responses if I can find them. Have to be
my own authority with him, as he is always his own
authority with a world in which he's unique. So
work with W. not just exhausting—exhilarating too,
along with strain, fear.

Am I growing braver? Not much choice.

Park again today (air-conditioning out at office).
Avoiding Lucille's phone calls from clinic (very reassuring that she calls despite quarrel, but don't
want to take all this up with her again). Also meeting W. in open feels saner somehow—wild creatures
belong outdoors? Sailboat pond N. of 72nd, lots of
kids, garbage, one beautiful tall boat drifting. We
walked.

W. maintains he remembers no childhood, no
parents. I told him my astonishment, confronted by
someone who never had a life of the previous generation (even adopted parent) shielding him from
death—how naked we stand when the last shield
falls. Got caught in remembering a death dream of
mine, dream it now and then—couldn't concentrate,
got scared, spoke of it—a dog tumbled under a
passing truck, ejected to side of the road where it
lay unable to move except to lift head and shriek;
couldn't help. Shaking nearly to tears—remembered Mother got into dream somehow—had
blocked that at first. Didn't say it now. Tried to rescue situation, show W. how to work with a dream
(sitting in vine arbor near band shell, some privacy).

He focused on my obvious shakiness: "The air
vibrates constantly with the death cries of countless
animals large and small. What is the death of one
dog?" Leaned close, speaking quietly, instructing.
"Many creatures are dying in ways too dreadful to
imagine. I am part of the world; I listen to the pain.

You people claim to be above all that. You deafen yourselves with your own noise and pretend there's nothing else to hear. Then these screams enter your dreams, and you have to seek therapy because you have lost the nerve to listen."

Remembered myself, said, Be a dying animal. He refused: "You are the one who dreams this." I had a horrible flash, felt I was the dog—helpless, doomed, hurting—burst into tears. The great therapist, bringing her own hangups into session with client! Enraged with self, which did not help stop bawling.

W. disconcerted, I think; didn't speak. People walked past, glanced over, ignored us. W. said finally, "What is this?" Nothing, just the fear of death. "Oh, the fear of death. That's with me all the time. One must simply get used to it." Tears into laughter. Goddamn wisdom of the ages. He got up to go, paused: "And tell that stupid little man who used to precede me at your office to stop following me around. He puts himself in danger that way."

Kenny, damn it! Aunt doesn't know where he is, no answer on his phone. Idiot!

Sketching all night—useless. W. beautiful beyond the scope of line—the beauty of singularity, cohesion, rooted in absolute devotion to demands of his specialized body. In feeding (woman in taxi), utter absorption one wants from a man in sex—no scorekeeping, no fantasies, just hot urgency of appetite, of senses, the moment by itself.

His sleeves worn rolled back today to the elbows —strong, sculptural forearms, the long bones curved in slightly, suggest torque, leverage. How old?

Endurance: huge, rich cloak of time flows back from his shoulders like wings of a dark angel. All springs from, elaborates, the single, stark, primary condition: he is a predator who subsists on human blood. Harmony, strength, clarity, magnificence— all from that basic animal integrity. Of course I long for all that, here in the higgledy-piggledy hodgepodge of my life! Of course he draws me!

*   *   *

Wore no perfume today, deference to his keen, easily insulated sense of smell. He noticed at once, said curt thanks. Saw something bothering him, opened my mouth seeking desperately for right thing to say —up rose my inward choreographer, wide awake, and spoke plain from my heart: thinking on my floundering in some of our sessions—I am aware that you see this confusion of mine. I know you see by your occasional impatient look, sudden disengagement—yet you continue to reveal yourself to me (even shift our course yourself if it needs shifting and I don't do it). I think I know why. Because there's no place for you in world as you truly are. Because beneath your various façades your true self suffers; like all true selves, it wants, needs to be honored as real and valuable through acceptance by another. I try to be that other, but often you are beyond me.

He rose, paced to window, looked back, burning at me. "If I seem sometimes restless or impatient, Dr. Landauer, it's not because of any professional shortcomings of yours. On the contrary—you are all too effective. The seductiveness, the distraction of our—human contact worries me. I fear for the ruthlessness that keeps me alive."

Speak for ruthlessness. He shook his head. Saw tightness in shoulders, feet braced hard against floor. Felt reflected tension in my own muscles.

Prompted him: " 'I resent . . .' "

"I resent your pretension to teach me about myself! What will this work that you do here make of me? A predator paralyzed by an unwanted empathy with his prey? A creature fit only for a cage and keeper?" He was breathing hard, jaw set. I saw suddenly the truth of his fear: his integrity is not human, but my work is specifically human, designed to make humans more human—what if it does that to him? Should have seen it before, should have seen it. No place left to go: had to ask him, in small voice, Speak for my pretension.

"No!" Eyes shut, head turned away.

Had to do it: Speak for me.

W. whispered, "As to the unicorn, out of your own legends—'Unicorn, come lay your head in my lap while the hunters close in. You are a wonder, and for love of wonder I will tame you. You are pursued, but forget your pursuers, rest under my hand till they come and destroy you.' " Looked at me like steel: "Do you see? The more you involve yourself in what I am, the more you become the peasant with the torch!"

Two days later Doug came into town and had lunch with Floria.

He was a man of no outstanding beauty who was nevertheless attractive: he didn't have much chin and his ears were too big, but you didn't notice because of his air of confidence. His stability had been earned the hard way—as a gay man facing the straight world. Some of his strength had been attained with effort and pain in a group that Floria had run years earlier. A lasting affection had grown between herself and Doug. She was intensely glad to see him.

They ate near the clinic. "You look a little frayed around the the edges," Doug said. "I heard about Jane Fennerman's relapse—too bad."

"I've only been able to bring myself to visit her once since."

"Feeling guilty?"

She hesitated, gnawing on a stale breadstick. The truth was, she hadn't thought of Jane Fennerman in weeks. Finally she said, "I guess I must be."

Sitting back with his hands in his pockets, Doug chided her gently. "It's got to be Jane's fourth or fifth time into the nuthatch, and the others happened when she was in the care of other therapists. Who are you to imagine—to demand—that her cure lay in your hands? God may be a woman, Floria, but She is not you. I thought the whole point was some recognition of individual responsibility—you for yourself, the client for himself or herself."

"That's what we're always saying," Floria agreed. She felt curiously divorced from this conversation. It had an old-fashioned flavor: Before Weyland. She smiled a little.

The waiter ambled over. She ordered bluefish. The serving would be too big for her depressed appetite, but Doug wouldn't be satisfied with his customary order of salad (he never was) and could be persuaded to help out.

He worked his way around to Topic A. "When I called to set up this lunch, Hilda told me she's got a crush on Weyland. How are you and he getting along?"

"My God, Doug, now you're going to tell me this whole thing was to fix me up with an eligible suitor!" She winced at her own rather strained laughter. "How soon are you planning to ask Weyland to work at Cayslin again?"

"I don't know, but probably sooner than I thought a couple of months ago. We hear that he's been exploring an attachment to an anthropology department at a Western school, some niche where I guess he feels he can have less responsibility, less visibility, and a chance to collect himself. Naturally, this news is making people at Cayslin suddenly eager to nail him down for us. Have you a recommendation?"

"Yes," she said. "Wait."

He gave her an inquiring look. "What for?"

"Until he works more fully through certain stresses in the situation at Cayslin. Then I'll be ready to commit myself about him." The bluefish came. She pretended distraction: "Good God, that's too much fish for me. Doug, come on and help me out here."

Hilda was crouched over Floria's file drawer. She straightened up, looking grim. "Somebody's been in the office!"

What was this, had someone attacked her? The world took on a cockeyed, dangerous tilt. "Are you okay?"

"Yes, sure, I mean there are records that have been gone through. I can tell. I've started checking and so far it looks as if none of the files themselves are missing. But if any papers were taken out of them, that would be pretty hard to spot without reading through every folder in the place. Your files, Floria. I don't think anybody else's were touched."

Mere burglary; weak with relief, Floria sat down on one of the waiting-room chairs. But only her files? "Just my stuff, you're sure?"

Hilda nodded. "The clinic got hit, too. I called. They see some new-looking scratches on the lock of your file drawer over there. Listen, you want me to call the cops?"

"First check as much as you can, see if anything obvious is missing."

There was no sign of upset in her office. She found a phone message on her table: Weyland had canceled his next appointment. She knew who had broken into her files.

She buzzed Hilda's desk. "Hilda, let's leave the police out of it for the moment. Keep checking." She stood in the middle of the office, looking at the chair replacing the one he had broken, looking at the window where he had so often watched.

Relax, she told herself. There was nothing for him to find here or at the clinic.

She signaled that she was ready for the first client of the afternoon.

That evening she came back to the office after having dinner with friends. She was supposed to be helping set up a workshop for next month, and she'd been putting off even thinking about it, let alone doing any real work. She set herself to compiling a suggested bibliography for her section.

The phone light blinked.

It was Kenny, sounding muffled and teary. "I'm sorry," he moaned. "The medicine just started to wear off. I've been trying to call you everyplace. God, I'm so scared—he was waiting in the alley."

"Who was?" she said, dry-mouthed. She knew.

"Him. The tall one, the faggot—only he goes with women too, I've seen him. He grabbed me. He hurt me. I was lying there a long time. I couldn't do anything. I felt so funny—like floating away. Some kids found me. Their mother called the cops. I was so cold, so scared—"

"Kenny, where are you?"

He told her which hospital. "Listen, I think he's really crazy, you know? And I'm scared he might . . . you live alone . . . I don't know—I didn't mean to make trouble for you. I'm so scared."

God damn you, you meant exactly to make trouble for me, and now you've bloody well made it. She got him to ring for a nurse. By calling Kenny her patient and using "Dr." in front of her own name without qualifying the title she got some information: two broken ribs, mul-

tiple contusions, a badly wrenched shoulder, and a deep
cut on the scalp which Dr. Wells thought accounted for
the blood loss the patient had sustained. Picked up early
today, the patient wouldn't say who had attacked him.
You can check with Dr. Wells tomorrow, Dr.—?

Can Weyland think I've somehow sicked Kenny on
him? No, he surely knows me better than that. Kenny
must have brought this on himself.

She tried Weyland's number and then the desk at his
hotel. He had closed his account and gone, providing no
forwarding information other than the address of a university in New Mexico.

Then she remembered: this was the night Deb and
Nick and the kids were arriving. Oh, God. Next phone
call. The Americana was the hotel Deb had mentioned.
Yes, Mr. and Mrs. Nicholas Redpath were registered in
room whatnot. Ring, please.

Deb's voice came shakily on the line. "I've been trying
to call you." Like Kenny.

"You sound upset," Floria said, steadying herself for
whatever calamity had descended: illness, accident, as-
sault in the streets of the dark, degenerate city.

Silence, then a raggedy sob. "Nick's not here. I didn't
phone you earlier because I thought he still might come,
but I don't think he's coming, Mom." Bitter weeping.

"Oh, Debbie. Debbie, listen, you just sit tight, I'll be
right down there."

The cab ride took only a few minutes. Debbie was still
crying when Floria stepped into the room.

"I don't know, I don't know," Deb wailed, shaking her
head. "What did I do wrong? He went away a week ago,
to do some research, he said, and I didn't hear from him,
and half the bank money is gone—just half, he left me
half. I kept hoping . . . they say most runaways come
back in a few days or call up, they get lonely . . . I
haven't told anybody—I thought since we were supposed
to be here at this convention thing together, I'd better
come, maybe he'd show up. But nobody's seen him, and
there are no messages, not a word, nothing."

"All right, all right, poor Deb," Floria said, hugging
her.

"Oh God, I'm going to wake the kids with all this
howling." Deb pulled away, making a frantic gesture toward the door of the adjoining room. "It was so hard to

get them to sleep—they were expecting Daddy to be here, I kept telling them he'd be here." She rushed out into the hotel hallway. Floria followed, propping the door open with one of her shoes since she didn't know whether Deb had a key with her or not. They stood out there together, ignoring passersby, huddling over Deb's weeping.

"What's been going on between you and Nick?" Floria said. "Have you two been sleeping together lately?"

Deb let out a squawk of agonized embarrassment, "Mo-*ther!*" and pulled away from her. Oh, hell, wrong approach.

"Come on, I'll help you pack. We'll leave word you're at my place. Let Nick come looking for you." Floria firmly squashed down the miserable inner cry, How am I going to stand this?

"Oh, no, I can't move till morning now that I've got the kids settled down. Besides, there's one night's deposit on the rooms. Oh, Mom, what did I do?"

"You didn't do anything, hon," Floria said, patting her shoulder and thinking in some part of her mind, Oh boy, that's great, is that the best you can come up with in a crisis with all your training and experience? Your touted professional skills are not so hot lately, but this bad? Another part answered, Shut up, stupid, only an idiot does therapy on her own family. Deb's come to her mother, not to a shrink, so go ahead and be Mommy. If only Mommy had less pressure on her right now—but that was always the way: everything at once or nothing at all.

"Look, Deb, suppose I stay the night here with you."

Deb shook the pale, damp-streaked hair out of her eyes with a determined, grown-up gesture. "No, thanks, Mom. I'm so tired I'm just going to fall out now. You'll be getting a bellyful of all this when we move in on you tomorrow anyway. I can manage tonight, and besides—"

And besides, just in case Nick showed up, Deb didn't want Floria around complicating things; of course. Or in case the tooth fairy dropped by.

Floria restrained an impulse to insist on staying; an impulse, she recognized, that came from her own need not to be alone tonight. That was not something to load on Deb's already burdened shoulders.

"Okay," Floria said. "But look, Deb, I'll expect you to

call me up first thing in the morning, whatever happens."
And if I'm still alive, I'll answer the phone.

All the way home in the cab she knew with growing certainty that Weyland would be waiting for her there. He can't just walk away, she thought; he has to finish things with me. So let's get it over.

In the tiled hallway she hesitated, keys in hand. What about calling the cops to go inside with her? Absurd. You don't set the cops on a unicorn.

She unlocked and opened the door to the apartment and called inside, "Weyland! Where are you?"

Nothing. Of course not—the door was still open, and he would want to be sure she was by herself. She stepped inside, shut the door, and snapped on a lamp as she walked into the living room.

He was sitting quietly on a radiator cover by the street window, his hands on his thighs. His appearance here in a new setting, her setting, this faintly lit room in her home place, was startlingly intimate. She was sharply aware of the whisper of movement—his clothing, his shoe soles against the carpet underfoot, as he shifted his posture.

"What would you have done if I'd brought somebody with me?" she said unsteadily. "Changed yourself into a bat and flown away?"

"Two things I must have from you," he said. "One is the bill of health that we spoke of when we began, though not, after all, for Cayslin College. I've made other plans. The story of my disappearance has of course filtered out along the academic grapevine so that even two thousand miles from here people will want evidence of my mental soundness. Your evidence. I would type it myself and forge your signature, but I want your authentic tone and language. Please prepare a letter to the desired effect, addressed to these people."

He drew something white from an inside pocket and held it out. She advanced and took the envelope from his extended hand. It was from the Western anthropology department that Doug had mentioned at lunch.

"Why not Cayslin?" she said. "They want you there."

"Have you forgotten your own suggestion that I find another job? That was a good idea after all. Your reference will serve me best out there—with a copy for my personnel file at Cayslin, naturally."

She put her purse down on the seat of a chair and crossed her arms. She felt reckless—the effect of stress and weariness, she thought, but it was an exciting feeling.

"The receptionist at the office does this sort of thing for me," she said.

He pointed. "I've been in your study. You have a typewriter there, you have stationery with your letterhead, you have carbon paper."

"What was the second thing you wanted?"

"Your notes on my case."

"Also at the—"

"You know that I've already searched both your work places, and the very circumspect jottings in your file on me are not what I mean. Others must exist: more detailed."

"What makes you think that?"

"How could you resist?" He mocked her. "You have encountered nothing like me in your entire professional life, and never shall again. Perhaps you hope to produce an article someday, even a book—a memoir of something impossible that happened to you one summer. You're an ambitious woman, Dr. Landauer."

Floria squeezed her crossed arms tighter against herself to quell her shivering. "This is all just supposition," she said.

He took folded papers from his pocket: some of her thrown-aside notes on him, salvaged from the wastebasket. "I found these. I think there must be more. Whatever there is, give it to me, please."

"And if I refuse, what will you do? Beat me up the way you beat up Kenny?"

Weyland said calmly, "I told you he should stop following me. This is serious now. There are pursuers who intend me ill—my former captors, of whom I told you. Whom do you think I keep watch for? No records concerning me must fall into their hands. Don't bother protesting to me your devotion to confidentiality. There is a man named Alan Reese who would take what he wants and be damned to your professional ethics. So I must destroy all evidence you have about me before I leave the city."

Floria turned away and sat down by the coffee table,

trying to think beyond her fear. She breathed deeply against the fright trembling in her chest.

"I see," he said dryly, "that you won't give me the notes; you don't trust me to take them and go. You see some danger."

"All right, a bargain," she said. "I'll give you whatever I have on your case if in return you promise to go straight out to your new job and keep away from Kenny and my offices and anybody connected with me—"

He was smiling slightly as he rose from the seat and stepped soft-footed toward her over the rug. "Bargains, promises, negotiations—all foolish, Dr. Landauer. I want what I came for."

She looked up at him. "But then how can I trust you at all? As soon as I give you what you want—"

"What is it that makes you afraid—that you can't render me harmless to you? What a curious concern you show suddenly for your own life and the lives of those around you! You are the one who led me to take chances in our work together—to explore the frightful risks of self-revelation. Didn't you see in the air between us the brilliant shimmer of those hazards? I thought your business was not smoothing the world over but adventuring into it, discovering its true nature, and closing valiantly with everything jagged, cruel, and deadly."

In the midst of her terror the inner choreographer awoke and stretched. Floria rose to face the vampire.

"All right, Weyland, no bargains. I'll give you freely what you want." Of course she couldn't make herself safe from him—or make Kenny or Lucille or Deb or Doug safe—any more than she could protect Jane Fennerman from the common dangers of life. Like Weyland, some dangers were too strong to bind or banish. "My notes are in the workroom—come on, I'll show you. As for the letter you need, I'll type it right now and you can take it away with you."

She sat at the typewriter arranging paper, carbon sheets, and white-out, and feeling the force of his presence. Only a few feet away, just at the margin of the light from the gooseneck lamp by which she worked, he leaned against the edge of the long table that was twin to the table in her office. Open in his large hands was the notebook she had given him from the table drawer.

When he moved his head over the notebook's pages, his glasses glinted.

She typed the heading and the date. How surprising, she thought, to find that she had regained her nerve here, and now. When you dance as the inner choreographer directs, you act without thinking, not in command of events but in harmony with them. You yield control, accepting the chance that a mistake might be part of the design. The inner choreographer is always right but often dangerous: giving up control means accepting the possibility of death. What I feared I have pursued right here to this moment in this room.

A sheet of paper fell out of the notebook. Weyland stooped and caught it up, glanced at it. "You had training in art?" Must be a sketch.

"I thought once I might be an artist," she said.

"What you chose to do instead is better," he said. "This making of pictures, plays, all art, is pathetic. The world teems with creation, most of it unnoticed by your kind just as most of the deaths are unnoticed. What can be the point of adding yet another tiny gesture? Even you, these notes—for what, a moment's celebrity?"

"You tried it yourself," Floria said. "The book you edited, *Notes on a Vanished People.*" She typed: ". . . temporary dislocation resulting from a severe personal shock . . ."

"That was professional necessity, not creation," he said in the tone of a lecturer irritated by a question from the audience. With disdain he tossed the drawing on the table. "Remember, I don't share your impulse toward artistic gesture—your absurd frills—"

She looked up sharply. "The ballet, Weyland. Don't lie." She typed: ". . . exhibits a powerful drive toward inner balance and wholeness in a difficult life situation. The steadying influence of an extraordinary basic integrity . . ."

He set the notebook aside. "My feeling for ballet is clearly some sort of aberration. Do you sigh to hear a cow calling in a pasture?"

"There are those who have wept to hear whales singing in the ocean."

He was silent, his eyes averted.

"This is finished," she said. "Do you want to read it?"

He took the letter. "Good," he said at length. "Sign it,

please. And type an envelope for it." He stood closer, but out of arm's reach, while she complied. "You seem less frightened."

"I'm terrified but not paralyzed," she said and laughed, but the laugh came out a gasp.

"Fear is useful. It has kept you at your best throughout our association. Have you a stamp?"

Then there was nothing to do but take a deep breath, turn off the gooseneck lamp, and follow him back into the living room. "What now, Weyland?" she said softly. "A carefully arranged suicide so that I have no chance to retract what's in that letter or to reconstruct my notes?"

At the window again, always on watch at the window, he said, "Your doorman was sleeping in the lobby. He didn't see me enter the building. Once inside, I used the stairs, of course. The suicide rate among therapists is notoriously high. I looked it up."

"You have everything all planned?"

The window was open. He reached out and touched the metal grille that guarded it. One end of the grille swung creaking outward into the night air, like a gate opening. She visualized him sitting there waiting for her to come home, his powerful fingers patiently working the bolts at that side of the grille loose from the brick-and-mortar window frame. The hair lifted on the back of her neck.

He turned toward her again. She could see the end of the letter she had given him sticking palely out of his jacket pocket.

"Floria," he said meditatively. "An unusual name—is it after the heroine of Sardou's *Tosca*. At the end, doesn't she throw herself to her death from a high castle wall? People are careless about the names they give their children. I will not drink from you—I hunted today, and I fed. Still, to leave you living . . . is too dangerous."

A fire engine tore past below, siren screaming. When it had gone Floria said, "Listen, Weyland, you said it yourself: I can't make myself safe from you—I'm not strong enough to shove you out the window instead of being shoved out myself. Must you make yourself safe from me? Let me say this to you, without promises, demands, or pleadings: I will not go back on what I wrote in that letter. I will not try to recreate my notes. I mean it. Be content with that."

"You tempt me to it," he murmured after a moment, "to go from here with you still alive behind me for the remainder of your little life—to leave woven into Dr. Landauer's quick mind those threads of my own life that I pulled for her . . . I want to be able sometimes to think of you thinking of me. But the risk is very great."

"Sometimes it's right to let the dangers live, to give them their place," she urged. "Didn't you tell me yourself a little while ago how risk makes us more heroic?"

He looked amused. "Are you instructing me in the virtues of danger? You are brave enough to know something, perhaps, about that, but I have studied danger all my life."

"A long, long life with more to come," she said, desperate to make him understand and believe her. "Not mine to jeopardize. There's no torch-brandishing peasant here; we left that behind long ago. Remember when you spoke for me? You said, 'For love of wonder.' That was true."

He leaned to turn off the lamp near the window. She thought that he had made up his mind, and that when he straightened it would be to spring.

But instead of terror locking her limbs, from the inward choreographer came a rush of warmth and energy into her muscles and an impulse to turn toward him. Out of a harmony of desires she said swiftly, "Weyland, come to bed with me."

She saw his shoulders stiffen against the dim square of the window, his head lift in scorn. "You know I can't be bribed that way," he said contemptuously. "What are you up to? Are you one of those who come into heat at the sight of an upraised fist."

"My life hasn't twisted me that badly, thank God," she retorted. "And if you've known all along how scared I've been, you must have sensed my attraction to you too, so you know it goes back to—very early in our work. But we're not at work now, and I've given up being 'up to' anything. My feeling is real—not a bribe, or a ploy, or a kink. No 'love me now, kill me later,' nothing like that. Understand me, Weyland: if death is your answer, then let's get right to it—come ahead and try."

Her mouth was dry as paper. He said nothing and

made no move; she pressed on. "But if you can let me go, if we can simply part company here, then this is how I would like to mark the ending of our time together. This is the completion I want. Surely you feel something, too—curiosity at least?"

"Granted, your emphasis on the expressiveness of the body has instructed me," he admitted, and then he added lightly, "Isn't it extremely unprofessional to proposition a client?"

"Extremely, and I never do; but this, now, feels right. For you to indulge in courtship that doesn't end in a meal would be unprofessional, too, but how would it feel to indulge anyway—this once? Since we started, you've pushed me light-years beyond my profession. Now I want to travel all the way with you, Weyland. Let's be unprofessional together."

She turned and went into the bedroom, leaving the lights off. There was a reflected light, cool and diffuse, from the glowing night air of the great city. She sat down on the bed and kicked off her shoes. When she looked up, he was in the doorway.

Hesitantly, he halted a few feet from her in the dimness, then came and sat beside her. He would have lain down in his clothes, but she said quietly, "You can undress. The front door's locked and there isn't anyone here but us. You won't have to leap up and flee for your life."

He stood again and began to take off his clothes, which he draped neatly over a chair. He said, "Suppose I am fertile with you; could you conceive?"

By her own choice any such possibility had been closed off after Deb. She said, "No," and that seemed to satisfy him.

She tossed her own clothes onto the dresser.

He sat down next to her again, his body silvery in the reflected light and smooth, lean as a whippet and as roped with muscle. His cool thigh pressed against her own fuller, warmer one as he leaned across her and carefully deposited his glasses on the bedtable. Then he turned toward her, and she could just make out two puckerings of tissue on his skin: bullet scars, she thought, shivering.

He said, "But why do I wish to do this?"

"Do you?" She had to hold herself back from touching him.

"Yes." He stared at her. "How did you grow so real? The more I spoke to you of myself, the more real you became."

"No more speaking, Weyland," she said gently. "This is body work."

He lay back on the bed.

She wasn't afraid to take the lead. At the very least she could do for him as well as he did for himself, and at the most, much better. Her own skin was darker than his, a shadowy contrast where she browsed over his body with her hands. Along the contours of his ribs she felt knotted places, hollows—old healings, the tracks of time. The tension of his muscles under her touch and the sharp sound of his breathing stirred her. She lived the fantasy of sex with an utter stranger; there was no one in the world so much a stranger as he. Yet there was no one who knew him as well as she did, either. If he was unique, so was she, and so was their confluence here.

The vividness of the moment inflamed her. His body responded. His penis stirred, warmed, and thickened in her hand. He turned on his hip so that they lay facing each other, he on his right side, she on her left. When she moved to kiss him he swiftly averted his face: of course—to him, the mouth was for feeding. She touched her fingers to his lips, signifying her comprehension.

He offered no caresses but closed his arms around her, his hands cradling the back of her head and neck. His shadowed face, deep-hollowed under brow and cheekbone, was very close to hers. From between the parted lips that she must not kiss his quick breath came, roughened by groans of pleasure. At length he pressed his head against hers, inhaling deeply; taking her scent, she thought, from her hair and skin.

He entered her, hesitant at first, probing slowly and tentatively. She found this searching motion intensely sensuous, and clinging to him all along his sinewy length she rocked with him through two long, swelling waves of sweetness. Still half submerged, she felt him strain tight against her, she heard him gasp through his clenched teeth.

Panting, they subsided and lay loosely interlocked. His head was tilted back; his eyes were closed. She had no desire to stroke him or to speak with him, only to rest spent against his body and absorb the sounds of his breathing, her breathing.

He did not lie long to hold or be held. Without a word he disengaged his body from hers and got up. He moved quietly about the bedroom, gathering his clothing, his shoes, the drawings, the notes from the workroom. He dressed without lights. She listened in silence from the center of a deep repose.

There was no leavetaking. His tall figure passed and repassed the dark rectangle of the doorway, and then he was gone. The latch on the front door clicked shut.

Floria thought of getting up to secure the deadbolt. Instead she turned on her stomach and slept.

She woke as she remembered coming out of sleep as a youngster—peppy and clearheaded.

"Hilda, let's give the police a call about that break-in. If anything ever does come of it, I want to be on record as having reported it. You can tell them we don't have any idea who did it or why. And please make a photocopy of this letter carbon to send to Doug Sharpe up at Cayslin. Then you can put the carbon into Weyland's file and close it."

Hilda sighed. "Well, he was too old anyway."

He wasn't, my dear, but never mind.

In her office Floria picked up the morning's mail from her table. Her glance strayed to the window where Weyland had so often stood. God, she was going to miss him; and God, how good it was to be restored to plain working days.

Only not yet. Don't let the phone ring, don't let the world push in here now. She needed to sit alone for a little and let her mind sort through the images left from . . . from the pas de deux with Weyland. It's the notorious morning after, old dear, she told herself; just where have I been dancing, anyway?

In a clearing in the enchanted forest with the unicorn, of course, but not the way the old legends have it. According to them, hunters set a virgin to attract the unicorn by her chastity so they can catch and kill him. My unicorn was the chaste one, come to think of it, and this lady meant no treachery. No, Weyland and I met hidden from the hunt, to celebrate a private mystery of our own. . . .

Your mind grappled with my mind, my dark leg over your silver one, unlike closing with unlike across whatever likeness may be found: your memory pressing on my thoughts, my words drawing out your words in which you may recognize your life, my smooth palm gliding down your smooth flank . . .

Why, this will make me cry, she thought, blinking. And for what? Does an afternoon with the unicorn have any meaning for the ordinary days that come later? What has this passage with Weyland left me? Have I anything in my hands now besides the morning's mail?

What I have in my hands is my own strength, because I had to reach deep to find the strength to match him.

She put down the letters, noticing how on the backs of her hands the veins stood, blue shadows, under the thin skin. How can these hands be strong? Time was beginning to wear them thin and bring up the fragile inner structure in clear relief. That was the meaning of the last parent's death: that the child's remaining time has a limit of its own.

But not for Weyland. No graveyards of family dead lay behind him, no obvious and implacable ending of his own span threatened him. Time has to be different for a creature of an enchanted forest, as morality has to be different. He was a predator and a killer formed for a life of centuries, not decades; of secret singularity, not the busy hum of the herd. Yet his strength, suited to that nonhuman life, had revived her own strength. Her hands were slim, no longer youthful, but she saw now that they were strong enough.

For what? She flexed her fingers, watching the tendons slide under the skin. Strong hands don't have to clutch. They can simply open and let go.

She dialed Lucille's extension at the clinic.

"Luce? Sorry to have missed your calls lately. Listen, I want to start making arrangements to transfer my practice for a while. You were right, I do need a break, just as all my friends have been telling me. Will you pass the word for me to the staff over there today? Good, thanks. Also, there's the workshop coming up next month. . . . Yes. Are you kidding? They'd love to have you in my place. You're not the only one who's noticed that I've been falling apart, you know. It's awfully soon—can you manage, do you think? Luce, you are a brick and a lifesaver and all that stuff that means I'm very, very grateful."

Not so terrible, she thought, but only a start. Everything else remained to be dealt with. The glow of euphoria couldn't carry her for long. Already, looking down, she noticed jelly on her blouse, just like old times, and she didn't even remember having breakfast. If you want to keep the strength you've found in all this, you're going to have to get plenty of practice being strong. Try a tough one now.

She phoned Deb. "Of course you slept late, so what? I did, too, so I'm glad you didn't call and wake me up. Whenever you're ready—if you need help moving uptown from the hotel, I can cancel here and come down. . . . Well, call if you change your mind. I've left a house key for you with my doorman.

"And listen, hon, I've been thinking—how about all of us going up together to Nonnie's over the weekend? Then when you feel like it maybe you'd like to talk about what you'll do next. Yes, I've already started setting up some free time for myself. Think about it, love. Talk to you later."

Kenny's turn. "Kenny, I'll come by during visiting hours this afternoon."

"Are you okay?" he squeaked.

"I'm okay. But I'm not your mommy, Ken, and I'm not going to start trying to hold the big bad world off you again. I'll expect you to be ready to settle down seriously and choose a new therapist for yourself. We're going to get that done today once and for all. Have you got that?"

After a short silence he answered in a desolate voice, "All right."

"Kenny, nobody grown up has a mommy around to take care of things for them and keep them safe—not even me. You just have to be tough enough and brave enough yourself. See you this afternoon."

How about Jane Fennerman? No, leave it for now, we are not Wonder Woman, we can't handle that stress today as well.

Too restless to settle down to paperwork before the day's round of appointments began, she got up and fed the goldfish, then drifted to the window and looked out over the city. Same jammed-up traffic down there, same dusty summer park stretching away uptown—yet not the same city, because Weyland no longer hunted there. Nothing like him moved now in those deep, grumbling streets. She would never come upon anyone there as alien as he —and just as well. Let last night stand as the end, unique and inimitable, of their affair. She was glutted with strangeness and looked forward frankly to sharing again in Mort's ordinary human appetite.

And Weyland—how would he do in that new and distant hunting ground he had found for himself? Her own balance had been changed. Suppose his once perfect, solitary equilibrium had been altered too? Perhaps he had spoiled it by involving himself too intimately with another being—herself. And then he had left her alive—a terrible risk. Was this a sign of his corruption at her hands?

"Oh, no," she whispered fiercely, focusing her vision on her reflection in the smudged window glass. Oh, no, I am not the temptress. I am not the deadly female out of legends whose touch defiles the hitherto unblemished being, her victim. If Weyland found some human likeness in himself, that had to be in him to begin with. Who said he was defiled anyway? Newly discovered capacities can be either strengths or weaknesses, depending on how you use them.

Very pretty and reassuring, she thought grimly; but it's pure cant. Am I going to retreat now into mechanical analysis to make myself feel better?

She heaved open the window and admitted the sticky summer breath of the city into the office. There's your enchanted forest, my dear, all nitty-gritty and not one flake of fairy dust. You've survived here, which means you can see straight when you have to. Well, you have to now.

Has he been damaged? No telling yet, and you can't stop living while you wait for the answers to come in. I don't know all that was done between us, but I do know who did it: I did it, and he did it, and neither of us withdrew until it was done. We were joined in a rich complicity— he in the wakening of some flicker of humanity in himself, I in keeping and, yes, enjoying the secret of his implacable blood hunger. What that complicity means for each of us can only be discovered by getting on with living and watching for clues from moment to moment. His business is to continue from here, and mine is to do the same, without guilt and without resentment. Doug was right: the aim is individual responsibility. From that effort, not even the lady and the unicorn are exempt.

Shaken by a fresh upwelling of tears, she thought bitterly, Moving on is easy enough for Weyland; he's used to it, he's had more practice. What about me? Yes, be selfish, woman—if you haven't learned that, you've learned damn little.

The Japanese say that in middle age you should leave the claims of family, friends, and work, and go ponder the meaning of the universe while you still have the chance. Maybe I'll try just existing for a while, and letting grow in its own time my understanding of a universe that includes Weyland—and myself—among its possibilities.

Is that looking out for myself? Or am I simply no longer fit for living with family, friends, and work? Have *I* been damaged by *him*—by my marvelous, murderous monster?

Damn, she thought, I wish he were here, I wish we could talk about it. The light on her phone caught her eye; it was blinking the quick flashes that meant Hilda was signaling the imminent arrival of—not Weyland—the day's first client.

We're each on our own now, she thought, shutting the window and turning on the air-conditioner.

But think of me sometimes, Weyland, thinking of you.

Here is a quietly evocative story of a reunion of four high school friends in the clear night of Wyoming. Perhaps ghosts can be seen more easily in clean air . . . and some of them may be older than the human race itself.

Edward Bryant has won two Nebula Awards for his short fiction. His books include *Cinnabar, Among the Dead, Wyoming Sun* and *Phoenix Without Ashes*, the latter written in collaboration with Harlan Ellison.

STRATA

Edward Bryant

SIX HUNDRED MILLION YEARS IN THIRTY-TWO miles. Six hundred million years in fifty-one minutes. Steve Mavrakis traveled in time—courtesy of the Wyoming Highway Department. The epochs raveled between Thermopolis and Shoshoni. The Wind River rambled down its canyon with the Burlington Northern tracks cut into the west walls, and the two-lane blacktop, U.S. 20, sliced into the east. Official signs driven into the verge of the highway proclaimed the traveler's progress:

**DINWOODY FORMATION
TRIASSIC
185–225 MILLION YEARS**

**BIG HORN FORMATION
ORDOVICIAN
440–500 MILLION YEARS**

**FLATHEAD FORMATION
CAMBRIAN
500–600 MILLION YEARS**

The mileposts might have been staked into the canyon rock under the pressure of millennia. They were there for those who could not read the stone.

Tonight Steve ignored the signs. He had made this run many times before. Darkness hemmed him. November clawed when he cracked the window to exhaust Camel smoke from the Chevy's cab. The CB crackled occasionally and picked up exactly nothing.

The wind blew—that was nothing unusual. Steve felt himself hypnotized by the skiff of snow skating across the pavement in the glare of his brights. The snow swirled only inches above the blacktop, rushing across like surf sliding over the black packed sand of a beach.

Time's predator hunts.

Years scatter before her like a school of minnows surprised. The rush of her passage causes eons to eddy. Wind sweeps down the canyon with the roar of combers breaking on the sand. The moon, full and newly risen, exerts its tidal force.

Moonlight flashes on the slash of teeth.

And Steve snapped alert, realized he had traversed the thirty-two miles, crossed the flats leading into Shoshoni, and was approaching the junction with U.S. 26. Road hypnosis? he thought. Safe in Shoshoni, but it was scary. He didn't remember a goddamned minute of the trip through the canyon! Steve rubbed his eyes with his left hand and looked for an open cafe with coffee.

It hadn't been the first time.

All those years before, the four of them had thought they were beating the odds. On a chill night in June, high on a mountain edge in the Wind River Range, high on more than mountain air, the four of them celebrated graduation. They were young and clear-eyed: ready for the world. That night they knew there were no other people for miles. Having learned in class that there were 3.8 human beings per square mile in Wyoming, and as *four*, they thought the odds outnumbered.

Paul Onoda, eighteen. He was Sansei—third-generation Japanese-American. In 1942, before he was conceived, his parents were removed with eleven thousand other Japanese-Americans from California to the Heart Mountain Relocation Center in northern Wyoming. Twelve members and three generations of the Onodas shared one of four hundred and sixty-five crowded, tar-papered barracks for the next four years. Two died. Three more were born. With their fellows, the Onodas helped farm eighteen hundred acres of virgin agricultural land. Not all of them had been Japanese gardeners or truck farmers in California, so the pharmacists and the teachers and the carpenters learned agriculture. They used irrigation to bring in water. The crops flourished. The Nisei not directly involved with farming were dispatched from camp to be seasonal farm laborers. An historian later laconically noted that "Wyoming benefited by their presence."

Paul remembered the Heart Mountain camps only through the memories of his elders, but those recollections were vivid. After the war, most of the Onodas stayed on in Wyoming. With some difficulty, they bought farms. The family invested thrice the effort of their neighbors, and prospered.

Paul Onoda excelled in the classrooms and starred on the football field of Fremont High School. Once he overheard the president of the school board tell the coach, "By God but that little Nip can run!" He thought about that; and kept on running ever faster.

More than a few of his classmates secretly thought he had it all. When prom time came in his senior year, it did not go unnoticed that Paul had an extraordinarily handsome appearance to go with his brains and athlete's body. In and around Fremont, a great many concerned parents admonished their white daughters to find a good excuse if Paul asked them to the prom.

Carroll Dale, eighteen. It became second nature early on to explain to people first hearing her given name that it had two r's and two l's. Both sides of her family went back four generations in this part of the country and one of her bequests had been a proud mother. Cordelia Carroll had pride, one daughter, and the desire to see the Hereford Carrolls retain *some* parity with the Angus Dales. After all, the Carrolls had been ranching on Bad Water Creek before John Broderick Okie illuminated his Lost Cabin castle with carbide lights. That was when Teddy Roosevelt had been president and it was when all the rest of the cattlemen in Wyoming, including the Dales, had been doing their accounts at night by kerosene lanterns.

Carroll grew up to be a good roper and a better rider. Her apprenticeship intensified after her older brother, her only brother, fatally shot himself during deer season. She wounded her parents when she neither married a man who would take over the ranch nor decided to take over the ranch herself.

She grew up slim and tall, with ebony hair and large,

dark, slightly oblique eyes. Her father's father, at family
Christmas dinners, would overdo the whiskey in the egg-
nog and make jokes about Indians in the woodpile until
her paternal grandmother would tell him to shut the hell
up before she gave him a goodnight the hard way, with a
rusty sickle and knitting needles. It was years before Carroll knew what her grandmother meant.

In junior high, Carroll was positive she was eight feet
tall in Lilliput. The jokes hurt. But her mother told her to
be patient, that the other girls would catch up. Most of the
girls didn't; but in high school the boys did, though they
tended to be tongue-tied in the extreme when they talked
to her.

She was the first girl president of her school's National
Honor Society. She was a cheerleader. She was the vale-
dictorian of her class and earnestly quoted John F.
Kennedy in her graduation address. Within weeks of graduation, she eloped with the captain of the football team.

It nearly caused a lynching.

Steve Mavrakis, eighteen. Courtesy allowed him to be
called a native despite his birth eighteen hundred miles to
the east. His parents, on the other hand, had settled in
the state after the war when he was less than a year old.
Given another decade, the younger native-born might
grudgingly concede their adopted roots; the old-timers,
never.

Steve's parents had read Zane Grey and *The Virginian*,
and had spent many summers on dude ranches in upstate
New York. So they found a perfect ranch on the Big Horn
River and started a herd of registered Hereford. They
went broke. They refinanced and aimed at a breed of
inferior beef cattle. The snows of '49 killed those. Steve's
father determined that sheep were the way to go—all
those double and triple births. Very investment-effective.
The sheep sickened, or stumbled and fell into creeks
where they drowned, or panicked like turkeys and smoth-
ered in heaps in fenced corners. It occurred then to the
Mavrakis family that wheat doesn't stampede. All the
fields were promptly hailed out before what looked to be
a bounty harvest. Steve's father gave up and moved into
town where he put his Columbia degree to work by getting
a job managing the district office for the Bureau of Land
Management.

All of that taught Steve to be wary of sure things.

And occasionally he wondered at the dreams. He had been very young when the blizzards killed the cattle. But though he didn't remember the National Guard dropping hay bales from silver C-47's to cattle in twelve-foot-deep snow, he did recall for years after, the nightmares of herds of nonplused animals futilely grazing barren ground before towering, slowly grinding bluffs of ice.

The night after the crop-duster terrified the sheep and seventeen had expired in paroxysms, Steve dreamed of brown men shrilling and shaking sticks and stampeding tusked, hairy monsters off a precipice and down hundreds of feet to a shallow stream.

Summer nights Steve woke sweating, having dreamed of reptiles slithering and warm waves beating on a ragged beach in the lower pasture. He sat straight, staring out the bedroom window, watching the giant ferns waver and solidify back into cottonwood and boxelder.

The dreams came less frequently and vividly as he grew older. He willed that. They altered when the family moved into Fremont. After a while Steve still remembered he had had the dreams, but most of the details were forgotten.

At first the teachers in Fremont High School thought he was stupid. Steve was administered tests and thereafter was labeled an underachiever. He did what he had to do to get by. He barely qualified for the college-bound program, but then his normally easy-going father made threats. People asked him what he wanted to do, to be, and he answered honestly that he didn't know. Then he took a speech class. Drama fascinated him and he developed a passion for what theater the school offered. He played well in *Our Town* and *Arsenic and Old Lace* and *Harvey*. The drama coach looked at Steve's average height and average looks and average brown hair and eyes, and suggested at a hilarious cast party that he become either a character actor or an FBI agent.

By this time, the only dreams Steve remembered were sexual fantasies about girls he didn't dare ask on dates.

Ginger McClelland, seventeen. Who could blame her for feeling out of place? Having been born on the cusp of the school district's regulations, she was very nearly a year younger than her classmates. She was short. She thought of herself as a dwarf in a world of Snow Whites. It didn't help that her mother studiously offered words like "petite" and submitted that the most gorgeous clothes would fit a wearer under five feet, two inches. Secretly she hoped that in one mysterious night she would bloom and grow great, long legs like Carroll Dale. That never happened.

Being an exile in an alien land didn't help either. Though Carroll had befriended her, she had listened to the president of the pep club, the queen of Job's Daughters, and half the girls in her math class refer to her as "the foreign exchange student." Except that she would never be repatriated home; at least not until she graduated. Her parents had tired of living in Cupertino, California, and thought that running a Coast to Coast hardware franchise in Fremont would be an adventurous change of pace. They loved the open spaces, the mountains and free-flowing streams. Ginger wasn't so sure. Every day felt like she had stepped into a time machine. All the music on the radio was old. The movies that turned up at the town's one theater—forget it. The dancing at the hops was grotesque.

Ginger McClelland was the first person in Fremont—and perhaps in all of Wyoming—to use the adjective "bitchin'." It got her sent home from study hall and caused a bemused and confusing interview between her parents and the principal.

Ginger learned not to trust most of the boys who invited her out on dates. They all seemed to feel some sort of perverse mystique about California girls. But she did accept Steve Mavrakis's last-minute invitation to prom. He seemed safe enough.

Because Carroll and Ginger were friends, the four of them ended up double-dating in Paul's father's old maroon DeSoto that was customarily used for hauling fence posts and wire out to the pastures. After the dance, when nearly everyone else was heading to one of the sanctioned after-prom parties, Steve affably obtained from an older intermediary an entire case of chilled Hamms. Ginger and Carroll had brought along jeans and Pendleton shirts in their overnight bags and changed in the restroom at the Chevron station. Paul and Steve took off their white jackets and donned windbreakers. Then they all drove up into the Wind River Range. After they ran out of road, they hiked. It was very late and very dark. But they found a high mountain place where they huddled and drank beer and talked and necked.

They heard the voice of the wind and nothing else beyond that. They saw no lights of cars or outlying cabins. The isolation exhilarated them. They *knew* there was no one else for miles.

That was correct so far as it went.

Foam hissed and sprayed as Paul applied the church key to the cans. Above and below them, the wind broke like waves on the rocks.

"Mavrakis, you're going to the university, right?" said Paul.

Steve nodded in the dim moonlight, added, "I guess so."

"What're you going to take?" said Ginger, snuggling close and burping slightly on her beer.

"I don't know; engineering, I guess. If you're a guy and in the college-bound program, you end up taking engineering. So I figure that's it."

Paul said, "What kind?"

"Don't know. Maybe aerospace. I'll move to Seattle and make spaceships."

"That's neat," said Ginger. "Like in *The Outer Limits*. I wish we could get that here."

"You ought to be getting into hydraulic engineering," said Paul. "Water's going to be really big business not too long from now."

"I don't think I want to stick around Wyoming."

Carroll had been silently staring out over the valley. She turned back toward Steve and her eyes were pools of darkness. "You're really going to leave?"

"Yeah."

"And never come back?"

"Why should I?" said Steve. "I've had all the fresh air and wide open spaces I can use for a lifetime. You know something? I've never even seen the ocean." And yet he had felt the ocean. He blinked. "I'm getting out."

"Me too," said Ginger. "I'm going to stay with my aunt and uncle in L.A. I think I can probably get into the University of Southern California journalism school."

"Got the money?"

"I'll get a scholarship."

"Aren't you leaving?" Steve said to Carroll.

"Maybe," she said. "Sometimes I think so, and then I'm not so sure."

"You'll come back even if you do leave," said Paul. "All of you'll come back."

"Says who?" Steve and Ginger said it almost simultaneously.

"The land gets into you," said Carroll. "Paul's dad says so."

"That's what he says." They all heard anger in Paul's voice. He opened another round of cans. Ginger tossed her empty away and it clattered down the rocks, a noise jarringly out of place.

"Don't," said Carroll. "We'll take the empties down in a sack."

"What's wrong?" said Ginger. "I mean, I . . ." Her voice trailed off and everyone was silent for a minute, two minutes, three.

"What about you, Paul?" said Carroll. "Where do you want to go? What do you want to do?"

"We talked about—" His voice sounded suddenly tightly controlled. "Damn it, I don't know now. If I come back, it'll be with an atomic bomb—"

"What?" said Ginger.

Paul smiled. At least Steve could see white teeth gleaming in the night. "As for what I want to do—" He leaned forward and whispered in Carroll's ear.

She said, "Jesus, Paul! We've got witnesses."

"What?" Ginger said again.

"Don't even ask you don't want to know." She made it one continuous sentence. Her teeth also were visible in the near-darkness. "Try that and I've got a mind to goodnight you the hard way."

"What're you talking about?" said Ginger.

Paul laughed. "Her grandmother."

"Charlie Goodnight was a big rancher around the end of the century," Carroll said. "He trailed a lot of cattle up from Texas. Trouble was, a lot of his expensive bulls weren't making out so well. Their testicles—"

"Balls," said Paul.

"—kept dragging on the ground," she continued. "The bulls got torn up and infected. So Charlie Goodnight started getting his bulls ready for the overland trip with some amateur surgery. He'd cut into the scrotum and shove the balls up into the bull. Then he'd stitch up the sack and there'd be no problem with high-centering. That's called goodnighting."

"See," said Paul. "There are ways to beat the land."

Carroll said, " 'You do what you've got to.' That's a quote from my father. Good pioneer stock."

"But not to me." Paul pulled her close and kissed her.

"Maybe we ought to explore the mountain a little," said Ginger to Steve. "You want to come with me?" She stared at Steve who was gawking at the sky as the moonlight suddenly vanished like a light switching off.

"Oh my God."

"What's wrong?" she said to the shrouded figure.

"I don't know—I mean, nothing, I guess." The moon appeared again. "Was that a cloud?"

"I don't see a cloud," said Paul, gesturing at the broad belt of stars. "The night's clear."

"Maybe you saw a UFO," said Carroll, her voice light.

"You okay?" Ginger touched his face. "Jesus, you're shivering." She held him tightly.

Steve's words were almost too low to hear. "It swam across the moon."

"What did?"

"I'm cold too," said Carroll. "Let's go back down." Nobody argued. Ginger remembered to put the metal cans into a paper sack and tied it to her belt with a hair-ribbon. Steve didn't say anything more for a while, but the others all could hear his teeth chatter. When they were halfway down, the moon finally set beyond the valley rim. Farther on, Paul stepped on a loose patch of shale, slipped, cursed, began to slide beyond the lip of the sheer rock face. Carroll grabbed his arm and pulled him back.

"Thanks, Irene." His voice shook slightly, belying the tone of the words.

"Funny," she said.

"I don't get it," said Ginger.

Paul whistled a few bars of the song.

"Good night," said Carroll. "You do what you've got to."

"And I'm grateful for that." Paul took a deep breath. "Let's get down to the car."

When they were on the winding road and driving back toward Fremont, Ginger said, "What did you see up there, Steve?"

"Nothing. I guess I just remembered a dream."

"Some dream." She touched his shoulder. "You're still cold."

Carroll said, "So am I."

Paul took his right hand off the wheel to cover her hand. "We all are."

"I feel all right." Ginger sounded puzzled.

All the way into town, Steve felt he had drowned.

The Amble Inn in Thermopolis was built in the shadow of Round Top Mountain. On the slope above the Inn, huge letters formed from whitewashed stones proclaimed: WORLD'S LARGEST MINERAL HOT SPRING. Whether at night or noon, the inscription invariably reminded Steve of the Hollywood Sign. Early in his return from California, he realized the futility of jumping off the second letter "O." The stones were laid flush with the steep pitch of the ground. Would-be suicides could only roll down the hill until they collided with the log side of the Inn.

On Friday and Saturday nights, the parking lot of the Amble Inn was filled almost exclusively with four-wheel-drive vehicles and conventional pickups. Most of them had black-enameled gun racks up in the rear window behind the seat. Steve's Chevy had a rack, but that was because he had bought the truck used. He had considered buying a toy rifle, one that shot caps or rubber darts, at a Penney's Christmas catalog sale. But like so many other projects, he never seemed to get around to it.

Tonight was the first Saturday night in June and Steve had money in his pocket from the paycheck he had cashed at Safeway. He had no reason to celebrate; but then he had no reason not to celebrate. So a little after nine he went to the Amble Inn to drink tequila hookers and listen to the music.

The Inn was uncharacteristically crowded for so early in the evening, but Steve secured a small table close to the dance floor when a guy threw up and his girl had to take him home. Dancing couples covered the floor though the headline act, Mountain Flyer, wouldn't be on until eleven. The warmup group was a Montana band called the Great Falls Dead. They had more enthusiasm than talent, but they had the crowd dancing.

Steve threw down the shots, sucked limes, licked the salt, intermittently tapped his hand on the table to the music, and felt vaguely melancholy. Smoke drifted around him, almost as thick as the special-effects fog in a bad horror movie. The Inn's dance floor was in a dim, domed room lined with rough pine.

He suddenly stared, puzzled by a flash of near-recognition. He had been watching one dancer in particular, a tall woman with curly raven hair, who had danced with a succession of cowboys. When he looked at her face, he thought he saw someone familiar. When he looked at her body, he wondered whether she wore underwear beneath the wide-weave red knit dress.

The Great Falls Dead launched into "Good-hearted Woman" and the floor was instantly filled with dancers. Across the room, someone squealed, "Willieee!" This time the woman in red danced very close to Steve's table. Her high cheekbones looked hauntingly familiar. Her hair, he thought. If it were longer—She met his eyes and smiled at him.

The set ended, her partner drifted off toward the bar, but she remained standing beside his table. "Carroll?" he said. *"Carroll?"*

She stood there smiling, with right hand on hip. "I wondered when you'd figure it out."

Steve shoved his chair back and got up from the table. She moved very easily into his arms for a hug. "It's been a long time."

"It has."

"Fourteen years? Fifteen?

"Something like that."

He asked her to sit at his table, and she did. She sipped a Campari-and-tonic as they talked. He switched to beer. The years unreeled. The Great Falls Dead pounded out a medley of country standards behind them.

". . . I never should have married, Steve. I was wrong for Paul. He was wrong for me."

". . . *thought* about getting married. I met a lot of women in Hollywood, but nothing ever seemed . . ."

". . . all the wrong reasons . . ."

". . . did end up in a few made-for-TV movies. Bad stuff. I was always cast as the assistant manager in a hold-up scene, or got killed by the werewolf right near the beginning. I think there's something like ninety percent of all actors who are unemployed at any given moment, so I said . . ."

"You really came back here? How long ago?"

". . . to hell with it . . ."

"How long ago?"

". . . and sort of slunk back to Wyoming. I don't know. Several years ago. How long were you married, anyway?"

". . . a year more or less. What do you do here?"

". . . beer's getting warm. Think I'll get a pitcher . . ."

"What do you do here?"

". . . better cold. Not much. I get along. You . . ."

". . . lived in Taos for a time. Then Santa Fe. Bummed around the Southwest a lot. A friend got me into photography. Then I was sick for a while and that's when I tried painting . . ."

". . . landscapes of the Tetons to sell to tourists?"

"Hardly. A lot of landscapes, but trailer camps and oil fields and perspective vistas of I-80 across the Red Desert . . ."

"I tried taking pictures once . . . kept forgetting to load the camera."

". . . and then I ended up half-owner of a gallery called Good Stuff. My partner throws pots."

". . . must be dangerous . . ."

". . . located on Main Street in Lander . . ."

". . . going through. Think maybe I've seen it . . ."

"What do you do here?"

The comparative silence seemed to echo as the band ended its set. "Very little," said Steve. "I worked a while as a hand on the Two Bar. Spent some time being a roughneck in the fields up around Buffalo. I've got a pickup—do some short-hauling for local businessmen who don't want to hire a trucker. I ran a little pot. Basically I do whatever I can find. You know."

Carroll said, "Yes, I do know." The silence lengthened between them. Finally she said, "Why did you come back here? Was it because—"

"—because I'd failed?" Steve said, answering her hesitation. He looked at her steadily. "I thought about that a long time. I decided that I could fail anywhere, so I came back here." He shrugged. "I love it. I love the space."

"A lot of us have come back," Carroll said. "Ginger and Paul are here."

Steve was startled. He looked at the tables around them.

"Not tonight," said Carroll. "We'll see them tomorrow. They want to see you."

"Are you and Paul back—" he started to say.

She held up her palm. "Hardly. We're not exactly on the same wavelength. That's one thing that hasn't changed. He ended up being the sort of thing you thought you'd become."

Steve didn't remember what that was.

"Paul went to the School of Mines in Colorado. Now he's the chief exploratory geologist for Enerco."

"Not bad," said Steve.

"Not good," said Carroll. "He spent a decade in South America and the Middle East. Now he's come home. He wants to gut the state like a fish."

"Coal?"

"And oil. And uranium. And gas. Enerco's got its thumb in a lot of holes." Her voice had lowered, sounded angry. "Anyway, we *are* having a reunion tomorrow, of sorts. And Ginger will be there."

Steve poured out the last of the beer. "I thought for sure she'd be in California."

"Never made it," said Carroll. "Scholarships fell through. Parents said they wouldn't support her if she went back to the west coast—you know how 105% converted immigrants are. So Ginger went to school in Laramie and ended up with a degree in elementary education. She did marry a grad student in journalism. After the divorce five or six years later, she let him keep the kid."

Steve said, "So Ginger never got to be an ace reporter."

"Oh, she did. Now she's the best writer the *Salt Creek Gazette*'s got. Ginger's the darling of the environmental groups and the bane of the energy corporations."

"I'll be damned," he said. He accidentally knocked his glass off the table with his forearm. Reaching to retrieve the glass, he knocked over the empty pitcher.

"I think you're tired," Carroll said.

"I think you're right."

"You ought to go home and sack out." He nodded. "I don't want to drive all the way back to Lander tonight," Carroll said. "Have you got room for me?"

When they reached the small house Steve rented off Highway 170, Carroll grimaced at the heaps of dirty clothes making soft moraines in the living room. "I'll clear off the couch," she said. "I've got a sleeping bag in my car."

Steve hesitated a long several seconds and lightly touched her shoulders. "You don't have to sleep on the couch unless you want to. All those years ago . . . You know, all through high school I had a crush on you? I was too shy to say anything."

She smiled and allowed his hands to remain. "I thought you were pretty nice too. A little shy, but cute. Definitely an underachiever."

They remained standing, faces a few inches apart, for a while longer. "Well?" he said.

"It's been a lot of years," Carroll said. "I'll sleep on the couch."

Steve said disappointedy, "Not even out of charity?"

"Especially not for charity." She smiled. "But don't discount the future." She kissed him gently on the lips.

Steve slept soundly that night. He dreamed of sliding endlessly through a warm, fluid current. It was not a nightmare. Not even when he realized he had fins rather than hands and feet.

Morning brought rain.

When he awoke, the first thing Steve heard was the drumming of steady drizzle on the roof. The daylight outside the window was filtered gray by the sheets of water running down the pane. Steve leaned off the bed, picked up his watch from the floor, but it had stopped. He heard the sounds of someone moving in the living room and called, "Carroll? You up?"

Her voice was a soft contralto. "I am."

"What time is it?"

"Just after eight."

Steve started to get out of bed, but groaned and clasped the crown of his head with both hands. Carroll stood framed in the doorway and looked sympathetic. "What time's the reunion?" he said.

"When we get there. I called Paul a little earlier. He's tied up with some sort of meeting in Casper until late afternoon. He wants us to meet him in Shoshoni."

"What about Ginger?"

They both heard the knock on the front door. Carroll turned her head away from the bedroom, then looked back at Steve. "Right on cue," she said. "Ginger didn't want to wait until tonight." She started for the door, said back over her shoulder, "You might want to put on some clothes."

Steve pulled on his least filthy jeans and a sweatshirt labeled AMAX TOWN-LEAGUE VOLLEYBALL across the chest. He heard the front door open and close, and words murmured in his living room. When he exited the bedroom he found Carroll talking on the couch with a short blonde stranger who only slightly resembled the long-ago image he'd packed in his mind. Her hair was long and tied in a braid. Her gaze was direct and more inquisitive than he remembered.

She looked up at him and said, "I like the mustache. You look a hell of a lot better now than you ever did then."

"Except for the mustache," Steve said, "I could say the same."

The two women seemed amazed when Steve negotiated the disaster area that was the kitchen and extracted eggs and Chinese vegetables from the refrigerator. He served the huge omelet with toast and freshly brewed coffee in the living room. They all balanced plates on laps.

"Do you ever read the Gazoo?" said Ginger.

"Gazoo?"

"The Salt Creek Gazette," said Carroll.

Steve said, "I don't read any papers."

"I just finished a piece on Paul's company," said Ginger.

"Enerco?" Steve refilled all their cups.

Ginger shook her head. "A wholly owned subsidiary called Native American Resources. Pretty clever, huh?" Steve looked blank. "Not a poor damned Indian in the whole operation. The name's strictly sham while the company's been picking up an incredible number of mineral leases on the reservation. Paul's been concentrating on an enormous new coal field his teams have mapped out. It makes up a substantial proportion of the reservation's best lands."

"Including some sacred sites," said Carroll.

"Nearly a million acres," said Ginger. "That's more than a thousand square miles."

"The land's never the same," said Carroll, "no matter how much goes into reclamation, no matter how tight the EPA says they are."

Steve looked from one to the other. "I may not read the papers," he said, "but no one's holding a gun to anyone else's head."

"Might as well be," said Ginger. "If the Native American Resources deal goes through, the mineral royalty payments to the tribes'll go up precipitously."

Steve spread his palms. "Isn't that good?"

Ginger shook her head vehemently. "It's economic blackmail to keep the tribes from developing their own resources at their own pace."

"Slogans," said Steve. "The country needs the energy. If the tribes don't have the investment capital—"

"They *would* if they weren't bought off with individual royalty payments."

"The tribes have a choice—"

"—with the prospect of immediate gain dangled in front of them by NAR."

"I can tell it's Sunday," said Steve, "even if I haven't been inside a church door in fifteen years. I'm being preached at."

"If you'd get off your ass and think," said Ginger, "nobody'd have to lecture you."

Steve grinned. "I don't think with my ass."

"Look," said Carroll. "It's stopped raining."

Ginger glared at Steve. He took advantage of Carroll's diversion and said, "Anyone for a walk?"

The air outside was cool and rain-washed. It soothed tempers. The trio walked through the fresh morning along the cottonwood-lined creek. Meadowlarks sang. The rain front had moved far to the east; the rest of the sky was bright blue.

"Hell of a country, isn't it?" said Steve.

"Not for much longer if—" Ginger began.

"Gin," Carroll said warningly.

They strolled for another hour, angling south where they could see the hills as soft as blanket folds. The tree-lined draws snaked like green veins down the hillsides. The earth, Steve thought, seemed gathered, somehow expectant.

"How's Danny?" Carroll said to Ginger.

"He's terrific. Kid wants to become an astronaut." A grin split her face. "Bob's letting me have him for August."

"Look at that," said Steve, pointing.

The women looked. "I don't see anything," said Ginger.

"Southeast," Steve said. "Right above the head of the canyon."

"There—I'm not sure." Carroll shaded her eyes. "I thought I saw something, but it was just a shadow."

"Are you both blind?" said Steve, astonished. "There was something in the air. It was dark and cigar-shaped. It was there when I pointed."

"Sorry," said Ginger, "didn't see a thing."

"Well, it *was* there," Steve said, disgruntled.

Carroll continued to stare off toward the pass. "I saw it too, but just for a second. I didn't see where it went."

"Damnedest thing. I don't think it was a plane. It just sort of cruised along, and then it was gone."

"All I saw was something blurry," Carroll said. "Maybe it was a UFO."

"Oh, you guys," Ginger said with an air of dawning comprehension. "Just like prom night, right? Just a joke."

Steve slowly shook his head. "I really saw something then, and I saw this now. This time Carroll saw it too." She nodded in agreement. He tasted salt.

The wind started to rise from the north, kicking up early spring weeds that had already died and begun to dry.

"I'm getting cold," said Ginger. "Let's go back to the house."

"Steve," said Carroll, "you're shaking."

They hurried him back across the land.

PHOSPHORIC FORMATION
PERMIAN
225–270 MILLION YEARS

They rested for a while at the house; drank coffee and talked of the past, of what had happened and what had not. Then Carroll suggested they leave for the reunion. After a small confusion, Ginger rolled up the windows and locked her Saab and Carroll locked her Pinto.

"I hate having to do this," said Carroll.

"There's no choice any more," Steve said. "Too many people around now who don't know the rules."

The three of them got into Steve's pickup. In fifteen minutes they had traversed the doglegs of U.S. 20 through Thermopolis and crossed the Big Horn River. They passed the massive mobile home park with its trailers and RV's sprawling in carapaced glitter.

The flood of hot June sunshine washed over them as

they passed between the twin bluffs, red with iron, and descended into the miles and years of canyon.

TENSLEEP FORMATION
PENNSYLVANIAN
270–310 MILLION YEARS

On both sides of the canyon, the rock layers lay stacked like sections from a giant meat slicer. In the pickup cab, the passengers had been listening to the news on KTWO. As the canyon deepened, the reception faded until only a trickle of static came from the speaker. Carroll clicked the radio off.

"They're screwed," said Ginger.

"Not necessarily." Carroll, riding shotgun, stared out the window at the slopes of flowers the same color as the bluffs. "The BIA's still got hearings. There'll be another tribal vote."

Ginger said again, "They're screwed. Money doesn't just talk—it makes obscene phone calls, you know? Paul's got this one bagged. You know Paul—I know him just about as well. Son of a bitch."

"Sorry there's no music," said Steve. "Tape player busted a while back and I've never fixed it."

They ignored him. "Damn it," said Ginger. "It took almost fifteen years, but I've learned to love this country."

"I know that," said Carroll.

No one said anything for a while. Steve glanced to his right and saw tears running down Ginger's cheeks. She glared back at him defiantly. "There's Kleenexes in the glove box," he said.

MADISON FORMATION
MISSISSIPPIAN
310–350 MILLION YEARS

The slopes of the canyon became more heavily forested. The walls were all shades of green, deeper green where the runoff had found channels. Steve felt time collect in the great gash in the earth, press inward.

"I don't feel so hot," said Ginger.

"Want to stop for a minute?"

She nodded and put her hand over her mouth.

Steve pulled the pickup over across both lanes. The

Chevy skidded slightly as it stopped on the graveled turn-out. Steve turned off the key and in the sudden silence they heard only the light wind and the tickings as the Chevy's engine cooled.

"Excuse me," said Ginger. They all got out of the cab. Ginger quickly moved through the Canadian thistles and the currant bushes and into the trees beyond. Steve and Carroll heard her throwing up.

"She had an affair with Paul," Carroll said casually. "Not too long ago. He's an extremely attractive man." Steve said nothing. "Ginger ended it. She still feels the tension." Carroll strolled over to the side of the thistle patch and hunkered down. "Look at this."

Steve realized how complex the ground cover was. Like the rock cliffs, it was layered. At first he saw among the sunflowers and dead dandelions only the wild sweetpeas with their blue blossoms like spades with the edges curled inward.

"Look closer," said Carroll.

Steve saw the hundreds of tiny purple moths swooping and swarming only inches from the earth. The creatures were the same color as the low purple blooms he couldn't identify. Intermixed were white, bell-shaped blossoms with leaves that looked like primeval ferns.

"It's like going back in time," said Carroll. "It's a whole nearly invisible world we never see."

The shadow crossed them with an almost subliminal flash, but they both looked up. Between them and the sun had been the wings of a large bird. It circled in a tight orbit, banking steeply when it approached the canyon wall. The creature's belly was dirty white, muting to an almost-black on its back. It seemed to Steve that the bird's eye was fixed on them. The eye was a dull black, like unpolished obsidian.

"That's one I've never seen," said Carroll. "What is it?"

"I don't know. The wingspread's got to be close to ten feet. The markings are strange. Maybe it's a hawk? An eagle?"

The bird's beak was heavy and blunt, curved slightly. As it circled, wings barely flexing to ride the thermals, the bird was eerily silent, pelagic, fish-like.

"What's it doing?" said Carroll.

"Watching us?" said Steve. He jumped as a hand touched his shoulder.

"Sorry," said Ginger. "I feel better now." She tilted her head back at the great circling bird. "I have a feeling our friend wants us to leave."

They left. The highway wound around a massive curtain of stone in which red splashed down through the strata like dinosaur blood. Around the curve, Steve swerved to miss a deer dead on the pavement—half a deer, rather. The animal's body had been truncated cleanly just in front of its haunches.

"Jesus," said Ginger. "What did that?"

"Must have been a truck," said Steve. "An eighteen-wheeler can really tear things up when it's barreling."

Carroll looked back toward the carcass and the sky beyond. "Maybe that's what our friend was protecting."

GROS VENTRE FORMATION
CAMBRIAN
500–600 MILLION YEARS

"You know, this was all under water once," said Steve. He was answered only with silence. "Just about all of Wyoming was covered with an ancient sea. That accounts for a lot of the coal." No one said anything. "I think it was called the Sundance Sea. You know, like in the Sundance Kid. Some Exxon geologist told me that in a bar."

He turned and looked at the two women. And stared. And turned back to the road blindly. And then stared at them again. It seemed to Steve that he was looking at a double exposure, or a triple exposure, or—he couldn't count all the overlays. He started to say something, but could not. He existed in a silence that was also stasis, the death of all motion. He could only see.

Carroll and Ginger faced straight ahead. They looked as they had earlier in the afternoon. They also looked as they had fifteen years before. Steve saw them *in process*, lines blurred. And Steve saw skin merge with feathers, and then scales. He saw gill openings appear, vanish, reappear on textured necks.

And then both of them turned to look at him. Their heads swiveled slowly, smoothly. Four reptilian eyes watched him, unblinking and incurious.

Steve wanted to look away.

The Chevy's tires whined on the level blacktop. The sign read:

SPEED ZONE AHEAD
35 MPH

"Are you awake?" said Ginger.

Steve shook his head to clear it. "Sure," he said. "You know that reverie you sometimes get into when you're driving? When you can drive miles without consciously thinking about it, and then suddenly you realize what's happened?"

Ginger nodded.

"That's what happened."

The highway passed between modest frame houses, gas stations, motels. They entered Shoshoni.

There was a brand new WELCOME TO SHO-SHONI sign, as yet without bullet holes. The population figure had again been revised upward. "Want to bet on when they break another thousand?" said Carroll.

Ginger shook her head silently.

Steve pulled up to the stop sign. "Which way?"

Caroll said, "Go left."

"I think I've got it." Steve saw the half-ton truck with the Enerco decal and NATIVE AMERICAN RE-SOURCES DIVISION labeled below that on the door. It was parked in front of the Yellowstone Drugstore. "Home of the world's greatest shakes and malts," said Steve. "Let's go."

The interior of the Yellowstone had always reminded him of nothing so much as an old-fashioned pharmacy blended with the interior of the cafe in *Bad Day at Black Rock*. They found Paul at a table near the fountain counter in the back. He was nursing a chocolate malted.

He looked up, smiled, said, "I've gained four pounds this afternoon. If you'd been any later, I'd probably have become diabetic."

Paul looked far older than Steve had expected. Ginger and Carroll both appeared older than they had been a decade and a half before, but Paul seemed to have aged thirty years in fifteen. The star quarterback's physique had gone a bit to pot. His face was creased with lines emphasized by the leathery curing of skin that has been exposed years to wind and hot sun. Paul's hair, black as coal, was streaked with *firn* lines of glacial white. His eyes, Steve thought, look tremendously old.

He greeted Steve with a warm handclasp. Carroll received a gentle hug and a kiss on the cheek. Ginger got a warm smile and a hello. The four of them sat down and the fountain-man came over. "Chocolate all around?" Paul said.

"Vanilla shake," said Ginger.

Steve sensed a tension at the table that seemed to go beyond dissolved marriages and terminated affairs. He wasn't sure what to say after all the years, but Paul saved him the trouble. Smiling and soft-spoken, Paul gently interrogated him.

So what have you been doing with yourself?

Really?

How did that work out?

That's too bad; then what?

What about afterward?

And you came back?

How about since?

What do you do now?

Paul sat back in the scrolled-wire ice cream parlor chair, still smiling, playing with the plastic straw. He tied knots in the straw and then untied them.

"Do you know," said Paul, "that this whole complicated reunion of the four of us is not a matter of chance?"

Steve studied the other man. Paul's smile faded to impassivity. "I'm not that paranoid," Steve said. "It didn't occur to me."

"It's a setup."

Steve considered that silently.

"It didn't take place until after I had tossed the yarrow stalks a considerable number of times," said Paul. His voice was wry. "I don't know what the official company policy on such irrational behavior is, but it seemed right under extraordinary circumstances. I told Carroll where she could likely find you and left the means of contact up to her."

The two women waited and watched silently. Carroll's expression was, Steve thought, one of concern. Ginger looked apprehensive. "So what is it?" he said. "What kind of game am I in?"

"It's no game," said Carroll quickly. "We need you."

"You know what I thought ever since I met you in Miss Gorman's class?" said Paul. "You're not a loser. You've just needed some—direction."

Steve said impatiently, "Come on."

"It's true." Paul set down the straw. "Why we need you is because you seem to see things most others can't see."

Time's predator hunts.

Years scatter before her like a school of minnows surprised. The rush of her passage causes eons to eddy. Wind sweeps down the canyon with the roar of combers breaking on the sand. The moon, full and newly risen, exerts its tidal force.

Moonlight flashes on the slash of teeth.

She drives for the surface not out of rational decision. All blunt power embodied in smooth motion, she simply is what she is.

Steve sat without speaking. Finally he said vaguely, "Things."

"That's right. You see things. It's an ability."

"I don't know . . ."

"We think *we* do. We all remember that night after prom. And there were other times, back in school. None of us has seen you since we all played scatter-geese, but I've had the resources, through the corporation, to do some checking. The issue didn't come up until recently. In the last month, I've read your school records, Steve. I've read your psychiatric history."

"That must have taken some trouble," said Steve. "Should I feel flattered?"

"Tell him," said Ginger. "Tell him what this is all about."

"Yeah," said Steve. "Tell me."

For the first time in the conversation, Paul hesitated. "Okay," he finally said. "We're hunting a ghost in the Wind River Canyon."

"Say again?"

"That's perhaps poor terminology." Paul looked uncomfortable. "But what we're looking for is a presence, some sort of extranatural phenomenon."

" 'Ghost' is a perfectly good word," said Carroll.

"Better start from the beginning," said Steve.

When Paul didn't answer immediately, Carroll said, "I

know you don't read the papers. Ever listen to the radio?"

Steve shook his head. "Not much."

"About a month ago, an Enerco mineral survey party on the Wind River got the living daylights scared out of them."

"Leave out what they saw," said Paul. "I'd like to include a control factor."

"It wasn't just the Enerco people. Others have seen it, both Indians and Anglos. The consistency of the witnesses has been remarkable. If you haven't heard about this at the bars, Steve, you must have been asleep."

"I haven't been all that social for a while," said Steve. "I did hear that someone's trying to scare the oil and coal people off the reservation."

"Not someone," said Paul. "Some *thing*. I'm convinced of that now."

"A ghost," said Steve.

"A presence."

"There're rumors," said Carroll, "that the tribes have revived the Ghost Dance—"

"Just a few extremists," said Paul.

"—to conjure back an avenger from the past who will drive every white out of the county."

Steve knew of the Ghost Dance, had read of the Paiute mystic Wovoka who, in 1888, had claimed that in a vision the spirits had promised the return of the buffalo and the restoration to the Indians of their ancestral lands. The Plains tribes had danced assiduously the Ghost Dance to ensure this. Then in 1890 the U.S. government suppressed the final Sioux uprising and, except for a few scattered incidents, that was that. Discredited, Wovoka survived to die in the midst of the Great Depression.

"I have it on good authority," said Paul, "that the Ghost Dance was revived *after* the presence terrified the survey crew."

"That really doesn't matter," Carroll said. "Remember prom night? I've checked the newspaper morgues in Fremont and Lander and Riverton. There've been strange sightings for more than a century."

"That was then," said Paul. "The problem now is that the tribes are infinitely more restive, and my people are actually getting frightened to go out into the field." His voice took on a bemused tone. "Arab terrorists couldn't do it, civil wars didn't bother them, but a damned ghost is scaring the wits out of them—literally."

"Too bad," said Ginger. She did not sound regretful.

Steve looked at the three gathered around the table. He knew he did not understand all the details and nuancances of the love and hate and trust and broken affections. "I can understand Paul's concern," he said. "But why the rest of you?"

The women exchanged glances. "One way or another," said Carroll, "we're all tied together. I think it includes you, Steve."

"Maybe," said Ginger soberly. "Maybe not. She's an artist. I'm a journalist. We've all got our reasons for wanting to know more about what's up there."

"In the past few years," said Carroll, "I've caught a tremendous amount of Wyoming in my paintings. Now I want to capture this too."

Conversation languished. The soda-fountain man looked as though he were unsure whether to solicit a new round of malteds.

"What now?" Steve said.

"If you'll agree," said Paul, "we're going to go back up into the Wind River Canyon to search."

"So what am I? Some sort of damned occult Geiger counter?"

Ginger said, "It's a nicer phrase than calling yourself bait."

"Jesus," Steve said. "That doesn't reassure me much." He looked from one to the next. "Control factor or not, give me some clue to what we're going to look for."

Everyone looked at Paul. Eventually he shrugged and said, "You know the Highway Department signs in the canyon? The geological time chart you travel when you're driving U.S. 20?"

Steve nodded.

"We're looking for a relic of the ancient, inland sea."

After the sun sank in blood in the west, they drove north and watched dusk unfold into the splendor of the night sky.

"I'll always marvel at that," said Paul. "Do you know, you can see three times as many stars in the sky here as you can from any city?"

"It scares the tourists sometimes," said Carroll.

Ginger said, "It won't after a few more of those coal-fired generating plants are built."

Paul chuckled humorlessly. "I thought they were preferable to your nemesis, the nukes."

Ginger was sitting with Steve in the back seat of the Enerco truck. Her words were controlled and even. "There are alternatives to both those."

"Try supplying power to the rest of the country with them before the next century," Paul said. He braked suddenly as a jackrabbit darted into the bright cones of light. The rabbit made it across the road.

"Nobody actually *needs* air conditioners," said Ginger.

"I won't argue that point," Paul said. "You'll just have to argue with the reality of all the people who think they do."

Ginger lapsed into silence. Carroll said, "I suppose you should be congratulated for the tribal council vote today. We heard about it on the news."

"It's not binding," said Paul. "When it finally goes through, we hope it will whittle the fifty percent jobless rate on the reservation."

"It sure as hell won't!" Ginger burst out. "Higher mineral royalties mean more incentive not to have a career."

Paul laughed. "Are you blaming me for being the chicken, or the egg?"

No one answered him.

"I'm not a monster," he said.

"I don't think you are," said Steve.

"I know it puts me in a logical trap, but I think I'm doing the right thing."

"All right," said Ginger. "I won't take any easy shots. At least, I'll try."

From the back seat, Steve looked around his uneasy allies and hoped to hell that someone had brought aspirin. Carroll had aspirin in her handbag and Steve washed it down with beer from Paul's cooler.

GRANITE
PRE-CAMBRIAN
600+ MILLION YEARS

The moon had risen by now, a full, icy disc. The highway curved around a formation that looked like a vast, layered birthday cake. Cedar provided spectral candles.

"I've never believed in ghosts," said Steve. He caught the flicker of Paul's eyes in the rear-view mirror and knew the geologist was looking at him.

"There are ghosts," said Paul, "and there are ghosts. In spectroscopy, ghosts are false readings. In television, ghost images—"

"What about the kind that haunt houses?"

"In television," Paul continued, "a ghost is a reflected electronic image arriving at the antenna some interval after the desired wave."

"And are they into groans and chains?"

"Some people are better antennas than others, Steve." Steve fell silent.

"There is a theory," said Paul, "that molecular structures, no matter how altered by process, still retain some sort of 'memory' of their original form."

"Ghosts."

"If you like." He stared ahead at the highway and said, as if musing, "When an ancient organism becomes fossilized, even the DNA patterns that determine its structure are preserved in the stone."

GALLATIN FORMATION
CAMBRIAN
500–600 MILLION YEARS

Paul shifted into a lower gear as the half-ton began to climb one of the long, gradual grades. Streaming black smoke and bellowing like a great saurian lumbering into extinction, an eighteen-wheel semi with oil-field gear on its back passed them, forcing Paul part of the way onto the right shoulder. Trailing a dopplered call from its airhorn, the rig disappeared into the first of three short highway tunnels quarried out of the rock.

"One of yours?" said Ginger.

"Nope."

"Maybe he'll crash and burn."

"I'm sure he's just trying to make a living," said Paul mildly.

"Raping the land's a living?" said Ginger. "Cannibalizing the past is a living?"

"Shut up, Gin." Quietly, Carroll said, "Wyoming didn't do anything to your family, Paul. Whatever was done, people did it."

"The land gets into the people," said Paul.

"That isn't the only thing that defines them."

"This always has been a fruitless argument," said Paul. "It's a dead past."

"If the past is dead," Steve said, "then why are we driving up this cockamamie canyon?"

AMSDEN FORMATION
PENNSYLVANIAN
270–310 MILLION YEARS

Boysen Reservoir spread to their left, rippled surface glittering in the moonlight. The road hugged the eastern edge. Once the crimson taillights of the oil-field truck had disappeared in the distance, they encountered no other vehicle.

"Are we just going to drive up and down Twenty all night?" said Steve. "Who brought the plan?" He did not feel flippant, but he had to say something. He felt the burden of time.

"We'll go where the survey crew saw the presence," Paul said. "It's just a few more miles."

"And then?"

"Then we walk. It should be at least as interesting as our hike prom night."

Steve sensed that a lot of things were almost said by each of them at that point.

I didn't know then . . .

Nor do I know for sure yet.

I'm seeking . . .

What?

Time's flowed. I want to know where now, finally, to direct it.

"Who would have thought . . ." said Ginger.

Whatever was thought, nothing more was said.

The headlights picked out the reflective green-and-white Highway Department sign. "We're there," said Paul. "Somewhere on the right there ought to be a dirt access road."

SHARKTOOTH FORMATION
CRETACEOUS
100 MILLION YEARS

"Are we going to use a net?" said Steve. "Tranquilizer darts? What?"

"I don't think we can catch a ghost in a net," said Carroll. "You catch a ghost in your soul."

A small smile curved Paul's lips. "Think of this as the Old West. We're only a scouting party. Once we observe whatever's up here, we'll figure out how to get rid of it."

"That won't be possible," said Carroll.

"Why do you say that?"

"I don't know," she said. "I just feel it."

"Woman's intuition?" He said it lightly.

"*My* intuition."

"Anything's possible," said Paul.

"If we really thought you could destroy it," said Ginger, "I doubt either of us would be up here with you."

Paul had stopped the truck to lock the front hubs into four-wheel drive. Now the vehicle clanked and lurched over rocks and across potholes eroded by the spring rain. The road twisted tortuously around series of barely graded switchbacks. Already they had climbed hundreds of feet above the canyon floor. They could see no lights anywhere below.

"Very scenic," said Steve. If he had wanted to, he could have reached out the right passenger's side window and touched the porous rock. Pine branches whispered along the paint on the left side.

"Thanks to Native American Resources," said Ginger, "this is the sort of country that'll go."

"For Christ's sake," said Paul, finally sounding angry. "I'm *not* the anti-Christ."

"I know that." Ginger's voice softened. "I've loved you, remember? Probably I still do. Is there no way?"

The geologist didn't answer.

"Paul?"

"We're just about there," he said. The grade moderated and he shifted into a higher gear.

"Paul—" Steve wasn't sure whether he actually said the word or not. He closed his eyes and saw glowing fires, opened them again and wasn't sure what he saw. He felt the past, vast and primeval, rush over him like a tide. It filled his nose and mouth, his lungs, his brain. It—

"Oh my God!"

Someone screamed.

"Let go!"

The headlight beams twitched crazily as the truck skidded toward the edge of a sheer dark drop. Both Paul and Carroll wrestled for the wheel. For an instant, Steve wondered whether both of them or, indeed, either of them were trying to turn the truck back from the dark.

Then he saw the great, bulky, streamlined form coasting over the slope toward them. He had the impression of smooth power, immense and inexorable. The dead stare from flat black eyes, each one inches across, fixed them like insects in amber.

"Paul!" Steve heard his own voice. He heard the word echo and then it was swallowed up by the crashing waves. He felt unreasoning terror, but more than that, he felt— awe. What he beheld was juxtaposed on this western canyon, but yet it was not out of place. *Genius loci*, guardian, the words hissed like the surf.

It swam toward them, impossibly gliding on powerful gray-black fins.

Brakes screamed. A tire blew out like a gunshot.

Steve watched its jaws open in front of the windshield; the snout pulling up and back, the lower jaw thrusting forward. The maw could have taken in a heifer. The teeth glared white in reflected light, white with serrated, razor edges. Its teeth were as large as shovel blades.

"Paul!"

The Enerco truck fishtailed a final time; then toppled sideways into the dark. It fell, caromed off something massive and unseen, and began to roll.

Steve had time for one thought. *Is it going to hurt?*

When the truck came to rest, it was upright. Steve groped toward the window and felt rough bark rather than glass. They were wedged against a pine.

The silence astonished him. That there was no fire astonished him. That he was alive— "Carroll?" he said. "Ginger? Paul?" For a moment, no one spoke.

"I'm here," said Carroll, muffled, from the front of the truck. "Paul's on top of me. Or somebody is. I can't tell."

"Oh God, I hurt," said Ginger from beside Steve. "My shoulder hurts."

"Can you move your arm?" said Steve.

"A little, but it hurts."

"Okay." Steve leaned forward across the front seat. He didn't feel anything like grating, broken bone-ends in himself. His fingers touched flesh. Some of it was sticky

with fluid. Gently he pulled whom he assumed was Paul
from Carroll beneath. She moaned and struggled upright.

"There should be a flashlight in the glove box," he said.

The darkness was almost complete. Steve could see
only vague shapes inside the truck. When Carroll
switched on the flashlight, they realized the truck was
buried in thick, resilient brush. Carroll and Ginger stared
back at him. Ginger looked as if she might be in shock.
Paul slumped on the front seat. The angle of his neck was
all wrong.

His eyes opened and he tried to focus. Then he said
something. They couldn't understand him. Paul tried
again. They made out, "Goodnight, Irene." Then he said,
"Do what you have . . ." His eyes remained open, but all
the life went out of them.

Steve and the women stared at one another as though
they were accomplices. The moment crystallized and shattered. He braced himself as best he could and kicked
with both feet at the rear door. The brush allowed the
door to swing open one foot, then another. Carroll had
her door open at almost the same time. It took another
few minutes to get Ginger out. They left Paul in the truck.

They huddled on a naturally terraced ledge about halfway between the summit and the canyon floor. There was
a roar and bright lights for a few minutes when a Burlington Northern freight came down the tracks on the other
side of the river. It would have done no good to shout
and wave their arms, so they didn't.

No one seemed to have broken any bones. Ginger's
shoulder was apparently separated. Carroll had a nose-
bleed. Steve's head felt as though he'd been walloped
with a two-by-four.

"It's not cold," he said. "If we have to, we can stay in
the truck. No way we're going to get down at night. In
the morning we can signal people on the road."

Ginger started to cry and they both held her. "I saw
something," she said. "I couldn't tell—what was it?"

Steve hesitated. He had a hard time separating his
dreams from Paul's theories. The two did not now seem
mutually exclusive. He still heard the echoing thunder of
ancient gulfs. "I'm guessing it's something that lived here
a hundred million years ago," he finally said. "It lived in
the inland sea and died here. The sea left, but it never
did."

"A native . . ." Ginger said and trailed off. Steve touched her forehead; it felt feverish. "I finally saw," she said. "Now I'm a part of it." In a smaller voice, "Paul." Starting awake like a child from a nightmare, "Paul?"

"He's—all right now," said Carroll, her even tone plainly forced.

"No, he's not," said Ginger. "He's not." She was silent for a time. "He's dead." Tears streamed down her face. "It won't really stop the coal leases, will it?"

"Probably not."

"Politics," Ginger said wanly. "Politics and death. What the hell difference does any of it make now?"

No one answered her.

Steve turned toward the truck in the brush. He suddenly remembered from his childhood how he had hoped everyone he knew, everyone he loved, would live forever. He hadn't wanted change. He hadn't wanted to recognize time. He remembered the split-second image of Paul and Carroll struggling to control the wheel. "The land," he said, feeling the sorrow. "It doesn't forgive."

"That's not true." Carroll slowly shook her head. "The land just *is*. The land doesn't care."

"I care," said Steve.

Amazingly, Ginger started to go to sleep. They laid her down gently on the precipice, covered her with Steve's jacket, and cradled her head, stroking her hair. "Look," she said. "Look." As the moon illuminated the glowing sea.

Far below them, a fin broke the dark surface of the forest.

Medieval Europe wasn't completely filled with knights, princesses, wizards, swords and high adventure. There were many more low adventures, involving highwaymen and rogues, coshes and curses. The following story includes one of the most dire curses of all.

Mary C. Pangborn has been writing for her own amusement all her life, but only since she retired has she begun to let the rest of us see her stories, which have appeared in *Universe* and *New Dimensions*.

THE CONFESSION OF HAMO

Mary C. Pangborn

SET DOWN ALL I TELL YOU, BROTHER AL-
bertus, and may the devil fly away with you if you bend
any of my words from their true meaning. Give them a
better sound if you will, you with your book learning, but
the truth is strange enough; let there be none of your
clerkly twistings and turnings to make either more or less
of it. Forty days I'll be here in sanctuary; we have plenty
of time.

Yes, I confess myself guilty of taking a life, though I
do not admit it was murder, no, for I never meant to hurt
that silly fat merchant, only to relieve him of part of his
superfluity. How was I to know he had a skull as frail as
an egg? But it was robbery on the highway, and so they
would hang me. I've no mind to yield myself to that.
When my forty days are gone, happen I'll abjure the
realm as the law commands, and wade out into salt water each day until there's a ship to take me away. Time
enough.

You see no need for my words to be written down? Ah,
you *will* see, sir, I promise you. For I have that to tell
which might be scoffed at for an idle tale were there only
my word for it, yet when it is written soberly in ink on
good parchment, it will be known for truth. More, good
father: there is a very dreadful sin weighing on me, the
telling of which I must approach in fear and trembling;
bear with me then, for it may need many words to make
all clear.

I'm told I was born in the same year as our valiant King Harry, who killed so many Frenchmen at the great battle of Agincourt some three years past. And they say the King's grace was some eight and twenty years of age when he fought that battle—now God forbid I should name my poor self in the same breath as the King, yet I call myself a true freeborn Englishman even as he is, the saints preserve him. So there is time ahead of me before I can count two score winters; I'm not ready to let them take me and hang me by the neck. And it may be you can feel with me in this, for you cannot be so many years older than I, though you are somewhat fatter.

Where was I? Oh aye, I was born. Hamo of York they call me, and sometimes Hamo the Red, for my hair. I was some twelve years old when my mother died, and I wearied of the kitchen service in my lord's household and ran away. I doubt they ever thought me worth the chasing —a weazened bony snippet of a boy, idler and trouble-maker. Here's a handful of sins at the beginning: idleness and mischief, that's sloth, and disobedience, running away from my rightful lord. Eh well, there's worse to come.

Not much to be said of my early years on the road, before I met with Tom—begging, a bit of thieving, lending a hand to the jugglers at fairs—sometimes I'd even work, if my belly was empty enough. It wasn't a bad life. I'd tramped the length of the realm before I was twenty, Lands End to Berwick, and found warm welcome all along the way, from young wenches and honest wives both. . . .

Now, with respect, Brother, that is a foolish question. How could I know? Was I ever in one place so much as two months, to say nothing of nine? How can a man guess how many bairns he may have sired? I'd not be surprised if England is well peppered with my redheads. But I will swear by any godly oath you like, I never took a wench against her will and liking. Willing they were, and pleased with me. I'll not tell you about one or another. I do here-by confess myself guilty of the sin of lechery—*mea maxima culpa*—let one confession stand for all of them.

But this is not what your abbot is hoping I may tell you.

Most kindly the noble abbott received me, when I knelt before him begging for sanctuary; most patiently he heard me as I confessed my crime of robbery. Of that he said nothing; he stroked his holy chin, and eyed me thoughtfully, and he said, "I am told you spent some time journeying with a man known as Moses the Mage." And I said this was true, for how should I deny my friend? Then he said, "It is rumored that this so-called mage has made a study of the art of alchemy, the search for the Elixir, called by some the Philosopher's Stone." And again I said, this rumor is true. Then he said no more except to promise I should receive sanctuary, and that he would send me a confessor to assist me in cleansing my soul of sin. And for this grace, and especially for his sending you to me, I am most deeply and humbly grateful. Now it would be presumptuous in me to suppose I could read the abbot's saintly thoughts, yet it did seem to me he felt that any knowledge of the secret work of alchemy might be too heavy a burden for such a simple soul as mine, and only by divesting myself of that burden, yielding it up to one too holy to be corrupted by it, might I hope to save myself. Wherefore, if you will but hear my confession and write as I bid you, I will reveal to you—for the abbot's ear—all that I know of the making of gold.

Let me first tell you about Moses the Mage.

He had already taken that name when I met him first, but he was baptized Thomas—Tom o' Fowey, a Cornishman. Maybe you know they have a language of their own, not like any other; it would make you wonder if you were in any part of England. When I joined him he was mostly making weather magic, and a marvel it was to hear him lashing out in his strange tongue, all the folk gowking at him—he could switch to priestly Latin fast enough if anyone smelling like a bailiff came near. He'd been raised for a priest, until he decided the life would not suit him, and he had more clerkly learning than many of them, saving your presence. Now the spirits that bring wind and rain surely understood Cornish, for Tom's weather sayings were usually right.

He could make an awesome figure of himself: tall and thin he is, with a mighty beak of a nose, and when he appeared as Moses he wore a black patch over one eye. Folk whispered he had sacrificed that eye in a pact with some evil spirit, in exchange for secret knowledge. Times we'd be in peril of a charge of sorcery, and the bailiff's men would be looking for a tall dark one-eyed man; when they'd find us, I'd be sitting there with the black patch on me, a harmless little redheaded beggar, and Tom with his two great solemn dark eyes whole and sound, a holy pilgrim fingering his rosary; so the fellows who described him would be put to shame. Once it was a near thing, when the sheriff's man pulled off my eye patch, but he backed away fast, terrified and cursing, seeing my eye horribly red and dangerous. We never traveled without an onion.

Weather magic wasn't our only business; we also traded in drugs and herbal mixtures, and sometimes we'd have a stock of the rare alicorn, which is the powdered horn of the unicorn, as you know—a strong cure for all poisons. Now there are rogues without bowels or conscience who will sell you a mess of powdered chalk and call it alicorn. We never did such a thing, though I'll not deny we might have mixed the true stuff with other matters, so as to have enough for everyone. One market day we had our stall set up and Tom was crying our wares in his big voice while I went among the people to take their money: "Here it is," he cries, "the only true alicorn, the one remedy for all poisons, that brave sailors bring you at great peril from strange and far places!" and he gives them a generous earful of Cornish to show how far and strange it was. "Here you see a piece of the horn itself—come close, friends, handle it, see for yourselves!" And then I saw a little man off at the edge of the crowd laughing to himself. Tom saw him too, and flung his Cornish speech at him, and when next I looked that way the man was gone. Scared off, I thought.

Alicorn fetches a good price, and we'd sold all we had, so we were enjoying a good hot supper at the inn when here comes that same little man sidling up to us, grinning and ducking his head at Tom. "Give ye good den, Master Moses," says he, "and will you not drink with me?"

Tom was scowling at him, and I held my breath, for Tom can be a fearsome man in a rage—the gust of his anger will blow you as high as the church steeple, till the sun comes out sudden and he's your good friend again. But this time he only growled a bit. "You'll be a Cornishman?" he says, begrudging it. The fellow lays a finger to his nose and puts his head to one side, as though he had to think about the answer. "Not exactly," says he, "but some of the words I know, yes. Black Jamie I am called, at your service."

Dressed all in black he was, and black-haired he might have been once, but the trifle of hair he had left was all white, only a bit of it sticking up over each ear; a small sharp face with the nose and chin pointing at you like knives, and little no-colored eyes watching from ambush. Still, he spoke to us quiet and friendly-like; Tom offered him our salt, and he made a ceremony of taking some of it, to show he meant us no harm. So bit by bit we fell to talking easily, the good ale warming us; we could tell he was one of us, of the company of the road.

Jamie said, "You'll be somewhat of a scholar, Master Moses?"

"Now how would you know that?" says Tom.

"Why, you're too modest, man, you're better known along the road than you think," and Jamie winked at him. Fumbling at his pouch, he got out a little book, a shabby dirty old thing, no more than a dozen pages sewed together. Held it out in his left hand. "I'll warrant you can read this," he says.

Tom took the book over to the light of the torch by the fireplace, grumbling and grunting over it. "Aye, I can read the words," says he. "It is alchemy, I can see that much." We knew about alchemy; we had friends on the road who made a good living at the art, in the way I'll be telling you.

"*Words,*" says Jamie. "Strong magic in grand long words, Master Moses, none knows it better than yourself."

We did know. Tom was trying over the big words on his tongue, tasting and liking them, and Black Jamie watching his face. "I'll be honest with you, my friends," says Jamie (now surely we ought to have been on our guard when he said that!). "I've learned all the words in that book, I do not need it, and if you like, I will sell it to you for one silver penny. And you can lose nothing, for if you do not find you have a good bargain of it, I will buy it back from you for two pennies the next time we meet."

"So you're thinking we'll meet again?" I asked him.

"That shall be as God wills," says he—said it solemn enough, but I did notice he never made the sign of the cross. Tom gave him a penny for the book, and I don't remember that we took leave of him; the next time we gave a thought to him, he was gone.

We spent some days studying the book, Tom reading out the words and I putting them all away in my memory, and true enough there never was a book with finer treasure of long words in it, far more than a penny's worth. Yet they would not be sufficient, as we knew and I said, "This is all very well, Tom, but it takes gold to make gold."

"I know," he said, and sighed. "Ah, I do wish we had a bit of gold."

Now everyone knows you ought to have a care how you speak those words *I wish,* for there is no knowing who or what may be listening. Yet I will swear Tom spoke no more than those innocent words, so there is no explaining what happened, unless maybe Black Jamie had a hand in it. For it was the very next day we came upon a man dead by the side of the road. A holy pilgrim, by his dress, lying there most peaceful, his hands folded on his breast, never a mark on him; you could tell it was only that his time had come to die, there where he was. His pouch was empty; he had a plain gold cross on a chain around his neck.

I did not like to take the cross off him. Tom said, "Surely 'tis the holiness that matters, not the gold," and he took off his own little wooden cross that had been blessed by Our Lady of Walsingham, and put that on the dead man instead of the gold one; and we went our way. It seemed an honest exchange, and we had done the man no harm. And I will swear neither of us had harbored any sinful thought of calling on the dark powers to help us—not then. . . .

Whatever, we made a good livelihood out of those mighty words in our book, as long as the pilgrim's gold lasted.

Now, Brother, I'd not be surprised if you have heard something of the way this is done. You must find yourself a patron, someone who is well endowed with the world's goods, yet feels he has not enough; a fat burgess is good, or the bailiff of a great lord—but you had best stay clear of the lord himself, he can too easily crush you like a louse between thumb and finger if you do not satisfy him. So, when you have found your man, you converse with him softly, slowly, at length, until you see he is enchanted; you discourse on *lunification,* on *tincture,* on *fixation,* on *dealbation;* on the secret names of Jupiter and Saturn, on the Black Crow, the White Eagle, the King and his Son, the Serpent who swallows his tail, and much more; thus it is beyond doubt that you are an adept, skilled in the lore of the mysterious East. We had an advantage, d'ye see, for if there was danger of being too clearly understood Tom would just speak a bit in Cornish.

Next, your man must build his furnace and supply himself with alembics and crucibles and many rare substances; meanwhile you are living at ease in his house, sleeping soft and eating well, and if you cannot put by somewhat when you go on errands to purchase his materials, you had better choose some other trade.

But you cannot let this go on too long; there will come a day when you must prove your work. You will let him place a bit of lead in his crucible, and throw in a bit of this and some of that, whatever; and finally you bring forth your magic powder. A black powder is good; you can use charcoal, with a sufficiency of powder of lead, and maybe the dried blood of a white cock. You should have him put it in with his own hand, making sure he tips it all in quickly, and then without delay you seal the crucible with moistened clay and place it in the furnace, for as long as you like. After the vessel has been well heated and the molten dross skimmed away, there will be a nugget of gold in the bottom, and why not?—for in your magic powder there was a fragment of gold covered with blackened wax.

Well now, your patron is happy, and so are you. You may decide to make another trial, and the second lump of gold will be a trifle larger than the first. But then, alas, you have only a little of the magic powder left, and you must make a long and costly journey to find the ingredients necessary to make more. He will eagerly help you on your way, and you will generously give him all the powder you have left, with many difficult instructions on the use of it, so that you shall be long gone before he despairs of success.

Yes, I know this is not the sort of gold-making your abbot wishes to learn, but remember it is said: *Blessed are the meek, for they shall be patient until the end of the story.* You would not have me omit any of my misdeeds from my confession? And before you lay a heavy penance on me, Brother, bethink you; this worthy patron I speak of has enjoyed a rare and strange adventure, and had great pleasure in it; has he not received good value for his money?

Well; so it went. The time came when all our stock of gold was gone, and we sat together by our campfire at the edge of a lonely road, considering what we might do next. We did not see Black Jamie come, maybe just out of the shadow of the trees; there he was.

"Well met, friends," says he, and sat down by our fire without any by-your-leave, the dancing shadows making horn shapes out of his two tufts of hair, and spread his left hand to the warmth of the fire—only that one hand, and I remembered he was left-handed, a mischancy thing. We were not wholly pleased to see him, but we did not like to be unfriendly, so presently we were passing our ale flask back and forth, and making small talk about the ways of the road; we were two stout young fellows to one old one, we saw no reason to fear him. After a while he said, "You'll have had good profit out of your book, I'm thinking. You'll not be wanting to sell it back to me?"

Tom says, "Nay, that we're not."

"Ah, you've used it well, I'll warrant! But, friends, have you not sometimes thought of the true art that lies concealed behind all that writing?"

"We might have put our minds to it," I said, and Tom frowned. But it needed no warlock to guess that such a thought would have come to us. For who would labor so mightily at all those mysteries, only to provide a few fellows like us with a chance of trickery? No, we knew there must be some truth in it. When we had argued this, Tom always said the secret was buried too deep for us. I was not so sure.

Black Jamie said, "Whatever, you'll be needing more gold."

"Who doesn't?" says Tom, a bit short, and Jamie laughed, a rusty-screechy noise with no mirth in it, a sound I did not care for. "Ah, a true word!" says he. "And there's more nor one way of getting it, am I not right?"

"I've heard so," says Tom.

Black Jamie yawned, like a man having no more to say and thinking of naught but sleep, and he says, tossing it out careless-like—"Well, there's the ancient mounds, and the red gold in them."

Now some folk will tell you those places are entrances

into faerie, and if you know the spell you may go in and
spend one day in delight at the court of a beautiful elfin
queen, but when you come out you will find a hundred
years have passed and all your friends are dead. Others
say these are only the burial grounds of old-time pagans,
not to be feared by anyone who can say his paternoster,
and men have broken into such mounds with pick and
shovel, finding old bones and sometimes the red gold. You
never do hear it told that those men have lived long and
happy lives thereafter. I said, "It's known that such gold
is accursed."

Jamie yawned again, and stretched out on the grass with
his back to the fire. "Ah," says he, "that's because the folk
do not know how to get it safely. You will please yourselves, friends, but I am going near one of those places
tomorrow, and if you care to walk with me I can show it
to you."

Then he was snoring, and it made us feel easier to hear
him. A snore is a natural and homely thing; you cannot
be afeared of a little bald wisp of a man who makes comical noises in his sleep.

So the next day we went along the road together, and
Black Jamie kept us merry with songs and tales of old
time, but never a word of himself or his own doings, and
we somehow forgot to ask ourselves what manner of man
he was. Near dusk he turned off the road into a great
moor spreading westward, and we said nothing, but followed him. I will not tell you where the place was. We
had lost sight of the highway when we came to the
mound.

"Yonder it is," said Jamie, "and I've a notion to camp
here for the night. You could join me and welcome, if
you cared to."

It was only a hillock rising from the moor; you would
think it a natural hill except for the smooth even shape of
it. No tree or bush grew there, only the sheep-cropped
grass, brighter and greener than common. Nothing fearsome about it. Tom says, "I've spent nights in worse
places."

We built ourselves a bit of a fire.

"Ah, there is pleasant," says Black Jamie. The dark
was sifting down around us. "It would maybe surprise
you," says he, "the things I know that I would not be telling to everyone. But since you have been so friendly as to

give me your comradeship, why, here is a secret you will not find in your book of alchemy. You will have heard that the gold found in the barrows is softer and redder than the common metal from the mines. Know, then, that this red gold of the ancient kings is not merely metal such as the goldsmiths use, but the very essence and spirit of gold. It is itself the Elixir."

I asked him, "Why then have the men who found this ancient gold not discovered what it was?"

"Ah, there is the heart of the matter. They have gone in roughly as mere grave robbers, d'ye see, and when the gold is stolen that way, the virtue goes out of it. You must enter the mound gently, humbly, and let the gold be given you as a free gift."

Tom said, "Are you telling us a mortal living man can do that?"

"It is not easy," says Jamie, "but I am the man who can tell you the way of it. Share and share alike, if you can get it."

We sat looking at him, thinking he mocked us, and he went on more urgently, "Of course, there is only one night in the whole month when it can be done," and even while he spoke the great silver circle was rising and peering over the lip of the moor at us. Night of the full moon.

I said, "If you know the way, why do you not get it for yourself?"

"*That* is why," he said, and thrust out his right hand at us, that he'd been keeping hidden. Half a hand it was, thumb and forefinger, three fingers gone. He said, "No one can enter the mound except he be a whole man."

It would have been childish to ask why not. "Well then," Tom was beginning, but Jamie put up that lonesome finger and shook it at him. "Not you." Now Tom had hurt his foot when he was a bairn and had lost the little toe off it: such a small old-time thing he'd nigh forgotten it himself. And Jamie had surely never seen him with his boots off, yet he knew. And now Jamie was studying me.

Let him look, I thought, and I began trying to remember my fights and beatings—scars enough I had for them, but nothing lost. I might now and then have stood in peril of losing an ear or so to the law, for this or that misdoing; still, it had not happened, for they never caught me. "Scars!" said Jamie impatiently. "Nay, how can anyone grow to manhood's years without scars? That is nothing. You could do it."

"I will, then," I said.

Now you see, Brother Albertus, here is that most deadly sin of which I spoke to you. For well I knew this was a trafficking with evil spirits, to the peril of my immortal soul, and yet I did knowingly enter upon it. Wherefore I will gladly suffer penance and go on pilgrimage if I may cleanse my soul of this thing.—Well; you must hear me out, to know how it was.

A black cross was to be set upside down, Jamie said, and he would teach me a spell in ancient Gaelic, and then—halfway through the telling of it he broke off and cocked his head sidewise at me. Smiling, if you could call it that. "There's a thing you ought to know, laddie, before you go on with this," says he. "You'll go in there a whole man, but you'll not come out without leaving some part of yourself in their hands. Whatever they choose to take."

I did not like the sound of that. I could imagine giving up a finger or a toe or two, even an ear, the red gold would be worth it; but there's other parts a man would not like to find missing off him, and I said as much to Black Jamie. "Never fear," said he, "they will play fair with you, they will take no more than you can spare. Even if they take one, they will leave you one," says he, and he let out that screech noise of his, laughter you might call it.

I'll be frank with you, Brother, I did not find much comfort in that reassurance, but it was too late for faint-heartedness. I came back at him cold and quick, the first words I found in my mouth: "Did *they* take your three fingers, then?"

He said nothing, said it in his ancient Gaelic, the little cold eyes freezing into me, and the silence might have gone on until we had all turned to blocks of ice where we sat, if Tom had not spoken. "Eh, well, get on with it, man," he says, "tell us what more we need to do." And so he did.

I had first to learn the words of the old Gaelic spell, and while the moon was climbing the sky Jamie strove most patiently with me to be sure I could say them right. I'd not have ventured to ask him what they meant, and surely he would not have told me—no need for me to know, only to speak them correctly. And at last he was satisfied I could do it. So I went up to the top of the mound and set that unholy cross in the earth, and walked three times widdershins around it saying the words I had learned; and I could not tell them to you now if I would, for as soon as they had served their purpose they went clean out of my head. Then I lay down on my back beside the black cross, and held my eyes open to the full light of the moon. And whether time passed while I lay there, or whether it stopped entirely, I do not know; I was not aware of anything happening, only that I found myself in another place.

I could feel walls enclosing space, and yet there was great distance, and no walls to be seen, nor any roof or sky; there was light—soft, not bright—you could not tell where it came from. Whisper of clean moving air; somewhere a darkness of trees, and a smell of old forest growing more thickly over the land than it does now. And there were men in the forest, though I could not see or hear them.

Then a man was standing in front of me, where there had been no one. He was no giant, but broad and thick, powerfully made, with a great gray beard and fierce old eyes frowning at me. He wore a short kirtle and a wolf-skin flung over one shoulder, and held in his hand a bright sword; and around his neck and on either arm he wore heavy circles of red gold. So I knew he was a king.

He spoke, and his voice was a deep rumble like the noise of drums; his words were strange to me, but the air of that place caught them up and twisted them around, the way sunlight spatters through leaves, making new patterns, and I knew what they meant. He said, "Is it time?"

I must have been gaping stupidly, for he moved impatiently, and there was a ringing sound from his sword. "Have you no ears, clod? Have you come at last to fetch me against the enemies of the Land?"

Now in the first breath I thought of great King Arthur, who is to return one day and fight for us; but everyone knows that Arthur is buried at Glastonbury, and moreover he was a chivalrous Christian knight, not a savage clad in the hide of a wolf. Then I saw how there might well be more than one ancient king standing guard over the Land. And at last I found my tongue, and answered him, "Sire, I thank you for your kindness, but I can tell you we've gotten the better of our enemies, for we have a strong warrior as king."

"Ah," he said, and nodded. "That is good. You have driven them back from the beaches?"

"Why, they never came so far," I told him. "It would glad your heart to see it, sir, the way our good King Harry went over the water after them to kill them, and came home to a great triumph."

"Good, very good. Then I may sleep awhile longer." His men had been coming out of the forest behind him; there was a gleam of eyes and a shadow of hands on clubs. He motioned them back. "You must be sure to keep a strong guard on the beaches," he said sternly. "That is the way they always come. . . ."

"We keep guard," I promised him. And then I bethought me one must mind one's manners in speaking to a king, so I went down on my knee and swept off my cap, as I should have done sooner. All this did not take as much courage as you might think, for something about that place made it seem right and proper for me to be there; it was all a part of the enchantment. "Great King," I said, "I have come here boldly to bring you word that the Land is safe, and you may rest in peace. Now in my time, sire, we hold that the bringer of good news merits a reward, and if it should please your lordship to think thus, I would only ask most humbly for a small token of your royal gold."

He smiled; and oh, Brother Albertus, you have never seen such a smile! You could see the naked skull grinning behind the flesh, and I knew that all my secret thoughts and my desires for the gold were transparent to him. Yet it seemed he was not angry. "Be it so," he said, and he drew the gold band from his left arm and gave it to me. The first touch of it burned my fingers like ice; then I felt the living warmth of my hand flowing into it, and it was no more fiercely cold than metal ought to be. I said, "Sire, with all my heart I humbly thank you."

My voice was flat and dull, and I was alone in a small dim space with barely enough light to see what lay before me in the dust, where I was still kneeling: clean old bones, undisturbed, arms straight at the sides; around the neck and the right arm were circlets of gold, but on the left arm nothing—only a fresh scar in the earth under the long arm bone, as though something had been taken away.

Then I was lying on top of the mound in the moonlight,

and I would have thought the whole thing a mere vision,
but that I held a golden armband in my hands: bright and
clean-shining, not like a thing dug out of old earth, and
now I could see a swirl of markings on it, like a sort of
writing. Down yonder by a fire were the shapes of two
men, waiting. In a little, I remembered who they were. I
went down to them and said, "Here is the gold," and fell
flat on my face.

There was a while I don't remember, and then I was
sitting beside the fire with Tom holding the flask so I
could drink, and the gold circle on the ground in the fire-
light.

Black Jamie put out a hand toward it, moving slow and
easy, the both of us watching him, Tom with his knife out
and ready.

"Given as a free gift, it was," I said.

Black Jamie said, "Yes, I know." He took it into his
hands, turning it over as though he could read the old
writing. It seemed a long time until he laid it down, carefully, never letting his eyes shift toward the gleam of
Tom's knife. "Now," says he, "we must divide it in three
pieces."

Not so easy; it was a lovely thing, we did not like to
hammer it roughly with stones. Jamie picked up an
ordinary-looking pebble and scratched a couple of lines
with it on the gold, muttering some of his Gaelic words,
and passed it once quickly through the fire. "Now strike
it with your stone," he said. I struck it, and there it lay,
split cleanly into three pieces. One piece, a trifle smaller
than the others, had the greater part of the writing on it.
Tom and I sat still, not touching the gold, waiting.

Jamie picked up the smallest piece and tucked it into
his pouch. Then he leaped suddenly in the air and clacked
his heels together, thumbing his nose at us, and *psst!* like
that, he was gone.

We both crossed ourselves quickly, all ashiver, fearing
we had dealt with the devil himself. But then I said, "He
is maybe a Welshman, or even a Scot, but I think he is
not a demon, for then why would he have needed our
help? And you must remember how he snored, like any
natural man."

"Eh well," says Tom, "we knew he was a warlock."

Whatever he was, we were free of him, and now I told
Tom everything that had happened, just as I have been

telling it to you. He shook his head and sighed, "Ah, Hamo, Hamo! What a marvelous adventure! Could I but have gone with you!"

Then I remembered why he could not go, and the rest of it, and now my fingers were shaking with impatience to get all my clothes off, Tom helping me. I could scarce breathe till I might discover what had been taken from me. We looked carefully, both of us, and there was no part of me lacking, nothing, not so much as a toenail. Tom laughed. "Ah, I'll warrant he was mocking you—it would seem a merry sort of jest to him, the black-hearted bastard he is, man or demon."

But I could not help wondering: if they had stolen nothing from my outward and visible body, what had they taken instead? I considered myself—not an easy matter, Brother, though easily said—and I felt myself to be the same man I had always been. Ah well; I was accursed, but I did not know it; not yet.

Tom heaved another great sigh, deep out of his guts, and he said, "Think now, Hamo, what a marvelous song it would make! To speak with an old dead king, and win the red gold. . . ."

I knew what was in his heart. It was always his deepest longing to be a bard, a minstrel; not to wrench a livelihood out of the folk by clever trickery, but to win it with praise and joy, as a singer of tales. He could not do it; he had no gift for it, no more than I have myself. What do you think, Brother Albertus? Does everyone cherish some deep unhealing sorrow for the one splendid thing he can never do?

We could not make the song; we only sat quietly there together until it grew light enough for us to see each other's faces, and the two broken pieces of the red gold lying there on the ground between us.

Neither of us moved to touch it. The light grew, and the sun rose, and a finger of sunlight reached down along the mound, pointing at the gold. We'd not have been surprised if it had crumbled into a bit of dust, as they say faery gold does at the touch of morning. But no: it brightened in the sun, it soaked up the light and gave it back in glory, you might think it was a living thing that had suffered from darkness all those years under the earth and now sang with joy. It was ours, the true red gold. . . .

Now am I come to the sad and sorry part of my tale,

Brother Albertus, and I ask you to hear me with compassion.

We lost no time in finding ourselves a snug place where we set up our furnaces and crucibles, and we labored earnestly to do all that was said in the book, employing our red gold as the Elixir, of which a tiny bit should suffice to change all the melt into its own pure nature, into true gold. Well. In a word, we could never get back more gold than we put in.

One day I found Tom sitting with his head in his hands, nigh to weeping, and he said, "I am greatly to blame, Hamo, I have made you think me a greater scholar than I am. I can read the secret words in our book, saying *Seize and slay the dragon, lift out his entrails, bring the green lion to the current of the Nile,* and so on, but I do confess to you I have no notion at all what these things mean, nor what the old masters are telling us to do."

I had been wondering about it myself, but it grieved me to see my poor friend taking the whole weight of our failure on himself, and I said, "Tom, I am thinking we ought not to have been so ready to trust yon fellow Jamie."

"Why, did he not have a potent spell? Did it not get you into the mound as he said it would? And surely he knew the value of the red gold, for he desired it for himself."

"He did," I said, "but I am not sure he wanted the gold as much as he did the secret writing on it. Most likely that was some excellent ancient magic."

"Do you mean—? Are you saying—?" Tom was swelling slowly to full fury, his face turning red. "When he told us that the red gold was the Elixir—?"

"I would not say he was lying," says I, "I was only wondering about it."

Tom was not wondering. He crashed his great fist on the table so the spoons jumped to the floor. "Why, that misbegotten limb of Satan! That—that *creature—he* to cozen *us?* I will have the heart out of him with my bare hands, by God's bowels I will! I will hang him up by the heels and cut out his tripes to feed him—I will . . ."

I don't know what more he planned; the rest was in Cornish. I waited until he grew weary and then I said, "We have no power to hunt him down, Tom, well you know it. Here we be two simple fellows trying to make an honest living, and him a warlock."

He did know it, and he sat drained and spent, the way he does when the anger has run out of him, and he said, "So, then, we must go back to our old trade. We have gold. . . ."

And so we did. I cannot bear to spend many words on this, Brother, for the horror is still with me. We found a patron, we sat at drink with him, and Tom spoke with him learnedly, as we had so often done; I, the humble assistant, waited until Tom should turn to me and say, "Now my good man here has somewhat to show you," and I was to unwrap the little bar of red gold and say, "Look you, master, a small bit of the gold we have made."

And I could not do it. I felt the words fighting each other in my throat, and knew what would happen if I spoke; I had just enough wits to fall on the floor, foaming at the mouth, and I heard Tom say, "Poor fellow, he's not had one of these fits for a month," and somehow he got me away. Truly feared for me he was, thinking of poison or some dread illness, for well he knew I never had fits.

Ah, the case was far worse than he thought! For I was accursed; I knew now what dire mutilation the old King had wrought on me. He had taken away my power to lie.

Better, far better, he had stolen an ear or even an eye! Only think, Brother, how easily your welfare or even your life may depend on your ability to lie! Never tell me the monastery is different from the rest of the world in that way, I would not believe it. Could you face even one day in which you knew that you could utter no word other than the truth, however great the need? Would you not be forced to a vow of silence? Can you not pity me, Brother Albertus? Yes, I see you do, I thank you for your tears. I could not have wept better in my evil old days, no, not even with the best of onions. . . .

I have striven against my fate, hoping to find the curse weakening with time. Often, while I have been speaking with you, I have tried to cheat just a little, not wishing to deceive you but merely as one might test a wounded arm to see if it has healed enough for use. All to no avail; the words I sought to bend have come out of my mouth straight, I have not been able to tell you anything except the exact truth.—You shake your head, you think such a

thing impossible? But consider, Brother, you have the
best possible reason to believe it. Am I not the one who is
telling you? And I am Hamo the Accursed, who cannot
lie.

Now when I had made Tom understand what had happened to me, I begged him to let me go my separate way,
for I was surely no use to him. "My poor friend," said he,
"you could never make your way alone in the world under such a curse. Let us think what we can do."

I will not spin you a long tale of those dreary days. In
our despair, we thought of setting up an honest mercer's
shop, but we had not the gift for it; nothing went right, in
no time at all we were deep in debt, and my poor Tom
whisked off to the debtors' prison. We still had our red
gold, buried in a safe place, but it would not have been
enough, and anyway we could not let them have it.
There's much virtue in it, even if it may not be the Elixir.

So I gave the sheriff's men the slip, and whispered Tom
that I'd make the money to set him free, and then I took
to the greenwood, as we ought to have done in the first
place. I had almost enough for his needs when I had the
misfortune to kill that merchant on the highway, and
there, but for the holiness and kindness of your sanctuary,
would have been the end of my pitiful tale.

You might think that for a man who has seen such adventures as mine it would be tedious merely to go on living from day to day, but I do not find it so; I am truly
grateful for this enchanted world God has given us, and
who knows what further joys and wonders I may find in
it? So I have decided not to wait out my whole forty days
in sanctuary. My good friend Tom is out of prison now—
never ask me how it was arranged—and he is waiting for
me. We'll try our luck with our comrades in the greenwood, or maybe on the high seas; there's Tom's cousin,
captain of his own ship, a free trader—I suppose some
folk would call him a pirate.

It's useless to struggle, Brother Albertus, I am stronger
than you. I do not wish to hurt you; have we not enjoyed
these days and hours of friendly converse? However, I
must win time to leave this place quietly, you see, and so
I must tie your hands and feet—I hope that is not too
tight? Yes, your habit fits me quite well, I knew it would.
I am sorry I cannot leave you my breeches, but you may

have this old coat to keep you warm until your brothers find you. It will not be long.

Oh aye, the abbot. You say I promised to tell him how he could make gold from lead?

With respect, Brother, that is not what I said. Look back at your writings; you will find my words were: *I will tell you all I know of the making of gold*—and is not this just what I have been confessing to you? One moment; I must tie this cloth over your mouth. I cannot have you crying out too soon. —Very well, you shall learn the final secret. Tell your abbot to take all his silver plate and jewels and his tools of whatever metal, and all his papers that tell of the wealth of the abbey in land and in sheep, and he shall go to the master goldsmith in London town and say, Give me gold enough for these things. Thus he may transmute any object whatever into gold. This is the exact and perfect truth: I, Hamo, have said it.

Does something trouble you, Brother Albertus? Nay then, do not fret your kind heart with fears for my safety, I shall be well away before any pursuit can set out. Farewell; remember me in your prayers. *Pax tecum.*

The sins of a father can be visited upon his children, as we've often heard and sometimes known. In this case, the father was a sea captain who kept his secret sins to himself, and tried to control what his four daughters had become. They outlived him and his safeguards, and we come in on the scene a century later. . . .

Bob Leman began selling his fantasy stories more than ten years ago, evidently as a hobby. In the past few years, he's been writing more and in greater depth; he's begun to attract an avid readership.

FEESTERS IN THE LAKE

Bob Leman

BONELESS PALE CREATURES WITH RAGGED mouths full of teeth lived at the bottom of the lake. We called them *feesters*. My Uncle Caleb said we called them that because that was their name. He said they were once a family who lived in the abandoned big house beside the lake, and long ago something very strange happened to them, so that now they could live only down there in the darkness, in the cold mud.

Sometimes at night they would come in close to the shore, he said, and rise to the surface and cry. They cried like lost little children who have given up hope, a sound that was infinitely sad and desolate, a piteous sobbing that awakened in the hearts of unwary womenfolk a powerful desire to rescue and comfort. Those who succumbed to the desire were not heard of again. So Uncle Caleb told me when I was eleven.

I half believed him. Telling stories was one of his specialties. In those days I spent my summers in Sturkeyville with my grandparents, and all summer long I was in Uncle Caleb's company as much as he would allow. There were a good many reasons for that, and the most important one was my fear that I was going to miss a story if I strayed from his side. I was always glad I did not miss the one about the feesters.

Uncle Caleb had heard it, he told me, from his father, my Grandpa Scoggins, whose father had actually known Captain Feester and indeed had been his lawyer. The

258

story went like this: Elihu Feester was a ship's master
sailing out of Boston in the middle years of the nineteenth
century. On one of his voyages, blown off course in the
South Pacific, he made a landfall at a populated island
that did not appear on the charts, and he and his crew
were forced to spend some time there while they repaired
their storm-damaged ship. There was apparently a quarrel
of some sort with the natives, and the Americans fled the
island, leaving behind a number of dead, both crewmen
and natives.

They took with them, however, their doom: a germ or
a parasite or perhaps a curse. Before they had completed
their trading along the China Coast, Feester found it necessary to execute several of the crew. (This was not reported until much later, by the captain of another China
trader.) No one knows what happened during the return
voyage. The ship burned to the waterline a few miles outside Boston harbor on June 16, 1851, and only Captain
Feester came ashore.

There was a great scandal, and a Board of Inquiry was
called. Feester's story never varied: they were hardly out
of the China Seas, he said, when the men began to fall
sick, and one by one they died. The last leg of the voyage
was accomplished with only himself, the second mate,
and one able-bodied seaman left alive, and both of these
had succumbed during the last days. He had no idea why
he should have been spared. He had burned the ship because he was the only one left to do it, and most certainly
his vessel had by then become a pest ship and might have
infected the whole of Massachusetts. The bodies of the
mate and the A.B. were still aboard at the time of the
burning. He had nothing to add.

His story was highly circumstantial, a detailed account
of high fevers and delirium, of black vomit and dreadful
pain, of sores and pustules. He produced the ship's log in
evidence. Nonetheless, he was not wholly believed. But
because he had been half-owner of the ship, a vocal mi-
nority held that his arson had in fact been a praiseworthy
and sacrificial act, and in the end he was absolved. It was
clear that he would never be given command of another
vessel, but that fact did not appear to cause him any concern, and indeed he was heard to say that once he was
free to do so, he intended to go where he would never
have to look at the sea again. He left Boston the day the

board cleared him, and he had been gone for more than a year when the trader captain brought home his account of the killings Feester had committed off China. They talked of re-convening the board, but no one had any idea where Feester might be found.

He was, as it happened, far to the west in the town of Sturkeyville, a somnolent county seat in the northern Appalachians. He was building a house there, a few miles out of town near the shore of Howard's Lake. And by the time the house was completed he had acquired a wife to live in it, the only daughter of Ezra Stallworth, the banker who had sold him the land.

There was a crazy streak in the Stallworths, Grandpa Scoggins told Uncle Caleb, a stubbornness that went far beyond anything rational, and Agatha Stallworth Feester's stubbornness had as much to do with the final horror as did the germ or parasite or curse or whatever it was that Feester carried. For a long time she persisted in a blind refusal to accept the fact that her children were what they were, and when at last there was no escape from the truth, it was too late.

Uncle Caleb's voice deepened dramatically at that point: "It was *toooo* late." Sepulchral, doom-laden. He enjoyed telling the story. It was plain, even to me, that he'd have preferred to be telling it at midnight in a room with shadowy corners, to a larger audience than one young nephew. But he was a story teller, and I had asked. I was getting the full performance.

It was impossible for me to tell whether or not he believed any of it. He put the same sincerity into all of his stories, both the demonstrably true and the obviously fictional. It is quite certain that on the day he told me about the feesters he did not yet know the whole story himself; it would be another five years before Grandpa Scoggins explained all the details to him and passed on the responsibility. What Uncle Caleb told me that day was simply the folklore of the town, and although I was too young to perceive it, I suppose there was a good bit of irony in his narration.

I was very fond of my uncle Caleb. He was thirty years old that summer (it was 1934), a bachelor, still making his home with my grandparents in the big house a block north of the square. He practiced law with my grandfather in chambers above Staub's Hardware, across from the courthouse. My grandfather owned the building. He owned a considerable part of the town, to tell the truth.

Uncle Caleb always had time to spare for me, and I appreciated it. I did not realize until a number of years later that he had plenty of time to spare, that he worked very little, if at all. There was no real reason why he should have, of course. He and my mother were the only children of their generation in the Scoggins family, and the deaths of several maiden aunts and great-aunts had settled upon Uncle Caleb all the money he would ever need. He was nominally a partner in the law firm, and I suppose he handled the odd conveyance or probate from time to time, but his chief occupations were those of a sportsman and man-about-town—if the term was applicable in Sturkeyville. He hunted and fished and rode his horses, and played a great deal of golf at the country club. He belonged to clubs in New York and Philadelphia, and he had kept in close touch with friends from prep school and undergraduate days. So he was often away, leaving the family to learn of his activities from the Society pages of the city papers.

My grandfather viewed Uncle Caleb's way of life with something less than enthusiasm, but the two of them did not, I believe, quarrel about it. I think that that was because Grandpa more or less agreed with Grandma's frequently expressed view that Caleb would in due course settle down like everybody else and that he deserved a little amusement to take his mind off what Dorothy Hodge had done to him.

What Dorothy Hodge had done to him was to marry Holmes Ungelbauer, his oldest and closest friend. She did not exactly jilt Uncle Caleb; there was never an engagement. There was not even an understanding, beyond the understanding the three of them had had since they were children, that some day she would marry either Holmes or Caleb. The three of them had been a close, closed triad almost from the time they were toddlers, musketeers who invariably snubbed any would-be d'Artagnan. They had their private jokes and private slang and private laughter at the efforts of their contemporaries in the town to copy their speech and dress and comportment. My mother always said that they were rotten little snobs during their teen years, but she was watching them from a six-year advantage in age, and I have a notion that in her time she may have been much the same.

I don't think they were snobs, exactly, but it would have been odd if they had not been aware of their position in the town. The Scogginses and Ungelbauers and Hodges were the three main families in Sturkeyville. The Scogginses had land and the bank, the Ungelbauers had coal, and the Hodges had the foundry. Scogginses and Ungelbauers and Hodges served together on the boards of the businesses and on the vestry of the church, and they tended to marry each other. But my grandparents' generation produced only four children: Holmes, Dorothy, my mother, and Uncle Caleb; and my mother astonished the town by marrying a young man from—of all places—Chicago. That left one marriageable daughter and two marriageable sons in The Families, and it was wholly taken for granted that Dorothy would marry one of the two.

In the event, she chose Holmes. I have no idea why. Family lore has it that she made her choice by flipping a coin, because she prized both young men equally. It could be true. It was said that up to the very day she announced her choice she had never given the slightest indication that she preferred Holmes to Caleb.

Uncle Caleb, as might have been expected (and as would have been expected of Holmes, had their positions been reversed) was wholly the good sport. He gave the couple, as a formal gift, an elaborate coffee service from Tiffany's, and, in addition, in recognition of the old comradeship, a facetiously inscribed silver cup. He stood as best man at the wedding, fulfilling his duties efficiently and with aplomb. He was the organizer of the housewarming party that welcomed the honeymooners home from Europe and into their new house on Wetzel Avenue. He became the very model of Old Family Friend.

But he had been more grievously wounded than anyone realized, and he changed. It was not quick or obvious, but after a time it became evident that some sort of spark had been extinguished or arrested, that he had elected, for a time at least, to become more spectator than participant. Although his demeanor did not alter perceptibly, those around him were aware of a certain detachment, of an ironical and sometimes almost sour amusement at most matters that would, under other circumstances, have been the chief concerns of his life. He declined to take serious things seriously. He pretended to an unchanged attitude, but he was not serious even about the pretense, and after a time he gave up pretending and frankly spent most of his time at play.

Thus he had plenty of time for me. He taught me the rudiments of golf that summer (it was now five years since the marriage), and a good deal about guns, and made of me an excellent rider, for my age. He owned three very fine hunters, and one of them, a bay mare grown placid with age, was temporarily mine. We spent a great many afternoons perfecting my seat and practicing low jumps, and at least once a week we would pack a lunch and spend the day on horseback, exploring the dusty back roads of the county. It was during one of these rides that he told me about the feesters.

We were riding that day up a disused road called Dexter Lane, a narrow strip of soft white dust that climbed crookedly through a forest of pin oak and locust to the three abandoned mountain farms it had once served. The day was hot, and we rode at a peaceful walk, to the agreeable sounds of slow hooves in the dust and birdsong from the branches.

My eye was caught by the entrance to a road that seemed even more sunken in desuetude than Dexter Lane. "Hey, Uncle Caleb," I sang out, "where's that road go?"

"That?" he said. "Why, that's the back road down to Howard's Lake."

"A lake? Can we go down there to eat our lunch? Can we, Uncle Caleb?"

He hesitated, and then said, "Why not?" We turned the horses in at the old road and began the descent. The road fell steeply, zigzagging in sharp switchbacks; I do not believe that a car could have negotiated it even in its best days. Years of erosion had cut a complicated system of foot-deep gullies, which sometimes followed the direction of the road and sometimes cut across it, so that we had to watch very carefully where the horses placed their feet. The trees grew more thickly here, their lowest branches spanned the road not far above our heads, so that we traveled in a twisting green tunnel. A silent tunnel, I suddenly realized: the normal small noises of the forest had unaccountably ceased. The only sound was the soft thud of hooves and the creak of our leather.

We emerged from the trees quite suddenly, into bright noon sunlight. We had come into a steep clearing, and from our position on its upper side we were looking over treetops down to the lake below and the house that stood beside it.

They were black. The lake lay like an irregular slab of polished anthracite, utterly black, utterly without motion, utterly lifeless except for the profusion of coarse hairy weeds that blanketed the hundred yards or so between the edge of the water and the edge of the woods. Across the lake the house rose from the weeds, a building disproportionately narrow and tall, topheavy, somehow four stories high and two rooms wide. It was built of black stone, great heavy blocks that would perhaps have suited a manor house of ducal dimension, but which, in this gaunt structure, conveyed an unpleasant sense of materials ill-used and weight wholly at variance with size. The weeds grew close all around it; there were no outbuildings. It towered in silent paradox there beside the black dead lake, grotesque and menacing.

"Boy," I said. "Boy. That's pretty spooky, Uncle Caleb. Who lived there?" I said "lived." It was clear that the house had been uninhabited for a long time. It was in excellent condition, though. No vandals had sported here.

"Feester," Uncle Caleb said. "Captain Elihu Feester. Shall we have our lunch now?"

We moved back into the shade of the outermost trees and tethered the horses, and then, as we ate our sandwiches and apples, Uncle Caleb told me what he knew or had invented about Elihu Feester and the feesters in the lake.

When Uncle Caleb told me a story, I never asked whether it was true or made up. It never occurred to me to ask how he had come to learn of Captain Elihu's disastrous voyage and all the events preceding his arrival in Sturkeyville, or how he was able to describe in such detail the grisly metamorphoses that were visited upon Feester's family. Fact or embroidery, it was all part of the story, part of the spell Uncle Caleb wove around me that day. Those poor doomed children came alive for me, they and their crazed mother, immured in the gloom of the locked and shuttered house, creeping with sticky sounds through the airless hot darkness of its hallways, struggling against the lure of the black waters of the lake just beyond the door. They were quite innocent, then, and so was their wretched mother, and even Captain Elihu was guilty of nothing more than theft from simple savages, an act not counted a great crime in those times.

That was what Feester had done, Uncle Caleb said. He had stolen treasure of some sort from the inhabitants of that remote South Sea island. And with the treasure he took, all unknowing, something dreadful: a curse, as the superstitious would have it, or, alternately, in the opinion of the more enlightened (among whom Uncle Caleb included himself), a microbe or enzyme or something else that would no doubt in due course be susceptible of scientific explanation.

Whatever it was, it turned human beings into something quite inhuman and thoroughly dangerous, and by the time Feester's travels brought him to Sturkeyville he had experienced things that might well have driven him into lunacy. Perhaps they had, but if so, he concealed it well. He arrived in town with style and élan, riding a spirited horse and bringing with him a heavy wagon driven by a burly man who carried a pistol in his pocket and never strayed more than a few feet from the wagon by day or night. Feester took a room in the hotel and began to explore the countryside, each day taking a different road out of town. Each evening he dined at the hotel and then entered the bar to spend a couple of hours drinking the famous local rye whiskey and conversing with the inquisitive regulars. He was genial enough, but conveyed a minimum of information: his name was Feester; he was retired; he was looking for a quiet place to settle down and enjoy his retirement; yes, he thought it might be here.

He extracted more information than he dispensed, and by the end of a week he had learned a good deal about the people of the town and the geography of the county. He had also, it transpired, selected a location for his house. One morning he turned up at the bank and spent several hours with Ezra Stallworth; before the day was out, he had duly recorded a deed to the old Phillips place, twelve hundred acres of steep forest land surrounding Howard's Lake. The town observed with interest Stallworth's respectful—indeed, almost obsequious—manner toward Feester and drew the obvious conclusion: Feester was very rich. It was said that he had paid spot cash in gold, counting off the coins from a heap dumped out of a heavy leather grip onto Stallworth's table, and that the pile was

hardly diminished by removal of the substantial sum paid
for the acreage. The rest of the gold, gossip had it, was
left with Stallworth on deposit. It seemed likely. Certainly,
from that day on, Stallworth became Feester's sponsor in
the town, and, in due course, when Feester began to pay
court to Agatha, Stallworth extended every possible en-
couragement. But then Stallworth would have encouraged
Agatha to marry a toad, the town said, if the toad had
enough money.

Feester continued to live in the hotel while the house
was being built. The burly man left town, and the wagon
stood empty behind the livery stable, its contents un-
loaded one night and hidden, presumably somewhere on
the Phillips place. The house grew slowly and expen-
sively beside the lake, much visited by Sunday-afternoon
buggy riders who had heard rumors of its surpassing ugliness. It was finished at last, and wagon loads of furniture
were moved into it, and on a rainy morning in April
Agatha Stallworth, spinster, and Elihu Feester, bachelor,
were united in holy matrimony at St. David's Church.

They were not a romantic couple. The bride was pushing thirty and had inherited the craggy Stallworth look,
and the groom, two inches shorter and square in build,
wore a seafaring beard that seemed to Sturkeyville to be
more than a little raffish. But they appeared to be fond
enough of each other, and they lost no time in populating
the strange house by the lake with children, four little
girls born by the time they had been four years married.
Feester, in naming them, displayed an unexpected touch
of classical learning: he called them Clio, Thalia, Urania,
and Polyhymnia, causing a minor scandal by the outland-
ish names. By the time Polyhymnia was born, Clio had
begun to change.

Because it was still there, the old curse or disease. If it
was a disease, Feester was only a carrier, not subject to
the symptoms but infecting those around him; and if a
curse, then one that doomed him to remain free of the
horror but compelled to watch as it destroyed first his
crew, and now his family. Little Clio's sturdy legs, just
coming fully under her control, and much used for running and jumping, became traitors; they bent at odd angles and would not support her weight. Her bones were
softening; not just in her legs, but all the bones of her
body, becoming not bone but flexible cartilage or baleen.

Her small, even teeth fell out and were swiftly replaced by new ones, twice as many as she had had before, crooked, crowded and pointed, changing the shape of her softened jaw. Her skin turned deadly pale, and then a sick frog-belly white. Her legs began to fuse together, and her arms to fuse to her sides.

That was the beginning. It was to be several years before the change was complete, but it proceeded steadily and inexorably through all those years. Clearly, it moved more slowly in children than in adults; on the ship, as Feester's crew was stricken one by one, it had been only a matter of weeks from the first onset to full, feral metamorphosis, only weeks from the first weakness of the legs to the time when they slipped overboard to assume the life of the sea creatures they had become, or began to try to devour their shipmates and had to be shot.

Each of the children began at an age earlier than her next older sister; the baby Polyhymnia never in all her life had legs that could walk. Perhaps she was never in her life truly human. By the time Clio was six the change was equally advanced in all of them, and almost complete; they continued to grow, but they were now what they would be when they achieved full size. And they were probably already dangerous.

But Agatha never accepted that. Indeed, it remains a question whether she accepted even the fact of the changes that were occurring before her eyes. Her behavior suggests that she had removed herself entirely from reality. She seemed to believe that the pallid cylinders humping wetly aross the floors of the dark house (dark because their great lidless eyes could not abide light) were still her four little girls, to be played with and sung to and tucked in at bedtime.

Feester no doubt attempted to reason with her, but there was no possibility that he could say anything capable of penetrating her madness. The more urgent he became, the more she perceived him as a monster, a Saturn bent upon the destruction of his own offspring. But some part of her understood quite well that there was absolutely no way for her to flee with these children, and she never attempted it; instead she created for herself a state of siege, setting up an ingenious system of barricades and locked doors that made a redoubt of the cellar and several ground-floor rooms. Here she lived in the dark in per-

petual terror, lavishing love and tenderness upon the four
small horrors that had been her children, crooning children's songs to them in the clammy blackness of a cave-
like room in the cellar which had come to be their lair.

One can imagine a desperate Feester prowling at night
through his part of the house, scourged by an absolute
conviction that the creatures must be destroyed and simultaneously stretched on the rack of an agonized and hopeless grief for his lost children. He wept sometimes, it may
be supposed, or raged incontinently and cursed God for
allowing his ship to survive the storm. He temporized
and procrastinated. And in the end he waited too long,
and it was too late.

"It was *toooo* late," Uncle Caleb said and fell silent. It
was a storyteller's trick. He was waiting for me to say,
"Why? Why was it too late? What happened?" And of
course I said it: "What happened?"

"Well, no one knows, really," he said. "Of course no
one ever saw Agatha again. I think we have to conclude
that they ate her. And then, it seems, they left the house
and went into the lake, down into that black water, down
to live in the mud where they were meant to live. *And
there they live to this very day."*

It was very dramatic, and very well done, and despite
any theories about the proper setting for the narration of
a spooky story, it seemed to me at that moment that I
was in just exactly the right place to enjoy the maximum
thrill from this one. Looking down at that blind, black
house I found myself elaborating and enlarging upon Uncle Caleb's brisk summation of those last events, wondering whether Agatha, in her last desperate seconds, beset
by greedy teeth, might have had a flash of bright, hard
sanity and realized, in her moment of lucidity before the
final darkness took her, that these were not—were not
by any means—her children. And it seemed to me quite
easy to visualize the flight after the feast: the silent opening of a ground-floor door and the faint gleam of four
pale shapes in the darkness moving soundlessly across the
weeds to slide without splashing into the black water. And
in the house, silence.

We led the horses back up to Dexter Lane and
mounted. Uncle Caleb said, "Shall we go on to the end of
the road?"

"What's up there?" I asked.

"Three farms. All abandoned for, oh, forty years. Kraft, MacTavish and Love were the farmers. The Krafts and the MacTavishes are farming over in the valley now, but I don't know what became of the Loves. Nobody will farm those places any more. They've got a reputation for being hard-luck farms. Something to do with the feesters in the lake, I imagine."

"Aw, come on, Uncle Caleb. There aren't really any feesters, are there?"

He grinned. "Why, I think you'll have to make up your own mind about that one, Nick. But I'll tell you this: there was indeed a man named Elihu Feester, and he built that house and married Agatha Stallworth and had four daughters. And it's in the archives that Agatha and the four daughter disappeared. Feester reported to the sheriff that Agatha had taken the children and run away. Stallworth backed him up, and the story was accepted, if not necessarily believed in all quarters. As to the curse and monsters in the lake—a good many people in the country believe it."

"But you don't, do you, Uncle Caleb?"

He continued to grin. "I always keep an open mind, Nick. 'There are more things . . .'—you know the quotation. Who can say?"

By unspoken mutual consent we had turned the horses toward home. Being pointed toward the stables aroused thoughts of oats in their heads, and despite the heat they tended to insist on trotting. Even this unaccustomed liveliness in my old Salome did not wholly take my mind off the feesters, however, and after a while I said, "Well, I know stuff like that's just in stories. Or movies. Not in Sturkeyville."

"But you'd like to believe it, is that it?"

"Well, you know. The house and the lake. They're really spooky, boy. You can believe it when you look at them."

Uncle Caleb said, "They belong to your grandfather, you know. The house and the lake. They still call it the Phillips place. For some reason it never did get to be called the Feester place."

"Grandpa? Grandpa owns it?"

"He does. And one of these days I'll own it."

"Gosh. Gosh. What'll you do with it, Uncle Caleb?"

"Why, nothing. Absolutely nothing at all. Except pay the taxes. That was your great-grandfather's arrangement with Captain Feester."

"Hey," I said. "Wait a minute. You never told me that part."

"So I didn't," he said. "I'll tell you now. A postscript, really." He paused. "Feester went away not too long after that. Went away, and wasn't seen or heard of again. He told your great-grandfather that he was accursed, that he would have to go where there were no people, and he needed legal advice before he went. The arrangement he wanted to make was this: he asked your great-grandfather to take the proper legal steps to insure that the house and the lake would stay undisturbed for as long as possible— forever, if that could be done. But there was no such thing as the modern trust in those days, and the law forbade entail. So there appeared to be no way to accomplish what he wanted. The upshot finally was that the two men shook hands on a gentlemen's agreement: Feester would deed the land to your great-grandfather in exchange for his word that the property would be kept in the Scoggins family in perpetuity, if possible, and that it would be kept forever undisturbed. The idea was that each Scoggins would deed the property to his eldest son as soon as the son was of responsible age and temperament, and that the sons were to be impressed with the importance of preserving things as they were.

"Some money went with the deal. Quite a lot of money, apparently. The Scoggins money dates from then. It seems that Feester's gold had arrived just in time to save Stallworth's bank from some sort of fatal default that had resulted from old Ezra's loony stubbornness, and Feester had taken a controlling interest in the bank in exchange. Your great-grandfather got Feester's stock in the bank, and Lawyer Scoggins was suddenly in the banking business. He was good at it too, and greedy, and he tended to keep properties he foreclosed. So by the time two or three panics had come and gone he owned a fair percentage of this end of the county. We still have most of it.

"And so in a few years your grandfather will be making a deed to me, and then it'll be my responsibility to see that everything is preserved intact. And to begin to think about what to do about the next generation."

He fell silent. I was riding a little in the lead, and I

turned to look at him. On his face was an expression I
had never seen him wear before, an expression, I now
realized, of an emotion very close to despair. I knew,
from overhead parental conversations, something about his
loss of Dorothy Hodge, and I was able to make the connection between that and the remark about the next generation. I blurted, "You mean you're *never* going to get
married, Uncle Caleb?"

The bleak look intensified for a moment and then disappeared, and he grinned again. "Oh, I wouldn't say that,
Nick. Time will tell. But if it should happen that I don't
marry, I expect you've figured out that you're next in
line. In twenty or thirty years I may well be deeding the
place to you."

"I don't want it," I said, instantly and without having to
think about it. "I don't want it."

That was during the summer of 1934. What Uncle
Caleb had told me was, I have no doubt, all he then
knew, or had heard, about the feesters. It was not
until five years later that he learned something further,
when, on his thirty-fifth birthday, Grandpa Scoggins
handed him a deed to the Phillips place and told him the
rest of the story. I was sixteen then, still spending my
summers in Sturkeyville, and once every summer Uncle
Caleb and I made the excursion up Dexter Lane and ate
our lunch in the clearing. The house and the lake never
changed at all from year to year, and even though I was
five years older now, and (I firmly believed) reasonably
sophisticated, the place still seemed pretty spooky. I said
as much to Uncle Caleb.

"Yes," he said. "I want you to promise me something,
Nick. Promise me that you'll never go down there. That
you won't even come this far unless I'm with you."

I stared at him. He appeared to be perfectly serious.
"You believe it!" I said, incredulously. "You believe
there's feesters in there!"

"I didn't say that. I just said I don't want you going
down there. I mean it, too."

And he did. His expression left no doubt about it. It
was quite obvious that this was a matter he took very
seriously. I said, "Well, sure, Uncle Caleb. Sure. I promise."

I was more than a little intimidated. He had never used
that tone with me before. I was not wholly surprised,

though. Each summer I was finding him a little changed; somewhat more detached, a bit gloomier, a touch more cynical. My mother and grandmother did a lot of worrying about him, although they simultaneously seemed to find a certain melancholy romantic satisfaction in his state of mind: "An old-fashioned broken heart," they said. For myself, I found it totally unsatisfactory; I wanted my old Uncle Caleb back.

Then Holmes Ungelbauer died. He died around Christmastime, suddenly, of pneumonia. He was a wiry polo player of thirty-six, the sort of person of whom it is said that he never had a sick day in his life; the fact of his death was difficult for the town to accept. He left no children, only his widow, the former Dorothy Hodge.

My grandmother's letters to my mother that winter as usual concerned themselves largely with Uncle Caleb and his state of mind, and we were easily able to infer from what she wrote that despite his undoubted grief over Holmes's death, a faint but perceptible improvement in his spirit was coming about. Within a year he was openly paying court to the widow, and during the summer after the courtship began—my last summer before going into the army—he was a different man altogether; he was, I think, very much like the young man who had lost Dorothy to Holmes ten years before, the young man I did not remember because I had been too young when it happened. He was playful and funny and his ironies had lost their bitter edge. He was a happy man, a man who clearly believed he was going to recover a thing of value that he had given up as forever lost.

He did not get it, of course. He had bad luck, Uncle Caleb. I was in the army by then, and my mother's long, chatty letters, reaching me in Fort Benning and Camp Shelby, and then in a series of forlorn places in Western Europe, kept me up to date (more up to date than I thought really necessary, to tell the truth) on events in Sturkeyville. The villain was a man named Willing, Otis R. Willing. At any rate my mother and grandmother thought of him as a villain. But then Dorothy was someone they had always known, and Willing was a newcomer, and so it was natural of them to assign the guilt (if guilt there was) to him, not to her.

He was vice-president and general superintendent at the foundry, a big, serious engineer from Purdue or perhaps Michigan State, a former Bright Young Man at Big Steel, who had been lured away by a challenge to put the moribund Hodge Brothers Foundry back on its feet. He had burst violently into the musty corridors of the old firm a few years before, an expensive expert with a reputation to uphold and a fierce joy in his work. He began with a merciless pruning of deadwood, ridding the offices of a puttering horde of routine-bound functionaries who had long since ceased to do any productive work, but who, by tradition, had every reason to believe they would remain on the payroll until at last their infirmities precluded even token appearances at work. He turned then to the denizens of the executive wing and found that he could not depose them; they were, after all, members of the family. But he bypassed them ruthlessly, so that within a few months they were left as functionless ornaments in their elegant offices, free to practice their putting on the carpet or gather together for futile indignation meetings or otherwise fill pointless days. Their responsibilities were assumed by men who came with Willing, men like himself, competent, assured, socially graceless, and, by Sturkeyville's standards, without backgrounds. They came with their prairie accents and degrees from unknown colleges and remade the plant; well before the arrival of the fat contracts of the war the foundry was moving steadily toward profitable operations.

An executive position in the foundry carried with it a social position in the town; Willing was immediately and automatically a member of the country club and the hunt (a purely honorary membership; he did not ride at all) and was invited to take his lunches at the round table at the Updegraff Hotel. If he had had a wife she would have been asked into the Hospital Guild and the Bridge Whist Society. But he had no wife, and that lack made it difficult to fit him into social life at the level of his entry. There was, furthermore, a whiff of wickedness about his reputation: Fred Ungelbauer, who sat on boards of directors in Pittsburgh, had brought back rumors of a mistress of long standing, and that, together with his age (he was probably forty), set him somewhat apart from the manageable classification of Eligible Bachelor. But, although it was an awkward situation, it was not a real problem because for the first couple of years he appeared quite literally to have no time for anything but his work. Then

he married the widow Ungelbauer, and there was no
longer any question about his place in the scheme of
things.

They presented the town with a *fait accompli*. One
Monday morning Wetzel Avenue awoke to see Willing's
car parked in Dorothy's driveway. The street watched
avidly until Willing emerged from the house and drove off
to the foundry, and then it began to telephone Dorothy.
By noon the whole town knew that they had been married
on Saturday in a county seat a hundred miles away.

I never learned where Uncle Caleb heard the news, or
what his initial reaction was. He was not the sort of man
who displayed emotion in public, and he may have managed not to show what he felt. But the shock must have
been enormous. He had lost Dorothy again, and not only
lost her, but lost her to a man who could never have entered his head as a rival, a man he would have thought
of only as hired help, a worthy person, no doubt, but not
the sort who had any right even to dream of someone like
Dorothy. I think I understood Uncle Caleb's mental pro-
cesses pretty well, and it seems to me that this action of
Dorothy's—this action that he surely at first flatly disbe-
lieved—must have been a humiliation almost beyond bearing. When he lost her to Holmes he lost her to an equal.
But Otis R. Willing—ah, that was humiliating.

In November I stepped on a land mine in a vinyard
above the Moselle, and by Christmas I was in the hospital
in Baltimore, with a right leg that was going to be a per-
manent problem, but comforted by the knowledge that I
would never again have to spend my days and nights in a
frozen hole. My parents came, and my mother cried over
me for a time, and got over it, and then cried again when
I asked about Uncle Caleb. When she left the room to
seek a vase for the flowers she had brought, I put the
question to my father.

"He's in bad shape, Nick," he said. "Drinking hard.
Turning into a hermit. He moved out of grandpa's house
a year ago, and he's living alone in the country with his
horses. He's fixed up an old farmhouse out by Howard's
Lake, and even your grandparents don't see him more
than once a month. It's bad."

It was indeed. Not long after V-J Day I finally got
back to Sturkeyville, and on the second day of my visit I

borrowed grandpa's car and drove up to the end of Dexter Lane, where Uncle Caleb had set himself up in the old Kraft farmhouse. I was appalled. Although he had not in fact changed in appearance very much, nor become dirty and slovenly, as I had half expected, he had undergone a change of character. Or of personality, at least. His old detachment and gentle irony had soured and curdled and become an unnerving blend of pessimism and cynicality. I found myself almost disliking him. We sat in the big room he had created by knocking out all the first-floor walls except those of the kitchen, and I listened to his bitter commentary with sorrow and incredulity. He had reached the point of viewing all accomplishment—including the war just ended—as futile and pointless; all human effort, in his black view, was inspired by sordid and ignoble motives; all human beings were knaves, and women were the worst of the lot. Not that they were entirely wicked and malicious, he said; they were simply empty and thoughtless and without character, and hence easily susceptible of being led by evil men into discreditable behavior. And such men were the basest and lowest of our low race.

I knew he was talking about Willing, and he knew I knew, and soon he began to use the name. He had been drinking pretty steadily, and as his rage and resentment fed upon themselves his speech began to lapse into incoherency. I was a little frightened, and I tried—as I had been trying all afternoon—to change the subject.

"What do you hear from your neighbors down at the lake?" I said.

"Neighbors?"

"The feesters. They're your neighbors now, aren't they?"

He gave me a startled, suspicious glare. "The feesters? What do you know about the feesters?"

"Why, I know all about them," I said. "You told me yourself. Five-foot aquatic maggots with shark's mouths. Members of the local gentry until The Curse of Hoog, Fish-God of the South Seas, fell upon them. Named for selected Muses. I've always wanted to meet a maggot named Polyhymnia."

His face changed expression several times as I spoke, altering from suspicion to anger, and then to an odd combination of fear and something akin to smugness. "Care-

ful, there, Nick," he said. "Be careful. Don't make fun of
things you don't know anything about. You might be
sorry."

"Now what the hell does that mean? 'Might be sorry.'
You mean the feesters might come and eat me?"

"You might be sorry."

"Oh, for God's sake," I said. I felt sick. He was deadly
serious. This was not just drunken maundering, it was
lunacy. I shouted at him: "For God's sake, Uncle Caleb,
what are you talking about?"

"Never mind," he said. "Never mind. Believe what you
like. Call it what you like. Just stay away from Howard's
Lake, that's all."

And that was all I got out of him. I had to report to my
grandparents not only the total failure of my attempt to
lure him back to real life, but also my conviction that it
was hopeless to try. He had, to put it simply, gone off his
head; I saw nothing to do but wait, and hope for some
sort of recovery. I was very wise at that time, with a far
greater certainty of the answers to hard questions than I
possess today, and it was perfectly clear to me that a man
who believed in ancient curses and monsters at the bottom of the local lake was, *ipso facto*, insane. But I thought
it was only temporary, a consequence of preserving into
advanced age (he was over forty) emotions that were
seemly only in the young. It had been, to be sure, a bitter
experience for him, to lose Dorothy twice; but I myself
had loved and lost, and recovered very nicely, and I saw
no reason why Uncle Caleb, an older man whose feelings
could not possibly be as deep as mine had been, should
not show an equal resilience in recovering from his geri-
atric infatuation.

Then he lost her for the third time. That is how he saw
it, at any rate. It might plausibly be argued that in none
of the three cases had he lost her, because he had never
in fact had her. But when she was once more widowed,
he allowed himself a certain amount of hope again, and
when that small hope was extinguished, he went irretriev-
ably over the edge.

It had been a foolish hope, to be sure. Dorothy had rejected him twice and apparently had been entirely con-
tented through all the years with Holmes and Willing.
After Willing's murder and the attendant turmoil and
publicity, no reasonable person could have expected her

to stay in Sturkeyville and take up with Uncle Caleb. But Uncle Caleb was by then very far indeed from a reasonable person.

He was a suspect in the murder. The prime suspect, the only suspect, really, except for the general fear of a vagrant madman. As it happened, Uncle Caleb was investigated and absolved almost immediately, and the crime was generally believed to have been the work of an insane hobo, who had probably caught the next freight train out of town. The case went down on the books as an unsolved murder. And the town went in fear.

Their fear was quite sensible; it had in truth been an atrocious crime. Willing had been working late that night, as was his habit. He was building an entirely new plant for the foundry, south of town in the direction of the lake, and the last weeks before production was to begin were hectic in the extreme. A night watchman saw him leaving the building at about eleven o'clock. It was a night of torrential rain, and water had shorted out some of the new wiring, so that there were no lights in the parking lot. Willing's was the only parked car.

The watchman's later testimony was that he had heard what he thought might be a scream, coming faintly through the roar of the rain. He went immediately to the door that gave onto the parking lot, and peered out. He could see nothing. He ran (as fast as he could; he was an old man) to his cubicle for the flashlight he should have been carrying. He threw its beam out into the parking lot. Then he stood frozen in the doorway for a little time, retching and trembling. When he was able to overcome his paralysis, he ran (faster this time) to the telephone.

The sheriff was an experienced lawman who had seen his share of grisly sights. but he admitted afterward that he had been shaken by what had been done to Willing. "Get the tarp, for God's sake," he said to a deputy. "Jesus Christ. I never saw anything like that. That's crazy." He stopped. "Crazy," he said. "Caleb Scoggins, by God. That's Otis Willing, there. Got to be Scoggins. We'll just go out there and get him. Keebler, you stay here till the meat wagon comes. Stark, you come with me. By God, we'll beat him home."

They slipped and slewed up Dexter Lane through the downpour. "No car's been down this road," the deputy said. "Not a track."

"He went down before the rain started."

"That was early this morning," the deputy said.

"He walked, then. Or rode his horse. Watch what you're doing."

The Kraft house faced the end of the road, and the headlights lit up its front. There was no sign of life. The deputy swept about with the spotlight. "Nobody's used the front door," he said. "Not a track."

"You take the flashlight and go around the house," the sheriff said. "I'll watch the front."

The deputy disappeared into the rain. He was back in a few minutes. "Nobody's been in or out since it started raining. Not a human track. Looks like maybe a dog dragged something through. But no Caleb Scoggins."

The sheriff felt a sense of triumph, as he never failed to mention when he told about it. "I figured I had him, then," he said. "I figured to hide the car in the woods, and then me and Stark would lay low till he got there. I thought he'd probly come back over the hills and wouldn't see the car tracks. And right then, by God, was when the front door opened, and there stood Caleb in his pajamas, blinkin' in the headlights."

So Uncle Caleb was cleared, and the town was left with the mad hobo theory and went in fear at night. Dorothy was not one of the fearful: she left town immediately and never came back, except many years later, to be buried. I suppose there were too many memories of tragedy in the town for her to stay, but her flight also served to save her from the terrors of the next few years. Because there were more murders.

Two of them, both crimes of the most appalling gruesomeness. There was a disappearance as well, which added to the general disquiet, although it appeared to have nothing to do with the murders. But then it was a frightened town in those years, apprehensive of the darkness and suspicious of strangers. The sensational press had a feast, spreading the story of the Sturkeyville Butcher from coast to coast and seizing the opportunity to recount once more the stories of Jack the Ripper and other mass murderers.

And Uncle Caleb, bereft now for the third time, disintegrated rapidly, crawling further into the bottle and wholly abandoning any effort to live a life of normal sociability. News of him came from Mattie Helms, my grandmother's housekeeper and my old friend, who was my only correspondent in the town since my grandfather's death and my grandmother's stroke. Mattie wrote, "Well Nick you would not believe your Uncle Caleb, I think the poor man has left his senses entirely, he does not wash and is very dirty and drunk. It is safe to say that Dorothy Hodge has a lot to answer for but God will judge. Now he has left the Kraft farm, he has moved to the old Feester house by Howard's Lake which is said by the country people to be haunted as I guess you know. It is almost a hundred years since anyone lived there, what it must be like inside I can not imagine. I wish you and your mother would come Nick and see if you can help him."

But I saw no way to help him, and indeed I was beginning to have certain small doubts about wanting to. The suspicions that nagged at me were of course unmentionable; I hardly let myself think about them, let alone discuss them with anyone else. It seemed to me, though, that I could read the same fear between the lines of Mattie's letter, and my mother's near-hysteria when Uncle Caleb's troubles were discussed seemed perhaps a touch excessive even for concern about a beloved brother's disintegration. Mother and Mattie were, of course, no more anxious to put their dread into words than I was, and we all kept our own counsel.

What troubled us was this: we had, reluctantly and unwillingly, been forced to conclude that all three of the murdered men stood in a relationship to Uncle Caleb that might have seemed to him—given the decrepit state of his mentality—to be inimical: first Willing, the contemptible man who had snatched away Dorothy and exposed Uncle Caleb to ridicule; then Gunther Hodge, who had brought Willing to Sturkeyville; and then Stark, the young deputy who had come to arrest him on the rainy night of Willing's death. These were not pleasant thoughts. But the person who had disappeared could in no way, I was grateful to note, be connected to Uncle Caleb: she was Wanda Karsky, a seventeen-year-old miner's daughter with a reputation for wildness, and no one but her parents thought there was much of a mystery about her disappearance. The consensus was that she had run off with a man and would end up on the street of a big city.

But the murders were a continuing occasion for brooding and black speculation. What could not be said aloud

festered at the back of my mind, and no matter how
much I tried to persuade myself that my conjectures mal-
igned Uncle Caleb most grievously, and that he was,
after all, hurting no one but himself by his lunacy, I remained prey to grim suspicions. And, although not a word
was spoken, I think my mother, to some degree, had the
same apprehensions.

The result was that for a long time I did not go to
Sturkeyville. My mother visited my grandmother from
time to time, but not nearly as often as she would have
done under other circumstances, and she never saw Uncle
Caleb at all. During this time I completed law school and
became a minor cog in a very large firm on LaSalle
Street. I acquired a wife, and a house in Winnetka, and a
son. Then my grandmother died, and I went to Sturkeyville again after all the years.

Uncle Caleb came to the funeral, an apparition that
bore only a remote resemblance to the Uncle Caleb of
old. It seemed to me now that he was hopelessly lost. He
was emaciated and slovenly in his dress, of course, and
afflicted with strange tics; but that was not what was ulti-
mately disquieting. It was his face. His eyes, especially,
were strange. He held them open to their utmost, in a
round, unblinking stare that seemed to be focused on
something other than his surroundings. He held his mouth
so that his lips were drawn into thin lines, keeping his
teeth always partially exposed. And he was pale, pale beyond belief, with a dead-white, shiny, almost translucent
pallor that was faintly disgusting.

"You need more sun, Uncle Caleb," I said. "You're
looking kind of bleached."

"Sun," he said. "I don't go out in the sun much. Both-
ers me. Stay inside most of the time. Too bright right
now." It was in fact a dull December day, the sun a wa-
tery, weak disc behind a thin cloud cover. "Oh, much too
bright," he said. His eyes were turned toward me, but the
focus of his enormous stare seemed to be somewhere to
my rear. "I'm living out at the Feester house now, you
know, Nick," he said. "As soon as all this is over, I want
you to come out there with me. Will you do that?"

"Sure, Uncle Caleb," I said. It was exactly what I
wanted. I believed that I had puzzled out some of the
answers, and I wanted to talk to him, to have the thing
out, to satisfy myself that my ugly ideas were only black

fictions. I was quite ready, now, to accept my uncle as a harmless lunatic, but the idea of homicidal mania had to be laid to rest.

The coffin was lowered into the grave. The ritual words were said, and everyone hurried to the waiting cars, grief suspended for the moment in the sheer discomfort of the day's bitter cold. The undertaker had assigned Uncle Caleb and me to the same car. My wife was not with me; she had given birth to our second son five days before and was snug at home in Winnetka. In the car he said, "You'll have to drive me back to the lake. I don't have a car that will run any more. Hostettler sent one of these things out to get me this morning." Hostettler was the undertaker.

Sturkeyville still favored funeral baked meats, and there was no way to avoid the customary luncheon at the house, an enormous heavy meal catered by the ladies of the Moravian Church. Uncle Caleb was not at table; he had disappeared upstairs, where, it transpired, he had hidden a bottle, perhaps years before. After everyone had eaten too much and departed, and Mattie Helms and my parents and I were sitting over a final cup of coffee, he appeared suddenly in the doorway. "All right, Nick, let's go," he said.

"Oh, Caleb," my mother said, "I *did* want to talk to you. It's been so long."

"Next time, next time. Come on, Nick." He was swaying in the doorway, glaring with that great round stare at some indeterminate point behind us, a scarecrow figure in a wrinkled expensive suit that was now several sizes too large for him. I seemed to have no choice. I said, "OK, Uncle Caleb. Let's go."

And so at last I found myself entering the Feester house. We drove in by the lower road, which came within a mile of the lake. The driveway in from the road, impassable for half a century, had been cleared and repaired, but it remained crooked and pitted and had to be negotiated slowly. I concentrated on my driving. The driveway ended abruptly, after making a sharp, steep turn around a limestone embankment, and we were suddenly out of the trees and facing the house.

The years had not improved it: it stood there among the frozen weeds with the same suggestion of paradox and seedy menace I had felt looking at it from the hillside long ago. It loomed blackly above us against the gray sky, top-heavy and brutal, a shuttered receptacle of old tragedy. Smoke was coming out of one of the gaunt chimneys, a human touch that compounded the paradox. I shivered and said, "Jesus, Uncle Caleb. How come you live out here?"

"Why, it's mine," he said. "Where else would I live?" He seemed to think that the answer was responsive. "Come on," he said. "It's cold out here."

It was anything but cold in the house, at least in the front ground-floor room where he lived. A great cast-iron stove, its pipe plugged roughly into the chimney above the mantel of the old fireplace, was pouring out heat in suffocating quantities. We entered into an oppressive unclean atmosphere of human odors long sealed in an overheated room, a staleness of unwashed bedding and a hermit's cooking utensils. It was pitch-black after the front door closed behind us, and Uncle Caleb led me by the arm into the room and struck a match and lighted an oil lamp. The bloom of yellow light illuminated a shadowy confusion of bulky furniture, with all the paraphernalia of his life scattered upon and among it in incondite heaps: groceries, tools, books, bottles and trash, indiscriminately piled together on table and chairs and floor. The bed in the corner was in shadow; I could not tell whether the welter upon it was part of the same rancid accumulation or only bedclothes long unchanged. I felt a little queasy.

"Have a seat, there, Nick," he said. "I'll stoke up the stove and fix us a drink. I've got some things to tell you. It's time, now." His face seemed to float at the edge of the shadows, the great round eyes staring out of it at something behind me. "That chair there," he said. "Just throw the stuff on the floor." I did as he commanded, but my skin crawled a little when I sat. I refused the drink; nothing could have induced me to put my lips to anything in that room.

"Now, first of all, I've got this for you," he said. He passed me a sheet of paper. I took it with extreme reluctance. I knew very well what it was, but I held it to the light and confirmed it: a warranty deed to the Phillips place.

"Uncle Caleb, I told you twenty years ago I don't want it," I said. "The old promise has been kept long enough.

If it was ever made at all. Sell the place, or let the county take it for taxes. This house ought to be torn down."

He paid no attention. "It's your responsibility now, Nick. A sacred trust. Family honor and all. You're bound to keep everything intact. Keep it intact and deed it to one of your sons. And set up a trust in your will to preserve it for as long as the law allows, in case you die before you can make a deed. I want your word. Your oath."

"Just a minute," I said. "Hold on. I said I didn't want it. I meant it. I'm going to put this thing in the stove. I see it hasn't been recorded, so that will be the end of it."

An expression of really appalling viciousness came over the pale face, and his voice went to the edge of a scream: "You will not. You will accept your responsibility. You are responsible now for four lives. You cannot cast that off."

"My God," I said. "You mean the feesters."

"Why, yes," he said, his voice suddenly quite reasonable. "Of course, the feesters. What else do you think this is all about?"

I took a deep breath. "Uncle Caleb." I said, "let's drop this bilge about the feesters. They're a campfire story to scare boy scouts with, and we both know it. But I do believe you're serious about wanting to keep the place intact and in the family, and I think I've figured out why. Shall I tell you?"

He gave me a sly look. "You're wrong, you know. The feesters are down there, all right. But go ahead. Tell me what you think."

"Here's how I've pieced it together," I said. "This isn't about superstition or curses and slimy things in the lake. It's about murder and conspiracy and scandal. The murders and conspiracy are a century old, now, but in Sturkeyville the scandal would be as fresh as ever, Sturkeyville being what it is.

"What I think, Uncle Caleb, is that our money—the Scoggins fortune—was founded on blackmail. I think that Elihu Feester murdered his wife and children and was caught or discovered by a couple of pillars of the community—one of them his own father-in-law—who proceeded to strip him of everything he had and then sent him off, a beggar threatened by the hangman.

"What did he have in that wagon of his? More gold

coin, maybe, maybe a big box of it. What'll you bet Great-
Grandpa and Ezra Stallworth got that, too? And then
Great-Grandpa beat Stallworth out of his share, somehow,
and got the bank as well.

"But the bodies were buried somewhere here on the
Phillips place. I don't think they'd have been put in the
lake, because sunken bodies have a way of surfacing
eventually. The bodies were buried here, and since their
discovery would raise the hue and cry for Feester, who
could be expected to talk if taken, they took steps to prevent any discovery. Great-Grandpa bought the place and
saw to it that it stayed wild and untenanted. He may even
have started the story of the curse and the feesters.

"I guess he must have told Grandpa all about it when
he deeded the place over, and impressed on him the importance of keeping those bodies hidden. Feester no doubt
would have been dead by then, but the discovery of the
bodies—or skeletons, I suppose—would have raised a lot
of questions. There must be no scandal. No, indeed. The
Scoggins were one of the First Families. Think what
Sturkeyville would do with a juicy morsel like that.

"And then it was your turn, Uncle Caleb, and you continued everything just as it was before, and now you want
me to take over. Well, I won't. I don't suppose the events
were exactly as I've put them together, but it has to be
something like that, and I want no part of it. Scandal
won't bother me. I don't live in Sturkeyville, and everybody's got a thief somewhere in his ancestry. Anyhow,
everybody involved in this thing has been dead for a long,
long time. So I'll say it again: I don't want title to this
place. I won't take it."

I was aware that my voice had become very loud and
that it shook a little. I leaned forward to peer at him,
searching for a clue to the effect of my thunderous pro-
nouncement. And Uncle Caleb tittered.

I am not sure what I had expected, but it was most certainly not that. He tittered and said, "Nick, you're crazy,"
—which, under the circumstances, struck me as grimly
comical. "Do you really believe the reason we've got to
save this place is just to prevent gossip?" he said. "Who
cares about that? I tell you the feesters are alive under
the ice down there. They're alive and they've got to be
kept a secret. You've got to see that."

He was passionately sincere, poor lunatic. I said, "Why, Uncle Caleb? Why do they have to be kept a secret?"

"Why, because they're dangerous," he said. "They kill people. They've done some really awful things these last few years. They've got to be watched. But if anybody finds out about it, they'll come down and destroy them."

"Well, why not?"

"Why not? Why not? Because it would be murder, that's why not."

"But they're murderers themselves, aren't they? And not even human?"

He answered quickly and glibly: "Oh, they're not responsible. It's their nature. You couldn't call it murder. Anyhow, they've only killed people who deserved it. If you look at it right, they actually ought to be thanked."

"You're talking about Otis Willing, aren't you? And Gunther Hodge and Tom Stark?"

"Yes, yes. Nobody could say *they* were any great loss to anybody. Oh, the feesters knew what they were doing. They're amazing, really. Justice is what they're interested in."

I had to pursue it to the end. "And how about Wanda? Wanda Karsky?"

He did not answer immediately. "Well," he said at last, "That one surprised me. The feesters didn't even know her. It's kind of a puzzle. But I'll tell you what I think. I think maybe they've begun to like it, that maybe sometimes they can't help themselves. That's why they've got to be watched. But don't you worry. I'll watch them. And when I'm gone, you'll have to do the watching. You see that now, don't you?" He sounded, suddenly, frightened and vulnerable.

For better or worse, I made a decision at that moment. I cannot say that I take any pride in it or that it shows a proper and responsible regard for the public weal; but my suspicions were still only suspicions, and he was my uncle and had been the light of my boyhood. I told myself that he was physically in very bad shape, that he could hardly have very long to live, and that to harass a dying man for something that was probably only a creation of my own imagination would be unforgivable. And it is quite possible—little as I care to admit it—that the fear of scandal, which I had just been deriding so strenuously, was the critical influence.

At any rate, I elected at that moment to take no action. I said, "All right, Uncle Caleb. I'll keep the deed. And you keep watch on the feesters. You watch them very carefully, very carefully indeed. Because if they ever get loose and harm someone, I promise you it will be the end of them, and a pretty terrible end, too. Do you understand me? Do you grasp what I'm saying?"

"Oh, I do, Nick, I do," he said. "You don't have to worry about it. I'll be all right. From now on they'll stay in their place, down there in the mud where they belong. I'll see to that. And I'm glad you've decided to do your duty and take on the ownership. I knew you would, of course. You've never been one to shirk your responsibilities. I guess that takes care of everything. You can leave, now."

And that was that. We did not even shake hands. I heard the slam of the door and a clash of bolts behind me, and I stood on the step and took great breaths of the cold air, clearing from my lungs the fog of Uncle Caleb's noisome den. Then I drove back to town and told my mother some lies: that Uncle Caleb was living quite comfortably out there at the lake; that he was neither as drunken nor as crazy as we had supposed; that we need have no fear about his future behavior; and that he had sent his love to her. I think she half believed me, because she wanted to.

Back in Chicago the old suspicions continued to nag at me, augmented, I must admit, by stabs of conscience and an uneasy conviction that I had made a tragic error. But the months passed, and then the years, and no dire news came from Sturkeyville. I decided at last that I had after all been right. Uncle Caleb and his troubles became, with the passage of time, matters that I thought about only occasionally, and then not for long. Those rare occasions came when my mother entertained visitors from Sturkeyville, who would, at her delicate but ruthless insistence, reluctantly tell what they knew about how things were now with Uncle Caleb.

They always brought an account of a deteriorating situation, describing a hermit committed to the absolute extreme of solitude, a man upon whom no one had laid eyes for several years. The house and the lake remained inviolate, carefully avoided by the populace. Twice a year, perhaps, the sheriff would send a deputy to ascertain that the hermit Scoggins was still alive. The deputy would thunder at the door until he heard a voice from inside; having heard it, he would report to the sheriff that the nut still lived, and that would be Uncle Caleb's sole contact with the outside world until the next official visit. It was not a reassuring state of affairs, but no one doubted that it was better than having him locked away.

Then one day I saw on an inside page of the *Tribune* a story with a Sturkeyville byline that instantly collapsed my rickety defense against facing the truth about Uncle Caleb. Another murder had been committed, an atrocity as bad as the rest. As I read, I realized that I had been expecting it and that I had, without realizing it, already made plans. I knew exactly what I was going to do.

I arrived in the late afternoon. The lake was not frozen, now, and the weeds were green, and yet the house seemed even more forbidding than on the gray, bitter day when I had seen it last. There was absolutely no sign that any human being had ever been here, except for the fact of the house itself. I beat on the door, first with the heel of my fist and then, when that had no result, with a stone. The noise was great.

After a time there was a voice from the other side of the door. "Get out!" it said. "Go away!"

"It's me, Uncle Caleb," I shouted. "Me, Nick."

Silence. I let several minutes pass and then beat again with my stone. The voice said, "Go away."

"I'm not going, Uncle Caleb," I said, "and it's no use your saying 'go away.' I'm not going until you let me in or you come out. I won't go away until you've talked to me."

There was silence again for a time, and then I heard bolts being pulled and the snick of the lock. There was a pause, and he said, "All right, you can come in."

I pushed the door open. I saw no one. The doors to the right and left were both closed. From the darkness at the end of the hall he said, "Close the door."

"For Pete's sake, Uncle Caleb," I said. "Light your lamp, first."

"Close it," he said. I pushed it shut and stood there in total darkness. There was an unclassifiable noise and a creak of floorboards, and then I heard the opening of the door of the room on the left. In a moment his voice came from inside the room. "You can light a match, now." It was a strange voice, thin, flat, and without overtones, not much louder than a whisper.

The flare of the match showed the door standing open. I moved toward it cautiously. As I entered the room I encountered the smell again, so strong that it almost had to be physically breasted. "Lamp on the table," he said. I located and lit it. The wick was almost burnt out; even turned to the top, it was no brighter than the match had been, and I stood in a tiny island of light, surrounded by impenetrable shadow. His voice came out of the darkness: "What do you want, Nick?"

"I want you to do the right thing, Uncle Caleb," I said. "You know what it is. I've brought the pistol."

I heard a strange little sound that could have been either a whimper or a giggle. "Now why should I do a thing like that?" he said.

"You know why. You knew I'd be here. You were expecting me, weren't you?" He made no answer. I said, "We had an understanding. I believed you, God help me. And now there's another corpse up in town. Or part of a corpse. But it's the last one, Uncle Caleb. You can be very sure that it's the last one."

Silence again, and then the eerie voice out of the shadows: "That's got nothing to do with me. It's the feesters, Nick. The feesters."

"Yes, of course," I said. "But tell me, Uncle Caleb: does it seem to you that you know how it happened? Do you have a picture in your mind—something that seems almost like a memory—of what happened in the parking lot? As though maybe you know what the feesters are doing, are thinking?"

I was being the amateur psychiatrist, but I was at least partly right. He said, "Yes. Yes. Of course. I knew they were going to do it as soon as they started to think about it. I wished they'd stop thinking about it, but they wouldn't. And finally they did it. And it was awful. Nick, it was awful."

"Yes," I said. "You know you're going to have to do it, don't you, Uncle Caleb? You know it's the only thing that will make the feesters stop, don't you?"

There was only silence. I said, "Come out into the light, now, Uncle Caleb. It's time. You know it's time."

I heard it again, then, the noise I had heard in the hall, but still I saw only shadows. And then I looked down.

He was on the floor, wriggling out of the shadows into the small pool of light at my feet, naked, dead-white, moving like a worm on his belly. His arms were held tight against his sides, his legs were squeezed tightly together. He twisted his head to look up at me from the floor, and the wild growth of hair on his head and face, still the same straw color it had always been, looked very dark against his extraordinary pallor. The great round eyes glowed in the faint lamplight like a nocturnal animal's. Within the tangle of facial hair his teeth gleamed in what could have been either a smile or a snarl.

It was as horrifying a sight as I ever expect to see, both frightening and pitiful; but it was also more than a little ludicrous, and it was that fact that enabled me to hold fast to my resolution and do what had to be done. I said, "Oh, Uncle Caleb." And then: "Here's the gun, Uncle Caleb."

The teeth flashed yellow in the lamplight. "You know I can't use a gun, Nick. I haven't got any hands. Or arms."

"Or legs, I suppose," I said.

"That's right. No arms or legs. But I can get around all right."

"Yes," I said. "I know. You can indeed." I thought about it for a moment. I said, "Do you suppose you could pretend or imagine—just for a minute or so—that you have an arm and a hand? If I left the gun on the floor?"

This time when he spoke the voice had changed; under the toneless quack was a faint ghost of the voice of my Uncle Caleb, and I swallowed. He said, "No. No. I can't take the gun. But you're right. I've thought about it. The feesters have to be stopped. You'll want to be here won't you. To be sure that I do it. I'll do it now. But another way. Open the door for me, Nick. I can't, you know."

I might have asked him how he had opened it to let me in, but scoring debater points was not what I had come for, and in any case I suppose he would have found the question meaningless. I took the lamp and went to the front door and opened it.

There was a moon at the gibbous stage; it threw a pale oblong of light into the hallway. I extinguished the lamp and went down the steps and a little way out into the weeds. I stood there in the warm night watching the door.

In a little while he came out, a whiteness that bulged suddenly across the threshold and then moved in a silent squirm down the steps and away from the house. And then he was gone, a gleam of white humping with quite astonishing speed in the dim light toward the blackness of the lake. As he reached the edge, I called out, "Goodbye, Uncle Caleb."

There was no reply, only a small splash as the white shape disappeared into the water. And then silence. I walked back to the car and drove into town. On the way I stopped and parked at the side of the road for perhaps half an hour while I gave way to an unseemly emotional fit, howling and weeping and pounding on the steering wheel. When it was over I went to the sheriff's office and reported that I had been to the house, where I had discovered the door standing open and Uncle Caleb nowhere to be found. The sheriff said that he was not surprised and that he would investigate.

He was not surprised, and not much interested, either; and in Sturkeyville the name of Scoggins ended that night as an item of routine police business, a dingy and discreditable end for a proud name. The investigation was hasty and perfunctory: an inadequate search of the woods, and an attempt to drag the lake, which proved to be impossible because it was found to be very much deeper than anyone had suspected. A missing-person bulletin was circulated. A watch was kept on the lake for a while, to see if a body would surface, but it never did.

In due course there was a memorial service at St. David's. I sat sedately through it, remembering strange things. Afterward elderly people came to me and talked about the old days, when they and Uncle Caleb were young and the world was bright. Their conventional nostalgia evoked my own memories of enchanted summers on horseback in the hills above Sturkeyville before the shadows closed in upon Uncle Caleb, and an access of regret and grief and guilt seized and shook me. I might reason that what had occurred was no more than the timely suicide of a homicidal maniac, but what I felt was a terrible sense of loss.

I still feel that loss. It is more than a decade, now, since Uncle Caleb died, and I am a man closer to old age than middle, and Sturkeyville itself has changed almost beyond recognition, but I have noticed of late that my reveries increasingly tend to dwell upon those boyhood summers with Uncle Caleb. There is, of course, a proximate cause: it has now become imperative that I decide what I am going to do about the Phillips place and the lake. It will be my decision, and mine alone; I did, in the end, record Uncle Caleb's deed, and the property is mine in fee simple, the land and the lake. But not the house; I had it pulled down after Uncle Caleb's death, and its stones hauled away. The weeds grow uninterrupted now around the silent lake.

I have already consulted the Corps of Engineers and a contractor; the lake can be drained. It can be drained and the mud on its bottom exposed to the sun to dry and bake and crack. And anything buried there in the mud will dry and bake as well, and die, if it is alive.

That is the direction in which my mind has been running, the kind of plans I have been making. Sometimes it seems totally irrational, and indeed almost insane; but then I look at what has begun to happen again in Sturkeyville, and I am persuaded that these things must be done.

There have been more of the murders. They are the same in every respect as those of the past, monstrously savage and gruesome, ghastly rendings and mutilations under midnight rainstorms. The theory is that some unbalanced person was pushed over the edge by reading in a true-crime magazine one of the periodic rehashings of the Sturkeyville Butcher murders. It may be true, I hope so. Another maniac seems more acceptable, somehow, than what I have almost begun to believe.

And so I think I will drain the lake. If nothing else, it will free me of the obsessive imaginings that have plagued me since I first heard of the new murders. I am persistently visited by a terrifying picture, a picture of the lake. I see it from the hillside above, as I first saw it with Uncle Caleb. It is night in this picture, a night of violent summer rain, utterly black except for sudden lightning that sporadically freezes the scene in a momentary white glare. The surface of the lake is churned by rain.

In a flash of lightning I discern four white shapes in the water, making for shore. Moments later, in another flash, I see them squirming and humping through the weeds away from the lake, the foremost almost at the tree line.

I can give them names: Clio, Thalia, Urania, Polyhymnia.

Their name is Feester. Their name is Death.

And the next flash shows the lake as before, black, rain-lashed, lifeless, waiting. They will come back after they have done what they are setting out to do, wriggling back into the black water, sinking into the depths, burrowing into the mud, deep into the cold mud.

That is the vision that obsesses me. It is obviously egregious nonsense, the sort of thing that could be accepted only by the most credulous and superstitious, and I devoutly wish I could exorcise it. But it will not go away.

It will not go away, and indeed it becomes more elaborate. My imagination, fed no doubt by discreditable suppressed guilts and fears, has given the screw at last an unbearable turn, and now, as I lie tensely in bed or sit in my chair gnawing my knuckles, I have begun to imagine that there are not four shapes exposed by the lightning's glare, but five.

And I will not tolerate that. Uncle Caleb, whatever became of his mind, deserves better of me than that. I will drain the lake. I will drain it down to its bottommost mud. And in that mud we will find Uncle Caleb's bones.

I hope very much we will find Uncle Caleb's bones.

There are recurring patterns in our lives, caused by our personalities, our hopes, our fears . . . and what else? Our stars? Sheer chance?

Whatever their causes, patterns suddenly noticed can be startling; yes, and unsettling. Especially if a pattern seems to be widening.

Pat Murphy lives in southern California, and is one of many successful alumni of the Clarion writers' conferences. (Edward Bryant is another.)

DON'T LOOK BACK

Pat Murphy

A SMALL WATERCOLOR PAINTING HUNG OVER the fireplace. When Liz had lived in the rambling old house, one of her sketches had hung in that spot. With her eyes squinted half-closed against the late afternoon sun, Liz could almost believe that the watercolor was one of hers.

She leaned her head against the arm of the couch, where the velvet had long since been worn smooth. Amanda's golden retriever, Bristol, bumped his head against her leg, trying to get her attention, and she scratched his ears idly.

She had visited the house a year before. At the time, she had been living with Mark in San Francisco. "You're trying to live in the past," Mark had claimed when she had left to visit the old house. "You'll just make yourself unhappy. You can't go back." Lying on the couch with the afternoon sunlight shining on her face, Liz knew that Mark had been wrong. She was happy in her past. She was worried about her future.

Mark still lived in San Francisco, but Liz had moved on. For the past year, she had lived in Los Angeles. Now she was taking a job in New York, moving far away and leaving her family and friends behind.

Bristol bumped his head against Liz's leg again, and she resumed scratching his ears. "What a pair," Amanda said as she stepped into the room. The older woman set a teapot and mugs on the coffee table and sat cross-legged on the floor beside the dog. Despite her gray hair, Amanda was as casual in manner as the art students who lived in her house. "You always were that dog's favorite."

Bristol lifted his head. With an apologetic air, he moved away from Liz, stretched, and paced to the front door. Liz frowned and sat up on the couch. "I wonder what's up," she said.

"That must be Elsa," Amanda said as she poured the tea. "She lives in your old room now."

When Liz opened the door for the dog, he pushed past her. Liz stood in the doorway, watching the golden retriever frolic around and around a girl of about eighteen. The girl was laughing and whirling as if trying to keep her face to the dog. A bright flower was stuck in the braid of her long brown hair. Under her arm, she carried a sketch pad and several slim art books.

Liz watched, remembering when Bristol had greeted her after a long day, when she had carried a sketch pad under her arm and walked home from the bus stop with a flower in her hair.

"Elsa painted the watercolor over the fireplace," Amanda said from behind Liz. "She's quite good. She's working under Professor Whittier."

"Nothing but the best for him," Liz said, her eyes still on the girl and the dog. Whittier had been Liz's professor.

Liz stepped back from the door when the girl turned toward the house. Footsteps pounded up the wooden stairs and the girl and dog burst into the room. "Hey, Amanda," Elsa began. "I won't be here for dinner."

"Slow down, kid." Amanda smiled at the girl as indulgently as she used to smile at Liz. "Say hello to Liz Berke."

"Pleased to meet you," Elsa's voice was low, as if she were not quite certain she wanted to be heard. "Professor Whittier has one of your drawings hanging in his office. It's very good." When she hesitated, Liz was painfully aware that Elsa did not know what to say and she remembered how she had felt awkward when she had met Whittier's old students, people he spoke of with respect and affection. Elsa shifted her sketchbook from one arm to the other and looked at Amanda as if for release. "I'm going out to a lecture with some friends so I won't be around for dinner, Amanda."

As Elsa hurried from the room with Bristol close behind her, Liz felt a twinge of something like regret. "Is this her first year?" she asked.

Amanda pushed a cup of tea toward Liz and nodded. "That's right. "Why?"

"I don't know. When I first saw her, she reminded me of someone." Liz shrugged.

"Your lost youth, perhaps?" Amanda grinned.

"I don't know," Liz repeated, frowning. "I would have liked to talk to her, though."

Amanda laughed. "I think you overwhelmed her. All of Professor Whittier's students are dancing in your shadow, you know. You're a tough act to follow."

"Nobody says they have to follow." Liz's voice was resentful. She sat back down on the couch and sipped her tea, trying not to wish that the golden retriever's head still rested in her lap so that she could scratch the dog's ears.

Liz spent the evening with Amanda, reminiscing about the years that she had lived in the house. "It was good that you moved on, you know," Amanda said. "I remember that you almost came back here a year after you left."

"I was going to take a job as Whittier's assistant," Liz recalled. "I don't know why I didn't. Good pay, interesting work, a chance to come back. . ."

Amanda shook her head in quick denial. "I told you not to take it and for once you listened. You can't come back. There's no place for you here anymore." Though Amanda's voice was warm with affection, the words left Liz with a cold feeling: no place for her anymore.

The feeling lingered after Amanda bade her goodnight and headed upstairs to the attic bedroom. In the many-shadowed hallway, Liz paused at the door to the guest bedroom listening to Amanda's footsteps ascend the stairs. Though the hour was past one, Elsa had not yet come home. Liz turned from the guest room and pushed open the door to her old room.

A bouquet of daisies, backlit by moonlight, stood on the windowsill; Liz had always had flowers in her room. The desk was littered with sketches, books, designs. An easy chair—the same easy chair that she had used or else one just as misshapen—stood by the open window, an Indian muslin bedspread flung over it to hide the rips in its upholstery.

Through the open window and across the quiet yard, Liz heard someone whistling a fragment of song—just as she had whistled to keep back the darkness on her way home from coffeehouses, parties, late nights in the studio. Liz heard a footstep on the driveway and she fled to the guest room, listening in the darkness to the sound of Elsa's key in the lock and chiding herself for invading the student's privacy.

Liz woke early the next morning. The sunlight filtered through the leaves of the tree outside the window and created shifting patterns on the ceiling. The sunlight had made shifting patterns on the ceiling of the adjacent room when she had been a student. Liz heard the creak of bedsprings in the room next door, the sound of the closet door opening. She heard footsteps on the stairs but she lay in bed, watching the light dance as the wind moved the leaves, until she heard the front door open and close. She waited until the sound of footsteps on the gravel drive had faded in the distance before she got up and joined Amanda in the kitchen for breakfast.

After breakfast, she caught the same bus she had taken each day as a student. On the bus and on the walk through the campus to Professor Whittier's office, memories plagued her. Not good memories; not bad memories; just memories: I dropped my portfolio in front of this door when I was hurrying to class; I got caught in the rain and took shelter in this building; I used that fountain to fill an old jam jar with water for a bouquet of flowers; I stood right here the first time I went to see Professor Whittier; a sketch of mine hung on the wall just around this corner.

Just around the corner, a sketch hung on the wall. Liz stopped. She recognized the woman in the portrait as Amanda and she peered at the signature. Elsa Brant. Liz could not put words to the disquieting feeling that touched her—the same uneasiness that had kept her in bed that morning.

When she raised her hand to knock on Professor Whittier's door, she could not suppress the thought: I used to do this every day. And she could not avoid the thought that followed: Elsa probably does this every day.

Professor Whittier had not changed in her absence. The glacial old man nodded slowly when she told him about the work she would be doing in New York. They talked about the changes in the school, the growth in her work, and then she could not resist asking about his students.

He shrugged. Through the years, he had remained as slow and unstoppable as a mountain of ice. "All art students are alike: lazy, self-indulgent. That hasn't changed," he said. "Only one—the girl who works in your old studio—shows any promise. Her name is Elsa Brant."

Liz had fixed her gaze on the drawing that hung behind Professor Whittier's head, a sketch of Bristol that she had completed during her sophomore year. She remembered sitting in the living room on a warm afternoon while the dog slept in a patch of sunshine, trying to catch the smooth grace of the animal in pen and ink. She remembered the moment and clung to it. She was unique. No one else could have caught that moment in just that way.

"Yes," Liz admitted quietly. "I've seen Elsa's work. She does have promise."

On her way out, Liz passed by her old studio and paused at the door. Elsa stood with her back to the corridor, facing the open window. The girl's easel held a self-portrait that was almost complete. In the painting, Elsa wore the same twisted half-smile she had worn when the dog had greeted her in the yard. Liz stepped forward, about to speak to the girl, and as she did so, realized: I always painted with the window open. She turned and fled.

"I thought you were going to stay for a while," Amanda complained as Liz stowed her suitcase in the trunk of her car. "You said you didn't plan to start driving to New York for a week or so."

"I know. I just . . ." She met Amanda's gaze. "I don't belong here anymore." She hesitated. She had been about to say—"I've been replaced"—but she had thought better of it. "You've been telling me that for years. I just now realized you were right."

Amanda looked worried. "Where are you going, then?"

"I've already called Mr. Jacobs, the man I worked for in San Jose. I'm going to be taking him to lunch." She tried to force a light-hearted note into her voice. "Oh, don't worry about it, Amanda. I'm just too restless to stay in one place just now." She hugged the older woman goodbye and got into the car. With the engine running, she reached out the car window to squeeze Amanda's hand. "I'm sorry, Amanda. I just have to . . ." She hesitated, uncertain of what it was she had to do. "I'll write you from New York," she said.

Liz reached the small silkscreening company in San Jose well before lunchtime. She had held her first design job here, drawing logos and designs for T-shirts.

She sat at Mr. Jacobs' desk in one corner of the workroom while the elderly man finished packing an order of T-shirts. Mr. Jacob's pipe lay unattended in an ashtray on one corner of the desk, giving off a scent that touched old memories. Mr. Jacobs stood with his back to her, folding shirts and layering them neatly. She had offered to help, but he had turned her down, saying it was quicker to do it himself. She watched him work —a wirey old man dressed in jeans and a blue workshirt. He had always worn jeans and a blue workshirt. Liz suspected that if she returned in five years he would still wear jeans and a blue workshirt, still have just the same bald spot in his thinning gray hair. Liz tilted her chair back, resting her feet on the oak desk top, and relaxed.

As Mr. Jacobs worked, he complained about his unreliable help—high school students who worked long enough to buy new wheels for their cars, then quit. When the car needed a new paint job, they asked to be rehired.

"I'll bet you still hire them back, don't you?" Liz accused, grinning at the old man.

"He sure does." A woman stepped from Liz's old office and answered her question. "You're supposed to be going out to lunch with your friend," the woman continued. "I said I'd pack those."

"See what kind of help I have, Liz," Mr. Jacobs said. "Libby is always ordering me around, just like you used to."

Liz put her feet back on the floor and let her chair return to an upright position. Libby wore blue jeans and had long straight hair. When she smiled at Liz, her smile was crooked—a slightly cynical line.

Mr. Jacobs scowled at the younger woman unconvincingly. "Watch yourself there. You can be replaced you know."

They went to the dinette a few blocks from the silk-screen company for lunch. Liz was uneasy and distracted. Feeling awkward, but unable to avoid the question, Liz asked about Libby. "She looks like an interesting person. Is she a good designer?"

Mr. Jacobs nodded. "She sure is. She's a good kid—I'm fond of her. She reminds me a lot of you when you first started working for me."

Liz caught a glimpse of her own face in the mirror behind the counter. Her brown hair hung straight to her shoulders and her mouth had a cynical twist. She looked away.

"She'll be moving on, soon enough, just the way you did," Mr. Jacobs was saying. "She has to grow up . . ." Liz tried to listen but she was distracted by her own reflection. The dinette seemed too crowded and noisy and Mr. Jacobs' joking words to Libby beat in Liz's head: "You can be replaced, you know. You can be replaced."

"How's that young man of yours?" Mr. Jacobs asked. The question cut through the noise of her thoughts and the noise of the dinette.

"You mean Mark," she said. She had not realized how long it had been since she had talked to Mr. Jacobs. "I haven't seen him for a while. We broke up over a year ago." She fidgeted with the silverware on the formica countertop and when she looked up Mr. Jacobs was watching her with concern. "It's all right," she said, and her voice seemed too loud, as if she were protesting too much and too soon. "We were just going in different directions, that's all. If we had both been older and ready to settle down, it might have been different." The sudden silence in her mind reflected the words as an echo: it might have been different.

From Mr. Jacob's office, Liz called Terry, an old friend who lived in San Francisco. She tried to keep her voice light, fighting the panic that rose in her. "Terry, can I come to visit tonight?"

"Sure, I'd be glad to see you before you head east." Terry's voice was calm. She had always served as a balance for Liz, a relaxed and soothing presence. "But I thought you were going to drive east from Santa Cruz."

"Plans have changed." Liz could hear the tension in her own voice.

"You're not chickening out on this job in New York, are you?" Terry asked. "You better not be."

In the workroom behind her, Liz could hear the rumble of Mr. Jacobs' voice, then the sound of Libby's laughter. She wanted to run away. "Please, Terry, can we talk when I get there. Please . . ." When Liz hung up, she slipped out the front door without saying goodbye.

At Terry's apartment, Liz tried to relax. She sat on the couch, staring at the cup of tea that her friend had given her, trying to think of a way to explain why she had been upset by meeting two women with brown hair holding jobs that she once held.

"You aren't planning on visiting Mark before you go, are you?" Terry asked. Her friend sat in an easy chair across the room, her hands clasped in her lap, her eyes intent on Liz's face. Liz knew that Terry was worried about her—but she could not help imagining another woman sitting on the couch, telling Terry about her problems while Terry listened intently.

"I'd thought of it," Liz admitted. She had imagined a reconciliation; she had imagined a mature, but tender, final farewell; she had imagined a confrontation with a dim figure—a woman with brown hair and a twisted smile.

"That wouldn't be a good idea," Terry said. "You know that."

"Yeah, I know. I just . . ." Liz hesitated. The dim image of the woman who followed her had grown clearer in her mind. Liz saw the woman's face—a younger version of her own. She imagined herself patting the woman on the back and saying: "Good luck. You've got a great past ahead of you, kid." She shook her head. "No," she said—half to herself, half to Terry. "I guess it wouldn't be a good idea."

In honor of Liz's visit, Terry took the next day off. At Liz's suggestion, they went to lunch at the café that had been her favorite when she had worked in the city. Just as they were leaving the restaurant, they met Dave, the editor of the magazine where Liz had been layout artist.

"Liz! I didn't even know you were in town." Dave clapped her on the shoulder. "You have to come to my party tonight. Everyone will be there." He hesitated, frowning. "Ah . . . you and Mark are still friends, aren't you?"

"Of course," she replied, a little too quickly. "It would

be good to see him again." She managed an unconcerned smile. "What time should we show up?"

When they left the café, Terry put her hand on Liz's arm. "You aren't fooling me, you know. If you don't want to see Mark . . ."

"It's okay," Liz insisted. "I do want to go to the party. And I'd like to see Mark again."

"I hope you want to see him out of spite—that's a good healthy motive. I hope you want to show him how well you're doing without him." Terry was watching Liz's face. "I just hope you don't want to see him for old time's sake. You can't go back, you know."

"I know," Liz said. "I really do know."

She realized at the door of Dave's house in the hills above Oakland that she really had not known—until she saw the lady on Mark's arm. The lady's long brown hair was tied up on her head so that wisps of curls floated down around her face. Though she looked a few years younger than Liz, her mouth had a cynical twist. And seeing Mark woke Liz's old doubts: could they have worked it out? should they have stayed together?

Dave took their jackets and followed Liz's gaze to the couple. "That's Lillian," he said. "She has your old job."

"Oh, really?" Liz maintained her calm facade, but when Dave turned away, she spoke to Terry under her breath. "That's not all she has."

"If you want to leave . . ." Terry began

Liz shook her head. "It's okay." She knew by the way that Terry touched her arm that her friend realized that it was not really okay, but would not blow her cover. Liz smiled and started across the room toward the couple, stopping on her way to greet old friends from the magazine, to tell people that, yes, she had moved to bigger and better things; yes, the rumors that she was moving to New York were true; no, she had not forgotten them, not at all. Even as she laughed and chatted, she kept an eye on Mark and Lillian and noticed when the lady left Mark to join another group of people.

"Well hello, Mark," Liz said at last. "How's life treating you?" She hugged him in greeting—they had parted as friends, after all. "You're looking good."

"Sounds like things are going well for you," he said. "From all the rumors that I've heard the job in New York will be a step up."

"It should be a challenge," she agreed. Across the room, she could see Lillian talking to Dave. "She looks like a really nice lady," Liz said. Lillian smiled at a remark, and Liz noticed again that her smile had a skewed look.

"She is." His voice had a guarded tone, and when Liz glanced at him she saw that he was watching Lillian too. "You don't remember her, do you?" She looked at him questioningly. "She was one class behind you in art school. Apparently she took a painting class with you."

Liz studied the woman's face, but could not remember having seen her before. "No, I don't remember her."

"She remembers you. Apparently she admired your work." He grinned wryly. "One of your many admirers."

Liz looked away from Lillian, meeting Mark's gaze. "I'll be in town tomorrow," she said. "I don't leave for a few days. I thought we might get together for lunch. Just to talk." She knew by Mark's expression that the question had been a mistake.

I'd rather not," he said. "Lillian and I . . . I think she feels threatened, seeing you here. You fit back in a little too well."

"I don't want to get back together or anything. I'm no threat. I just thought . . . we're still friends and . . ." She stopped, feeling she was making a fool of herself. "We spent a lot of time together and I still care what you're doing . . ."

"You still haven't learned to let go of the past, have you?" His voice held a slight edge. "You still hang on to it."

"And you don't?" She realized as soon as she spoke that she could not explain what she meant. She could not explain that Lillian's twisted smile was just like Libby's, like Elsa's, like her own.

"I *have* let go," he said, and she did not know how to refute it.

When Terry hailed her from across the room, Liz turned away with relief to join her friend by the fireplace. Later in the evening, she started to step out on the wooden deck that overlooked the ravine behind Dave's house, and stopped with her hand on the glass door.

Mark and Lillian stood on the deck, silhouetted by moonlight. Mark's hand rested on Lillian's shoulders and as Liz watched, he lifted one hand to touch her cheek.

In her mind, Liz could hear him saying: You're really very special to me, you know that?

Liz felt as if she were watching a replay of her own courtship. In the darkness beyond the figures, she imagined a long line of faces, each one framed by brown hair, each wearing a twisted smile. Behind her, she could hear music from the party; on an old album, Crosby, Stills, Nash, and Young sang: "And it seems like I've been here before . . ."

She ran away, knowing that she was running away. She persuaded Terry to leave the party. She insisted on leaving for New York the next day. Terry did not question Liz's sudden panic and Liz knew that her friend interpreted her need to be gone as stemming from a fear that she might be trapped into staying. Liz did not tell her otherwise.

As Liz drove cross-country, speeding along midwestern highways where every town looked the same, she admitted her cowardice to herself. But she kept her foot pressed to the gas pedal, staring at the road until her eyes ached and gripping the wheel to keep her hands from shaking. At a McDonald's, she ate a hamburger and gulped coffee that scorched her throat on the way down and burned in her stomach afterward. She spent one night in a roadside motel, sleeping fitfully and waking with the sensation that she was still moving, clutching the wheel and pushing down on the gas pedal. She was leaving them all behind.

A knot of resentment remained with her: Why did they follow her? Why was she chosen to be the leader, the Pied Piper with a pack of children dancing in her shadow?

She reached New York and began work, spending the first day setting up her office so that it suited her. The secretary for the art department said that Beth, the artist who had quit, would stop by and pick up the sketches that she had left behind.

Liz settled down to work at her new desk, trying to ignore the constant anger that knotted her stomach. When the door to her office opened, she looked up. The older woman who stepped inside wore her brown hair pinned back. Her mouth was twisted in an ironical grin.

"Hello," she said. "I'm Beth."

This is a very strange, very ordinary story; it probably won't frighten you. It takes place in a tiny English village that could hardly be quieter; its protagonist is a young man who's taken the unexciting job of postman. But there *is* a beautiful woman, surrounded by mystery and apparently in distress. And there are mysteries within mysteries. . . .

British author Robert Aickman is recognized as one of the finest writers of strange tales today. His most recent story collections include *Cold Hand in Mine*, *Painted Devils* and *Intrusions*.

LETTERS TO THE POSTMAN

Robert Aickman

THE SITUATION AT HOME HAD LEFT ROBIN Breeze entirely free to choose what he did with his life.

His father, the doctor, had never been particularly successful in his vocation, and had from the first taken care not to influence Robin even to think of following in his footsteps. Indeed, he always referred to medicine in disrespectful terms, even though he himself seemed noticeably adroit with cases that he took seriously, as Robin surmised. Dr. Breeze's main public complaint appeared to be the usual one that so little was now left to the individual practitioner, or given to the individual patient. Robin's mother had been simply a summer visitor, with whom the lonely young doctor had scraped up a flirtation. There were few summer visitors at Brusingham, which was six or seven miles from the coast. At that time, Robin's father had been the youngest partner in the practice. Now more and more of the patients were going a little further afield.

None the less, money had been found to send both Robin and his elder sister, Nelly, to non-coeducational private schools within the county. Little had been offered there in the way of "vocational guidance." Options continued to be left fully open. Nelly had soon found a niche in helping her mother, as the problems of running the house intensified year by year. Nelly could see for herself that she was invaluable, probably indispensable; and her mother was generous and sensible enough to confirm this daily. The family way of life would have collapsed in a moment, had it not been for Nelly. Nelly, therefore, had little ambition to type all day in a congested Midlands office, or to spend her life cauterizing farm animals, as assistant to a boozy young vet: to name two other options that offered. Robin remained less decided. One day he noticed an advertisement in the local weekly, which the doctor took in for professional reasons, though it was perennially in danger of folding finally or being taken over by a national syndicate and neutralized.

The advertisement stated that Lastingham was in need of a provisional postman. It was slightly more than a temporary postman. The exact background to the announcement was not stated, doubtless in order to economize on the number of words; but Robin divined that it might be something slightly special and unusual.

Lastingham was the community on the coast; hardly a village anymore, owing to the erosion of the low cliffs. Even the church had gone, except for the very west end. Dr. Breeze sometimes spoke of coffins and bones projecting from the cliff face as the churchyard fell away, but Robin and Nelly had never seen anything, often though they had been on their bicycles to look. The living had been merged with those of Hobstone and Mall. What had happened of late was that the fisherman's cottages and the little shops of Lastingham had been replaced by holiday shacks and inexpensive bungalows for retired persons; scattered at random over the landscape, and challenging permanence. None the less, the one filling station that had been attempted had failed almost immediately, perhaps from insufficient working capital. There remained a cabin for selling ice cream, meat loaf and crisps, though it was usually closed and padlocked. Robin and everyone else knew that the post office had been at last designated unsafe; so that all business was being transacted from the former lifeboat station.

Robin laid down the local weekly on a glass case of his father's specimens, mounted his bicycle, and rode off without a word to anyone.

As so many who undertake the job have discovered, the postal round was far more interesting than laymen would ever suppose. The overhanging threat, which made

Robin's position permanently provisional, was that
technological advance might at a moment's notice lead to
delivery by impersonal van direct from Corby or Nun-
eaton or some place even more remote. Dispatch from
such spots would alter all the postmarks into names
entirely misleading. The availability of Robin's own bicycle might help, though perhaps it was too much to
hope. At the outset, Robin was told that a retired postman would go around with him and show him the ropes.
Robin could only wheel his bicycle, as the old man was
past riding anything. The retired postman proved also to
be a retired fisherman, and was always talking of the
sea and the village market; the latter long closed.

They were in a region of unadopted roads, underde-
fined boundaries, random structures at uncoordinated
angles.

Robin pointed to a small house at the very far corner,
where the ground fell away. The road thither had been
made but once and for all; doubtless in the chicken-
farming period after the First World War.

"What about that one, Mr. Burnsall?"

"There's no post there," said the old postman and old
fisherman. He was rubbing his left knee with his right
hand. He had to stoop quite a long way to do this.

"You mean the house is empty?"

"Not empty, but there's no post."

"Who is it lives there exactly?"

"Miss Fearon lives there. She's said to be pretty like.
Lovely as a linnet. But she gets no post."

"Have you ever seen her, Mr. Burnsall?"

"No I never have properly seen her, Robin."

"How do people know she exists?"

"Take a good look!" said the old postman, patiently,
though he was not in a position to point.

Robin, as trainee, looked much harder than before. A
wisp of smoke was rising from the distant house's chimney. Robin fancied that he would not have seen it, had
not this been a pale and windless day.

"Likes to keep warm, does Miss Fearon. It's always the
same, winter and summer."

"Women are like that," Robin said, smiling.

"*Some* women, Robin," responded the old postman, at
last upright once more.

"I shall hope to set eyes upon Miss Fearon. Perhaps I

could go after her for a Christmas Box when the time comes."

"We don't do that with people like Miss Fearon. They receive no post, so there's nothing due from them."

"Has the house a name?" asked Robin.

"No name," replied the old postman. "Why should it have?"

"To deliver the coal," suggested Robin, still idly more or less.

"If she burns coal. Maybe she walks out at night and helps herself to the peat."

"I didn't know there *was* peat," said Robin, though all his life he had dwelled only six or seven miles away.

But the old postman had said enough on random topics for that morning and was already a few yards homeward, while Robin had been continuing to stare. If Robin really wished to glimpse pretty Miss Fearon, the old man had at least propounded a possible hour. As, pushing his bicycle, he followed the sturdy old figure, he felt manhood almost surging within himself. It could be a difficult sensation to cope with, as educationists are agreed.

Difficult in particular was the decision as to whether the nocturnal project would be seriously worthwhile. Six or seven solitary miles each way through the mist on the bicycle; a long, cold wait; the obvious unreliability of the old man's tale—put forward, moreover, even by the old man, merely as a surmise; above all, the extreme unlikelihood of picking the right night or nights. So far Robin had not even set up the scene with his father about the key.

In some ways, it would be far more sensible, at least as a start, to move in closer to the small house by full daylight; but Robin was deterred by his official prominence. Comment would almost certainly be made if at broad noon the postman were to ride so noticeably far from his paper round. People could complain quite justly that thereby the delivery of their own letters and parcels had been frivolously delayed; and that might be only the start of it. In the second place, Robin did not wish to be suspected by the house's occupant of mere snooping and spying. In the third place, Robin, if he were to be honest with himself, had no inclination to be suddenly sprung upon from within. What defense could he make? What excuse?

Problems, if meant to be solved, solve themselves more effectively than we can solve them. After Robin had been in the job for only seven and half weeks, a packet appeared plainly addressed to "Miss Rosetta Fearon." It was a questionnaire from the rating authority, and all the world would be receiving one sooner or later. The old man, who had accompanied Robin everywhere for the whole of this first week, had thus been proved right about three important matters: the name, the sex, and, it would appear, the unmarried status. There was reason, therefore, to suppose that he might probably be right about the fourth and most important thing. A wave of new confidence bubbled through Robin. On the other hand, the precise name, "Rosetta," strongly suggested an older person. Dr. Breeze had once taken his children to view the Rosetta Stone, clue to so many matters. It had been quite near the museum at the Royal College of Surgeons in Lincoln's Inn Fields, which had been the primary object of the expedition. They had seen the bust of Julius Caesar at the same time; since removed.

"She never gets anything," confirmed young Mrs. Truslove, who ran the temporary post office on a part-time basis.

It was quite true that the official envelope bore no address more precise than "Lastingham." The old man seemed to have been right too about the house being unnamed. But the Rating Authority knew that the detective department of the post office was one that could be relied upon. Everybody knows.

When he reached the place, Robin saw at once that the name of the house had simply fallen off. Very possibly the single letters could still be found among the long grass. Patterned curtains were drawn together in all the windows that Robin could see, downstairs and upstairs. He hesitated to prowl through the weeds to the rear of the structure, where the living room overlooked the sea. The familiar trail of smoke from the familiar chimney was rising, faintly green or greenish yellow, against the azure, and soon losing itself. Robin could see that this could hardly be coal smoke, trusty and dependable. He did not know in what hue peat burned. There was no other sign at all of the little property being tenanted. Robin had laid his bicycle carefully against the rough hedge, before giving the gate a stout push. Now he was clasping the packet.

The letter box was not in but alongside the front door. It appeared to be a box indeed, a distinguishable capacious object built into the brickwork and removable *en bloc* with a hacksaw. The flap was unusually wide. Postmen suffer everywhere from the smallness of orifices, and so does the correspondence they handle.

As it was an almost ceremonial occasion, comparable, perhaps, to the service of a writ, Robin pushed back the flap with his left hand, proposing to insert the communiqué with his right. But as soon as he touched the flap, something white erupted from it and fell at Robin's feet.

It was a letter, folded tightly in upon itself, and quite skillfully. It was boldly superscribed "To the Postman." Robin pushed the effusion from the Rating Authority back into his satchel, and proceeded to read. He might be receiving special instructions concerning delivery. The handwriting continued large and legible:

Something strange has happened to me. I find that I am married to someone I do not know. A man, I mean. His name is Paul. He is kind to me, and in a way I am happy, but I feel I should keep in touch. Just occasional little messages. Do you mind? Nothing more, for God's sake. That you must promise me. Write to me that you promise.

ROSETTA. ROSETTA FEARON

Robin examined, as best he could, the mechanism by which the missive had been expelled. The flap of the letter box proved not to be attached to the top, but to swing upon a lower axis which made it just possible for a letter to be placed in position so that, with good fortune, it would fall outward as soon as the flap was touched. Miss Fearon had been in luck that the house had been built in that way. Or perhaps she had made a personal alteration.

Robin drew a Packet Undeliverable form from his pocket. He took his official pencil from inside his cap and wrote: I promise. Back next week. POSTMAN." He had been told always to sign "Postman"; never to give an actual name. He thrust the form into the house. He realized that he could be standing at the gateway to romance. Even though, as might now appear, a romance with a married woman.

His heart joined the larks everywhere overhead. He began to hum "Nearer, My God, to Thee," his mother's special hymn tune. The waves were crumbling against the low cliffs with a new impulsion.

Not until he had mounted and departed did he realize that Miss Fearon's rating questionnaire was still in his haversack. Properly, he ought to ride back, but that would attract more comment than anything he had so far contemplated. He shoved the questionnaire into his jacket pocket among the various forms. After all, he thought, he was still an apprentice.

"You're smiling," said Mrs. Truslove, when he arrived back at the temporary post office. It was half a cry of surprise, half an accusation.

That night in his room, Robin read Rosetta Fearon's odd letter again and again, and even deposited it under his pillow. In the morning, he realized from the state of the paper that this could not be done with the same letter every night. No matter. There would be further letters. They were as good as guaranteed.

Robin made no attempt to press. He had a long and treacherous road before him, but he saw that to rush things might be to lose all. He said nothing to anyone; not to Mrs. Truslove, not to his father or mother, not to Nelly, who was his mother's second voice, and her first voice more and more noticeably. The old postman and fisherman was rigid with lumbago. Bob Stuff, Robin's best friend, had gone to Stockport as a door-to-door insurance salesman. Not that Robin would have told Bob a thing like this, or Bob, Robin.

The seven days passed sooner or later, and Robin was leaning his bicycle against the rough hedge once more, but this time the bell was jingling and tingling as the rider trembled. The trouble was the cold rain of late April. It soaked and chilled everything. Robin was wearing official oilskins that had either survived from earlier postmen or been found in the disused lifeboat station. Mrs. Truslove never seemed to know which it was.

Robin picked up the second letter and stood holding it. The house offered no protection: not a veranda; not a porch; not an outhouse even. All the larks were holed that day. The waves moaned and clawed.

He is never unkind, not at all, but I cannot be at ease with him. He is a total stranger. Often I do not follow what he says, and it seems to make him sad. But I am not unhappy. There is goodness everywhere, and many compensations. Thank you for writing. Please keep in contact. No more than that, under any circumstances. It seems that I am not free. Give me your solemn undertaking. Your

ROSETTA

The words blurred as Robin read, keeping the water out of his eyes with an old handkerchief. The letter had virtually pulped in his hands before he had finished it. Also, the act of reading takes, at the best, two or three times longer when even light rain is falling.

Equally, Robin had no shelter in which to indite his reply, let alone to meditate. Rain was dripping from the circumference of his sou'wester. He grubbed out another form, dashed down, "I undertake. Back as usual. POSTMAN," and plunged the damp paper into the box.

In other circumstances, he might have essayed more warmth of expression; though, even then, "Your Postman" would surely have struck the wrong, improperly Yuletide, note, against which he had been indirectly cautioned. At that point, Robin realized that so far there had duly been no second communication for delivery to the remote little abode.

For that matter, the first communication was yet to be delivered. Robin supposed it to be lost. He had to acknowledge that he seemed to think of it only at the wrong moments. But, probably, nondelivery of a questionnaire made little difference to Miss Fearon or to her obscure feelings.

The third letter, discharged the due week later, read:

I cannot deny that sometimes it is pleasant. If only I knew more about him! I should wish to trust myself to him without reserve, but it is impossible. Do you understand what I am saying to you, Postman? Often I see him wrestling with himself. I do not understand how he came into my life. Accept these confidences, but expect no more. Surely I am committed to him? You have sworn. Your

						R.

Now it was zephyrous weather again, and Robin gave way to impulse. "I am your true friend," he wrote, and that alone; and he signed with the bare initial, "P."

The larks were chiming to the pulses in his body; the waves whispering. Everything set up a temptation to poke and pry, but Robin had his round to resume. Neither this week nor last had he any working business to be here at all, unless belatedly to deliver the original communication, which was probably gone for ever.

Before mounting his bicycle, Robin looked at the other side of the letter. Last week, it had been impossible to look as the letter had melted in reading. Now Robin saw that there was no superscription. Whether or not this was proof of advancing intimacy was hard to say; but it is permissible always to hope while breath is with us, and breath was much with Robin that morning as he pedaled away.

Soon the days were opening out wonderfully, and Lastingham was filling with summer visitors, as Brusingham could never hope to do. There were lengthening queues outside the small public lavatory block, outside the picturesque little snack bar, beneath the LOST CHILDREN sign, all around the miniature bus station. Cars were parked right to the cliff edge, regardless of the Parish Council's warning notice, regardless of the witness offered by the ruined church and deserted post office. Men were arguing on all sides as to which filling station was nearest; which was cheapest; which could still supply. Women were beginning to suffer and to long for home. Children raged and rampaged. The larks flew higher than ever. The waves lapped erotically.

Robin might possibly have forgotten Rosetta Fearon. He could have taken his pick, it may be supposed, from the girls and women flat on the shingle; first, of course, discarding his uniform. He and Nelly had paid odd visits to Lastingham during bygone summers, but that was

very different from seeing the sights daily. One trouble
was that too many visitors were themselves there for the
day only, as the Parish Council ceaselessly lamented. If
a romantic relationship was to be sustained, Robin
might have had constantly to travel to Stroud Green or
Smethwick or Chorlton-on-Medlock. That he simply
could not afford. Nor at the moment was it practicable
to migrate for the rest of his life to one of those places,
however ardent he might find himself. Rosetta Fearon
was on the spot; even, up to a point, on his round.

Among the loitering throng Robin began to notice a
woman always in a summer dress, different each day,
that made her look more beautiful, still more beautiful.
Sometimes she wore a loose summer coat; often a tilted
summer hat. Her hair was perfect. Her complexion was
perfect, perhaps because the hat kept off the worst of
the sun. Her step was swift and sparkling. Her shoes and
ankles were such as Robin had never dreamed of. For
example, these were not among his own mother's assets,
and it was doubtful whether they ever had been. Nelly
had bicyclist's limbs.

No such woman as this would come to Lastingham as
a visitor; not even by the week. Robin could never have
supposed it. Robin thought that she was Rosetta Fearon
immediately he spotted her.

That was two days after he had received Miss Fearon's third letter. There had always been one last claim
made by the old postman and fisherman that needed to
be confirmed. And now? Good old postman and fisherman! Salt of two elements in equal parts! It was sad that
according to Mrs. Truslove, the poor old chap was now
suffering from urticaria as well. She wondered what
would happen to him, all alone.

Robin made no attempt to draw close. That would
have been to challenge fate, to upset made arrangements. Furthermore, he would have had to be quick,
even though the crowd might well have made a passage
for the postman. But he was able to see that the woman
often or always, was carrying what might have been an
elegant, foreign bag in which, presumably, to place purchases. Like any other woman, she was shopping, forever shopping. No further explanation of what she was
doing was really needed. Sometimes he glimpsed the
lovely vision at least twice in a single day—and not

within ten or twenty minutes, but at wide intervals,
sometimes when he was still delivering, sometimes during an approved rest period. The woman wore long
gloves, stretching up casually over her wrists, or over the
sleeves of her slim dress, different every day. Always she
seemed about to smile.

Bicycling around the unadopted roads was hot work
as the sun began to burst itself; and the trouble was that
no winter satchel would contain the rigmarole demanded
by the weekly visitors: cans of babyfood, flasks of anti-
diuretic, grandma's Botticelli wig in tissue paper, picture
postcards by the bushel each day of identical places in
interchangeable weather. If all the daily visitors had become weekly visitors as the Parish Council wished, then
acting supplementary postmen or postwomen would have
been unavoidable, and perhaps a motor scooter. More
likely would have been the dreaded transfer of delivery
and dispatch to that unpredictable distance. Frequently
removing his cap for a moment or two, Robin toiled on,
staving off the inevitable.

When for the fourth time he leaned his machine
against Miss Fearon's boundary, he saw that all the buds
were proclaiming and all the thorns mobilized. He ventured to lay his cap on the hedge top, and the pencil
within it.

He mopped at his face and his neck with one hand,
and held Miss Fearon's letter in the other.

*He is behaving more and more weirdly. Though it
may not be weird at all for those who have the key,
which I have not. I feel that he would like to con-
fine me here. Even when I wash my hair, there is
challenge. And yet he is always so kind, so gentle
to me. I may have to make an appeal. Ask no more
of me at this moment. Your own*

                                                    R.

And the initial was followed by what Robin could only
take to be a kiss; a single kiss; a very tiny St. Andrew's
Cross. By then, Robin was almost fainting from the heat.
Certainly he was staggering as he stumped back up
the cracked path to the sinking gate. Certainly he sank
upon his back as if the stony road outside had been the

shingly beach below. Certainly he lost all count of time, all sense of eyes peeping through bargain binoculars from the middle distance, all recollection of hearts that hated him for having received an actual paper kiss from gorgeous Miss Fearon.

Strenuously, Robin tried to integrate himself and his thoughts. He swallowed a couple of the quick-revival pills with which his father kept his family always supplied, and constantly had recourse to himself. Robin put the big summer postage sack, fabricated by reluctant convicts, under his burning head. It seemed to him that the main definable development or advance in the correspondence had been in the expression of regard for him, the postman. What development could be more to the point? In the end, Robin managed to extract one of the usual forms from his overheated pocket. For the burning of boats this was precisely the weather. Robin rose to get his official pencil. Then he sat again in the bad thoroughfare and simply wrote: "I shall answer your appeal. I ask nothing more. POSTMAN." It was a moment for the word in full.

He thought for a long time, back and forth; sometimes even sucking the official pencil. Then he subscribed not one St. Andrew's kiss, but two. He might as well be hanged not for filching a single postal order but for seizing the entire General Post Office, as in Ireland. Robin almost ran to deliver the note. Now that the decision was made, his step would be light for a whole hour or two hours. He would hardly notice the heat. He would breathe like a young boy.

The larks had ascended so high that they were inaudible. The sea was so unnaturally flat that no wave broke anywhere. Holidays were to dream of; in retrospect as in advance. The one chimney still emitted faintly viridian smoke.

Two days later, with the lovely woman floating about everywhere, like a blue bird, a parcel turned up at the temporary post office addressed to "Miss Rosetta Fearon, Lastingham," and no more.

"If it's too heavy, wait till tomorrow, dear," suggested kindly Mrs. Truslove.

"I'll manage," responded Robin, as if he had been the postman in a publicity film.

He had spoken before lifting the parcel.

"What do you think's in it?"

"Something on appro. You're lucky it's not C.O.D."

Robin toiled out into the heat with the heavy summer bag and the heavy parcel, the heaviest parcel he had yet struggled with. In more advanced places, there was of course a different postman for the parcels. Robin found it difficult to keep his burdened bicycle on course. The heat had been doing something to the tires.

In order to unload the parcel as swiftly as possible, Robin rode past a number of structures at which he should have stopped. So to proceed might be in the interests of good and imaginative personal organization, but he left a series of disappointed and weeping children; at least temporarily.

If there had ever been a bell at or in Miss Fearon's front door, it had been taken out or boarded up. The letter-box flap was so hung that it would not rattle properly, though Robin tried several different methods. He was reduced to thumping on the door itself, like the police in a film. He still hesitated to thump loudly. The nearest neighbor was not more than a third of a mile away.

Fortunately, there was no need. Robin could hear steps.

He tore off his cap. Postmen were not supposed to do this, but not every postman had to confront lovely Miss Fearon for the first time, or for the first time acknowledged; and in so remote a place. Robin just had time to pick the pencil off the ground and hide it in his shirt.

The door opened, and it was no Miss Fearon who stood there, but a man in old checked shirt and dirty trousers, like any other Englishman.

"Parcel," said Robin.

He got the word out, as the regulation prescribes, but was so taken aback that he omitted to lift the package from the step.

The man was under no obligation to lift it for him. "What's in it?" he asked, with extraordinary suspicion. He was a suspicious-looking man, at best: brown-whiskered, small-eyed, unfeatured.

"It's on appro.," said Robin.

"Don't know about that," said the man.

"It's very heavy," said Robin, volunteering a trifle

more, though under no requirement to do so. Correspondents must accept or refuse items as they are delivered. The right of refusal may soon be withdrawn. It goes back to the days before the penny post."

"So what?" enquired the man suspiciously.

Things were approaching a deadlock. Robin had learned by now that this sometimes happens, but in the present case he could have cried from disappointment. However, a lifeline was thrown to him; whether frail or stout was difficult to say.

A woman's voice spoke from within the abode: a most musical voice, Robin thought, though he really knew little about music, and though the voice uttered merely a monosyllable.

"Paul!"

"All *right*," said the man irritably, and without turning towards the loveliness within, or ceasing to glare at poor Robin.

"I don't want it," said the man, and gave the parcel a heavy kick. It came to Robin at once that this might be a dangerous thing to do, when neither of them apparently knew what the parcel contained; dangerous and silly.

"It's not addressed to you," Robin pointed out; whether or not so required.

"Paul!" cried the musical voice from within. Robin was almost certain that it came from nearer. In seconds, something most unexpected might happen.

Robin put his hand on the door. Now might be his moment; possibly his finest hour as yet.

"You can keep the—thing," bawled the brown-whiskered man.

Robin could see that both the man's eyes were bloodshot. Living in the country, he had never before seen such eyes. He continued to lean his slightly extended arm against the open door, though as unobtrusively as possible.

"Paul!" cried the musical voice; nearer still, as Robin would have sworn.

"—you postman," bellowed the man. At the same time, he struck down Robin's right arm with a blow as from a crossbar, and stamped on his left foot with a heavy boot that might very well have been soled in iron. It was as if Robin had "put his foot in the door" like a travelling salesman, which postmen are bade never to do in any circumstances whatever. The door was shut with a slam that should have torn a door like that from its hinges, and must certainly have traveled that third of a mile on such a still day as every day now was.

Robin, injured in two places, was left with the heavy and enigmatic parcel. He half hoped, half feared that the door would open again, but it did not. There was the total silence within the house that by now he could almost describe as usual. Vulnerable though his position was, he was too upset to move for what seemed to him a long time.

Then, something really strange happened. Robin, without thinking, put his hand into one of his jacket pockets, and, from among all the official forms and other documents, drew forth the communication from the Rating Authority that he should have delivered to this very house weeks ago! He reflected that he must have been looking unconsciously for his pencil.

It was time for Robin to pull himself together. He rose to his knees, and, in the kneeling position, put the questionnaire timidly into the box.

As he did so, the usual letter fluttered out, though nothing like a week had passed since the last one.

This time, Robin was seated on the actual step as he read.

> *I lie crushed beneath his weight, and I ask Who is he? Nothing he does for me reconciles me. Postman, I have this to say: there is no lasting happiness anywhere. Your true*
>
> R.

And Robin's two kisses had been exchanged for two others. He noted particularly that for the first time no assurance had been sought from him. None at all. Either his word had been accepted, or, by implication, his past promises were now waived. As in the matter of his career, he was left free himself to decide for the best.

How had the man, Paul, not seen the replies that the postman had already made, and had delivered unsealed? How had such a man left unslain the musical-voiced woman, if he had seen them? How, living with such a man, and, as she claimed, knowing almost nothing about him, had the musical-voiced woman the courage to continue such a correspondence with a postman she could only have examined, if at all, through some crevice? The most likely explanation came to Robin even as he stood there. It was simply that such a man might not be able to read; and probably not.

Robin managed to drag another of the familiar forms from his pocket, together with the familiar pencil. "Live with me instead," he wrote. At the moment, his injured arm hardly permitted him to write more. He mused about the signature. He returned to "P." That seemed best; and with a single, almost austere, little cross. The completed form followed the municiple missive into the house.

Robin resumed his cap and limped to the gate. He left the parcel on the step. That was often done; in the absence of an alternative. Robin might bicycle back later in order to see if anything had happened to it.

Where were the larks now? What the waves?

On his way home that evening, Robin diverged (a fair distance, too) in order to look. As far as he could see, certainly as far as his duty went, the parcel had been "taken in." He fancied that the normal thieving hypothesis hardly arose here. The little house might be kept under observation from afar, let alone the fabulous occupant; but there were no callers other than the postman, no visitors. That simple probability explained in itself several aspects of what had happened. However, the greenish smoke could this evening hardly be seen. Swarming gnats would have tinged the air more noticeably.

Very soon, Rosetta Fearon might be emerging, quite differently arrayed, to gather peat.

Robin decided that it would be both unwise and impracticable to take a chance on it.

Robin had been keeping the three surviving letters in a red betel nut box which his Uncle Alexander had brought back from the East as a young man and had given to Robin on Robin's thirteenth birthday.

Uncle Alexander lived in retirement at Trimingham. His continuing contribution to life was a ceaseless lament for Trimingham railway station, and for the entire M.

and G.N. network that once served the region so spar-
klingly. He spoke always of the bright yellow rolling
stock, immaculate time-keeping, and totally painless
fares. Uncle Alexander had hardly left the house since
the line closed, but cronies of his own generation came to
see him almost every evening for negus and talk about
the past. Two of them had worked in the M. and G.N.
yard at Melton Constable; two others in the timetable
department; one old fellow on the track itself, in and
around the Aylsham area.

Until now, Robin had been unable to find any particular use for the box. Never had he dared to surmise a
use so ideal as this one. The box was now a casket.
Robin covered Miss Fearon's last letter with kisses; every
moment kissing the woman he had seen amid the listless
throngs of Lastingham. The promise in the different letters was indeed by implication only, perhaps even remote implication; but Robin knew that this was how
attractive women proceeded. For a woman to speak
plainly was an admission. Robin hid away the casket
amid the worn-out pajamas and running gear in his
tuckbox and turned the key twice. He then changed out
of his uniform.

All the time he could hear his mother singing. She was
cooking his supper, as best she could without Nelly.
Nelly was holidaying for a week or two on the shores of
The Wash with a girlfriend who was slightly crippled.

"... Say ... Goodbye ... to Daddee.
He's ... gwine away to ... the War."

The heavily accentuated dance tune was her favorite air.
She came back to it always. She seemed to have been
singing it since Robin had been in his cradle, which had
once been her cradle also, and of course Nelly's, in between the two of them.

Robin's father was out that night, professionally or
merely by way of a change.

As the two of them ate together, Robin's mother
talked about the different men who had admired her before she married. It was her invariable topic when she
was alone with Robin; which, after all, was not very
often. In those days, she had worked in a pharmaceuticals factory near the Thames, and had been promoted

several times. Pharmaceuticals had been a common interest with Robin's father when they had first found one another. If Robin's father were present, Robin's mother seldom said anything in particular, and neither did he. It is acknowledged officially that medical practitioners are greatly given to gloom. More of them actually kill themselves than anyone else. Nelly could be depended upon nowadays to do most of the talking at meals, and at other times.

Robin had been through a particularly hard day, physically and emotionally. He might well have been unable to eat very much, especially as it was still so hot, and as his mother hated an open window. But, surprisingly, he devoured all that was set before him, and then requested a further helping. His mother beamed nostalgically as he ladled it forth.

"Rex had such soft hands," she said.

Robin nodded. His mouth was once more too full for words.

"And the most lovely arms."

"Good for him," responded Robin, with articulation still impaired.

"Right up to the shoulders."

"Not like my arms," said Robin, now able to grin.

"You have lovely arms, Robin boy. You too," affirmed Robin's mother. "I often wonder about them. I wonder. I wonder."

"They carried a very heavy parcel today, Mum."

"It's a shame you have to work so hard."

"I see the world, Mum."

"It's time you had a nice girl and a home of your own. I must think what I can do. I've had experience, you see."

In the end, Robin rubbed wedge after wedge of sliced bread round the heavy gravy which nothing else would remove from the plate.

"Hungry hunter!" exclaimed his mother affectionately.

"I've got responsibilities, Mum." He felt quite differently about his mother when, occasionally, they were allowed to be alone together.

Without a word to anyone, Robin, in plain clothes, set out the next afternoon to look for a room to let in Jimpingham. It was one of his rest periods, and Mrs.

Truslove had let him change in her toilet. She had also undertaken to look after his uniform until the evening. She had even winked at him.

Jimpingham was a village much like Brusingham, though a little further from the sea: possibly nine or ten miles away. Between Brusingham and Jimpingham was Horsenail, much like both of them. Robin thought, or rather hoped, that in Jimpingham no one would have a very precise idea who he was. His father's understanding with the partnership excluded him from ministering in that direction. With the other partners, much older men, a chance would have to be taken. From Miss Fearon's house, one could reach Jimpingham with hardly an inhabited structure en route, though the route was not very direct.

As will be seen, Robin had considered long and carefully. If Rosetta were to cast herself upon him, he could not bring her home to his parents and Nelly. A room in Lastingham would hardly avail: he himself was known by now to everyone, and marked out by his uniform; Rosetta seemed to flit about there almost all the time; the rent would be based upon holiday values. Least of all did he see himself trying conclusions with Paul for possession of the existing hearth. Moreover, the need might arise upon an instant. If there were no place reasonably near for Rosetta to lay her head, she might fly at once to London or somewhere.

Possession of the little house might of course come about later, supposing that Robin was really prepared to live with Rosetta where Paul had lived with her, but in the interim somewhere entirely unobtrusive was required, and not too demanding, in that the harboring of a beautiful wounded blue bird was the primary intention. Fortunately, there had been talk all the time among the boys at Robin's non-coeducational school about love nests in the different villages: over one kind of honest habitat; under another; behind a third; within a fourth, though with no proper window. It is probable that little of the talk derived from first-hand experience, but Robin was confident that he knew the basic ropes. Shyness was not precisely his problem, in any case; but something less definable.

Robin looked around Jimpingham for some time before making a first plunge. There was plenty for visitors

to look at without their being called upon to explain
themselves: the remains of an ornamental pump and a
pale green pond, upon which perhaps the pump had
once drawn; a milestone said to be linked with King
Charles II; a blacksmith's forge now selling comb honey
and souvenirs; the fair maid's grave in the old part of the
churchyard; Dr. Borrow's grave in the new. Dr. Borrow
had been a prominent local mathematician and preacher;
descended collaterally, it was claimed, from Lavengro
himself. Not all of these things had Robin previously in-
spected with any care.

Robin's first choice of a possible tenancy led almost at
once to an embarrassing conversation of a character he
had not allowed for, though he realized that he should
have done. He had been warned often enough. He
brought the conversation to an end by affecting to be
simple; a device that still has its uses in the less sophisticated parts of the countryside.

True courage was required to try again; within minutes; within only a certain number of yards. But Robin
would not have said that courage was what he lacked,
and this time his choice was better, for he lighted upon
the helpful Mrs. Gradey, a refugee from Dublin itself,
with no proper man behind her and her living to make.
There were seven children, away just then at school, but
Mrs. Gradey said that they would make no sound of a
noise. Mrs. Gradey was most accommodating about the
rent and about every other matter that Robin could think
to raise, such as the whereabouts of a bathroom. She even
promised to cook steaks and french fried potatoes for
the poor blue bird, if the need arose, and if the costs and
so forth could be settled in advance.

Robin stated that at this point he would like to·rent
the furnished room by the month only, as he did not
quite know when the blue bird would be free to move in.
He implied that only a little later, he and she might well
book a suite, a penthouse, the entire grand edifice.

After his last experience at Rosetta's house, Robin saw
no reason why he should visit her only once a week, or
when there was a heavy parcel in need of delivery.
There might never be another parcel. On the morning
after he had driven his bargain with Mrs. Gradey, he sat
writing to Rosetta while his mother repeatedly summoned

him to piping hot breakfast below. In Nelly's absence for a few more days, he had taken from her room a sheet of her pink writing paper, and had meticulously cut off the vertical heather sprig, using the official scissors with which every postman is theoretically equipped.

"Linger no longer," he wrote. But that sounded like one of his mother's songs, and Robin cut away a horizontal strip also.

"Come away at once." At times like these, Robin, as everyone else, proved not to have been taught Shakespeare for nothing.

"Come away at once. I await you respectfully. Here is the address. Take a taxi, if necessary. Act now. Have trust. POSTMAN." Robin knew that a woman in Rosetta's position would fly more readily to the protection of another woman, even an unknown one. He had therefore fully particularized Mrs. Gradey's identity and whereabouts. He could not offer a telephone number, because Mrs. Gradey could not manage a telephone. However, there was plainly no telephone at Rosetta's house either: nothing but a wisp of greenish smoke, tiny but undying; that and silence. Robin subjoined no little cross. The moment was too serious for that.

He folded his letter into its matching pink envelope, but made no attempt to stick it up, as he might easily think of something to add. Since it was even possible that he might wish to rewrite the whole thing, he also helped himself to a spare sheet. He put the cut-off heather into the pocket of his shirt for good luck. It would lie near to his heart until Rosetta came to him.

He tore downstairs, now rampant for breakfast, albeit belated.

"Your father didn't come home last night."

"Nothing new about that."

Robin's mouth was full of scrambled egg, bacon, half-a-beef-sausage, grilled tomato, pigsfry. On such a morning, what did it matter that piping hot was meaningless? All the easier to get down as things were.

"I sometimes worry about him."

"Nelly will be back soon."

"I sometimes worry about all of you."

"No need to worry about *me*, Mum."

Robin's mother glanced quickly at him as he fed. He should have been on his bike ten minutes ago; clean out

of Brusingham; pedalling hard; remembering his round.
Robin's mother began to weep.

She was always doing that, but, when, infrequently,
they were alone together, just the two of them, he loved
her none the less because of it.

"Oh, Robin."

He chucked down his knife and fork. He had almost
cleaned the busy plate, in any case; surely with record
speed? He laid aside his heavy cup, not bothering with
the saucer. He scrambled round the faded but familiar
room, and pressed himself against his mother's deep
bosom.

"*You're* mine, anyway," said Robin's mother, crying
all the more profusely. "Mine. Mine."

Robin laid his left cheek, newly shaven as the regulations stipulated, against his mother's bare throat and
front. He looked downwards at her tight black petticoat.

"It's *such* a struggle," said Robin's mother, dissolving
anew.

"One day you'll get away from it all."

She stopped crying for a second, and looked at her
son hard and seriously.

"Do you really think so? Do you believe it?"

"Of course I do, Mum." He gave her an extra hard
and special squeeze. "Now I must go. All those letters.
All those parcels. Etcetera."

Before finally releasing him, she gave him a serious
and deliberate kiss. Tears were rolling all over her. She
said nothing more.

"Bye, Mum."

He raced to unlock his bike. Every moment, his left
hand was on the packed but unsealed letter, and on the
spare sheet of heathered paper beside it.

When the time came, it seemed the merest trifle to
wander off course and make his delivery. Who cared that
morning about the cracked old telescopes, half rusted-up
and with whole lenses missing; about the battered
Brownie cameras; about the hearts dry as boleti when
their season is over? All were well lost if this were love.

Robin strode along the fragmented path as if he had
every right to be there, and official business to do. He
struck up his letter and persuaded it through the idio-
syncratic flap as if it had been a Last Demand. For the
first time, nothing dropped out as he did so. He gave

hardly a look to the house as he rode away, though he did check the timid green effluvium. There it was, and there, he could not but suppose, was the snail on the thorn, and all things 'like it! Quite unconsciously, as he pedaled he began half to sing another of his mother's favorites: "Dreamy bridegroom. Dreamy bride. She's the sweet one by his side. Father's darling. Mother's pride."

Four days later, Robin was sitting alone in the room he had rented.

He had managed to take in Rosetta's abode each morning, but each morning he had gently tilted the funny flap without result. He did not need to be told that Rosetta must be in inner turmoil. He no longer even noticed her skipping blithely from shop to shop in Lastingham. She was facing the crisis of her life. There might not be another such crisis for her until he himself had a sudden heart attack or total nervous breakdown. If all went well, that is.

Robin was not merely alone in his room. He was alone in the house. Mrs. Gradey and all her brood were out scavenging. They seemed to do it every evening, when the weather permitted. They brought back objects amazing in their variety, which Mrs. Gradey spent much of each day sorting through and rendering marketable.

Mrs. Truslove had told Robin that the old man had died the day before. Something fearful had set in finally, and the end had come as a release. "When people begin to go, they crumble like trees," Mrs. Truslove had remarked poetically. She had been sorting out postal orders as she spoke.

The bell rang: long and loudly. Robin remained fairly calm. Mrs. Gradey had visitors at many hours, and so did her two eldest daughters, and her eldest son, whose name was Laegaire. Robin was schooled already in discounting all expectation.

However that might be, he was greatly surprised this time. At the door was Nelly, back from the coast, brown as a seadog (or female equivalent), firm as a rock.

"I'm coming up," were her only words at that stage.

Robin stood in the middle of the carpet he had rented, partly fawn, partly woodnut. Nelly wore a flowered traveling costume.

"It's all I can afford," said Robin, smiling around. "For the present, that is."

"I hope she's got short legs," said Nelly, looking at the bed, which might well have been in fumed oak.

"I don't really know," said Robin, smiling still.

"Who is it, Robin? Better come clean with me. Then we'll be in it together."

"Her name is Rosetta Fearon. It won't mean anything to you."

"Won't it just! She's that piece who prances round Lastingham getting in everywhere first."

Robin's heart, and much else within else, turned right over. Only then did he realize how very far from sure he had so far been. It would take two or three minutes for him to regain confidence. Still, yet again the old and invalid postman and fisherman had been confirmed in his words.

"You *are* simple!" said Nelly; much as she had addressed Robin from his very earliest days.

"You won't tell people, Nelly?"

"No. But you'll never get that one into bed. Not into this bed or any other."

"It's not the point, Nelly. It's not the only thing there is."

"No," said Nelly. "Not the *only* thing."

Robin glanced at her. She was at such an advantage with everybody, and always had been; starting with their mother, let alone their father. Nelly had simply been born like that.

"Sit down, Nelly," said Robin gravely, "and please tell me just what you mean about Miss Fearon."

Instinctively, Nelly seated herself on the only chair that was fully sound. She had not needed even to shake or test the others. Nelly pulled down her skirt sharply, as if she were with a stranger. There was a sense in which Nelly was always with a stranger. Robin sat upon the floor, drawing up his legs to his chest.

"She's not the kind for anything like that," said Nelly. "For one thing look at the way she's dressed. Clothes like that aren't meant to take off."

"I think she dresses beautifully."

"A woman knows," claimed Nelly. "Besides, there's something funny about her."

"Such as?"

"She knows nobody and doesn't want to."

Robin let his legs stretch themselves a little. "Nelly! Can you honestly blame her?"

"'And nobody wants to know *her*. I can tell you *that*."

"They wouldn't know what to say."

"She holes herself up and no one knows what she does."

Robin stared upwards at Nelly from the floor. "Nelly, how can you or anyone else possibly know, when no one even speaks to her?"

"I'm talking to you, Robin. You can take it or leave it."

Robin reflected for a moment. "Tell me," he said. "How did you find out about me? About this place?"

Nelly smiled for the first time—and quite affectionately, Robin thought.

"Everything *you* do or think about is an open book to me, Robin. Always has been, and always will be. You must know that."

Robin reflected once more. Nelly had not even set eyes on him since he had moved in.

"There are times when I'm frightened by it all. I admit that."

"Robin," said Nelly earnestly, or seemingly so, "I advise you to give it up and return home."

"I think most chaps are frightened for some of the time," said Robin, following his line of thought, and remembering his chums, squared up in memory, jumbled together in the break.

"It's not for you, Robin," said Nelly; softly, and therefore perhaps even more in earnest. "Come back home."

"I've not left home, Nelly."

"Then what's all this?" Nelly's gesture would have comprehended the entire long guest wing at Sandringham.

"This is something additional. That's all."

Nelly looked hard at him. "That's not possible, Robin. I tell you. It has to be one thing or the other."

Robin lowered his knees and intersected his legs in the supposedly Turkish manner. "I can't go back now," he said. He was trying hard to seem at once resolved, unmoved, and in control.

"You certainly can't come back with me," said Nelly, as if he had been speaking literally. She had risen to her feet and was examining the state of her tights, first one leg and then the other. "I've got to go and help Mother, and Mother would only wonder if you arrived with me. No doubt I shall see you later. If you're not interrupted first, that is. I've said what I have to say."

"It's nothing like as desperate as that, Nelly," said Robin, smiling again; which this time required an effort. "Of course you'll see me. My stomach's beginning to gnaw. How did you get here, anyway? Are you on your bike?"

"Boulton gave me a lift from Trapingham. He's waiting for me now."

"Where is he waiting?"

"In the Peck of Peas. He's another reason why you can't travel with me, little brother."

Boulton Morganfield was from outside the region; basically from near Coventry. He looked unlike anyone else.

"Are you gone on Boulton?"

"Not in the least, Robin. Not one little bit. Not one tittle."

That time, Robin managed almost to laugh.

"Take care of yourself, Robin. Do try."

But all that happened after this necessarily disturbing talk, was that Robin gave things another half hour by his official watch, and then bicycled slowly home. Though he was very hungry, it would be no good hurrying. The preparation of the evening meal always took his mother and Nelly a long time, because the task was always being interrupted by confidences. There had been no sight or sound of the returning Gradeys.

On the very next morning a letter fell at Robin's feet as he tipped Miss Fearon's flap. He unbuttoned his jacket or tunic before reading it.

"I can suffer no more. I throw myself upon you here and now, certain that you will treat me with respect. ROSETTA." And there were two crosses; this time larger.

All day Robin had difficulty in remembering the order of the different structures and shacks; in not wheeling leftwards at crossings where it behooved him first to wheel right. At about half-past eleven, he almost ran down a Mrs. Watto, who wrote books for older women, and who always wore a full smock, concealing who-knew-what.

"You have quite broken my train of thought," murmured Mrs. Watto, her eyes glinting, her lips parting.

In the late afternoon, Robin bicycled over to Jimpingham. Naturally, it was at the earliest possible moment; though Rosetta had not been able to specify a very precise time. At some distance from the homestead, Robin perceived that the Gradeys were already out and about. There were manifestations which one had learned to interpret from quite far off.

Robin locked his bicycle, and slowly went upstairs. He opened his door cautiously, as always; it being necessary structurally.

The beautiful Rosetta was seated within. Like Nelly, she had found the one dependable chair.

Rosetta rose upon her lovely legs. "Are you my postman?" she enquired in her musical voice, higher than Robin was used to, but rippling like a cascade in the sun. She held out her hand. She was holding her gloves in the other hand.

"My name is Robin Breeze," said Robin quietly. "I am only a provisional postman. I think I should say that right away. I shall be doing something else soon."

He would not have expressed himself so positively even three minutes ago. Rosetta's voice had inspired him; her hand, so precisely right in warmth, texture, and grip, had already strengthened him.

"So shall I!" said Rosetta, and laughed like tiny pieces of purest silver falling into a sunlit pool. She resumed her chair.

"Do sit down," said Rosetta; very much the hostess, receiving. Robin thought it wisest to sit on the bed. He had first shut the door, though it was close in the room.

"Where is everybody?" asked Rosetta.

"Out at work. It's a family named Gradey. A mother and some children. I hope you don't mind."

"I shan't be here for ever," said Rosetta.

"I've arranged for Mrs. Gradey to cook for you, if you would like that. Pretty simple, I'm afraid. Rather like we get at home." Robin thought it well to make clear as soon as possible that he had no idea of himself moving in on Rosetta immediately; not even into another room in the cottage, supposing one to be free. Besides, the way he had spoken should lighten the tone of their conversation; make it perceptibly more familiar and intimate.

"I've not been eating very much for some time," said Rosetta, dimpling a little. "I've been through rather an ordeal, you know."

"So it seems," said Robin, aiming at an air of mastery. To his delight, Rosetta could not be much more than ten years older than he was, even now that he could closely examine her, at about four feet distance, in sunlight, and newly relaxed. "How long have you lived in Lastingham?"

"I was left the house by my uncle. In his will, you know. Mr. Abraham Mordle. Perhaps you have heard of him?"

Robin shook his head. As it happened, he had indeed heard of Abraham Mordle. He was known to all the kids as the Spook King. It seemed best for Robin to shut up on the subject.

"And you moved in?" he asked politely, though he had been slightly shaken.

"There seemed nothing better to do," said Rosetta. "I found plenty to occupy myself, though it is an easy house to run. You know it used to be called *Niente*."

"What does that mean?" asked Robin.

"It is the Italian for Nothing. The name fell off and before I could arrange for it to be put back, Paul was there."

"Couldn't *he* put it back?" Robin asked; facetiously no doubt, but more and more familiarly, which was the real point. Every second second, he was glancing at the subtle neckline of Rosetta's dress; every intermediate second, at the perfectly placed hemline.

"Paul could do *nothing*. Have you heard of H. H. Asquith?"

"Just."

"Asquith's wife—his second wife—said: 'Herbert who couldn't strike a match!' It's the one thing everyone remembers about Asquith. Paul was like that too."

"He didn't *look* like that," said Robin. "I saw him once, you know."

"Paul was very different from his looks. That was something I soon learned. *One* thing I learned."

"I had to deliver a parcel," said Robin. "It was addressed to you. Did you ever get it?"

"I expect so," said Rosetta. "Parcels were always coming along."

Robin managed somehow to stop himself from saying "They were *not*."

"Paul did what he thought best with them. He *was* my husband, remember. Not that he was inconsiderate. I told you he was not."

"You told me things I couldn't quite follow," said Robin. "I suppose you didn't feel like going into details. Perhaps you could tell me more now? I don't want to ask, if you would rather not talk about it."

"There's little to tell," replied Rosetta, again dimpling, and this time completely. "One day I woke up and found myself married. Just like Lord Byron. I have never understood how it happened. It was like a dream, and yet not. You say you saw Paul for yourself. No one could just dream up Paul."

Robin nodded. He had no wish of his own to talk about Paul. "We had better think more about the future, hadn't we?" he suggested.

Rosetta laughed her sunlit pool laugh. "How practical you are!"

"That's best, isn't it?" asked Robin, somewhat at sea.

If he himself wished to be practical, it was, he thought ruefully, in a quite different way. He tried to take in the complete glorious totality of Rosetta, from cornfield hair and mignonette eyes to slender feet and figment shoes. Suddenly he wondered how ever she had made the journey. He could not see this vision gathering peat. There at least the old man had been mistaken.

Rosetta spoke definitively. "I think I had better just remain here for several weeks at least. Incommunicado, you know. Except sometimes to the postman."

Robin caught her eye.

"But only sometimes."

"We could plan what to do next," Robin said, trying to turn her proposition to account, though feebly, he felt.

"I shall use the time for resting, and then perhaps I shall go abroad. You must understand, Postman, that I have no money. Only what's in my handbag. Paul was very stringent. It was one reason why I left. One among several. I *had* to leave. I had no choice."

Robin felt that he had turned paler with every sentence of this confusing narrative.

"But—" he said; without entirely knowing what words he was proposing to use next.

Rosetta spared him. "It is best for me to tell you this quite clearly, Postman. Of course I shall repay you every penny in the end. When I am strong enough, I shall go aboard. I can make my way there. Not in England. But for my uncle's legacy, I might have starved for all my so-called friends and rotten family cared. There was a little money from Uncle Mordle, as well as the house. You have no idea what people are really like, Postman. At least I hope you haven't. I shall let no one near me ever again. Paul was the last."

It was a speech with elements of bitterness, to say the least of it, but Rosetta spoke it gaily, like the middle-distance chiming of medieval bells.

"I shall do everything I can," said Robin; though by now he had no idea how he could do anything much. It was much as when, through inexperience, he had swallowed an entire lemon sorbet at one of his father's professional banquets—the only one that either of them had attended. Like every worthwhile young man, he had supposed that romance would provide its own mysterious wherewithal. At least to the true believer; he who had faith. No young man who supposes otherwise deserves consideration.

Rosetta was regarding him with a smile in her blue eyes. "I shall pay you interest as well," she said. "Of course I shall. In the meantime, I throw myself upon you." It had, of course, been the expression she had used in her last letter.

But the Gradey family was back. Robin had been hearing their miscellaneous rattlings and crashes for some time, though hardly listening to them. Rosetta had of course made no remark. The dialogue between her and Robin had been of great intensity.

There was a tap on the door.

"Enter," said Rosetta. It was the first time in Robin's hearing that she had spoken as perhaps a foreigner speaks. At home, his father said "Come in" to each patient alike.

Mrs. Gradey entered, still spotted with rust and dung. "How are you, my dear?" she enquired sympathetically.

"Fairly well," said Rosetta, remaining in her chair. "Tired after my ordeal." She smiled; as it were, bravely.

"I knew well you had arrived. It is a gift that I have. Robin will tell you that."

"You were quite right about it," said Rosetta.

"My children have the gift too," said Mrs. Gradey.

Rosetta nodded slowly and graciously.

"Did Robin tell you about my children?"

"Yes, of course. I am sure I shall make friends with all of them. Have they got bicycles? It's so good round here."

"Bicycles they have, but some other things they have not."

"I must see what each of them most wants."

"That's very thoughtful of you, my dear. They are quiet, good children. You'll not hear one sound as far as they are concerned. You'll sleep in peace. I promise you that." In fact, there were still thuds and clankings outside, but Mrs. Gradey's eyes were roving round the simply appointed room, comparing it with the simply elegant Rosetta. "If there's anything you'd want me to buy for you, I'll send the eldest into town for it."

"Thank you. I'll make a list."

"It's not a steak you'll be wanting for your supper! What about a nice plump guinea fowl? And a bottle of fine French wine from the Peck of Peas? They've surely a splendiferous off-license at the Peck."

"Thank you," said Rosetta. "Between ourselves, Mrs. Gradey, I am quite hungry for the first time since I can remember."

"Call me Maureen," said Mrs. Gradey, breaking out into a broad simper, albeit her face was still filthy from toil.

Rosetta smiled back, though she did nothing more.

"And will Robin be staying for everything?" asked Mrs. Gradey.

"No," put in Robin, "I can't. I can't possibly."

There was a long and curious pause among the three of them, as in *tableaux vivants*. It could not be said that there were little crosses in the air at the moment, though one could perhaps hope.

"I have to go home," said Robin. "I'm expected. I shall come round tomorrow evening at the same time or a little later."

How desperately and confusedly he wished that he

could have added "with a thousand pounds in bank-notes"—even if only to himself!

But, he reflected in his bedroom that night, it was not only money that was a problem and a question mark. Romance was singularly lacking in everything that had happened, and practicality all too intrusive. At the evening meal, Nelly had noticeably shown no further interest in him, and had applied herself entirely to organize the morrow's tasks with their mother. Arrears had accumulated in quantity during Nelly's absence. Their father had turned the pages of the evening paper back and forth, as he often did; spent by the day's struggle with intangibles and intractables.

When Robin reached Jimpingham the next evening, Mrs. Gradey was awaiting his arrival, in order to hand him a bill for thirty-nine pounds odd.

"A few little extras to brighten up the room," she said.

Then she handed him a second bill, for forty-seven pounds exactly.

"I don't entirely know the nature of that," she said, "but I think it's all right." She was standing expectantly; intercepting Robin on his way to the delights above. Robin was more than forty minutes later than on the previous occasion, in any case.

He was in no state to assimilate or analyze the financial details. "You want the money now?" he asked. It was all he could ask.

"Sure and I can't give credit," said Mrs. Gradey, with a new thread of militancy in her tone.

How had the cash been found to pay the different shops and businesses and the fares for Laegaire or Emer to reach them, probably absenting themselves from school for the purpose? Doubtless from Mrs. Gradey's strongbox buried deep beneath the praties and watched over by little people.

"I'll bring it tomorrow, Mrs. Gradey."

Fortunately, he had as much as a hundred and eighteen pounds invested—naturally, in the Post Office.

"Or I'll bring as much as I can. I have to give three days' notice to get the rest."

Mrs. Gradey said nothing. Robin could hear the children playing Micks and Prods in the garden. At previous times they had made only noises connected with their business.

"I think it's three days." Robin was finding it difficult to be certain about anything.

"Sure, and she's a charming lady," said Mrs. Gradey enigmatically.

"But don't you go buying anything else for her," said Robin. There was more of fear than of firmness in his voice. "I can't afford it." In the hope of a little understanding, even fellow-feeling, he did his best to smile at Mrs. Gradey.

"Slim purse never bought fair lady, don't they say? Up you go, Robin, while still you can."

Tapping at Rosetta's door, Robin noticed how much his hand was once more shaking.

"One moment." That lovely voice was unlikely to quell Robin's tremor.

He waited. Mrs. Gradey was taking up tiny tasks immediately below. All the time, she could see him standing there.

"One moment," said the lovely voice a second time.

Right away, Robin would very probably have dissolved into nothingness for ever, had the opportunity been offered him.

"You may enter now."

Rosetta was in a different lovely dress, as always when he saw her in Lastingham; but the odd thing was that he could see no change to the room at all, nothing added, nothing subtracted. Not even the air seemed to have changed.

But there was a small dog trotting up and down the room on business of his own; a fluffy terrier, puttycolored.

"Where did *he* come from?" asked Robin; trying not to make his meaning too obvious.

"I found him in the room when I woke up," said Rosetta. "First Paul, and now a puppy." She laughed. "I'm not much better with a pet than I was with a husband. I wonder if you could do something with him?"

"I can't take him home," said Robin quickly. "My father won't have a dog in the house. He's a doctor."

"Then *don't* take him home," said Rosetta.

Rosetta had not as yet suggested that Robin sit. They stood looking at one another with the terrier darting about them and among their legs. Probably it was only because he was so young. Robin knew it was what people would say.

"I don't think I could take him to the vet either," said Robin slowly.

"Perhaps he'll turn into a handsome prince," suggested Rosetta.

"I'm your handsome prince," replied Robin; after only a few silent seconds had passed.

He could only hope that this time he had chosen the right moment for the boat-burning that was at intervals essential.

"I *have* a prince," said Rosetta. "You never seem to realize that, though surely I made it clear in all my letters?"

"No," said Robin. "Actually you didn't. Where is this prince?"

"Abroad. I'm on my way to him. I told you."

Robin continued to gaze at the scrubby carpet; far too familiar after perhaps six sightings. The dog crossed and recrossed his field of vision.

"So that's all there is to it?" he inquired.

"There's no need to be disagreeable," said Rosetta, rippling with reasonableness. "I told you from the first. Anything else is entirely in your own imagination."

"What about Paul?"

"I shall divorce him. I have grounds enough. Though you don't really need grounds nowadays."

"What about me?" Robin was improvising blindly; gaining time and extenuating reality; unlikely to achieve.

"I'm very grateful for all you've done and I hope you'll continue doing it for a few more weeks. Of course I don't expect you to visit me every day. I said that too. The Gradey children will go between us, if necessary. They are fine kids. I've given them all machine guns. Girls don't like being left out nowadays."

"*I* don't like being left out much," said Robin, without one leg to stand on, not one toe.

The little dog seemed busy as ever, though what the business was no ordinary person could tell. Robin was sure of that.

"If you'll sit down for just a moment," said Rosetta, "I'll tell you exactly what to do."

Of course the very last thing that Robin wished was

to go, so he seated himself; naturally upon the bed, leaving the good chair to his hostess.

Rosetta came at once to the point. "Give up all the wild ideas that buzz round you like wasps. Or like blue-bottles. Oh, yes I know. I know all there is to know about men. I can read them through a brick wall. Find a nice, ordinary girl, not too attractive or you'll be jealous all the time, not too bright or you'll be anxious all the time, not too rich or you'll have nothing to strive for, not too original or she'll upset people. There are plenty of them, and all of them are available to a young postman like you. Those are the terms offered."

The terrier had come to a sudden standstill, as if he had been a white gun dog on one of the estates.

"*You* don't live like that," said Robin from the bed.

"I don't live at all," replied Rosetta. "Haven't you realized?"

"Perhaps I have." Now Robin was staring at her: momentarily still that muggy evening; for seconds rigid as the dog.

Rosetta smiled. "I am the person every postman meets in the end."

"I'm a provisional postman only. I told you that clearly," remarked Robin, starting once more to relax.

"Do what I tell you. What else is there for you? Only wasps and bluebottles."

"It seems that I have to meet the bills, none the less," said Robin. He could feel them at this moment in his jacket or tunic pocket.

"Only till I can repay. And with interest."

Robin must have looked in some way sceptical, though it was not with intent.

"I promise." Rosetta even leaned toward him. The dog too had recovered mobility, and had begun to lick Rosetta's ankles.

Robin made a second supreme effort in the course of that short meeting. "Take off your dress," he said; hoarsely in the still, worn air.

"All right," said Rosetta, quietly but immediately. Her eyes were on his.

She went to work at once. Robin continued to sit on the bed, affecting calmness, convincing none.

Rosetta had removed the lovely bluish dress, and it lay there, with the little motley dog now sniffing round it.

But she was wearing a dress still; a lovely pinkish dress.

"Take it off," said Robin, now almost growling with masculinity.

Again she went to work, and a second dress lay before him, near the first dress, and with the dog pattering interestedly and indecisively between them. Rosetta now wore a lovely dress that was greenish. She was smiling placidly. She reseated herself in the sound chair. For the first time, Robin noticed her green earrings, long but light.

"Postman, I'll write to you always," said Rosetta. "I promise."

He would have to borrow; but from whom could he do so? Only from Nelly that he could think of; who was likely to have ideas of her own. It had to be remembered that rent to Mrs. Gradey would have to be paid too, for as long as Rosetta cared to remain, though Mrs. Gradey might well be among the least of his prospective creditors.

"Always?" inquired Robin.

"Always."

Now he could stand up. It seemed hardly right merely to shake hands, as when yesterday they had met; and Robin suspected that Rosetta's kisses were strictly and exclusively epistolary.

"I'll not say Goodbye then?"

"Never say Goodbye." Rosetta was standing too. The dog was looking up at them, from one to the other, half interested, half apathetic, and with its tongue beginning to hang out.

Mrs. Gradey was lurking below.

"Tomorrow then?" she demanded. "With some of it? As much as you can manage? I'm not the Queen of Tara, you know."

"You are the queen of my heart," responded Robin jauntily; "which is far better."

RECOMMENDED READING
—1980

Terry Carr

Robert Aickman: "The Fetch." *Intrusions.*

Orson Scott Card: "Tinker." *Eternity Science Fiction*, Vol. 1, No. 2.

Glen Cook: "Call for the Dead." *Fantasy and Science Fiction*, July 1980.

———: "Soldier of an Empire Unacquainted with Defeat." *Berkley Showcase*, Vol. 2.

Richard Cowper: "The Web of the Magi." *Fantasy and Science Fiction*, June 1980.

Avram Davidson: "There Beneath the Silky-Tree and Whelmed in Deeper Gulphs than Me." *Other Worlds 2.*

Thomas M. Disch: "Josie and the Elevator." *Omni*, May 1980.

David Drake: "Than Curse the Darkness." *New Tales of the Cthulhu Mythos.*

Joseph V. Francavilla: "Deletions." *New Dimensions 10.*

Robert Henderson: "Master of the Revels." *The New Yorker*, Jan. 14, 1980.

R. M. Lamming: "The Ink Imp." *Fantasy and Science Fiction*, May 1980.

Janet E. Morris: "Raising the Green Lion." *Berkley Showcase*, Vol. 1.

Richard Purtill: "Others' Eyes." *Fantasy and Science Fiction*, May 1980.

Chelsea Quinn Yarbro: "Cabin 33." *Shadows 3.*